As the two vehicles came to a stop, Liz came out the house's front door. She was naked, her long lean body hard-looking, her eyes hidden behind large dark sunglasses. It was Liz' style to be aggressive and challenging; neither Peter nor any of the others would remark upon her nakedness.

Getting out of the Impala, Peter opened the rear doors of the van and there they were. Koo Davis, head still enclosed in the burlap sack, lay face down on an old double-bed mattress. Mark, bearded and stolid, sat at this end of the van, his feet stretched out over Davis' legs, while Larry perched uncomfortably up front by Davis' head. "Very good," Peter said. "Get him out of there."

Davis didn't speak as they helped him out to the blacktop; Peter, taking his arm to assist, felt the man trembling.

"Just walk," he said...

D0556064

**SOME OTHER HARD CASE CRIME BOOKS
YOU WILL ENJOY:**

361 *by Donald E. Westlake*
THE CUTIE *by Donald E. Westlake*
MEMORY *by Donald E. Westlake*
SOMEBODY OWES ME MONEY
*by Donald E. Westlake*
LEMONS NEVER LIE
*by Donald E. Westlake writing as Richard Stark*

FIFTY-TO-ONE *by Charles Ardai*
KILLING CASTRO *by Lawrence Block*
THE DEAD MAN'S BROTHER *by Roger Zelazny*
HOUSE DICK *by E. Howard Hunt*
CASINO MOON *by Peter Blauner*
FAKE I.D. *by Jason Starr*
PASSPORT TO PERIL *by Robert B. Parker*
STOP THIS MAN! *by Peter Rabe*
LOSERS LIVE LONGER *by Russell Atwood*
HONEY IN HIS MOUTH *by Lester Dent*
QUARRY IN THE MIDDLE *by Max Allan Collins*
THE CORPSE WORE PASTIES *by Jonny Porkpie*
THE VALLEY OF FEAR *by A.C. Doyle*
NOBODY'S ANGEL *by Jack Clark*
MURDER IS MY BUSINESS *by Brett Halliday*
GETTING OFF *by Lawrence Block*
QUARRY'S EX *by Max Allan Collins*
THE CONSUMMATA
*by Mickey Spillane and Max Allan Collins*
CHOKE HOLD *by Christa Faust*

# The Critics Applaud
## THE COMEDY IS FINISHED!

"One of the best Westlake novels I've read."
— *Washington Post*

"A terrifying sprint for redemption and rescue with the reader kept in agonizing suspense until the literal last page. Not to be missed."
— *Mystery Scene*

"This is a major novel by Westlake at the top of his craft… It is an astonishment and it is also deeply, profoundly relevant."
— *Barry Malzberg*

"Possibly the best kidnapping novel ever written."
— *Bibliodiscoteque*

"That didn't take long. Halfway into January and we already have the first great book of [the year]…some of the finest work of the author's career. And that is truly saying something."
— *Vince Keenan*

"A true literary find and masterpiece…a brilliant work of nonstop suspense and richly developed characters."
— *Book Reporter*

"A fascinating time capsule and a strong character-driven crime novel."
— *Seattle Post-Intelligencer*

"We're all in the presence of the master one last time."
— *Open Letters Review*

"A tense, compelling story…painfully insightful."
— *Booklist*

"Sharply written…a worthy addition to Westlake's lengthy catalogue."
— *Publishers Weekly*

"A real page-turner…Westlake's book is hot with fear, remorse, lust and violence…a fine novel in all respects."
— *Ed Gorman*

"This is more than 'just' a pulp novel; Westlake does nothing less than peer into the soul of a nation."
— *Book Geeks*

"Worth the wait. *The Comedy Is Finished* is one of the best books Westlake ever wrote…one of the best suspense thrillers of the year."
— *Rambles*

"Rife with unexpected scenes of great emotional power and poignancy…You just don't expect a razor-wire read like this to be so full of feeling…*The Comedy Is Finished* is a perfect capper to a brilliant career."
— *Tom Piccirilli, The Cold Spot*

# The COMEDY
# *Is* FINISHED

## *by* Donald E. Westlake

A HARD CASE CRIME NOVEL

**A HARD CASE CRIME BOOK**

(HCC-105)

*First Hard Case Crime edition: February 2012*

Published by

Titan Books
A division of Titan Publishing Group Ltd
144 Southwark Street
London SE1 0UP

in collaboration with Winterfall LLC

Copyright © 2012 by the Estate of Donald E. Westlake

Cover painting copyright © 2012 by Gregory Manchess

*If you purchased this book without a cover, you should know that it is stolen property. It was reported as "unsold and destroyed" to the publisher, and neither the author nor the publisher has received any payment for this "stripped book."*

All rights reserved. No part of this book may be reproduced or transmitted in any form or by any electronic or mechanical means, including photocopying, recording or by any information storage and retrieval system, without the written permission of the publisher, except where permitted by law.

*This book is a work of fiction. Names, characters, places, and incidents either are the products of the author's imagination or are used fictitiously, and any resemblance to actual events or persons, living or dead, is entirely coincidental.*

Print Edition ISBN 978-1-78116-781-6
E-book ISBN 978-0-85768-409-7

Design direction by Max Phillips
*www.maxphillips.net*

Typeset by Swordsmith Productions

The name "Hard Case Crime" and the Hard Case Crime logo are trademarks of Winterfall LLC. Hard Case Crime books are selected and edited by Charles Ardai.

Printed in the United States of America

*Visit us on the web at www.HardCaseCrime.com*

## PUBLISHER'S NOTE

*Donald Westlake began writing this book in the late 1970s. In the early 1980s, he sent a carbon copy of the finished manuscript to fellow crime writer Max Allan Collins, with whom he'd been corresponding for more than ten years. Shortly afterwards, Don decided not to publish the book, in part because Martin Scorsese had just released the movie* The King of Comedy *and Don thought some readers might feel the movie's premise and the book's were too similar. Max packed the manuscript away in a box in his basement, where it sat for the better part of the next three decades.*

*When Hard Case Crime published* Memory *in 2010, describing it as "Donald Westlake's final unpublished novel," Max informed us of this one's existence, unearthed the faded typescript, and sent it to us in the hope that the book would finally see print.*

*That it has is thanks to Abby Westlake and to Larry Kirshbaum, agent for the Westlake Estate, who agreed to let us publish it—but all three of us owe special thanks to Max Allan Collins, without whom* The Comedy Is Finished *might never again have seen the light of day.*

*This is for Brian Garfield, who knows what I'm doing better than I do.*

*Sometimes people call me an idealist. Well, that is the way I know I am an American. America is the only idealistic nation in the world.*

PRESIDENT WOODROW WILSON
SIOUX FALLS, SOUTH DAKOTA
SEPTEMBER 8, 1919

*THE COMEDY IS FINISHED*

*1*

"Welcome to television, folks. If you're very very good, we'll renew ya for next week."

Koo Davis is onstage, hand mike negligently held just below his round pink chin. He looks like that portrait of him done by Norman Rockwell over twenty years ago; *everybody* has that same warm pink latex face in Norman Rockwell portraits, but Koo Davis has it in real life. He's the ultimate justification for the Norman Rockwell palette: "See? It *is* realistic!"

"This thing here," Koo Davis is telling his studio audience, "is called a camera, and that thing there is called a cameraman. If he's a union cameraman he's called 'sir'."

The place is a television studio, with a wide shallow bleacher along one wall, on which sits a studio audience of two hundred fifty people. There isn't any actual stage, simply the black-composition-floored work area, made into cubicles by muslin-walled sets, with three cameras in position: left, right, center. The center camera operates in a central break in the bleachers, so it isn't in anybody's view. The floor is here and there covered with neutral gray carpet, and everywhere strewn with cables, like strings of black and silver spaghetti. Three television sets hang from the ceiling, facing the audience; they are dark now, but during the taping they'll show the progress to the audience as it's being put together. Sitting on the rows of folding chairs on the bleachers are the first two hundred fifty people from the line that formed earlier this afternoon outside the studio. They all came in for free, and they're looking forward to a good time.

"Now," Koo tells them, "we're gonna be together the next hour or so, while we put this show on tape, and if you're a student of television and you wanna just sit there and watch the camera angles, that's okay. And if you wanna laugh so hard you get a stitch in your side and fall down on the floor and roll around helpless with laughter, that's okay, too. And we'll be watching you all with monitors, and after the show we'll tell you which of you can go home."

Koo Davis does his own warm-ups. There are lesser comics who wait in their dressing rooms, talking with their agents and their accountants, while warm-up specialists (jolly-faced fiftyish failures with memorized repertoires) pep up the audience with semi-dirty jokes, get the audience already chuckling away, comfortable in its seats and ready to roar. But that isn't Koo Davis' style; his style is to find them where they are, grab them by the lapel, hit 'em with some yocks, hit 'em with some more yocks, and between times grin at 'em and walk around. He does *confidence*, that's what Koo Davis does, because an audience digs confidence.

"We're gonna have a couple special guests here on the show," Koo Davis tells the people. "They're actors, but you ought be nice to them anyway. I wanna tell ya, I'm always nice to actors. I learned my lesson. Last time I fired an actor, he got a job as Governor." Little pause, grin at them while they laugh. "He wasn't a very good actor, either."

This is a new line of territory for Koo, a new kind of politics in the jokes, and he's easing into it very cautiously, like into a tub of too-hot water. Behind the confident grin, the faintly swaggering walk, he's watching how that Governor gag goes down, he's waiting to see if they'll accept it. That is, if they'll accept it from *Koo Davis*. He's got some fence-mending to do, and he's not exactly sure how to go about it.

The trouble began with the goddamn Vietnam thing. That

goddamn war cut the country in half, it put the white male middle class over on this side and every damn body else over on that side, and when it finally ended, for some damn reason Koo couldn't let go. Others could, Duke Wayne and Shirley MacLaine right away kidding each other at the Academy Awards, but for Koo it was as though to admit the last step had been wrong meant admitting everything before it had also been wrong, and that he just couldn't do.

The bitch of it is, Koo always stayed *out* of politics. He started on radio back in '39, and it was the normal road then to follow the Will Rogers recipe; a couple jokes about Congress not doing anything, some jokes about Roosevelt's alphabet soup, every comic in the business was doing it. But not Koo. He had an instinct, it said times change, it said people don't really want to laugh at their leaders, it said leave the messages to Western Union. So Koo told jokes about the railroads, about the army, about automobiles and radio and California weather. And when World War Two came along he told jokes about nylons and chocolates and V-girls and let the other comics tell their jokes about the Nips. (Nobody told jokes about the Nazis; they weren't funny enough.)

You always knew what year it was from Koo's material, but never what the issues were. Housing shortage. Vets in college. Fins on cars. Men in space. Let Mort Sahl come onstage with a newspaper, Koo Davis walked on with a golf club. But then came the goddamn Vietnam thing, and the country was divided as it had never been before, and Koo just couldn't help himself. Like everybody else, he had to come down on one side or the other:

*"I didn't know if it was a boy or a girl, and it turned out to be a sheepdog."*

*"Of course, Canada's a fine place for people with cold feet."*

Nobody needs a majority more than a comic. You're standing there in front of all those faces and you say your line, and you don't want six jerks in the corner with a tee-hee, you want every face split open. If you don't have the instinct for the majority, you don't make it as a comic. Koo went over to politics because the audience wanted it. Inside himself he had two conflicting instincts—give them what they want; stay out of politics—and he had to choose.

"Also with us tonight, a wonderful actress from Sweden, Birgit Söderman—that's the way you pronounce it, folks. I said it wrong in a smorgasbord restaurant the other night and got pig's knuckles. I used to make the same mistake with Juanita Izquerta, but then I got *her* knuckles."

Poor reaction, drop-off in audience response. Koo walks around, grinning—"But I wanna tell you, I *love* working TV"— and in fifteen seconds he's got them back, and he's forgotten the dead spot. Most mistakes he remembers, but gags like the Juanita Izquerta he keeps in no matter how bad the response. The trouble is, not enough people remember the name. She was never a big star, Juanita, she made a dozen pictures in the early fifties and that was it. But Koo had her along on some of his USO tours—the boys in Korea, that decade—and his female co-stars, the starlets and has-beens and almost-wases he trouped and shtupped on those tours, are always fresh in his mind, as though they're still this minute young hard-breasted terrific chicks knocking them dead tonight in Vegas or Miami Beach just as Koo himself is knocking them dead here at this taping of *The Koo Davis Special* in beautiful downtown Burbank, California. It's as though there's a loyalty he owes those girls, to pretend they're still hot stuff, still hot, that it could still be any one of them appearing on this show with him instead of the latest blonde, Jill Johnson, a laid-back girl comic of the new school, twenty-six and a sexual bearcat, with whom he would be cheerfully expending his post-tape hard-on. (Performing has always been good for his sex life.)

Even the first of the blondes, Honeydew Leontine, on his premier tour—Hawaii, Australia, a few shitty islands, a couple aircraft carrier flight decks—even Honeydew, a girl whose movie career never got higher than stooge for the Ritz Brothers and was over even before the end of World War Two, even Honeydew still shows up from time to time in his monologues, and the last time he'd trouped and shtupped with Honeydew was—Christ on a crutch, it was over thirty years ago! The *first* time, in Hawaii, was *thirty-six years ago*! Jesus! Honeydew and her big tits and her collection of stones—stones from every goddamn beach she'd ever walked on, she carried them around in burlap bags, everywhere she went—Honeydew must be almost sixty fucking years old by now. And Koo himself, if he stops to think about it, which he never does, is sixty-three.

"Of course, television is different from the movies. When I started in pictures—I won't say how long ago that was, but I taught William S. Hart how to ride—and in the old days you'd shoot the same scene over and over until the director was satisfied. It got to be a habit to repeat things until you got them right. It got to be a habit to repeat things until you got them right. It got to be a habit to repeat things until you got them right. It got to be a—"

Which is about par for that gag; the laugh starts at the beginning of the first repeat, a trickle that dwindles off, picks up again at the beginning of the second repeat, lulls, then picks itself up again *before* the finish of the second repeat (the audience anticipating the third), so Koo is pushing the third repeat into a growing laugh. Then he can stop and do his own laugh, and grin, and shake his head, and walk around, selecting the next gag while the audience works on the last one.

It was the USO taught Koo how to be a comedian. He'd done vaudeville, he'd done radio, he was already what was then called a "headliner," but it was the USO tours that taught him how to live with an audience, how to make it want to like him, how to make it feel afterward that he didn't just make them laugh, he made them happy. In those early days he was just another radio comic, and the point of the touring shows was to give the troops a safe acceptable look at American tits and asses, so what he had to do when he stepped out on that temporary stage was give the GIs a reason to be happy to see him. Give them topical jokes ("Actually, I'm just here to buy cigarettes."), give them local jokes ("General Floyd sent me a message not to fraternize with the natives. At least that's what the mama-san told me, when she hung up the phone."), then bring out Honeydew or Juanita or Laura or Linda or Karen or Lauren or Dolly or Fanny, run a couple dumb-blonde routines, leave the chick out there to sing a song, come back with the local commander (they were *all* hams at heart, every last one of them), do a little uplift, cut it with some mild sex gags, send the General or Admiral or Colonel or Commander off with Juanita or Linda or Lauren or Dolly, give their exit an innuendo the troops could enjoy, and by then they were his, because *he was their link to special status*. They were dogfaces, retreads, grunts, and he was hanging around with Generals and blonde chicks, but he was one of them. He could come on like the rawest of raw recruits ("Colonel O'Malley's being terrific to us all. He's gonna watch Honeydew for me while I go up all by myself to the rest camp at Bloody Nose Ridge." Or Pork Chop Hill, or St. Lo, or wherever the most dangerous spot in the neighborhood might be.), and he could come on like the cool wiseguy the troops all wished they were, and they learned to love him for it, and he learned to love them for loving him.

He got a lot of good press for the USO work, and in truth he deserved it. He made no money out of it, not directly, beyond the expenses of the troupe. He'd started the tours in the first place because he was medically 4-F in 1940 (bad ear *and* bad stomach *and* bad knee), and he felt guilty about it, and this was something he could do to make up for not being "in it." (He wound up "in it," in fact, more than most guys in uniform, being under fire or otherwise in danger countless times while riding in jeeps or trucks or planes or helicopters or transport ships or—once, on Okinawa, when three kamikazes came plunging through the ack-ack—in a rickshaw. "We have some wild drivers in California," he told the troops that afternoon, "but those three that came through this morning were ridiculous.")

And when the goddamn Vietnam thing came along, how was he supposed to know it was *different*? Why wasn't it the Pacific Theater all over again, Korea all over again? It hadn't been wrong to cheer our side ever before, and these were the same kids, weren't they? Fighting the same slant-eyed son of a bitch gooks, weren't they? So what the hell was the difference?

Permissiveness, it seemed like. A lot of fat, soft college kids hanging around on their campuses, young snotnoses, didn't know their ass from their elbow. You looked at the real kids marching along in the same uniforms as before, you knew you had to make a choice, and Jesus the choice seemed easy. It should have been *Stage Door Canteen* all over again, it *should* have been, but it wasn't.

Koo did the USO tours the same as ever, but when he was in the States the great National Debate was creeping into his comedy, and for the first time in his career he was coming out on stage and getting *booed*. Half the under-twenty-fives out there in America thought he was some sort of goddamn baby raper or something. He just couldn't figure it out, and it made him mad, and the jokes got more and more political, and everything was just simply out of control.

He still doesn't know why the goddamn Vietnam thing was different, but fairly early on he understood it *was* different. Maybe the slant-eyed gooks were the same (he wasn't even sure about that anymore), and maybe the American uniforms were the same, but the kids inside that olive drab were something else. They laughed at the space-shot jokes and the bureaucracy jokes and the sex jokes ("I was supposed to do a nude center-fold for *Cosmopolitan* but it didn't work out. They said all the interesting parts were behind the staple."), but there were tried-and-true lines they *didn't* laugh at. "The General's being terrific to us all. He's gonna watch Dolly for me while I go up all by myself to the rest camp at Khe Sanh." They gave him a polite chuckle. They didn't want to embarrass him, the sons of bitches, and they were *polite* to him!

You're polite to a comedian, you're killing him.

Then, when Vietnam ended, you couldn't throw an asparagus spear without hitting six hypocrites. But not Koo; he wasn't sure why he even *had* these convictions, but he'd stick by them. The career was thinning out, TV sponsors weren't picking up their options, it was getting tougher to find writers whose mate-rial Koo could even *understand*, and he began to think long thoughts about retirement. He remained steadfast through the Nixon resignation and the Ford pardon, he even stuck when nobody invited him on that goddamn aircraft carrier in New York on Bicentennial Day; July 4, 1976, the Tall Ships, and Koo watched it on *television*. He'd offered to work for the Ford campaign, and they'd gently let him down, and it wasn't till later he figured it out; Koo Davis had become a reminder of too much bad history. *Koo Davis!*

But what did it for him at last was the investigations into the CIA, where it was made public that for several years in the sixties they'd had a phone tap and a mail check on *him*! On *Koo*! And when the asshole involved was asked by the Senate Committee why Koo Davis, the answer was that Koo had a lot of liberal friends. Did have.

Right after that came the revelations about the CIA experiments on human beings in hospitals, and that just put the icing on the cake. Maybe nobody else remembered what the Second World War had been all about, but Koo did, and he got mad: "The purpose of the experiments was to see if a human being could live without a brain. It turns out he can, if he's in the CIA." And when it occurred to him he was now telling *anti*-government jokes, he realized the time had come to end his own long war. Back to civilian life, back to the home front, back to the world he'd left behind.

"And if you don't like the show, folks, you'll get a full refund at the door. But I know you're gonna love it, and now I gotta go get ready, we're in kind of a hurry today, the manufacturer is recalling my pacemaker."

With a grin, with a wave, Koo tosses the mike to a waiting stagehand and trots off. "It's a good audience," he tells somebody on the way by, but that's just words, he doesn't even know who he's talking to. They're all good audiences for Koo Davis, they've been good audiences again for a year now. The split is over, the trouble's over, everybody's a good guy after all, and Koo is happy to relax once more into who he really is; a funny man, a funnyman, a good comic, an honest uncomplicated human being, living like every comic in the eternal Now, the Present, the Hereheisfolks, the Nowappearing. It's a good life, safe at last, and it's always happening right Now.

Koo has three minutes to drink a little ice water, get the makeup adjusted, have a quick last look at the script, play a little grabass with Jill, and then come out stage center into a group of eight tall lean dancing girls and his opening line of the show: "I can remember when legs like that were illegal." Now, he moves briskly along a cable-strewn alley created by the false walls of stacked sets, toward the door to a corridor leading to his dressing room, and as he reaches that first door somebody on his left says, "Mr. Davis?"

Koo turns his head. It's one of the scruffy bearded young crew members; these hairy sloppy styles never will look to Koo like anything but shit. Behind the kid is a side exit from the studio, the red *Taping* light agleam above it. Koo is in a hurry, and he wants no problems. "What's up?"

"Look at this, Mr. Davis," the kid says, and brings his hand up from his side, and when Koo looks down he is absolutely incredibly dumbfounded to see the kid is holding a pistol, a little black stubby-nosed revolver, and it's pointed right at Koo's head. *Assassination!* he thinks, though why anyone would want to assassinate him he has no idea, but on the other hand he has in his time played golf with one or two politicians who were later assassinated, and in his astonishment he opens his mouth to holler, and the kid uses his free hand to slap Koo very hard across the face.

And now a bag gets pulled down over his head from behind, a burlap bag smelling of moist earth and potatoes, and cable-like arms are grabbing him hard around the upper arms and chest, imprisoning him, lifting him, lifting his feet off the floor. He's being carried, there's a sudden rush of cooler air on the backs of his hands, they're taking him outside. "Hey!" he yells, and somebody punches him very very hard on the nose. *Jesus Christ*, he thinks, not hollering anymore. *Now they're punching me on the nose.*

# 2

Peter Dinely watched the blue van with Joyce at the wheel jounce slowly over the speed bumps at the studio exit and turn right toward Barham Boulevard. Were Mark and Larry in the back, out of sight? Did they have Koo Davis back there? Peter gnawed the insides of his cheeks, willing Joyce to look this way, give him some sort of sign, but the van turned and drove unsteadily away, an enigmatic blue box on small wheels, its rear windows dark and dusty. Peter followed, in the green rented Impala, the ache in his cheeks a kind of distraction from uncertainty.

The habit of gnawing his cheeks was an acquired one, chosen deliberately a long long time ago and now so ingrained he could no longer stop it, though the inside of his mouth was ragged and even occasionally bleeding. If he ever could stop chewing on himself he'd be glad of it; but then would the blinking come back?

Peter was thirty-four. To break an early habit of blinking when under pressure, he'd been chewing his cheeks in moments of tension for fifteen years. Eleven years ago a dentist had reacted with horror, telling him the interior of his mouth was one great raw wound, since when he had stopped going to dentists.

Now, Peter followed the blue van west on Barham Boulevard, and it wasn't until the turn onto Hollywood Freeway northbound that he could angle into the middle lane, run up next to the van, look over at Joyce's tense profile, and tap the horn. She looked at him almost with terror, not seeming to understand what he wanted—or possibly even who he was—until he gave her an angry questioning glare while pointing with jabbing fingers at the back part of the van. Then she gave a sudden jerk of understanding, and an exaggerated nod. Yes? he asked, demanding with head and face and arm, and she nodded again, with a small tense smile and a quick jerky wave of the hand.

All right. All right. Peter became calm, his shoulders sagging, his jaw muscles relaxing, the blood oozing into his mouth, his foot easing on the accelerator. The Impala dropped back and tucked in once more behind the blue van. Everything was going to be all right.

The house was in Tarzana, up in the hills south of the Ventura Freeway. Peter waited behind the van as Joyce stopped at the gate and her hand reached out to ring the bell in the metal pole beside the driveway. There was a pause—up above, Liz must walk to the kitchen, ask for identification through the speaker, receive reassurance from Joyce, then press the button—and then the wide chain-link gate slowly opened and the van jolted up the hill. Peter followed, seeing in the rearview mirror the gate automatically swing shut.

At the top, the blacktop driveway leveled off into a flat area in front of the wide garage. Next to it, the house was a broad ranch-style in brick and wood; as the two vehicles came to a stop, Liz came out its front door. She was naked, her long lean body hard-looking, her eyes hidden behind large dark sunglasses. It was Liz' style to be aggressive and challenging; neither Peter nor any of the others would remark upon her nakedness.

Getting out of the Impala, Peter opened the rear doors of the van and there they were. Koo Davis, head still enclosed in the burlap sack, lay face down on an old double-bed mattress. Mark, bearded and stolid, sat at this end of the van, his feet stretched out over Davis' legs, while worried-looking Larry perched uncomfortably up front by Davis' head. "Very good," Peter said. "Get him out of there."

Davis didn't speak as they helped him out to the blacktop; Peter, taking his arm to assist, felt the man trembling. "Just walk," he said.

Liz led the way into the house. When she turned her back the scars were visible; twisted rough-grained white lines that would never take a tan, criss-crossing down the middle of her back.

The interior of the house was cool with central air conditioning. Pale green carpet on all the floors muffled sound. While Joyce and Mark stayed behind, Peter and Larry guided Davis through the house, following Liz. In the kitchen, she opened a narrow door and they went down a narrow staircase to the left. Here, beneath the house, were the utilities, in a small square concrete block room without frills. Cardboard wine cartons were messily piled in one corner, behind the pool heater. On a side where it wouldn't be expected was a door, which Liz opened, revealing a fairly long narrow room which extended out from the house underneath the sun deck as far as the swimming pool. At the far end of the room was a thick glass picture window, with the green-blue water at the deep end of the pool restlessly moving against its other side. Daylight filtering through that water made a cool gray dimness in here, until Liz touched a switch beside the door which brought up warm amber indirect lighting.

The first owner of this house had been a movie director, who had added several ideas of his own to the architects' plans, including this room, in which it was possible to sit and have a drink and get a fish-eye view of one's guests swimming in the pool. The director had enjoyed this idea so much he'd had the setting written into one of his movies, and shot the scene in this room.

The room was plain but comfortable, with maroon cloth on the walls, low overstuffed swivel chairs, dark carpeting, soundproofed ceiling, built-in bar sink and refrigerator, several small low tables, and in one corner a door leading to a small lavatory, with shower, sink and toilet. In readiness for Koo Davis, the refrigerator had been stocked with simple foods, more ready-to-eat food was stacked on the shelf above it, some plastic plates and cups and spoons had been placed on a table, and even a plastic decanter filled with inexpensive Scotch had been provided.

Once they were all in the room, Larry pulled off the burlap bag, and Peter looked at the familiar face of Koo Davis. His sense of accomplishment was so strong that this time he had to bite his cheeks not to ease tension but to keep himself from smiling.

Davis had had a nosebleed, which had stopped, leaving smudges of brown under his nose and along his left cheek. He looked frightened but cocky, as though he'd decided his game plan was to tough it out.

Larry, of course, reacted big to the nosebleed, saying, "Oh, we're sorry about that! Your nose!"

Davis looked at him in mock astonishment. "You're sorry about my *nose*? If you'll notice, you took the whole body."

Peter said, "If *you'll* notice, you're in a room with one door, which we'll keep locked. You have food there, drink there, and a toilet over there."

Glancing around, Davis said, "Okay if I open the window?"

"This isn't a joke," Liz told him. She had removed her sunglasses, and her eyes and voice were as hard as her nude body.

Davis grinned at her. "I'll be able to identify *you* later on," he said. "Anyway, I'm looking forward to the lineup."

"That fine, Koo," Peter said, permitting himself a small

grin. "You keep your spirits up." To Liz and Larry he said, "Come on."

Davis, suddenly less jocular, said, "Do I get a question?"

Amused, Peter said, "Which question? Why? Who? What?"

"I thought kidnappers didn't want to be recognized. Unless they figured to kill the customer."

Jumping in, looking very intense, Larry said, "We're not going to kill you, Mr. Davis."

"Assuming things go well," Peter said. "Assuming everybody is sensible, Koo, including you."

"That's a big relief," Davis said. Terror was pulsing just beneath his cocky surface, like a kitten under a blanket. "As long as I go on being sensible, I'm okay, right? I mean, sensible like you people."

"That's right," Peter said.

# 3

"So here I am on the bricks," Mike Wiskiel said. He felt god-damn sorry for himself. "Lemme tell ya, Jerry, the worst word in the English language is the word 'retroactive.' You can forget all about 'it might have been' and 'nevermore' and all that crap, the word is 'retroactive.' It'll fuck ya every time." And he swallowed another mouthful of vodka and tonic, while Jerry chuckled his friendly, agreeable, meaningless realtor's chuckle.

Mike Wiskiel was a little drunk, at four in the afternoon; not for the first time. He'd spent the morning talking to women who'd sent in eleven bucks for a scalp-invigorator that when they'd tried it made their hair fall out, and by lunchtime he'd seen enough bald women to last him the rest of his life. So he'd come here to the club for a quick game of tennis and the Daily Special lunch—today it was avocado followed by abalone, washed down with a Napa Riesling—and then he'd run into Jerry Lawson in the bar and here he still was, sitting at a table by the tinted-glass windows, having another little drink, at four on the clock in the pee em. And at this moment he and Jerry were the only members present in the bar.

Jerry Lawson was a real estate agent, and probably Mike's closest friend out here, apart from the people at the Bureau. Mike had met him—Jesus, almost a year ago—when he'd been transferred to the L.A. office and had made the exploratory trip to find a new house for Jan and the kids. He'd walked into the real estate office on Ventura Boulevard, and the first thing he'd ever said to Jerry was, "I know you from someplace," and he

remembered thinking, *Jesus, maybe this guy is on the hot list.*
But Jerry had gripped and said, "I'm the guy shot June Havoc
in *The Sound of Distant Drums*," and wasn't that L.A. for you?
Your real estate man turns out to be a one-time actor.

And a good friend. Jerry had found them a perfect house, up
in the hills in Sherman Oaks, and had even put up Mike's name
for his country club, El Sueno de Suerte, here in Encino. Of
course, it's true that in Los Angeles realtors keep in closer
touch with their former clients than elsewhere, since the average
turnover of a middle-level-and-up house in that city is two and
a half years, but Mike was convinced in this case it was more
than the usual business friendship. He and Jerry enjoyed tennis
together, drinks together, poker and barbecue and a good laugh
together, and the wives got along, and even the kids from both
families didn't seem to hate each other one hundred percent of
the time. Jerry's friendship had helped a lot to soften the blow
of having been transferred out here through no fault of his
own. After all those years, back on the bricks.

He repeated it aloud. "Back on the bricks. I tell ya, Jerry, I
had it made at the Head Office, it didn't matter who the Director
was. They knew I was a reliable man, they knew I was loyal,
they knew I delivered. 'I don't want excuses, I want results,'
that's what the Director used to say, and nobody *ever* heard an
excuse from me."

"I know," Jerry said sympathetically, though he could only
know what Mike told him. "You got your nuts in the wringer,
that's all. That's all that happened."

"Retroactive," Mike said, dealing with the word as though it
were a pebble he was moving around in his mouth. " 'Do this,'
they said, 'it's your patriotic duty.' 'Oh, yessir,' I said, and salute
the son of a bitch, and I go *do* it, and when I come back there's
some *other* son of a bitch in there and he says, 'Oh, no, that wasn't

patriotic, it was *illegal* and you shouldn't of done it.' And I say, 'Why I got my orders right here, I'm covered, I got everything in black and white, *this* is the guy told me what to do,' and they say, 'Oh, yeah, we know about him, he's out on his ear, he's in worse trouble than you are.' So that guy's ass is in a sling and my nuts are in a wringer and Al Capone is up there at San Clemente in a golf cart. And who's loyal now, huh? Who do you trust now, the shitter or the shit-upon?"

"It's a tough racket," Jerry said. He was a terrific sounding board, he never confused the conversation with a lot of dumb suggestions.

"You're fuckin A," Mike told him, and turned to point at Rodney the barman. "Twice again," he called, and the beeper in his jacket pocket went EEEEEEEEEEEEEEEEEEE. "Shit," Mike said, under the noise of the machine, and reached to shut it off.

Jerry looked interested. "The office?"

"More fuckin bald women," Mike said, and twisted around the other way to holler over at Ricci the waiter, "Bring me a phone, will ya, Rick?"

The phone came first. Ricci plugged it into the jack under the window, then went off to get the drinks while Mike phoned the office.

"Federal Bureau of Investigation."

"Extension twelve."

A few burrs, and then: "Agent Dodd."

"Mike Wiskiel here. I was just buzzed."

"Hold on, Redburn wants you."

The drinks arrived while Mike was holding on, and he signed for them with the receiver tucked in against his shoulder. Jerry said, "What's up?"

"Dunno yet."

Ricci took the tab away, Mike slugged down about a third of

the new drink, and the voice of Chief of Station Webster Redburn came on the line: "Mike? Where are you?"

"At the club, Wes. I spent all day on that mail fraud case, I just came in for a little late lunch."

"Forget the mail fraud *and* lunch," Redburn said, and went on to tell him what had happened. Mike's eyes widened as he listened, and he knew there'd be no more paperwork, no more routine slog, no more bald women and low-IQ bank robbers and stolen cars, no more day-by-day boring bullshit, not for hours, not for days, maybe even not for weeks. "So get there fast," Redburn finished.

"I just left," Mike told him, and cradled the phone.

Jerry looked as inquisitive as a cat who's just heard a noise under the refrigerator. "What's up?"

"A james dandy," Mike told him. "Somebody put the snatch on Koo Davis! Would you believe it?" And, getting to his feet, he downed the rest of his drink and trotted from the room.

I need this, Mike told himself. I gotta do good on this one. Fuzzy from that last vodka, he sped east on the Ventura Freeway while a golden future opened up before his bleary eyes; if he did good on this Koo Davis thing. Yes, sir. They'd *have* to transfer him back to Washington then, they'd have no choice. Back where he belonged.

Yes, sir. Old Mike Wiskiel, fucked over because of Watergate, kicked out of D.C., rescues *Koo Davis* from the kidnappers! Talk about your media blitz! Mike could see his own fucking face on the fucking cover of *Time* magazine. "Tough but tender, FBI man Mike Wiskiel counts persistence among his primary virtues." Writing the *Time* article in his head, pushing the speed limit, not quite grazing the cars to left and right, Mike Wiskiel raced to the rescue.

•

The gate guard at Screen Service Studios gave Mike's ID a very careful belligerent screening. Mike didn't need this shit; he was more sober now, but the buzz of vodka was steadily souring toward a headache. He said, "Locking the door now the horse is gone, huh?"

The guard glared but made no remark, simply handing back the ID and saying, "Soundstage Four. Past the pile of lumber up there and around to your left."

Mike grunted, and drove cautiously forward. The speed bumps weren't that good for his head.

Following the guard's directions, Mike soon saw a large black number 4 painted on an otherwise featureless gray wall, above a gray metal door. Several cars, most of them official-looking, were parked in a cluster along the wall, and two Burbank cops were standing together outside the door, chatting in a bored way and looking around for stars.

There weren't any stars, not right now. Except for the two Burbank cops there was nobody in sight. Mike didn't know those two—his acquaintanceship among the bewildering multiplicity of police forces in the Greater Los Angeles area was very low—but he waved to them anyway as he drove by, looking for a place to park. They responded with flat looks, and when he left the car and walked back these Burbank cops also gave his ID a tight aggressive inspection. Mike said, "I understand the snatch took place about three-thirty, am I right?"

"That's right."

"Then *that* was the time to check ID. One thing you're not gonna get right now is the kidnappers sneaking back in here disguised as FBI men."

They both looked sullen. One of them said, "You *could* be a reporter."

"Flashing Federal ID? I'm some fucking stupid reporter." And he went inside.

Almost any of the other agents in the Los Angeles office, with their local police contacts, would have been better qualified than Mike to be liaison on this case, except that the victim was Koo Davis; a famous name, a celebrity, and a man with lots of official friends back in D.C. No one lower-ranking than Assistant to the Chief of Station could possibly be sent to cover the first day, when legally the FBI's connection with kidnapping—a state, not federal, crime—was advisory only; which was why it was Mike's baby. And his big chance.

He had no idea, on walking into Soundstage Four, whether the local law would welcome him with open arms or closed faces, but it turned out he was in luck. The local man in charge, a tall leathery old duff called Chief Inspector Jock Cayzer, seemed both friendly and competent, and started right off by saying, "FBI, huh? Good to have you aboard."

Cayzer had a hard strong handshake. He wore a brown suit and a string tie and a Stetson, and he talked with the gruff slow twang of Texas or Oklahoma, but the deep creases in his face and the knobby knuckles of his blunt-fingered hands said plainer than words that he was the real thing and not one of the million imitations spawned in the Los Angeles area. Despite the strong handshake, and the keen look in his silver-flecked blue eyes, and his strong deep voice, he was surely older than the mandatory retirement age, so his still being here, actively in charge, meant he either knew his business or knew the right people. Probably both. So Mike had better be careful with him.

He knew his business, that much was sure. He took Mike around the building, explaining the situation, and Mike could only agree with everything Cayzer had so far chosen to do. What had happened, Koo Davis had been on stage talking with the studio audience before taping his program, and on his way back to the dressing room—down this corridor, through this door, along that hall—he'd disappeared; probably out this door, leading to this alley. Presumably he'd been snatched, though so far there'd been no word from the kidnappers. On the other hand, the kidnapping (if that's what it was) had taken place barely half an hour ago: "They might not even be gone to ground yet," Cayzer said.

As to who they were, and how they might have done it, there were some clues, beginning with that studio audience. In normal movie studio fashion, Triple S was under controlled access, with high walls or fences all around the property and only two usable gates, both manned by private guards. The minute the alarm had reached Cayzer's office, he had ordered the lot sealed; no one off, no matter who they were or what their reason, and only police and other authorized officials on. The result was, the studio audience that had come to see Koo Davis was still here, undergoing a kind of thrilled boredom. They'd been told what had happened and that they wouldn't be permitted to leave just yet, so they knew they were involved in a very dramatic moment, but on the other hand they were just sitting there on those bleachers, with nothing to do and nothing to see.

And they were two short. "They keep a headcount," Cayzer explained. "They get a mob comes to these things, but they only let in the first two hundred and fifty, that's final, no more and no less. I've had three of these studio fellas swear to me up and down and sideways there was exactly two hundred fifty people let in today, and we done our own headcount, and now there's two hundred forty-eight."

"So that's how they got in," Mike agreed. "The next question is, how'd they get out?"

"I do believe we got a hint on that," Cayzer said. "Two of my men talked to the fellas on the main gate, asking who come in and out during the ten minutes between Davis disappearing and us closing the place down, and we got one good-looking prospect. A Ford Econoline van, belongs to one of the girls works in the studio offices. The fella on the gate remembered it because she only brings it in on Fridays and she usually leaves later in the day. Girl's name is Janet Grey, she's been working here less than two months, she didn't ask her boss' permission before she took off early."

"Sounds good," Mike said. "You got an address?"

"Down in West L.A. County boys looking into it now."

"She won't be there," Mike said.

Cayzer grinned, making another thousand creases in his face. His eyes were meant for seeing across open miles, they seemed too powerful for small rooms, small concerns. "I'll be surprised, there's even such an address," he said.

Mike said, "What about the family?"

"Well, that's sort of a problem," Cayzer said. "Seems Davis's separated from his wife, she's out in Palm Beach, Florida. Then he's got two sons, both grown up, one of them in the television business in New York, the other one lives in London. Your boss said—"

"Webster Redburn."

"That's him; Chief of Station. He said his people would see about notification of the family. We got no relatives around this part of the world at all. The closest we can come is Davis' agent, a woman called Lynsey Rayne. She's heading to my office right now, hoping for news."

"We could all use some news," Mike said. "What's your next move?"

"I have men searching this whole lot," Cayzer said. "Indoors and out. Don't expect they'll come up with anything."

"Probably not. These people hit and run."

"That's right. Then there's that audience. I think I might's well let them go, unless *you* want them."

"This is your show," Mike said. "I'm just an observer."

"Oh, I think we could work together right from now," Cayzer said. His grin, it seemed, could develop a sly twist at the left corner. "Less you'd *rather* wait till tomorrow."

"Anything I can do to help," Mike promised, "just let me know."

"Fine. Think I oughta let that audience go home?"

"Did you talk to them about pictures?"

Cayzer looked blank. "Pictures?"

"Snapshots."

"Well, goddamn it," Cayzer said. "Sometimes I don't know if I was stupid all my life or if I'm just getting stupid with old age. Come on along, you can ask them yourself."

Mike followed Cayzer to a large soundstage full of sets and cameras, with an audience-full line of bleachers along one side. A technician gave him a hand mike, and he stepped out into the floodlights, where forty minutes ago Koo Davis had been making people laugh. Now his absence was making the same people wide-eyed with anticipation, and Mike was strongly aware of all those eyes glittering at him out of the semi-dark. He was also strongly aware of the floodlights; they were making his headache worse. His eyes felt as though the pressure behind them would make them pop out onto the floor; and good riddance.

With the bleachers so broad and shallow, the audience was much closer to the stage than in a normal theater, and Mike immediately had the sense that these people were *still* an audience, still spectators rather than participants. They were waiting for him to amuse them, thrill them, capture their interest.

He did the latter merely by introducing himself: "Ladies and gentleman, my name is Michael Wiskiel. I'm an agent with the Federal Bureau of Investigation, here to assist Chief Inspector Cayzer in his inquiry." *His* inquiry; the social niceties are important everywhere. "Now, I imagine some of you nice people are tourists in this area, and all of you have your own lives you want to get on with, so we'll try not to hold you up very much longer. I suppose some of you brought cameras along today, I wonder if any of you have Polaroids. Anybody?"

A scattering of hands was raised; Mike counted six.

"Fine. So any pictures you folks took today, you've already got them in your pocket or purse, all developed and ready to be looked at. I wonder, did any of you people happen to take any pictures while you were out on line, before you got in here, and would those pictures show anybody *else* in the line?"

A stir in the audience, as two hundred forty-two people turned in their seats to watch six people self-consciously leaf through little clusters of photographs. Four of them eventually turned out to have pictures of the sort Mike had in mind, and ushers brought these photographs to the stage.

Seven snaps. Mike looked at the first, and saw four more-or-less distinguishable people behind the smiling squinting foreground lady who was the obvious subject of the photograph. He called out, "Could we have some light on the audience?" and immediately a bank of overhead spots came up, lighting the audience as though *it* had become the stage.

"Let's see now," Mike said. "Here's a young man in a pale blue sweater, black hair, wearing sunglasses. Anybody?"

The young man was found, and when he stood and put on his sunglasses Mike matched him to the photograph. Also the lady wearing the white scarf and green polka dots. And also the elderly couple in matching white turtleneck shirts.

And so on through the seven Polaroids. Every identifiable face was still among the two hundred forty-eight. Either the two kidnappers had been very careful or very lucky.

"Well, it was worth a try," Mike told the audience, when the pictures had been returned to their owners. "So now let me ask about other cameras, where you've still got the film inside. Anybody?"

More: thirty-five hands went up. Mike arranged with Cayzer to have police officers collect the film rolls, identifying the owner of each, and promising that the pictures would be developed, all developed prints and negatives would be returned to their owners, and reimbursement would be made for unused parts of rolls.

"Now, one last thing," Mike said, when the film had been collected. "We'll want group pictures of you all. If you were wearing something outside on line that you're not wearing now, like sunglasses or a hat, please wear it in the picture." There's something about standing on stage with a hand mike that compulsively brings out the ham in everybody; Mike couldn't resist adding, "And if you're here with somebody you shouldn't be, don't worry, we won't say a word to your wife." The answering chuckle, from two hundred forty-eight throats, delighted him.

While Cayzer's men took the pictures, section by section, and copied down the names and addresses of everybody present, with their location in each photograph, Mike and Cayzer had a talk behind the set, Cayzer saying, "My people finished their search of the lot. Nothing, nobody, no report."

"What we expected."

"That's right. You want to talk to Janet Grey's co-workers?"

In a cracking, terrible falsetto, Mike said, "Oh, I just can't *believe* Janet would be involved in anything like this. She was always such a *quiet* girl, she just kept to herself all the time, a *very* good worker, never made any trouble or called attention to herself in *any* way."

Grinning, nodding, Cayzer said, "You just saved yourself an hour and a half. So what do you want to do next?"

"Hear from the kidnappers," Mike said.

# 4

Koo Davis is in trouble, and he knows it, but he doesn't know why. And he doesn't know who, or how, or even where. Where the hell *is* this place? An underground room with a bar and a john and a cunt-level view of a swimming pool; the naked girl with the scars on her back spent half an hour paddling around in the water out there, after Koo was locked in. She swam and dove, the whole time pretending there wasn't any window or anybody watching, and all in all Koo was very happy when she finally got her ass out of the pool and left him in peace. She has a fantastic body when you can't see the scars, but she doesn't turn him on. Just the opposite: having that cold bitch flaunt herself like that shows just how little he matters to these people. They kidnapped him, they probably figure to sell him back for a nice profit, but other than as merchandise they couldn't care shit about him, and that makes Koo very nervous.

*Why me?* he asks himself, over and over, but he never comes up with an answer. Because he has a few bucks? But Jesus, a lot of people have a few bucks. Do they think he's a millionaire or something? If they ask for too much money, and if they don't believe the answer they get, what will they do?

Koo doesn't like to think about that. Every time his thoughts bring him this far, he quickly switches to another of his questions; like, for instance, *Where am I?* Still somewhere in the Greater Los Angeles area, that's for sure. He estimates he was no more than half an hour in that truck or whatever it was. From the turns, this way and that, when they took him away from Triple S, he's come to the conclusion they drove first on the Hollywood Freeway and then either the Ventura Freeway west or the Pasadena Freeway east; probably Ventura, out across the Valley. Then at the very end they did some climbing, with a particularly steep part after one fairly long stop. So he's most likely on an estate somewhere in the Hollywood Hills, on the north slope, overlooking the Valley. And not some cheapjack place either, not with this room next to the pool. Somebody spent money on this layout.

Why do they want to keep him from identifying this place, yet they don't care if he sees their faces? And why the fuck would rich people play kidnapper? These clowns operate like they're at home here, they're not worried about the owners coming back and interrupting the operation, so they must—

Unless they killed the owners.

Time to switch to another question. Like: Who exactly do they deal with, these kidnappers, who do they put the arm on? The network? Chairman Williams and the vice-presidents, that crowd of Easter Island statues? You can't get blood from stone faces; if Koo knew his businessmen—and he did—Williams wouldn't pay more than three bucks to get his sister back from Charles Manson.

But who else was there? Lily? "Hello, we got your husband Koo here, you remember him. He's for sale." How much would Lily pay for a living Koo Davis?

Koo is something of a showbiz oddity, a man who's been married to the same woman for forty-one years; but that isn't quite the record it sounds. As he once explained to an interviewer (in an answer cut from the published interview at Koo's insistence), "You want my formula for a happy marriage? Marry only once, leave town, and never go back."

Which is almost the truth. When twenty-two-year-old Koo married seventeen-year-old Lily Palk, back there in nineteen thirty-six, how could he know he was going to be bigtime any minute? Naturally he had his dreams, every kid has dreams, but there was no reason to believe *his* dreams were any less bullshit than anybody else's.

If an insecure punk kid marries a practical girl, and if three years later the punk is a radio star in New York while the practical girl is a housewife and mother in Syosset, Long Island, the prognosis for the marriage is unlikely to be good: "I won't be home tonight, honey, I'm staying here in town." As he commented one time to a gagwriter pal named Mel Wolfe, "I got to put that on a record. Then somebody in the office can call the frau and play it at her. 'Hi, honey, I won't be home tonight, I'm staying in town.' Then a little pause and I say, 'Well, I wouldn't if I didn't have to. Everything okay there?' Then another little pause and I say, 'That's fine.' One more pause and I say, 'You, too. Have a good night, honey.' And meantime I'm in Sardi's."

"Hey, listen," Mel Wolfe said. "I got a terrific— Feed it to me. Do the record."

"Yeah?" Grinning in anticipation, Koo said, "Hi, honey, I won't be home tonight, I'm staying in town."

In a shrill angry falsetto, Mel Wolfe replied, "I went to the doctor today, you bastard, and *you* gave me the *clap*!"

"Heh heh," Koo said, and went on with his script: "Well, I wouldn't if I didn't have to. Everything okay there?"

"The *house* burned down this afternoon, you prick!"

"That's fine."

"You've got a *woman* there!"

"You, too," Koo said, cracking up. "Have a good night, honey." And eventually they used a cleaner version of the idea in the show.

For a while, Koo appended excuses to his calls home ("Meeting with the sponsor." "Script trouble, gotta stay up with the writers."), but soon he gave up even that much pretense, as his evenings "in town" grew to outnumber his evenings "at home." He stayed at

the Warwick on Sixth Avenue below Central Park, he traveled
with a funny, bright, invigorating crowd, and it became more
and more difficult to force himself to make appearances in that
other life. By 1940 he was solemnly vowing to spend at least
one night a week with the family, and most weeks he wasn't
making it.

The finish came in February of 1941. Koo joined a bon voyage
party seeing off some Miami-bound friends at Penn Station,
and awakened next morning to find himself still on the train,
which was highballing south. "By God, I'm having my ham and
eggs in Carolina." Once in Miami, he had to make several ex-
planatory phone calls to friends and business people back in
New York, and every one of those conversations was sprinkled
with hilarity, except the call to Syosset. "I won't be home
tonight, honey," Koo started, intending a gag line on his present whereabouts, but before he could deliver it Lily said, "I
know you won't. You haven't been here for three weeks."

What surprised Koo, even more than the words, was the
voice. Maybe the long-distance wire had a distorting effect, or
maybe he was actually *hearing* Lily for the first time in years.
In any case, she sure as hell didn't sound like the girl he'd married. This Lily sounded like a head nurse: flat, tough, dispassionate, uncaring. Sitting there in his warm hotel room in hot
Miami, listening to that cold voice, Koo shivered. He tried to
go on with his gag—"A funny thing happened, uh, on the
way…"—but at that point he simply ran down. You can't swap
swifties with a zombie.

"I can't talk long," Lily said. "Frank just woke up from his
nap." At that time, Barry was three and Frank one. Koo had
offered to pay for nurses, nannies, but Lily had refused, in-
sisting she would bring up her own children herself. What
Koo didn't understand at the time—what he still doesn't
entirely understand, though it doesn't make any difference

now—is that Lily was afraid of his life in New York. She was afraid of fame, afraid of glamour, afraid of the same bigtime that Koo reveled in.

But Koo couldn't see that. All he saw was that Lily had turned herself into a drudge, and that she was unhappy, and that her unhappiness was dragging him down. Now, he couldn't even mention Miami, not in the presence of that frigid misery. "I'll call you later," he said, all the fun gone from his voice. He sounded as bad as she did.

And that was the moment, when he heard his own voice pick up her flat deadness. His other phone calls had involved problems—a meeting rescheduled, a rehearsal cancelled, a newspaper interviewer given an apology—but they'd been solved, hadn't they? And solved without spoiling the *fun*. Koo Davis was a free and happy man, so free and happy that he could suddenly be in Miami *by mistake* and the main result was only laughter. Koo loved laughter, not only audience laughter when he was performing but also his own laughter when something tickled him, laughter around him when he was with his pals. What did he *need* with this specter from the Grim Beyond?

The specter was saying, "Will you be home this weekend?" But she didn't ask as though she cared about the answer. It was more as though he was another of the problems in her life, like Frank waking from his nap, or Barry's bed-wetting.

"I don't think so," Koo said. Huddled on the edge of the bed in the Miami hotel room, phone pressed to the side of his face, free hand over his eyes, he looked like a clockwork toy waiting to be rewound.

"When will you be home?"

Koo could never resist a straight line. "Nineteen sixty-eight," he said, and hung up.

And that was it. He was terrified, the instant the line was out of his mouth and the phone was out of his hand, but not for a

second did he think of turning back. Once it was done, once
he'd blurted out the words that made the change, he wanted
nothing except to stay with the action already done. But still
the change terrified him, so he promptly left that hotel room
and got drunk with friends, stayed drunk until three days later,
when the network sent people down to collect him and bring
him back to New York for his next weekly show. He sobered up
on the northbound train, but thought no more about his break
with Lily until the next week, when she phoned him at the
Warwick to ask if he wanted a divorce.

"A *what*?" He was palling around with one girl in particular
at that time, a dancer named Denise (in fact, they'd just had an
argument in this very room, about money), and at the word
"divorce" an image came into his mind of Denise as a great
hunting bird, an eagle or a hawk with talons, swooping down
on him. If he were no longer safely tied by marriage, if he were
a single man and available, what would not Denise do? "No
divorce!" Koo said.

Lily said, "Koo, I want to know where I stand."

"I'll get back to you," Koo promised, but in fact it was Koo's
lawyer who got back to her later that week, and by the time the
legal details were worked out Koo himself was off on his first
USO tour; the one with Honeydew Leontine. In the years since,
there has never been any one woman with whom he's wanted to
spend the rest of his life, and what other reason for divorce is
there except remarriage?

So Lily Palk Davis is still Koo's wife, though the last time he
saw her was 1965, when Frank was married. She was friendly
enough then, the old rancor long since dead and buried, but
what kind of answer are these clowns likely to get if it's Lily
they hit up for the ransom?

*Or* the boys. What Koo did wrong back there in 1941, and in
the busy crowded events of his life it was easy not to notice the

mistake at the time, when he split with Lily he also split with his sons. It was nearly three years before he saw either of them again, and that time was only because Barry got pneumonia and was in the hospital, maybe not to live. Koo was terrified during that crisis, moving into the hospital, cancelling all his work, gasping along with every struggling breath rattling through that skinny little body, and for the first time—almost the last time—really *feeling* that body as a part of himself; flesh of his flesh, bone of his bone, an extension of Koo Davis into the future, a part of him that walked and moved and lived when he wasn't around.

But the feeling was too intense. There wasn't any comedy in it, he couldn't wrap himself around it. He wasn't in charge of his emotions there, they were in charge of him. At night in the hospital, when sleep did come, it was accompanied by confused, roiling, blundering dreams, and by day he lived with nervousness and fear, a jittering clammy stumbling sense of his own helplessness. His stomach, never healthy, was in turmoil. When the crisis finally ended, when Barry at last came out of the hospital, followed by cartons of toys, comic books, stuffed animals and game sets, Koo hugged him and kissed him and put him away, and went right back to the world he knew, in which he could be comfortable and in control.

It wasn't, in fact, until Barry was thirteen and Frank eleven that Koo made any intense effort to be a father. In his late thirties by then, successful in the movies and reaching out for his first success in television, secure at last in his long-term status as a star and becoming truly aware for the first time that he was aging, he was no longer the fast-talking hotshot radio comic of a dozen years ago, he found himself finally conscious of those two boys he'd helped to create just before he'd become the real Koo Davis. They were both in boarding school, Lily at that time living in Washington, an unpaid consultant on various welfare projects, and when Koo phoned her to ask if he could have the boys on one of their vacations she was sardonically amused—she wasn't afraid of his comedy anymore—but she did agree; he could have the boys for two weeks in April.

And it was a disaster. Koo didn't know children, and more importantly he didn't know *these* children. He had the use of a mountain ranch in Colorado, complete with horses to ride, streams to fish, hills to climb, real-life cowboys as ranch-hands, and even some of Koo's showbiz pals dropping in for a day or two. But the whole thing went to hell in a handbasket, and by the end of the two weeks Koo was drinking all day long and shooting zingers at his own kids.

The almost constant rain didn't help much, of course, but the real problem lay deeper than that. Children, particularly when just entering their teens, tend to become absorbed in one or two special interests, and to ignore everything else that life has to offer. At eleven years of age, Frank was utterly wrapped up in music: swing music, that being the very end of the big band era. Ralph Flanagan, Sauter-Finegan, Billy May: those were Frank's heroes, and his dream in life was to be a big band arranger. Cowboys and mountains had no place in Frank's life, and he spent the entire two weeks fretfully hunkered over the ranch's only radio, a huge pre-war monster that could barely bring in Albuquerque. He clearly saw himself as a prisoner—an innocent prisoner at that—with Koo as the evil jailer.

As for thirteen-year-old Barry, his passion was even farther from trout streams and backpacking; he was a science-fiction fan, a voracious reader and a constant designer on graph paper of rockets and space stations, all prominently featuring the American Air Force star-in-a-circle. (This was before Sputnik dampened the science-fiction fans' more chauvinistic sentiments.) Barry ran out of reading material the fourth day and graph paper the sixth. Also, Koo made the mistake of ordering him out of the house and onto a horse, during one break in the rain. It was probably sulky Barry's fault that the normally placid horse eventually threw him into a rail fence and broke his arm. ("Two weeks from now," a misguided pal told Koo, "you'll think back on this and laugh." Koo gave him a look: "Twenty *years* from now," he said, "if anybody mentions this and laughs, I'll kill him.")

This disaster didn't stop Koo from trying. He knew at last he'd made a mistake in shutting those kids out of his life, and he was determined to make up for it, so over the next several years he took the children from time to time on their vacations from school, and gradually learned to leave them alone with their enthusiasms. A kind of distant respect grew up on both sides, an aloof sort of tolerance. The boys were never warm toward Koo, but they liked him well enough, as though he were a long-term friend of the family; not of their generation, but basically all right. Koo, feeling the guilt of his earlier omission, circled cautiously around the boys, accepting whatever affection they could show him.

Did he love them? He never asked himself that question, wouldn't have considered it in any way to the point. The point was to get them to love him; his own feelings didn't matter. In truth he did love them, fiercely and with terror, but that love had only surfaced the once, during Barry's pneumonia. He— and they—remained essentially unaware of it, and operated at a much cooler and less passionate level. The fact was, the missing years could not be reclaimed. Koo was not their father any longer; he had waited too long.

With the children's maturity, the pressure eased. It was permissible, after all, to leave grown children to their own devices. Koo helped where he could, stood ready to answer any call, but didn't push himself forward. Barry wanted Yale, and Koo got it for him. Frank wanted UCLA, and Koo arranged that. Frank's ardor for music gradually shifted to an interest in movie music, then to movies, and finally to television; with Koo's help, he was taken on by a network affiliate station in Chicago after graduation from UCLA, and now he's a middle-management executive in the network's home office in New York. Barry's interests having swung much more wildly between future and past, he is now a partner in a highly profitable antique dealership in London, selling chandeliers, sideboards and firescreens to Arabs and Texans.

Koo's learning about Barry's homosexuality was, in fact, the only real trauma in his relationship with either of his children once they'd grown up. Barry, visiting Koo in L.A. with his "friend," announced the fact of his inversion with a kind of unblinking defiant vulnerability that touched Koo almost as deeply as the pneumonia-racked skinny body had one day almost twenty years before. He didn't *want* the boy to be queer, he didn't want Barry to face the complications and the suffering and the loneliness that Koo felt convinced were the inevitable complements of homosexuality, but he didn't dare say aloud even one word of what he thought. His reaction was instinctive and immediate and based on his ingrained perception of the relationship between himself and his children. What he thought of them or about them didn't matter; it didn't even matter who in fact they were; all that mattered was that somehow he must, in a permanent and clear cut way, win their love—as he had long since won the affection and the (granted much shallower) love of the American audience. "It's up to you, Barry," he said, at once, "but remember; if you and Len have any children, I want them brought up Catholic."

What if—Koo isn't sure he even dares to phrase this question, the answer means so much to him—what if, now... What if (all in a rush) these people go to *Barry*, or to *Frank*? "We've got your father. Mortgage your house, empty your bank accounts, convert everything you own to cash, give it all to us, and we'll give your father back." Back? Have they ever actually had Koo, have they ever really thought of themselves as having a father, who happens to be this fellow here, this Koo Davis?

What would they do? Barry and Frank, how would they react? Do they love Koo Davis? Do they love him enough to trade all their money for him?

Well, that isn't even a sensible question, and Koo knows it, because he knows who'll pay. He himself, he'll pay; that's who. These people grabbed him because he's supposed to've piled up a lot of bucks over the years and they want some. The only question is who they'll deal with on the outside, and the fear in Koo's mind is not that Barry and Frank don't love him enough to buy him back; the fear in his mind is that the boys don't love him enough to *deal*: "Who? The old man? Why not talk to his agent? Her name is Lynsey Rayne, she's the one closest to him. Hold on, I'll give you the number."

Oh, Jesus, Jesus, would they do that? Koo can't bear the question, much less the answer. He can't bear any questions, locked away here in this cavern under the waves—imprisoned king, in the cave beneath the sea. "I refuse to ask myself any more questions," Koo says aloud, "on the grounds I may incriminate myself."

The fact is, Lynsey Rayne really *is* closer to Koo than anybody else in his life. She used to be Max Berry's assistant, and when Max retired Lynsey came to Koo and said, "I'm taking over Max's client list."

Koo was already looking around among established agents for a Max replacement, so all he said was, "Oh, yeah?"

"Yeah," she said. "And there's two reasons why I want you to stick with me."

"Name them."

"Number one, you're easy. Everybody knows who you are, I don't have to go out and sell you. I just sit in the office, say yes to one offer in ten, skim my percentage and live fat."

Laughing, Koo said, "Now I *got* to hear the other one."

"Max has been sick a long time," she said. "I've *been* your agent for the last five years. Nobody knows you better than me."

And she was right, wasn't she? "Nobody knows you better than me." Jesus Christ, when Koo casts around in his mind for his closest relation, his nearest and dearest, he comes up with his *agent*. Lynsey's a terrific lady, one of the best—*not* one of the blondes to be trouped and shtupped—but is this any way to run a life? Your next of kin is your agent?

A distraction, a distraction. He paces his small soft-surfaced carpeted prison, trying to push all the bad thoughts, the horrible questions, right out of his mind. Death, love, money…

Hunger. How about that one? *There's* something he can think about, because the fact of the matter is, Koo is getting damn hungry.

There's a lot of food in his room, bread and cereal and milk and even what smells like bargain basement Scotch, but Koo won't touch any of it. It's the booze that makes him nervous about the rest. Why give him so much, and why throw in whiskey? Maybe it's drugged, huh? They've left him alone a couple hours, so maybe they're just waiting for the drug to take effect. Koo doesn't know how or if he can help himself out of this jam, but one thing is sure: if he's doped up, he can't take advantage of any break that *might* come along.

As for his cell, his cage, his prison, Koo looks around and says out loud, "I been in worse places, and paid forty bucks a night." It has become his habit in recent years to talk to himself, but only in the form of one-liners, asides, comments on the action of his life. This remark is unfortunate, though, because it leads his thoughts directly to the next question, which is: how much will *this* room cost? All or most of his assets? His life?

"Then there's the view," Koo says, hurriedly. "It overlooks the garden. Completely. And the weather's been so *wet* recently." Turning, pacing the small room, making fretful hand gestures, he says, "I wish I had a cigarette, and I don't even smoke. I'd use it to point at things."

Koo used to smoke. For nearly thirty years, one of his trademarks was the cigarette between the first two fingers of his left hand, used in casual gestures, mostly with gag lines where something was being dismissed. "I told him, Sergeant, I don't want to be in the Army at *all*." A silhouette drawing used in the logo of his weekly television show back in the fifties showed his profile and his waving left hand with the cigarette and a curl of smoke coming up around his face. But seven years ago his doctor told him to stop, giving him a lot of medical reasons that Koo refused to hear, and Koo stopped. Like that. He's never been willing to think about death, about his own mortality or any of the grimmer steps along the path, the aches and pains, the accidents and illnesses and gradual wasting away that must come to every human being in time. He doesn't want to think about all that shit, and he won't think about all that shit, and there's nothing more to be said about it. He's got enough money to hire good doctors, so he hires good doctors, and he does what they tell him to do, and if they insist on telling him *why* he just nods and grins and doesn't listen.

There's no way out of this room. The door is securely locked, and it opens outward so there's no way to get at the hinges. Shortly after he was left alone in here Koo did some poking at the fabric covering the wall, working low on the corner nearest the door, and behind the cloth he found Sheetrock and behind that concrete block. "No way am I gonna dig through concrete block," he told himself, and searched no further.

The next question was the window. After the bitch with the scars vacated the pool, Koo spent a while studying that window, considering the possibility of maybe throwing a chair through it or something. Water would rush through the opening, but long before the room filled up the pool would have emptied below the window level. It would be like a James Bond flick; heave the chair, brace himself against the side wall until the water level in room and pool equalized, then *swim to freedom*!

Yeah; carrying an American flag and shooting Roman candles out his ass. "When I was *twenty* I couldn't pull a stunt like that." Also even when he was twenty the noise and racket involved in wrecking a swimming pool would attract a certain amount of attention. *Also* also, this window happens to be two thicknesses of very heavy-grade plate glass, and if he did throw a chair at it probably the chair would bounce off and crack open the Koo Davis skull. "I got trouble enough," Koo reluctantly decided, and since then he's had no further thought of escape. He's stuck here with these meatheads until they decide to do something else.

*Scrabble click*. Koo looks over at the door, where the sound came from, the sound of a key in the lock, and he can't help a little thrill of fear, that buzzing adrenalin surge like when you've just had a near miss on the freeway. "Company," Koo says. "And me not dressed."

The door opens and two of them come in. One is the sarcastic-looking fellow who was in here the last time, and the other is the sullen-faced bearded character who showed him the gun at the studio. The bitch with the scars isn't along, for which Koo is grateful, but on the other hand neither is the worried-looking guy who apologized for Koo's nosebleed. Koo misses that one, he was the only touch of common humanity in the whole mob. And speaking of mobs, just how many of these people are there?

The two young men come in, closing the door behind themselves. The bearded one puts a small cassette tape recorder on the nearest table, then stands silently with his back against the door and his arms folded over his chest, like a harem guard in a comedy, while the sarcastic-looking fellow says, "How you doing, Koo?"

"I got nothing to say, warden," Koo snarls. "To you *or* the D.A."

"That's good," the fellow says, then looks in mild surprise at the plastic container with the whiskey in it. "Not drinking? Wait a minute—not eating either?"

"I'm on a diet."

The fellow frowns at Koo, apparently not understanding, then suddenly laughs and says, "You think we're trying to *poison* you? Or drugs maybe, is that it?"

Koo doesn't have a comic answer, and there's no point giving a straight answer, so he just stands there.

The fellow shakes his head, amused but impatient. "What's the percentage, Koo? We've already got you." Then he goes to the counter beside the bar, lines up three plastic glasses, and pours a finger of whiskey in each. "Choose," he says.

"I won't drink it."

"Just *pick* one, Koo."

"How come you call me by my first name? You're no traffic cop."

"*I'm* sorry, Koo," the fellow says, with his most sarcastic smile. "I'm just trying for a more relaxed atmosphere, that's all. For instance, you can call me Peter, and this is Mark. Now we're all friends, am I right?" He gestures at the three glasses. "So decide. Which one?"

"My mother says I can't play with you guys anymore. I got to go home now."

The bearded one—Mark—says, "Pick a glass." There's nothing comic in his manner at all. In fact, there's the implication in his voice that if Koo *doesn't* pick a glass, this guy is going to start using his fists again.

Shrugging, Koo says, "Okay. I say the pea is under the one on the left."

"Fine," says the sarcastic-looking fellow: Peter. He picks up the other two glasses and hands one to Mark. "Happy days," he says, toasting Koo, and then they both drink the whiskey. "Not bad," the leader says, and extends the third glass toward Koo, saying, "Sure you won't join us?"

Oh, the hell with it. "I'll hate myself in the morning," Koo says, taking the glass, and he sips a little. It tastes nothing at all like Jack Daniel's, Koo's favorite whiskey, but it does spread an immediate warm alcohol glow through his body.

Peter has now taken some folded sheets of typewriter paper from his jacket pocket. "You're going to make a recording for us now, Koo," he says.

Koo had guessed that from the cassette recorder. He gives Peter what's supposed to be a defiant look. "I am?"

Peter glances over his shoulder at the tough guy, Mark, then grins again at Koo. "Yes, you are," he says. Holding out the sheets of paper toward Koo, he says, "You may want to look it over first. You'll begin with some personal remarks of your own, some statement to convince your family and your close friends that it's really you, and then you'll follow up by reading this. Exactly as written, Koo."

Koo takes the papers. There are three sheets, messily type-written, with many pen and pencil alterations in various hand-writings. It isn't easy to read, but very soon the thrust of the message makes itself clear, and Koo looks up at these bastards and says, "You're out of your fucking minds."

"That's okay, Koo," Peter says, unruffled. "You don't have to agree with it, you just read it. Like it was a movie script."

"They'll say no," Koo tells him. "And then what happens?"

"Tough for you," says Mark.

"That's what I thought."

"Oh, don't be pessimistic," Peter says. "You're an important man, Koo, you've got a lot of important friends. I think they'll come through for you, pal, I really do. That's why I picked you."

"They won't do it," Koo says.

Peter looks a bit troubled, a bit grim. "I hope you're wrong, Koo. For your sake, I hope so." Turning, he says, "Mark, get the machine ready."

Koo can't believe this is happening to him. "Killed," he mutters. "Murdered to death by assholes."

# 5

Lynsey Rayne parked her Porsche Targa behind the Burbank Police Headquarters annex. A tall and fashionably dressed woman of forty-one, wearing many bracelets, she entered the building through the rear door, and asked directions to "the Koo Davis office." That was what Inspector Cayzer had told her to ask for, on the phone, and it produced a uniformed police-woman to escort her down brightly lit bare corridors to a small crowded office with the hastily assembled air of a campaign headquarters, where she identified herself to another police-woman working as receptionist: "Lynsey Rayne. I'm Koo Davis' agent, I spoke to Inspector Cayzer earlier."

"One minute, please."

Apparently this set-up was not yet organized enough to have intercoms; but the kidnapping and its investigation were still less than two hours old. Lynsey waited while the policewoman went to an inner office to report, then came back and said, "Yes, Miss Rayne, you can go in."

Entering the inner office, equally small and ramshackle but somewhat less crowded, Lynsey saw two men rising from their desks. The one on the right was Inspector Cayzer, an old man but, she had been assured by Mayor Pilocki, a good one. "So you found us," he said, smiling, and extended his hand, which she took, saying, "Any news?"

"Not yet, Ms. Rayne."

"Inspector," she said, and echoed his own earlier words to her, "surely they've gone to ground by now."

"Kidnappers work at their own pace, Ms. Rayne," Cayzer said. "I'm afraid there's nothing we can do to hurry them along.

May I introduce Agent Michael Wiskiel of the Federal Bureau of Investigation? Agent Wiskiel, this is Ms. Lynsey Rayne, Koo Davis' agent."

"How do you do," Wiskiel said. He had come around from behind his desk in anticipation of the introduction, and as Lynsey shook his hand she studied him carefully, needing to understand him; he had suddenly become very important to Koo. The reports she'd gotten on Wiskiel from her calls to friends in Washington, after Cayzer had mentioned his name, had been ambivalent. He'd had something minor to do with Watergate, and had been demoted. He had a reputation as a hotshot, a right-winger, a tough man but not a subtle one. Nothing in his heavy good looks did anything to dispel this impression. Feeling the need to let him know at once that she was not easily dismissible, she said, "You haven't been out here long, have you?"

"About a year." His grin was easy, loose, sensual. "What told you? Not enough tan?"

"I'm an old friend of Webster's," she said, releasing his hand, referring to Wiskiel's immediate boss, Webster Redburn. "I spoke with him on the phone about an hour ago."

A film seemed to settle over Wiskiel's face, though his expression hardly changed at all; perhaps something faintly mocking entered his smile. "Is that right," he said, and turned away to gesture at something on the side wall. "I don't suppose that face means anything to you."

"Is she one of them?" Lynsey stepped closer to the drawing, holding her glasses at a tight angle to her face. The sketch showed an anonymous standard type; about thirty, long straight hair parted in the middle, and a plain half-formed slightly worried face, as though she'd been taken from the oven before ready. "She doesn't look the part, does she?"

"That's why they had her out front. She was the one worked at the studio."

"More like a flower child," Lynsey said. "In fact..." Struck by something, she leaned closer to the drawing, trying to capture the brief impression that had just flashed by. But it was no good; stepping back, releasing her glasses, shaking her head, she said, "No."

"Don't tell me you thought you recognized her."

"Not from actually seeing her, no," Lynsey said. "Not in the flesh. But I thought— For just a second she reminded me of a newspaper photo, or something on television. Was it the anti-war people? Or, you remember the period when they were attacking banks."

"Very well," he said.

"Could she have been involved in that?"

He looked at the sketch, something moving behind his eyes, some old battle still not resolved. She turned to gaze again too at that characterless Identikit face, the smooth plain features untouched by experience, the flat expressionless eyes. A flower child, yes; but it's been winter a long time.

"She could have been involved in anything," Wiskiel said.

Lynsey waited in the office, even though there was nothing happening and Jock Cayzer several times promised to call her the instant they heard anything new. The phone number here had been announced over the radio and television as the place to call "if you have any information on the disappearance of Koo Davis," so it was likeliest this was the way the kidnappers would make contact. "The minute they call, Ms. Rayne," Cayzer said, "I'll let you know."

But she wasn't to be moved. "They'll call tonight," she answered, matter-of-fact but determined. "I want to be here, in case they let Koo say anything. I'll know...how he is, from the way he sounds."

During the next two hours the phone did ring from time to time, and Lynsey on each occasion became once more tense,

all concentrated eyes and ears, but it was only the usual cranks
and clowns. Then, a little before eight-thirty, the next event
came, not from the phone but from the workroom next door,
where three police officers studying snapshots taken from
Koo's audience suddenly hit paydirt. Two faces had emerged
that were not to be found anywhere in the main group photographs. In the darkened workroom they all stood looking at
the blown-up slide on the wall, the two strangers clearly visible
behind and to the right of the smiling ten-year-old boy who was
the photographer's primary focus.

"They're young," Lynsey said. She felt both surprised and
obscurely annoyed, as though their youth somehow made things
worse.

They *were* young, both about thirty, slouching and round-
shouldered in an even more youthful manner. The one in profile
had thick curly black hair, a full beard and sunglasses, and wore
a yellow T-shirt with some unidentifiable saying or picture on
it, plus a short blue denim jacket and jeans. His companion,
facing the camera, also wore sunglasses, but his rather bony
worried-looking face was clean-shaven. His hair, over a high
rounded shiny brow, was a wispy thinning brown, blowing in
the breeze. He was wearing a light plaid open-collar shirt, what
looked to be a light brown suede zipper jacket, and chinos.

"Those are just soldiers," Jock Cayzer said. "We haven't seen
the general yet."

"When we do, Jock," Wiskiel said, "he'll look a lot like them."
And he switched on the workroom lights.

The phone rang in the other room. "Not another one," Lynsey
said.

"I'll get it," Wiskiel said, and went back to the other room.

All phone calls were being taped, on equipment also in this
workroom. A monitor was on, so Lynsey and the others in here
could listen to both parts of the conversation, beginning with

the click when Wiskiel picked up the receiver and said, "Seven seven hundred."

The voice on the other end was young, male and very uncertain. It struck Lynsey that either of those young men in the photograph could conceivably sound like this. "Excuse me," it said. "Is this the number for, uh, if you know something, if you want to talk about Koo Davis?"

"That's right. This is FBI Agent Wiskiel here."

"Oh. Well, uh, I think I've got something for you."

"What would that be?"

"Well— It's a cassette recording, I guess it's from the kidnappers. It's got Koo Davis' voice on it. It's pretty weird."

The boy was twenty. A tall slender blond California youth, his name was Alan Lewis, he lived in Santa Monica with his parents, and he attended UCLA, where he was an assistant features editor on *The Californian*, the university's daily newspaper. According to his story, he'd been watching television when a phone call had come from a woman who wouldn't give her name but who said, approximately, "You can have a scoop for your paper. We have Koo Davis, we are holding him in the name of the people. Look in your car. On the front seat you'll find a tape. It isn't too late, the people *still* can win."

"At first I thought it was a joke," the boy explained. "But I couldn't figure out who she was. She didn't sound like any of the girls I knew. She sounded—I don't know—"

Wiskiel suggested, "Older?"

"Yeah, I guess so. No, not exactly. Well, maybe older, but mostly, well, *sad*. You know? She was saying these things, 'The people *still* can win,' and all that stuff, but there wasn't any *pep* in it. That's why I finally figured maybe it was on the level, and I went out and looked in the car."

Where he had found the cassette recording on the front seat, as promised. Having his own cassette player, he'd listened to part of the recording, but once he'd satisfied himself he was really hearing Koo Davis' voice he'd immediately called the special number given on television. As to why he'd been chosen to receive the cassette, he could offer no explanation other than his job on the university paper: "She did say she was giving me a scoop." Nor could he identify either the Identikit drawing of "Janet Grey" or the two men in the photograph.

In the workroom again, Lynsey and the others waited while the technician inserted the cassette, arranged to simultaneously record it onto his own tape, and pushed the Play button. After a few seconds of rustling silence the familiar voice began, abruptly, loud and clear and unmistakable:

"Hello, everybody, this is Koo Davis. To steal a line from John Chancellor, I'm somewhere in custody. To tell the truth I don't know *where* I am, but it looked better in the brochure."

There was a handy metal folding chair; weak-kneed, Lynsey dropped into it, trembling and astonished at her reaction to that voice, known in so many ways, personal and public. Until this instant, now, when the voice proclaimed so clearly that Koo was still alive and unharmed, she had been hiding from herself the fear, the terror, that he was dead, or that awful dreadful things were being done to him. Now, her sense of relief was almost as strong as if he were already home again and safe; she felt the blood rushing from her head, she felt the overpowering physical need to faint, and she fought against it, digging her nails into her palms. It wasn't over; Koo wasn't home; he wasn't safe; she couldn't relax, not yet.

The easy, confident, astonishingly cheerful voice went on: "The crowd here is a lot like television people. Floor managers. Stand here, do that, talk into the mike, read this script. I don't know about these hours, though. Did you guys check this out with AFTRA?"

Lynsey felt Wiskiel frowning at her, and she elaborately and silently mouthed the explanation: "*The union*." He nodded.

"Anyway, folks," Koo was saying, suddenly speaking more quickly, as though one of the "floor managers" had off-mike ordered him to get on with it, "I'm supposed to say something here to prove I'm really me and not Frank Gorshin, so check with my agent Lynsey Rayne—are you sure this is the right gig for me, honey?—about the writer I call 'The Tragic Relief,' with the initials dee-double-u."

At Koo's mention of her own name, Lynsey's eyes had suddenly filled with tears, which she determinedly blinked away. And when she saw Wiskiel again frowning at her she nodded at him, to say that Koo's reference to The Tragic Relief had made sense to her.

"And now," Koo was going on, "I'm supposed to read this statement. Here goes: I am being held by elements of the People's Revolutionary Army—huh, think of that—and have so far not been harmed—except for the punch in the nose, let's not forget about that. The People's Revolutionary Army is not materi— Wait a minute. I don't usually get words like this in my scripts. The only really big word I know is BankAmericard. The People's Revolutionary Army is not ma-ter-i-a-lis-tic-ally or-i-en-ted—there—and so this is not a kidnapping in the ordinary capitalist sense. Well, that's a relief. We have chosen Koo Davis not because he is rich—smart, very smart—but because he has made a career of being court jester to the bosses, the warmongers and the forces of reaction. You left out the Girl Scouts. Okay, okay. The United States, which trumpets endlessly about civil rights in other nations, itself has thousands of political prisoners in its jails. Ten of these are to be released and are to be given air passage to Algeria or whatever other destination they choose. These ten are to be released within the next twenty-four hours, or a certain amount of harm will come to me. I don't think I like that part. Once the ten have been released and are safely at the destinations of their choice, I will be permitted to return to my normal life. If there is any delay, the People's Revolutionary Army will take what action toward me it deems fit. The ten people are: Norman Cobberton, Hugh Pendry, Abby Lancaster, Louis Goldney, William Brown—who are these people?—Howard Fenton, Eric Mallock, George Toll—sounds like a VIP list at the bus station—Fred Walpole, and Mary Martha DeLang. This complete recording is to be played on all network and Los Angeles area radio and television news programs beginning at eleven o'clock tonight, and is to be played on all network radio and television news programs during the day and evening tomorrow. If it isn't played according to these instructions, the People's Revolutionary Army will take appropriate action toward me. These demands are not negotiable. So that was, uhhhh, the message from our sponsor. And from the way it looks here, my only hope is I flunk the audition and they send me home."

# 6

Joyce and the others sat in the darkened living room together, all five of them, watching the eleven o'clock news on NBC, Channel 4. The lights outside the house were off, and through the long wall of glass doors at one side of the room moonlight reflected silver-gray from the breeze-ruffled surface of the pool. Beyond the pool and its cantilevered deck the Valley could be seen, a gridwork of dotted light-lines dividing the darkness into comprehensible bite-size chunks, while the greater darkness remained intact, surrounding and above.

The Koo Davis kidnapping was the major news story, the lead-in piece. The newscaster announced the fact of the kidnapping and then the cassette tape was played, in its entirety, while on the screen a photograph appeared, a publicity still; a smiling Koo Davis face, in color, confident and successful.

Joyce hadn't listened to the tape before it went out, and she didn't really listen now. This wasn't her part of the work, and it didn't interest her to know the details. She was content to be the one who entered the straight world, got the jobs, drove the van away from the studio, delivered the tape to the boy in Santa Monica, made the easy informational phone calls. And here in the house she was the den mother, she made the dinner, washed the dishes, did the laundry.

For Joyce, the group in the darkness around the flickering TV light was like some wonderful kind of camping out. In her childhood, in Racine, where the winters were so long and so cold, "camping out" had mostly meant what were known as "overnights": half a dozen giggling girls on mattresses or folded blankets on a living room floor, the host parents far away in their own part of the house, the girls clustering together like tiny delighted animals at the dry hidden warm bottom of the world, whispering and shushing at one another, young small bodies in the nightgowns trembling with exhilaration.

It was the group that Joyce loved, the very idea of being part of a group. In her childhood she had been a Brownie, later a Girl Scout and for a while simultaneously a Campfire Girl, also member of a Junior Sodality at church, the 4-H Club, other groups at school and college; and tonight she sat with her feet curled up under her at one end of the sofa, the complete group around her, the television offering its flickering light to the room, and she was back where it had all begun: an "overnight," with friends. Her hand over her mouth so no one would know, her eyes on the screen without seeing it, her ears ignoring the loping cadence of Koo Davis' voice, she giggled.

When the tape came to its end—"and they send me home"— the Koo Davis photograph on the screen was replaced by film of an office, where two men stood behind a desk while several photographers snapped their picture and newsmen asked them questions, some extending microphones. A voice said, "In charge of the investigation into the Koo Davis kidnapping is Chief Inspector Cayzer of the Burbank Police. Representing the FBI is Michael Wiskiel, Assistant to the Chief of Station of the Los Angeles office of the FBI."

"Wiskiel," Mark said, while an old man in a Stetson said on-screen that they didn't have much to go on so far. "He had something to do with Watergate."

"Hush," said Peter.

The announcer's off-camera voice had returned: "Agent Wiskiel was asked if the ten named individuals would be released from prison."

The scene cut from the old man in the Stetson to Wiskiel, a

heavyset fortyish man with too much self-conscious actorish good looks. Wiskiel said, "Well, it's early yet, and frankly I don't recognize every one of those names, we're not even sure yet they're all *in* prison. If they are, it'll be up to Washington to make a decision about their release. I don't know if the kidnappers are watching—"

"We are," Peter said. Joyce giggled, this time not repressing it.

"—but I hope they realize their time limit just isn't realistic. I want to get Koo Davis back as much as anybody, but they're asking for a decision that I just don't think can be made in twenty-four hours."

"Send them a finger," Mark said.

Joyce shivered, not looking toward Mark, trying to make believe to herself that she hadn't heard him. Mark frightened her whenever she was incautious enough to think about him; he was in the group but not of it, a cold separate presence, an anti-body. As much as possible, Joyce pretended that Mark didn't exist.

On the screen, Agent Wiskiel was saying, "In the meantime, from the sound of that tape they haven't up to this point actually harmed Koo Davis, and I'm very hopeful we'll be able to negotiate some sort of agreement with these people. I'll have to wait for word from Washington on the details, but it's my guess we'll have Koo Davis home and safe in a very short period of time."

"In a box," Mark said.

"*Hush*," Peter told him, and Joyce flashed Peter a grateful smile, which he apparently didn't see.

The television scene switched to the news set in the studio, where the announcer spent some time telling the audience how many famous people had publicly expressed their shock and outrage that a "great entertainer" like Koo Davis had been treated in such a barbarous fashion. An ex-President was quoted as referring to "this man who has brought the gift of laughter to millions."

Next, the announcer went on to a description of the four people so far identified by the media out of the ten whose release had been demanded, and a picture of each of the four in turn was shown on the screen while a biased inaccurate brief biography was given. One was Eric Mallock, and it was during his biography that Liz's name was mentioned:

"Eric Mallock, thirty-two, is currently in the Federal Penitentiary at Lewisburg in Kentucky, serving an indeterminate sentence on a number of convictions, including destruction of property and attempted murder. A member of a splinter group from the Weathermen, Mallock was captured in August of 1972 in Chicago when a building apparently being used as a bomb factory blew up, killing two people outright and severely wounding Mallock. Two associates of Mallock's believed also to have been in the building at the time, Elizabeth Knight and Frances Steffalo, disappeared and have not been seen since, though Federal warrants are out for both women."

"You're in the news!" Peter cried, with his sardonic bark of laughter.

Liz made no answer. Looking at her profile, Joyce saw her as expressionless as ever. Joyce envied Liz that coolness. What was Liz thinking, seeing her lover's face on the television screen after all these years? Nothing showed; and when the picture changed to another face, there was still not the slightest flicker from Liz.

Then, at the very end of the news story, Joyce had her own opportunity to react to a face on the screen; her own. Or was it her own? "The police sketch of the woman calling herself Janet Grey" was plain, glum, anonymous. Peter made another mocking remark, which Joyce was too agitated to hear. Appalled, she thought, Is *that* what I look like? Gazing at that pale sketch, she felt the heat in her own face as she blushed, and was afraid to look away, lest she meet someone's eye. If only she had some of Liz's unconcern.

The blank-faced sketch seemed to stay on the screen forever; then at last it disappeared, replaced by the mobile face of the announcer, moving on to other stories. Rising, Peter switched on a floor lamp and turned off the TV. Obviously pleased with himself, facing the others with his back to the receding-dot light of the TV screen, he said, "They'll produce. We picked the right horse, and they'll trade."

"You shouldn't have let him do all those jokes," Mark said. "I told you at the time, make him do it over, without the wise-cracks."

Peter shrugged; Joyce thought he showed astonishing for-bearance with Mark. He said, "What difference does it make?"

"Because he sounds like the winner," Mark said. "He sounds like *he's* got *us*."

"You worry too much about the appearance of things." Peter put a hand to his face, stroked his cheek with his fingertips, his expression pained. Joyce recognized that gesture; it meant Peter was troubled, struggling to retain control or composure. Joyce wished Mark would leave Peter alone, he had enough to think about as it was. "The important thing is," Peter said, "the other side knows he's alive and well. He's our trading counter, and he has to be recognizable."

"He made fun of us. He's the star and we're the stooges."

"Mark, so what? Would you rather be on top, with the power, or on the bottom making fun?"

"*He's* on top," Mark insisted. "*He* has the power."

"Then go downstairs and kick him a few times," Peter said,

obviously annoyed and bored. "Show him who's in charge."

Joyce was grateful when Larry chimed in then, awkwardly but earnestly changing the conversation, saying, "Um, Peter, what about the deadline business? What that FBI man said, that they can't get an answer out of Washington in twenty-four hours. Do you think that's true?"

Mark said, "They have to be pushed."

Peter smiled easily at Larry. "We'll send them another tape tomorrow night," he said. "And this time we'll let Mark direct the performance."

Larry looked disapproving, but didn't react directly. Instead, he said, "How much time will we give them, really?"

"We don't know, really. The minimum time possible."

"I wonder…" Larry said, musing, then said, "Peter? Do you think he's trainable?"

Peter seemed amused. "Koo Davis? You want to orientate Koo Davis in dialectical materialism?"

"An intelligent brain is capable of seeing truth," Larry said.

"Then give it a try," Peter suggested. Joyce saw that he was mocking Larry, and that Larry knew but didn't care. "Spend time with him tomorrow," Peter said, "discuss the theory of labor. How much is a man worth who tells jokes for a living?"

"All men are worth the same," Larry said.

Peter gave him a sly look. "More and more, Larry, your politics sound like religion."

Mark said, "I'll go look at Davis, check him one last time tonight."

He means to do something cruel, Joyce thought, looking at Mark's face, grim and angry behind the heavy beard. She was glad when Larry said, "I'll go with you."

Mark gave him a venomous look. "You can go instead of me," he said, and walked away, toward his bedroom.

"Leave Davis alone for tonight," Peter said. "He's all right down there."

"I didn't want Mark to see him alone."

"I know, Larry."

Liz abruptly got to her feet, saying, "Mark's right, we should push them, get this over with. Phone that number they gave, put Davis on, let Mark twist his arm. When they hear Davis holler, they'll start to move."

Peter shook his head, like a patient tutor with a backward pupil. "In the first place, they'd trace the call. In the second place, if we start with high pressure, where do we go from there? We begin calm, and we crank it up a bit at a time. If they stall we can still go way up. We can let Mark slice off his ears, for instance." Peter chuckled, a low comfortable sound. "Can you imagine that round neat head without ears?"

Joyce, who preferred to be silent, was driven to speech now, saying in a pained voice, "You aren't serious, Peter."

"Of course not," Peter told her, speaking easily, but Joyce watched his face and eyes, and she thought he might very well be serious, if the circumstances were right.

Liz said, "Peter. Do you want to fuck?"

He seemed to consider the question, without much enthusiasm. "Possibly."

"All right, then. Good night," Liz said, and walked from the room. Smiling slightly, Peter followed her.

Leaving Larry and Joyce. Open sexuality had been a postulate in the Movement in the early days, sexual relationships as a statement of political belief, so these five people had long ago completed the round of all the possible heterosexual couplings. But sex had long since faded as a primary factor with any of them; these days, only Liz would raise the subject in public, and particularly in that aggressive way.

The introduction of sex in that manner and these circumstances left Joyce embarrassed and uneasy. She didn't want Larry to feel obligated to make the same offer to her; she had no illusion that he might actually want to have sex with her. Casting about for a new topic, glancing over at the TV screen, she said, "Larry?"

"Yes?"

"Did that look like me?"

"Not a bit," Larry said. He sounded surprised at the question. "To tell the truth, I thought they did those things better."

"It must have looked *something* like me."

"I'll tell you want it looked like," Larry said, coming over and sitting at the other end of the sofa. "It looked like a *category* of person which includes you, but it didn't look like you. It looked like someone who might be you for two seconds from a block away, but then you'd say, 'Oh, no, that doesn't look like Joyce at *all.*' "

"It's not that I'm being vain." Joyce was always afraid people would think her too feminine. "It was just that she looked—dead."

"It wasn't accurate," Larry told her. "I promise."

She offered him a quick grateful smile. "Thank you." Then, looking at his earnest face, all the doubts she tried to keep buried came rushing into her mind, and she cried, "Larry, is it really going to work? Will it all come *out* somewhere?"

"Of course." He was surprised, and it showed. "We've had victories," he said. "We'll have more."

"Yes," she said, concealing her doubts.

But he leaned closer, saying, "Do you mean you fight without believing in the inevitability of success? Don't you know, historically, we *must* win?"

"Yes, of course. It just seems so long sometimes." Then she

smiled at him, knowing he needed the reassurance more than she did. "And I seem so short. Good night, Larry." She patted his knee, and got to her feet.

"Good night, Joyce."

"Don't bother about Davis tonight," she told him.

"No, that was just to protect him from Mark. He's all right down there, he'll keep until morning."

## 7

"My *brain* is happy to be here," Koo Davis says, "but my feet wanna be in Tennessee." That's a line from *Saturday Evening Ghost*, one of a series of comic spook movies Koo made in the early forties. Portraits with moving eyes, chairs whose arms suddenly reach up and grab at the person seated there, wall panels that open so a black-gloved hand can emerge clutching a knife; and Koo Davis moving brash and unknowing through it all. It was a genre then, everybody did the same gags: the candle that slid along a tabletop, the stuffed gorilla on wheels whose finger was caught (unknown to him) in the back of the hero's belt so he'd be tiptoeing through the spooky house with this gorilla rolling along behind him, the hero pretending to be one of the figures in a wax museum. The audiences didn't seem to care how often they saw those gags, and a recurring bit in Koo's movies was the point where he would suddenly *notice* all those weird things around him, and become terrified. Koo's bit of going from oblivious self-assurance to gibbering terror was one of his most famous routines, so much so that Bosley Crowther wrote in a review, "No one can make panic as hilarious as Koo Davis."

I'm scared, Koo thinks, but he doesn't say it aloud; it ain't that hilarious. Remembering how often he simulated fear in all those movies, and later on television, he's surprised at how different the real thing is. Of course, like everyone else he's known brief moments of fear in his life—mostly on those USO tours—but what he's feeling now is steady, growing, ongoing. He's afraid of these people, he's afraid of what will happen, he's afraid of his own helplessness, and he's afraid of his fear.

"Why would anybody be afraid of getting killed?" he asks. That's a line from *Your Genial Ghost*, and it was supposed to be a rhetorical question, but in fact death is not at all what Koo fears now. His imagination crawls instead with images of pain, images of humiliation. He's afraid they'll hurt him in some awful way, and he's afraid he won't be brave in front of them. He'd hate to live the rest of his life remembering himself groveling on the floor in front of these bastards.

What if they do something to his throat or his mouth, so he can't talk? What if they blind him or scar him in some awful way? What if they cut him—he's always been afraid of knives, sharp things.

"We've got nothing to fear but fear itself—and that big guy over there with the sword." *The Zombie Goes to College*. He keeps trying to reassure himself—they haven't done anything to him yet, have they? They haven't even threatened very much. But Koo remembers the look on that one guy's face, the bearded son of a bitch who showed him the gun way back at the beginning. He's probably also the one who hit him when the sack was over his head. And he doesn't talk, he just stands there and glares at Koo like he'd prefer Koo's head on a platter, with an apple in his mouth.

If only they wanted money. He'd been afraid earlier that they'd ask too much, but now he believes he could somehow have raised any amount they wanted. Ask for money, you bastards, and I'll find it, one way or the other I'll buy my way out of here. "Will you take a post-dated check?" Anything; ask for something I've got, ask for something that makes some kind of goddamn *sense*.

Ten political prisoners. The Feds won't do it, Koo is convinced they won't do it, and why the hell should they? Koo has no illusions about his "friendships" with generals and senators; one of the perks of being a general or a senator is to hang around with famous show biz people, and one of the perks of being a famous show biz celebrity is to hang around with generals and senators. "They come out ahead on *that* deal," Koo says, but he doesn't really mean it. He's always enjoyed the company of VIPs, playing golf with them, going on hunting weekends, cruising on their yachts, visiting at their ranches, and he knows damn well they've enjoyed him just as much, but that doesn't mean they're going to release ten weirdos and crazies in return for one Koo Davis.

They won't do it. *No negotiation with terrorists*, that's been the official position for years, and Koo has always agreed with it, and even where he is now he *still* agrees, because if you give in to these bastards it just encourages more of them.

Well, what encouraged *this* bunch?

Shit; Koo doesn't want to sit around thinking about it. He just wants to go home, back to his life, back to being what he's good at. He's no good at sitting here in the semi-dark, wondering what's going to happen next. "My mother didn't raise me to be a hostage."

What will they do when the Feds say no? They won't quit, not right away. They'll try to pressure the Feds to change their minds, won't they? And how will they do that? Koo knows how, but doesn't want to know, he doesn't want to think about it. He wants this over with, and he doesn't see any good way for it to end. If this is reality encroaching on his happy private world, he doesn't think much of it.

He also wishes to hell he had his pills. He's not what you could call *addicted* to sleeping pills, but he does more often than not take one or two little capsules before going to bed. Sleeping pills, prescription, from his doctor; in addition to all the other pills he takes every day. He doesn't know what the rest of them are for, and he doesn't want to know. He's simply made it clear to his doctors that he's too busy to get sick, he can't keep coming down with a lot of sniffles and aches, he's got schedules, appointments, deadlines, he's booked two full years into the future. So they give him these pills, and he takes one red-and-green every morning, and two whites after every meal, and a black-and-yellow every Wednesday and Saturday, and—

Well, he's got a lot of pills, except they're all back at the Triple S studio, in his dressing room, packed away in the brown leather carrying case made to his specifications by Hermes. And even somebody who *never* took sleeping pills would find it hard to doze off in Koo's present position. Koo is awake, wide awake. He doesn't know what time it is, but it must have been hours since the last light faded in the swimming pool water. He ought to sleep, if only to keep his strength up for whatever is ahead, but he just can't. When he turns off the lights, the fears swarm worse than ever in his mind, like worms, each carrying another horror. The lights are on a dimmer, so now he has them at their lowest setting, and he's lying on the long built-in couch with two blankets over him, but his mind just won't slow down. He's afraid, he's goddamn afraid.

And now it's affecting his digestion. For the last hour or so his stomach has been feeling worse and worse, and he's been refusing to admit that he might have to throw up. Ignore an upset stomach, he believes, and the chances are it'll go away by itself. Brood about the goddamn thing and the first thing you know you'll up-chuck.

Well, this time the theory isn't working. He's not brooding about his stomach, God knows, he's brooding about his fear of the unknown, but *something* is making the stomach worse and worse, in fact insistent, in fact it is going to happen, in fact he'd better get the hell to the toilet right—

He makes it; barely. He hasn't eaten much since he's been

here, and only had the one small glass of whiskey, so what the hell *is* all that coming out of him? Smells as bad as it looks. Koo keeps flushing the toilet, keeps bringing up more, keeps flushing the toilet, and when at last it's all over he's so weak he can barely stand. He reels over to the sink, rinses out his mouth, staggers back to the couch, plucks at the blankets, gives up with only his legs covered.

Jesus, he feels awful. Perspiration is pouring out of him now, his face and chest and arms are greasy with it. Foul-smelling perspiration, as though he hadn't bathed in a month. Is this the smell of fear?

The stomach again. "There's nothing left!" But, oh, God, it won't take no for an answer. He can't walk, he scurries on all fours, he only partly makes it this time. Oh, Jesus, Jesus, what *is* this stuff?

For a while, this time, he lies on the floor afterward, waiting for strength to return. Got to wash out the mouth, it tastes so *bad*. The perspiration runs along his body, his shirt is sopping wet. Finally he crawls to the sink, struggles upward, rinses his mouth, crawls to the bed, climbs into it, doesn't even try for the blankets.

He's shivering, and he's hot, and the skin of his temples is burning. The *skin* is burning.

This isn't fear. What in the hell is this? Some goddamn flu, maybe, there's always some goddamn flu going around. What a hell of a time to get sick.

Then he wonders, What's in those pills I take all the time? Jesus, do I really *have* something? What a joke—after all these years, it turns out I really need all my pills.

At the next attack, he can't leave the couch, but he manages to turn his face over the side.

# 8

It was one-thirty in the morning, and Mike Wiskiel had been
asleep less than an hour, when the phone rang with news of the
next development in the Koo Davis kidnapping. Mike mum-
bled into the phone, muttered a few words of explanation to his
half-asleep wife, and stumbled back into his clothing. He'd had
a couple quick bourbons before going to bed, which made him
even groggier now, and the first time he went out to the garage
he had to go back into the house for his keys.

His car, a maroon Buick Riviera, was a barely restrained
beast in his uncertain hands. It lunged from the garage, swayed
dangerously as it made the turn out of the driveway, and raced
heedlessly down out of the quiet sleeping residential hills of
Sherman Oaks. In an all-night taco joint on Ventura Boulevard
Mike got a rotten cup of coffee to go, and up on the Freeway
heading east he gradually came awake.

It had been a strange experience earlier tonight, listening to
that Koo Davis tape. Mike was just old enough to remember
Koo Davis as a regular weekly voice on the radio, so listening to
that tape had been for him an eerie double-layered experience
in which present drama and past comedy, his own middle-aged
self sitting there in that Burbank office and his past self as a
skinny child sprawled on the living room carpet in his parents'
home in Troy, New York, had combined like a movie montage
in his emotional reactions. He'd found himself smiling, ready
to chuckle, ready to laugh out loud, half expecting to hear the
old regulars from that distant radio program—the sharp-tongued
nasal-voiced script girl constantly correcting Koo's grammar or

pronunciation, the get-rich-quick brother-in-law with the voice like mashed potatoes and the endless series of goofy inventions and dumb money-making schemes, the bad-tempered neighbor with the weirdly roaring power mower—and it had been very hard to replace those voices (and his own childhood idea of what those people must look like) with the faces and the unfunniness and the grim intentions of the Identikit girl and the two sullen young men.

And now something else had happened; but what? "We've heard from them again," was all Jock Cayzer had said on the phone.

When Mike arrived the office contained, in addition to Jock and Lynsey Rayne, an elderly stoop-shouldered man with a Sigmund Freud goatee, and another agent from the local Bureau Headquarters, Dave Kerman. Lynsey Rayne, who had been here all along, was apparently prepared to stay until Koo Davis was released; surely service above and beyond the call of an actor's agent. She was gaunt and hollow-eyed by now, but showed no sign of weakening resolve.

Was there something sexual between this woman and Koo Davis? Of course, Davis was an old man and Lynsey Rayne probably wasn't much over forty, but even an old man likes to have a woman around, and the real Mrs. Davis was more than three thousand miles away. Lynsey Rayne wasn't behaving like a simple business associate, but did that necessarily mean it was sex? Somehow the *style* of her reaction wasn't like the tenterhooks fear of a loved one. She was more like…like an intensely involved nurse, like the competent older sister in a parentless household, or (farther afield, maybe ridiculous) like the bomber squadron commander in World War Two movies, waiting by the landing field to see how many of his "boys" have made it "home."

Jock Cayzer introduced the dapper bearded man. He was Doctor Stephen Answin, Koo Davis' personal physician. "I came as quickly as I could," the doctor said. He had a habit of ducking his head, as though apologetic, shooting quick glances over the tops of his spectacles, but the hesitant self-conscious manner was belied by his appearance; the goatee was as neat as a freshly clipped hedge, and his blue cashmere suit, raw silk ascot and gleaming pointed-toe shoes (all crying out their origin in male boutiques along Camden or Rodeo Drive in Beverly Hills) suggested a rather dandyish self-assurance.

"The kidnapper's due to call back soon," Jock said, looking at his watch.

Mike said, "Call back? You've got an appointment?"

"To talk to the doctor. Come listen."

They trooped into the workroom, where all incoming calls were being put on tape. An FBI technician named Menaged was there, with the earlier conversation already cued up. He played it, and Mike listened to the voices.

Receptionist: "Seven seven hundred."

Caller (cold emotionless male voice, in something of a hurry): "This the Koo Davis number?"

Receptionist: "Yes, sir."

Caller: "Davis is sick."

Receptionist: "Beg pardon?"

Caller: "You've got two minutes on this call, then I hang up. We checked Davis a while ago, and he's all of a sudden in bad shape. We didn't hurt him, but he's sick. He's throwing up, sweating, can't move. He's muttering something about pills in a dressing room. Is he on some kind of maintenance medicine?"

Receptionist: "Sir, I couldn't possibly—"

Caller: "Not you. This is going on tape, right? Get Davis' doctor, get those pills if he's got pills. I'll call back at two o'clock."

Receptionist: "I'm not sure I can— Hello? Hello?"

The technician switched it off, saying, "He'd hung up by then."

Mike checked his watch, and it was not ten minutes before two. Turning to the doctor, he said, "Does that make sense to you?"

"I'm afraid it does, yes."

"Davis is on some kind of medicine? What does he have?"

"It isn't that simple," the doctor said. Between his assured appearance and his bashful manner it was hard to get a coherent reading on the man, but Mike suspected in him a kind of embarrassment. Why?

The doctor was going on, saying, "If Koo were a diabetic, or had leukemia in remission, something along those lines, it would be much easier to define for you what the problem is. Let me explain; Koo Davis is not a young man. He's sixty-three, but he refuses to behave as though he were. He pushes himself far too hard, and he doesn't want to be hampered by illness *in any way*. He was medically unfit during the Second World War, you know, and one of his problems was with his digestion. He takes— I admit he takes a great deal of medicine. Half the things I've prescribed are to counteract the side-effects of some of the *other* things. He's lived that way for years, and so long as he has his medicines he can continue in the same fashion for many years more. But it has been a long long time since his stomach, his liver, his intestines, have been asked to deal with his food, for instance, in a completely natural way. They can't do it. Until he gets his medication, he won't be able to eat a thing, he won't be able to sleep or have proper elimination or even breathe without difficulty. If he doesn't receive his medicines, and I would say proper medical care, within the next several hours, the consequences could be very serious."

All of which was said with the doctor's combination of confidence and sheepishness, though it did seem to Mike that a true sense of unease came through the mixture. As perhaps it should; what the doctor was saying was that Koo Davis was a prescription junkie, a man hooked on preventive medicines, who simply couldn't live his normal life without them.

All of which had been created by this doctor, or by several doctors; or created by Davis with their acquiescence. There was undoubtedly some ethical ambivalence in the position in which Doctor Answin now found himself. "These consequences," Mike said, not particularly interested in smoothing things for the doctor, "how serious could they be?"

"He won't live." The doctor blinked behind his stylish spectacles, shrugged his shoulders, spread well-washed hands crosshatched with thick black hairs. "Within a week, possibly a bit more, he would simply die, from starvation, from shock, from any number of complications and contributing factors. In less time than that, in say two days, there could be irretrievable damage. Koo's health is a very delicate balance, between what his body can stand and what he insists on doing. We have made it possible for him to exceed his body's potential for years; this event could be extremely damaging."

Mike said, "What about these pills?"

"I've got them," Lynsey Rayne said. "As soon as that—creature—was off the phone, I called Ian Komlosy, head of Triple S; got him out of bed. He sent someone to open the studio and let me into Koo's dressing room. His pill case is in the other office."

Jock Cayzer said, "It seems to me the most important thing here is to get this man together with his medicines."

"It would be best if I could see him as well," Doctor Answin said, ducking his head.

"I doubt we can swing that, Doctor," Jock told him. "And if they did let you see him, they'd probably want to keep you right along with him."

"I wouldn't permit you to go," Mike said. Then, remembering the twenty-four hours weren't yet up, he was still merely an advisor, he added, "And I don't believe Jock would either."

"Sure not," Jock said. "But, Doctor, I will want you to talk to the fellow, when he calls back."

"Make them let him go," Lynsey Rayne said. Her gaunt face looked as though she too were about to be critically ill. "They can't keep him if he's sick, they'll have to let him go, start all over again with someone else."

"I doubt they'll see it that way," Mike told her.

"Then let *me* talk to them. Doctor Answin, *you* tell them; it isn't just the pills, it's medical attention, it's his age, it's all the risk involved."

Mike said, "Miss Rayne, that fellow said on the last call he wouldn't talk more than two minutes, obviously to keep us from putting a trace on the call. He'll surely do the same thing when he calls back. Doctor Answin should tell them the truth, answer questions as truthfully—and briefly, Doctor, please—as he can. If there's time, he can make an appeal for Mr. Davis' release, but you know and I know it won't do any good. If we do convince them Davis is in critical danger, they'll tell us that simply reinforces the tightness of their deadline. Negotiations of this kind aren't easy under any circumstances. If we tell them Koo Davis is a goner unless they release him, we're handing them a gun they can put at our heads."

"Then *release* those people," Lynsey Rayne said. "Ten left-over radicals, my *God*, what difference can it make anymore? Let them go to Algeria, anywhere they want, good *riddance*."

"I'm sorry, Miss Rayne," Mike said. "Nobody in this room can make that decision. And so far, I don't even think all ten have been positively identified, so it might be a bit early to characterize them all as simply harmless 'leftover radicals'."

"Whoever they are," she said, "getting them out of the country has got to be a good idea. Is Koo's life worth keeping these people in prison?"

"I don't know," Mike said. "We hope to get Washington's answer to that question tomorrow."

As he was speaking, the phone rang. Everyone stopped, looking at the tape reels suddenly turning, listening as the technician turned up the sound.

Receptionist: "Seven seven hundred."

Caller: "You know who this is. You got the doctor?"

Jock was pointing at a phone on one of the worktables. As Doctor Answin picked it up, the technician turned the taped sound down slightly; still, there was an odd echo in the room as the doctor's voice went into the phone and emerged a micro-millisecond later from the tape machine. "Doctor Answin here."

"What's the story? You got one minute."

"I should see him. He's not a young man, he should have proper medical care."

"No. Give me an alternative. Quick."

The doctor sighed and shook his head, then spoke in a brisk, matter-of-fact manner: "Koo Davis is a very sick man. He can't live more than a few days without his medications, and there would be irreversible damage before death."

"All right. You got the pills he was talking about?"

"Yes. We have Koo's pill case here."

"A whole case, huh? All right. One car—not a police car, no car with a police radio—should get on the San Diego Freeway northbound at the Sunset Boulevard entrance at three A.M. The car should identify itself with a white handkerchief tied at the top of the antenna. Drive at forty in the right-hand lane. When a car behind you flashes its highs, pull off the road, put the case outside the car, drive on. Do *not* get out of the car. If you get out of the car, or if you try to put more than one car on

the Freeway, we won't pick up the pills, and the bastard can
live or die. This is Davis' own case?"

"Yes."

"Don't bug it, don't switch it for another case. *Any* cute stuff
at all, and Davis doesn't get his pills."

Mike had scribbled on a piece of paper, "Make it 6AM," and
he now held this in front of the doctor's eyes. The doctor
nodded and said, "I don't think we could do it that soon. Make
it six A.M."

The caller laughed, a dry scornful sound. "When it's light
enough for choppers? No, Doc, you don't follow us home.
We'll make it three."

"I'm not sure I—"

The technician said, "He hung up."

The small metal object in Mike's palm was the size and shape of
a shirt button. "Look, Miss Rayne," he said. "They *won't* find
this. Some of those medicines are in capsule form. I can put
this in one of the capsules and how in God's name are they
going to find it?"

The button was actually a radio transmitter, capable of
broadcasting a single beam for a distance of perhaps a quarter-
mile. They planned to follow this transmitter to wherever
Davis was being held—except that Lynsey Rayne was putting
up an unexpected argument. "There's a *chance* they'll find it,"
she insisted. "Either looking for it or by accident. And you just
listen to that man's voice. He *wants* to hurt Koo, you can hear
it. Don't give him the excuse."

Mike was losing his patience. In ordinary circumstances he
would simply go ahead and plant the transmitter, but Lynsey
Rayne had already threatened once to phone Washington, to
throw Koo Davis' weight around and get a countermanding

order from Bureau Headquarters. The point wasn't whether or
not Koo Davis' name was influential enough to get the order
reversed; his name definitely *was* influential enough to get
Lynsey Rayne a hearing. It was now five-thirty in the morning,
Washington time, and Mike Wiskiel was not going to be the
man responsible for rousting a lot of important people out of
bed at this hour. The problem had to be solved here, in this
office.

Unfortunately, Mike had to fight the battle alone, Jock Cayzer
having artfully eased himself out of the conversation the instant
trouble began to emerge on the horizon. Jock was now in the
workroom next door, dealing with the arrangements for the
medicine delivery, while Mike was here in the main office,
alone with Lynsey Rayne. "Look, Miss Rayne," he said, and
tried very hard to control his impatience and contempt. But the
woman was getting in the way of the job to be done, arguing
tactics when what mattered was results. And basing her convictions on the sound of a voice on the telephone! "Look. The
important thing is to get Davis out of these people's hands."

"No, it is not." She wouldn't even accept that much. "The
important thing right now is to keep Koo alive. Don't you plan
to negotiate at *all*?"

"Washington negotiates," Mike said. "If we can do it a quicker
way, we do it. Miss Rayne, this isn't the kind of negotiation
you're used to, we're not dealing here with a bunch of calm
businessmen. These people are terrorists, they're criminals,
and they're most likely more than a little psychotic. If we *can*
deal with them, we will, but if we can get Koo Davis out of their
hands, that's the goal to aim at."

"You'll want it to finish with a shootout," she said bitterly.
"Everybody killed, and all you button-down types being manly
with your walkie-talkies."

Mike closed his eyes. "Miss Rayne," he said, "a shootout is

the last thing I want, I swear that on a stack of Bibles. I want Davis alive and safe just as much as you do."

"Then get the medicine to him and don't try to outsmart them." Her bone bracelets jangled when she waved her arms about, and her expression was becoming increasingly helpless and agonized. "I'm sorry," she said. "Mr. Wiskiel, I know I'm getting your back up and I am sorry, I don't mean to. I *know* you know your business, and I *know* you're right about the kind of people we're dealing with, but even by your description you can see we shouldn't take chances. They *are* criminals, they know their business as well as you know yours. That man knew you were thinking about helicopters the second Doctor Answin mentioned six o'clock; I didn't. He knows you'll want to try this transmitter thing, and he even warned against it, said don't bug the case. If you challenge them, if you try to be trickier than they are, and if they catch you at it, they'll be *insulted*. And they'll take it out on Koo. 'More than a little psychotic,' you said. But you want to taunt them while they've still got Koo!"

"It would be better if we could use a case or box of our own," Mike admitted, "with the transmitter already built into it. But the doctor let them know it was Davis' own case, so we have to stick with what we've got, and if we put this little gizmo *inside* a capsule, it won't be found."

"It *might* be found. You don't have the right to take that kind of chance with Koo's life. With anybody's life."

Dave Kerman, the other FBI man on duty here tonight, came in from the workroom to say, "Mike, we're ready to go. The doctor's typed up a set of instructions, what pills to give and what symptoms to look out for and all that, and we're set. And time's a little short."

Mike sighed and shook his head. "All right, Miss Rayne, you win. I think you're wrong, but you probably *can* throw a lot of weight around, so we'll forget it."

In victory, Lynsey Rayne looked unhappy, defensive. "It isn't whether or not I can throw weight around."

"Oh, yes it is," Mike told her. Turning away, he dropped the transmitter into Dave Kerman's palm, winking at him on the side away from Lynsey Rayne as he said, "Take this back to the office, Dave."

"Right," Dave Kerman said, and went off to install the transmitter in the pill case.

# 9

Mark Halliwell crouched in shrubbery on a front lawn, completely invisible. His lips stretched in a smile as he watched the slow-moving car ease along Sunset Boulevard, obliviously passing his hiding place. The police were so predictable, so inept. This car was as anonymous as it was possible for a white Ford Granada to be, but at this hour of the morning here in this residential section of Brentwood there was virtually no traffic, so any car traveling at five miles an hour on the four-lane-wide winding roadway of Sunset Boulevard would be bound to call attention to itself.

They were, of course, taking down—probably on film—the license numbers and particulars of all the cars parked in the neighborhood. After the delivery car had gone by at three o'clock, they would return to see what car was missing, and then have a description to broadcast to police waiting at every freeway exit for miles around. Mark, who almost never smiled in the presence of other people, luxuriated in a broad taunting grin as the Granada went by. Safe in the thick ornamental shrubbery on this lawn, he'd be invisible even if they were using infrared. He watched the Granada out of sight, then settled back to wait.

Mark burned with a pure fire. He knew what he wanted, and how to get it. The people who made pain in the world would be stopped. The uncaring, the smug, the self-confident, the lofty, too high and mighty to think about the people down below; they would all be toppled from their pedestals, and afterward the world would be clean. No more hatred, no more pain, no more suffering, no more pity. No need for pity in a world without pain.

"You don't feel sorry for *me*, you only feel sorry for *yourself*!" They'd both written that, in an exchange of letters, each accusing the other, and Mark had thought, If we make a joke of it, perhaps we can get past all this despair and love one another, mother and son at last. But he hadn't made the attempt, nor had she; neither ever spoke of the coincidence, the same sentence in both letters, crossing from bedroom to bedroom. Had she failed to notice the identity of the words? He knew she read his notes, she quoted selected pieces back at him out of context in her own subsequent writings. This was at a later stage, after the screaming and crying, when he was in high school, in the larger apartment with her own bedroom, so she was no longer sleeping on the convertible sofa in the living room. (How he hated her out there, heavy, humid, unconscious, imprisoning him in his room with her presence.) She had started leaving him notes on his pillow about cleaning his room, washing up after himself in the kitchen, putting out the garbage, and he'd responded at first with scrawled remarks at the bottom of her notes, placed on *her* pillow at night while she was out working at the bar. But soon what he had to say was too extensive for the remaining corners and margins of her notes, so he bought his own paper with money stolen from her purse, and the correspondence began.

Tonight, Mark had been the one to find Koo Davis, and now his mind kept filling with that extraordinary scene. After he'd heard Larry at last go to bed—*without* checking Davis—he'd got up again to see to Davis himself. The man's jokey treatment of the cassette still rankled; it was time he learned that everybody was serious.

Mark had expected to wake Davis, maybe put a little respect into him—*not* slap him around, Larry always overstated things—

but he hadn't at all anticipated what he'd actually found. There was good reason to believe he'd in fact saved Davis' life. What irony!

He'd gone down to the utility room, moved all the empty wine cartons concealing the door, unlocked and opened it, and there was Davis bubbling and strangling in a lake of his own vile vomit, his bloated red face streaked with it, his arms and legs twitching like an impaled bug. The *stink* of the place! And the helplessness, the terrible gross flabby weakness, of the man gargling and retching on the couch. Mark had rolled him over, pounded his back, got Davis at last breathing again, and had then gone off to wake Peter, who would have to decide what to do next.

The action had been instinctive, saving Davis' life. Now, after the event, would he repent at leisure? A dead Koo Davis would make no more tapes, of course, but he'd still be usable as a counter in the negotiations. The other side needn't know of his death until it was all over. And mightn't it be better, simpler all around, for Koo Davis to be dead? In imagination now, Mark saw himself *not* enter the room, *not* save Davis' life, but instead close the door, walk away, and never tell anyone he'd been down there that night.

There was nothing personal about it. There *was* nothing personal in it. The fact that Davis had been Mark's choice of subject—so subtly inserted into Peter's mind during the early discussions that Peter now believed Davis to have been his own idea—mattered little. In truth, Davis *was* the best bargaining chip they could have obtained, since government officials and other people closer to the center of power were all so much more carefully guarded.

True, Mark had reasons to hate Koo Davis for himself if he wanted to dwell on them, but that wasn't the point. Mark had left all that personal stuff behind, he was out of those emotional quagmires now, he behaved on the basis of logical necessity *only*. Whatever happened to Koo Davis, it would be due exclusively to the impersonal logic of the situation. Revenge, hatred, none of that would make any difference.

On balance, in fact, it was marginally better that Davis be alive. One or two more tapes should still be made—without the jokes. And it was tactically better that Davis remain a living redeemable counter in the game. So Mark's decision to save his life had also been logical, an immediate decision among alternatives, and not the result of any misplaced emotional reaction. He had done the right thing for the right reason.

At precisely three o'clock, a blue Dodge Colt rolled by, a white cloth fluttering flaglike from its antenna. Mark leaned forward to watch, hard-edged leaves brushing his bearded cheeks and the jungly smell of the shrubbery rich in his nostrils. No other car trailed the Colt.

The white Ford Granada eased by in the opposite direction at three minutes past the hour. Mark watched it out of sight.

At five past three he stood, stretching in the dark, his anklebones cracking. He waited there, in the darkness, and two minutes later the Impala came along, Peter at the wheel. Mark trotted out to the road, Peter stopped, Mark slid in on the passenger side, and Peter accelerated again, toward the freeway entrance.

"Blue Dodge Colt," Mark said. "Went through on the dot. Nobody followed it."

"Good. That package of yours smells."

Mark glanced at the brown paper bag on the back seat. "Can't," he said. "It's very securely sealed in a Baggie."

"It smells," Peter insisted. "Sniff for yourself."

Mark sniffed; there was a faint aroma, at that. "Maybe you farted."

Peter's mouth corners turned down. He was not amused. He

steered them onto the freeway, then accelerated to sixty. There were fewer than half a dozen vehicles anywhere in sight. Peter said, "It's a stupid gesture anyway, even if you're right."

"They'll understand," Mark said. "And I will be right."

"And if you're wrong?"

Mark shrugged. "Then it's cost me one Baggie and one cassette. Besides, they're already being cute." And he told Peter about the white Granada.

Peter obviously didn't like that. "What's the matter with them? Don't they realize we don't *have* to do this?"

"They can't help themselves. They've just got to play Counterspy."

Peter drove along, drumming his fingertips against the steering wheel. "Who knows what else they're doing? We'll call it off," he decided. "We'll phone them, tell them to do it right or not at all. They're the ones want Davis alive."

"No, Peter. Let them do it again later? They still won't be straight with us, you'll just give them more time to get set up. We do it now."

"I'm not interested in being caught."

"None of us is."

Peter gave him a sidelong look. "You just want to use your Baggie."

"There's that, too." Then Mark pointed forward. "In the right lane."

The Colt was moving at the modest forty miles an hour specified by Mark, and there seemed no other vehicle pacing it. Staying in a middle lane, Peter hung well back, and waited.

The San Diego Freeway north of Sunset Boulevard runs between two low barren treeless hills with virtually no buildings and an almost total lack of secondary roads. There's only one freeway exit before the Valley itself, five miles to the north. It's a strange landscape for the middle of a major metropolitan area, and it's quite dark at night. At one of the darkest spots, near the top of the long straight slope down toward the Valley, Peter drove forward to flash his high beams into the Colt's rearview mirror.

The Colt at once braked hard, swerving off onto the shoulder of the road. Peter did the same, dropping farther back, and the two vehicles stopped about four lengths apart. The Colt's driver's door opened, but from his angle Mark couldn't see what was happening. "Is he getting out?"

"No. He put the case on the ground."

The Colt's door closed, and the car at once spurted away, throwing gravel in its wake, leaving behind a small brown-leather case with a handle; it was about the right size and shape to carry two liquor bottles. Peter drove forward, stopped next to the case; Mark opened the door, picked it up, then slammed his door and Peter accelerated.

The case opened like a book, revealing in the faint glow of the map-light a dark blue plush interior separated into more than a dozen small compartments; it reminded Mark of cliff dwellings in photographs. A folded sheet of paper proved to contain the doctor's instructions; Mark put it away in a pocket and returned his attention to the case.

Each compartment contained a bottle or box, with a small plush strap across to keep the contents in place. Mark murmured to himself, "One of these buttons?" His thumb stroked the chrome snaps on each of the straps, feeling for one to be different. "No; they didn't have time for structural changes. In one of the bottles."

Peter meanwhile was driving rapidly down the slope toward the Valley, where the Ventura Freeway crossed this one, in an interchange with almost limitless options. While Mark went through the bottles, opening each, emptying the contents into his palm and then returning them, Peter took the exit ramp for the Ventura Freeway east, then switched back to the San Diego Freeway north, then at the last instant took another downramp to the local streets. His rearview mirror told him that no one had followed him through all his maneuvers.

Mark had finished his first scanning of the case by now, and had found nothing. He was frowning at it, thinking it over, stroking his beard, considering the possibilities. Peter said, "Nothing?"

"I don't believe it. Wait a minute. *Inside* a capsule!" He reached for a bottle, shook a dozen or more large capsules into his palm, then picked them up one at a time, shaking each next to his ear before putting it back in the bottle propped on his lap. The capsules were red and green, opaque, and contained something with the consistency of coarse sand; a faint rattling sound could be heard inside each.

Except one. Mark nodded in satisfaction when he reached it. "Right," he said.

Peter seemed honestly surprised. "Did they really?"

"Really." Dumping the rest of the capsules back into the bottle, Mark broke open the odd one, and there in his palm was the transmitter, a tiny bug no bigger than a shirt button.

"Those stupid bastards," Peter said.

A cold rage lived deep within Mark, ready to be stirred by almost anything. It was rising now, making his face bonier beneath the beard, making his voice softer and colder. "What we *should* do," he said, "is dump this whole case out into the street and let *them* decide if he dies first or they deal first."

"No," Peter said. "As long as he's alive and unhurt, they have to be cautious against us."

Mark held up the hand with the bug in it. "Like this?"

"Devious, but cautious. Go ahead and use your package."

"Right." Tucking the bug into his shirt pocket, Mark closed the pill case and put it on the back seat, then brought forward the brown paper bag, which seemed fairly heavy. He opened the bag, then reached in to remove the twisty sealing the Baggie within. When the Baggie was opened, a stench filled the car.

"Jesus!" said Peter.

"Won't be long." Mark dropped the transmitter into the Baggie, sealed it again, and closed the paper bag. "Stop at a mailbox."

They drove another two blocks, then Peter angled to a stop by a mailbox. Mark got out, dropped the paper bag into the mailbox, and then they drove on.

## 10

Koo Davis is sick and scared, he thinks he's dying, and he's stuck here in some kind of awful comedy. He asks himself: Do I deserve this? His stomach is so painful he can't stand it; in fact, he keeps passing out from the pain, particularly if he tries to move. His head hurts, his throat is on fire, perspiration streams from him and yet his mouth is so dry his tongue feels like a foreign body, some lumpy dry sausage cluttering up his head. I'm dehydrating, he tells himself, with useless medical assurance. But he's tried asking for water, and they've given it to him, and he's learned the hard way that he can't keep it down.

But the comedy is, there's some clown here talking to him about politics. This guy, and a woman Koo hadn't seen before, cleaned him up and cleaned up the room and have both spent a lot of time with him ever since, and have even told him their names—or anyway they've told him names they'll answer to, theirs or somebody else's. Larry and Joyce. Joyce just stands around looking worried, in traditional sickroom fashion, but this schmuck Larry *talks*.

"You're a bright man, Koo, you've seen a lot of the world, you must have seen the terrible inequity in the way different people live. Infant mortality in Central America, for instance, is *so much* higher than in the United States. Yet we all live on the same planet, don't we? In the last analysis, we're all a part of the same community. And the *resources* are there, Koo, everybody could have a decent life, enough food, proper shelter, a decent rewarding life. What stands in the way? Koo, isn't it obvious? It's the method of distribution, Koo, you can see that."

And: "Did you know Thomas Jefferson said America needed a new revolution every twenty-five years? Because otherwise the country would stagnate into just another power, just another nation like all the others."

And: "Marx tells us the means of production belong to the workers, and if you think about it you can see where that makes sense. The tenant farmer, the sharecropper, is the clearest example. His work makes the land productive. His *ongoing* work, clearing, seeding, crop rotation, makes the land productive for the long term and makes it increase in value in the only way that value matters, which is increased production. But he has to pay a portion of that production to someone else, who doesn't work the land, who doesn't have any connection with the land except a deed that says he *owns* it. Why does he own it? Because he bought it or inherited it from somebody who had the same relationship with it; that piece of paper. And if you trace it back, sooner or later you get to the man who started the piece of paper, and he either stole the land from somebody else or he made it his in the first place by *working* it. Of *course* land should belong to the farmer who works it and makes it productive, there really can't be any argument about that. So let's take the same concept into the factory."

It isn't bad enough that Koo is kidnapped, that he's sick and possibly dying; he also has to be nattered at by some soapbox birdy. If I throw up again, Koo promises himself, then somehow, somehow, I'm gonna throw up on *him*.

Koo sleeps or dozes or loses consciousness from time to time during this endless lecture, and there are weird intervals when he's neither awake nor asleep, but somehow floatingly present, and everything takes on the strange glow of fantasy; the calm persuasive stupid voice, the absurdity of a window facing only water, the long narrow dimly lighted room, the remaining stinks of his sickness, it all swirls together and he becomes Captain Nemo in the Nautilus, sailing through the limitless green oceans, sailing on and on, noiseless and omnipotent, gliding through the echoing ocean depths to save the world.

Yes, it all makes sense now; Captain Nemo will save the world, will give each man and woman and child his own portion of the planet, marked off on a grid, like a great monster checkerboard in green and brown, grassy green and dirt brown, green grass and brown dirt, and all the tall slender silent people with the solemn big eyes and the silent gratitude standing on the checkerboard, each person on his square, all around the world. And Captain Nemo sailing through the sky in his submarine, while the rain pours down on all the people, and the water crashes through the window, and now Koo *is* in the submarine, rising through yellow water toward the surface, and here he is on the hot wet sticky sheet atop the couch, with the water still imprisoned beyond the unbroken window—wasn't that smashed? he remembers something; no, it's gone—and the calm earnest reasonable intense committed intelligent thoughtful *stupid* voice going on and on.

Other times, his mind is clear, and he thinks his own thoughts within the persuasive drone. He knows this is what they call brainwashing, and he wonders if they poisoned him on purpose, to weaken his resistance. Their surprise and shock *seemed* real, but it could have been just an act. And in any event, what this guy is talking is straight party line, right enough.

The thing is…the thing is, the goddamn Vietnam thing might have been a mistake, and everybody now knows it was a mistake, but that doesn't mean the worldwide Communist conspiracy doesn't exist. It exists, all right, and now Koo's gotten tangled up in it; they picked him, he knows they picked him, because he broke his no-politics rule. So here's a rule about rules: Break the other guy's rules if you want, but don't break your own.

Those ten names he read into the cassette. A couple of them rang a bell, reminded him of headlines from a few years back, but clearly the whole crowd is part and parcel of the Communist plot. These people *exist*, they really do, and Koo now realizes what went wrong. The trouble was, the American government and the American intelligence community, starting from the time of Joe McCarthy and coming right on up, has played the part of the boy who cried wolf. They were seeing Commies and pinkos and fellow travelers and Comsymps and all those other chowderhead words under every bed, and the result is, too many people now don't believe there's a wolf out there at all. But there is, by Jesus, and just at the moment he's got Koo by the ankle.

Joyce comes in from time to time with a cool damp cloth to put on Koo's forehead. It helps a little, but the cloth gets as burning hot as his head within seconds. She comes in now with two wet cloths, puts one on his forehead, and swabs his face and neck with the other. Larry pauses in his monologue, and Koo whispers to Joyce (he can't talk anymore, not with this throat), "Thanks. It's better."

"Good. They've gone to get your medicine. They'll bring it soon."

She's said that before, but Koo can't work out what she means by it. Are they going to the drugstore for aspirin? They can't go back to Triple S, can they? "Excuse me, we're the people kidnapped Koo Davis, we came to get his pills." Makes no sense. Koo would like to ask her what she means, but the question won't phrase itself; his mind wanders before he can figure out how to ask her anything.

He drifts away now while she's still dabbing at his stubbly cheeks—he hasn't shaved since yesterday—and when he drifts back she's gone, the Larry doll has been wound up again, and a hint of gray smears the water beyond the window; it's becoming tomorrow.

He went to sleep with some question half-formed in his mind, but he wakes up with another one all ready, on the tip of his tongue. He turns his head a little and whispers, "Larry."

"—into the communal pot, and— Did you say something?"

"Question."

"Of course, Koo." Larry's sincere intern's face comes closer. "What is it?"

"Not an insult," Koo whispers. He can only bring out fragments of the sentences in his mind. "Really want to know."

"I understand, Koo. I promise I won't be insulted. What do you want to ask?"

"If you like—Russia—so much—why *don't* you—go live there?"

Larry doesn't look insulted, but he does look astonished. "Russia? Koo, what does Russia have to do with anything?"

"Commie—Communist—"

"Marxist, you mean." Larry smiles with indulgent understanding. "Marxism isn't Russia, Koo. Russia is at least as decadent and far more repressive than the United States. What we're talking about is a *new* order, something never seen on the planet before, a wedding of people and resources, and finally the salvation of the planet itself. Koo, do you think it's an *accident* that the developer of the aerosol spray can was a friend of Nixon's?"

This non sequitur is so striking that Koo can only stare at Larry in admiration. "I could use you—as a writer," he whispers, and the door is burst open and in marches the mean one, the tough guy with the beard. Koo first notices, in amazement and sheer unalloyed pleasure and delight, that in the tough guy's hand is Koo's pill case! By Christ, they've done it! Salvation is at hand! But then Koo notices that the guy is raging mad, and his delight turns to fear. Something bad is coming.

It is. The guy slaps the pill case onto a counter and says, "There it is." Pointing at Koo he says, "And you don't get it."

A terrible weakness runs through Koo's throat and into his eyes, and he can only stare, beaten down, unable anymore even to wonder why.

But Larry asks the question Koo might have asked: "Mark? You won't give him his medicine?"

"Not yet," Mark says. (So now Koo knows another name.) "Not for a while yet."

"But why not? *Look* at the poor man!"

"You look at him." Mark, the son of a bitch, leans over Koo and speaks loudly and angrily into Koo's face: "We didn't have to deal with them at all. We could have left it up to them, either release those people and get you back, or fuck around until you're dead. That's what *I* wanted to do."

You would, you bastard, Koo thinks. He stares in fear and hatred up at the angry face.

"But we were *humanitarian*," Mark says, twisting the word and giving a contemptuous quick glance over his shoulder at Larry. "We got your goddamn pills. But could they play it straight? They could not. They bugged the case, they put a directional transmitter in it. I *knew* they would. And *you're* going to pay for it." Turning to Larry, whose face shows he's full of protests, tough guy Mark says, "Out. *I'll* watch our beauty for a while."

Larry will argue, but he won't win; Koo can only watch, sharing Larry's helplessness as he says, "Mark, you can't ex—"

"I can. Go complain to Peter, and see what good it does you."

Koo stares across the room at his case. His stomach burns, it burns as though charcoal briquettes are smoldering there. Even a bastard like this fellow Mark wouldn't act like this if he understood the pain. Would he? I'm not going to cry, Koo promises himself, blinking.

## 11

Lynsey Rayne, having had her little "victory" over the question of the transmitter, had finally agreed to go home and get some rest, leaving Mike free to supervise the tracking operation from the office. There'd been no positive result from the sweep at the Sunset Boulevard end, so the transmitter was their last shot at the basket. Mike suspected Jock Cayzer had private doubts about the wisdom of using the transmitter, but that was why Jock was local and Mike federal; you had to know when to play hardball if you wanted to get into the big leagues. And at any rate, if Jock did have qualms, he kept them to himself.

One of Jock's people had come in with plastic cups of orange juice, and Mike had surreptitiously spiked his from the pint of hundred-proof vodka he kept in the glove compartment of his car, so he was feeling more relaxed now, more alert and sure of himself. He was in radio contact with the two monitor vans, and from their first reports things were going well; the subject car appeared to be moving in a fairly straight line northwestward across the valley. There'd be no attempt at visual contact until it came to rest.

The workroom, where Mike and a radio technician sat together at a table, was filling up with people; mostly men, with a sprinkling of women. Assembling here were uniformed and plainclothes officers from Jock Cayzer's force, plus FBI agents from the Los Angeles office, waiting for the suspects to settle back at last into their nest, which at exactly twenty-three minutes to four they did.

"Been in one place now for over a minute," the voice said

from Van Number One. "I think they've lit." The voice maintained the proper tone of professional detachment, but underneath the excitement could be heard.

It was infectious excitement, vibrating in the very air of the workroom, in the quick bright-eyed glances people gave to one another, in their inability to remain seated quietly in one place. Mike felt it as a kind of tingling sensation in the tips of his fingers, in his throat, buzzing through his body. They were going to wrap it up, they were going to put it on ice even before the statutory twenty-four hours and the FBI's official entry into the case. Beautiful. Beautiful. Washington, here I come.

It was another five minutes before the vans, moving cautiously, announced the location: "Intersection of White Oak Street and Verde Road, Tarzana."

"Can you give us a house address?"

Two minutes later they had it: 124-82 White Oak Street. Two of Jock's people got busy on telephones, and Jock came back with the result. "Family called Springer. Gerard Springer, forty-six, engineer out at Cal-Space. Wife, four kids. Owns the house, bought it five years ago."

Mike frowned. "That doesn't seem right. Unless they've invaded the house. Could be they're holding the family."

"At this hour of the morning," Jock said, "there's no way to check, find out if the kids've been at school, if Springer's been at work."

"Aerospace engineer, huh? Deep cover agent, do you think? Surfaced for this job?"

Jock Cayzer shook his head. "Mike, I do believe anything is possible."

Five hours of surveillance at the Springer house produced nothing out of the ordinary. Gerard Springer himself drove away at seven-forty, in a red Volkswagen Golf, taking with him two of the children. Two more children, dawdling and carrying bookbags, left at eight-oh-five. FBI agent Dave Kerman entered the premises at eight-thirty-five, showing ID from Pacific Gas and Electric and claiming to be a repairman looking for a potential gas leak; on his return to the mobile headquarters a block away he said, "It can't be right. I'll swear there's nothing going on in there."

Mike said, "Then they must have dumped it. Either they found the transmitter or they just dumped the whole package. Let's go take a look." And when they drove past the Springer house Mike and Jock Cayzer both said, at the same instant, "The mailbox."

In the mailbox they found the brown paper bag, and inside the bag was the transmitter, with a piece of human dung, inside a sealed plastic bag. Also another cassette. With an uneasy tremor beneath his anger and humiliation, Mike traveled back to Burbank to listen to this new tape.

It was shorter than the first, and the voice was not that of Koo Davis, but was recognizably the same as the individual who had done the phoning. It said: "I'm taping this ahead of time, and I'm having a nice shit ahead of time, too, because I know what you people are like. You have no ethics. You have no morality. You think you're on the side of good, and therefore it's impossible for you to do wrong. You'll promise not to plant a bug on us, but you *will* plant a bug on us. And I'll find it. And I'll send it back. I'm talking to *you*, Michael Wiskiel, I remember you from Watergate. We'll be listening to the radio news all morning. Until we hear an apology from *you*, Michael Wiskiel, in your own voice, Koo Davis gets no medicine."

That was it. In the profound silence that followed the harsh self-righteous voice, Mike sighed and said, "Lynsey Rayne is going to have my head on a platter."

## 12

Trying to distract himself, Larry Crosfield sat in his bedroom and wrote in his notebook, the most recent in a series of notebooks he'd kept over the years. He wrote:

> *The dreadful paradox, of course, is the absolute necessity to do evil in order to bring about good. To make the world a better place, one must be worthy. To be worthy, one must strive for sainthood (in the non-clerical sense of* total commitment *to unattainable but appropriate ideals), and yet the lethargic and static forces of Society are so powerful that it requires, specifically requires, extra-social acts in order to promote change. One must do evil* while knowing it to be evil *and at the same time one must strive for sainthood. This paradox—*

No. Larry couldn't go on, he couldn't stand it any longer. It was after nine o'clock, news broadcasts blared from radios throughout the house, cold-eyed furious Mark was standing guard over Davis and wouldn't let anybody in the room with him, and neither Peter nor anybody else seemed capable of doing anything about it.

But something *had* to be done. Putting away the notebook, Larry went out to the living room, found Peter pacing back and forth there amid the radio noise, and forced himself into the other man's awareness by standing directly in his path. Peter gave him a distracted irritable look, and Larry said, "Peter, listen to me."

Peter turned away. "Why?"

Following, Larry said, "What if they *don't* apologize?"

"They *will*."

"But what if they don't? Are you really going to let Davis die, with his medicine right here?"

"The ball's in their court." Peter was steadily, compulsively, stroking his cheeks, his face seeming more gaunt than usual, and he wouldn't meet Larry's eye. "They'll have to come through."

"But what if they don't?"

"They will."

"Give me a time limit," Larry insisted. "Peter, what time do we give it up and let Davis have his medicine? Ten o'clock?"

"No."

"When, then? Ten-thirty?"

"Larry," Peter said, pressing his cheeks with the backs of his fingers, "Larry, I can't set a time on it. They have to come through, that's all. If we back down, how can we negotiate later?"

"If we let Davis die, what do we negotiate *with* later?"

Peter violently shook his head, as though being attacked by bees. Desperately he said, "We have to stand by our promise, we have to, that's all. Mark's right."

"You're afraid of Mark."

"I *agree* with Mark!" Peter yelled, but he wouldn't meet Larry's eye. And he wouldn't set a time limit. He would do nothing, in fact, but pace the floor, stroking his cheeks and staring at the walls and refusing to be a *leader*.

Through the glass wall Larry could see Joyce and Liz out beside the pool; Liz in a yellow dashiki and dark glasses lay on a chaise longue, while Joyce in jeans and an orange T-shirt sat rather tensely on a pool chair beside her. If leadership couldn't function under present conditions, perhaps democracy could. Of if not democracy, precisely, then some sort of pressure group. Larry knew that Mark would not listen to either himself or

Joyce, but if he could get Liz to join them, might not all three together have some effect? Abandoning Peter, Larry slid open one of the glass doors and went out to the pool, where a portable radio spoke of life on Earth: Jew versus Arab, Greek versus Turk, Christian versus Muslim, Catholic versus Protestant, white versus black.

Joyce smiled wanly over Liz's unmoving body. "How are you, Larry?"

"Terribly worried about Davis," Larry told her. "Peter's just simply abdicated his leadership function." Pulling another chair over by the two women, he sat down and said, "If the three of us went to Mark, our combined weight might make him see some sense."

But Joyce shook her head, with the same wan smile. "Don't count Liz," she said. "She's tripping. I'm her buddy."

"She's what?" Looking down at Liz, seeing now the unnatural stillness of the face behind the large-lensed dark glasses, seeing the blotchy redness of the usually tanned skin, Larry said, "My God. We're all going crazy." It had been two or three years since any of them had dropped acid; that had been a phase, like open sex, like hop, like the sixties themselves. Larry hadn't even known there was acid left in anybody's possession.

"It's a strain," Joyce said. "It's a strain on all of us."

"We're going crazy. We can't stand it anymore, and we're going crazy."

Larry believed that to be literally true. In the past they had planned attacks, bombings, incursions, and the planning had been good, the acts themselves had been well performed and effective. This time, the planning, the act of kidnapping, all had been just as good and just as efficient as ever. But now they were into a different kind of scene, a waiting scene, an ongoing set-piece involving one specific human life, and they were all breaking down.

We can't hack it anymore, Larry thought, and looked out over the Valley, the crawling sun-bleached lifeless deadly Valley, glittering with smog like a fever victim. Thousands and thousands of people lived on that floor, in little white-pink-coral boxes, breathing the sharp glittery air, driving back and forth like ants under the dead sun. How could they be helped? How could they be saved? "Nobody can do anything," Larry said.

Joyce said, "Don't give up, Larry. Please. I need your strength."

Larry looked at her in surprise. "*My* strength?" And seeing her earnest eyes, her soft face, her trust in him, he thought without pleasure: I suppose in truth I do love her. If only we had lived in better times. We were meant for quiet lives, both of us, calm perhaps boring lives, ordinary lives. In a way, Joyce and I have both sacrificed more than Peter or Mark or Liz, all of whom in any era would have been impelled to some sort of extravagance. We have given up our ordinariness for a cause. We have been caught by the flow of history and swept far from shore, far from shore.

But he didn't want to think about that. And in any event, he couldn't keep his mind for long on anything but the one problem; he said, "What's the *matter* with Mark, why does he have to be this way? He's the one making everything impossible. What's he *doing* down there?"

"Listening to the radio," Joyce said. "Like the rest of us."

"But why is he locked in, why won't he let anybody else even *see* Davis?" Then, in a sudden decision, he said, "I'm going to see for myself," and started to strip off his shirt.

"Don't confront Mark, it won't do any good. You'll just make him worse."

"I won't confront him." Larry stepped out of his trousers and shorts, shoes and socks, then, naked, went down the pool steps and swam across to the deep end, making as little disturbance in the water as possible. Above the window he inhaled deeply, then plunged.

The window; from an angle a cold clear shimmering sheet, from straight on a transparency. Larry's arms and legs moved, fighting his body buoyancy, and he looked through the window into the dim-lit room.

It was like a picture in a dream, like some kind of fantastic television. It was as though Larry were tripping, rather than Liz; these shimmering shapes, this underwater quality, had been present sometimes in trips he'd taken before quitting acid, four or five years ago. Through a yard of water, through the twin thicknesses of the glass, was spread the diorama of the room; Koo Davis lying on the couch, twitching from time to time, his head occasionally turning fretfully on the pillow, his eyes closed or no more than slightly open, a sheet half covering him and leaving exposed his panting chest, while seated across from him, unmoving, waited Mark. Still, silent, Mark seemed relaxed in his chair, but he was gazing without pause at Koo Davis, staring at him as though the very appearance of the man contained the answer to some urgent question. The shifting water made vision uncertain, so that Larry couldn't be certain of the expression on Mark's face. It seemed bland and calm, yet intent; was that possible? The usual rage, coldness, unrelenting dissatisfaction, none of that seemed present now in Mark's face, though it could merely be an ambiguity of the water that made him seem so tranquil. He would be listening to the radio in there, the same news, the same planet; but it seemed a planet far far away from the room.

Larry's lungs were hurting, but the scene held him, the sick older man and the black-bearded young man together in tableau in their underwater cave. It seemed to Larry the scene somehow *meant* something, that it was both a question and an answer, and

if he could comprehend what he was seeing he would understand everything. He fought to remain under the surface, while
his lungs and chest and ears strained and his heart pounded,
until he suddenly realized that what he was seeing, whether he
understood it or not, was *too private*. He wasn't supposed to
know this. Afraid all at once that Mark would turn his head, see
him, and never forgive this knowledge, Larry relaxed his arms
and floated to the surface, then swam slowly back to the shallow
end.

Liz was still in the chaise, the same as before, but Joyce had
risen and was standing by the edge of the pool when Larry
climbed out. She said, "He isn't hurting him, is he?"

"He's just watching him. Sitting there unmoving. Koo seems
unconscious, but I suppose that's best for him. But Mark just
sits there." Larry looked back down at the water, as though
Mark lived down in those chlorinated blue depths. "There's
something weird about him. Weirder than usual."

Joyce managed a laugh, and said, "I suppose you're right, we
all are going crazy a little bit, at least for—"

"Wait."

Larry had heard the announcement begin, from the tinny
portable radio on the tiles by Liz's chaise. "The Los Angeles
office of the Federal Bureau of Investigation has asked all radio
stations in this area to present the following taped statement at
this time." And then another voice came on, sounding strained
and hurried:

"This is Michael Wiskiel of the Los Angeles office of the
FBI. I have been involved on the FBI side in the Koo Davis
kidnapping. Early this morning, we delivered to the kidnappers
medicines necessary to keep Koo Davis alive. Although we had
promised not to use this humanitarian act as an opportunity to
capture the kidnappers, we felt that certain legal, moral, and
medical considerations were more urgent than our promise,

and so we inserted a form of tracking device in with the medicine, hoping to follow its transmission and rescue Koo Davis. Unfortunately, the kidnappers found the device and returned it to us with a taped message. Here is part of that tape."

Now Mark's cold angry voice pushed itself into the sunny day: "We'll be listening to the radio news all morning. Until we hear an apology from *you*, Michael Wiskiel, in your own voice, Koo Davis gets no medicine."

"Ah, Jesus," Larry said.

The Michael Wiskiel voice had come back: "The most important consideration, of course, is Koo Davis' health and safety. I certainly do apologize for my decision to use the tracking device, since it clearly has resulted in increased danger for Koo Davis. I not only apologize, I am voluntarily removing myself from further connection with this case. I can only hope this delay has not caused irretrievable harm to Koo Davis. I beg the kidnappers, *please*, to give Koo his medicine *now*."

Peter had come out during the statement, looking both jubilant and relieved, and when it was over Larry turned on him, angrily saying, "Do you like that victory? Peter? He took it away from us, it's a *triumph* for them. They broadcast as much of what Mark said as they wanted—and what a wonderful voice he has to play a villain!—and they made it sound as though it was their idea to turn over the medicine. Are you *really* pleased with that?"

"Be quiet, Larry," Peter said. "They apologized, didn't they? Let's go downstairs and give the man his medicine."

# 13

Koo lies on the couch, his head propped by pillows, and eats spoonfuls of oatmeal fed to him by the woman called Joyce. "After this," he says, still whispering because of his ragged throat and still gasping with fatigue, "will you—read me a story?" To his complete surprise and embarrassment, she responds with an utterly tragic and despairing expression of face; two large tears ooze from her eyes and roll unhindered down her cheeks. They look hot, and the skin itself looks both hot and dry. All in all, her appearance is in Koo's eyes unhealthy, as though she doesn't eat right, doesn't sleep right, doesn't have good medical advice. "Hey," he whispers, lifting one weak hand from his side, "you trying to—break my—self-confidence?— That's the worst—reaction to a gag—I *ever* got."

She turns away, fumbling the oatmeal bowl onto the counter, swabbing at the tears with shaky fingers of her other hand. Then she covers her face with both hands and just sits there, huddled over like a refugee in a bombed bus station.

Koo frowns at her. His strength is slowly returning, and with it the determination somehow to help himself, be of some use to himself.

For instance, he knows where he is. It came to him in one of his deliriums, and now that he's once again more or less in his right mind he's convinced he's right. He's never been here before, but he definitely knows where he is. Could the knowledge be turned to use?

He also wonders if he could work some sort of deal or something with one of the kidnappers. So far he's seen five of them, and is beginning to get a sense of each as an individual. There's the leader, probably the one referred to as Peter; he likes to stay behind the scenes, put in an occasional dramatic or sardonic appearance, and then fade away again. The old *eminence grise* routine. Along with him there's Vampira, the naked blonde chickie with the scars; Koo doesn't know her name, and would be perfectly happy never to see her again, with or without clothing. Another nut is Larry, the lecturer in Advanced Insanity; there's a weird sort of sympathy inside Larry, but it's probably useless to Koo, since Larry clearly is a True Believer, one of those intellectual clowns who can't see the goods for the theories. A completely *un*sympathetic type is Mark, the tough guy with the chip on his shoulder; Koo *knows* that fellow is just waiting for an excuse to do something really drastic.

Which leaves this girl here, Joyce, who looks tragic and unhealthy, and who cries at Koo's jokes. Can he make some sort of useful contact with this one? "Hey," he whispers. She doesn't respond, she remains huddled, face covered, shoulders trembling slightly, but Koo knows she's listening. He licks dry lips and whispers, "Your pal Mark—is gonna kill me—can you help me out of here?"

Her head moves, a quick negative shake.

"Tonight," he whispers, pressing harder, feeling the urgency as he says it. He reaches out, but she is just too far away to touch, and he isn't strong enough yet to sit up. "I can hack it— till tonight," he says, as though she's already agreed to help and all that's left to get organized is the details. "I'll be stronger then—able to walk—just get me away—from the house—it's my only chance—you don't want—Mark to get me."

"But Mark has you," says the cold voice, from behind Koo, back by the door.

Joyce goes rigid, then lifts her tear-stained face to stare toward the doorway. Koo closes his eyes, sighing, trying not to be afraid. He's so *weak*, so goddamn weak. What will the son of a bitch do now?

Talk; for the moment, that's all, just talk. "Joyce wouldn't do it," he says. Koo opens his eyes, and now Mark is standing next to Joyce, his hand on her shoulder, his coldly triumphant eyes on Koo, and in his other hand the cassette recorder. "And if she would do it," he tells Koo, "she couldn't. Not a chance. Right, Joyce?"

"I was feeding him," Joyce says, trying to reach around Mark for the bowl.

"He's had enough to eat. He shouldn't get his strength back too fast. Go on, now, he's about to make another record."

"I should finish feeding him."

"Later, Joyce."

Joyce flashes Koo a quick frightened look, then gets to her feet and leaves the room. Koo isn't sure about that look: Is she afraid *for* me or *of* me? Maybe there's other stuff inside her, and the sympathy won't matter.

But now the problem is Mark, who sits where Joyce was sitting and says, "Davis, you're helpless. I could beat you to death now, if I felt like it. You live or you die according to what *we* want. You're healthy or unhealthy according to whether or not *we* let you have your medicine. You're in no position to make mistakes. What you were saying to Joyce was a mistake."

Koo doesn't speak; he doesn't want to make another mistake. This guy is a time bomb, and Koo doesn't want to set him off; but on the other hand Koo himself has always had a certain amount of pride, and he doesn't want to grovel before the son of a bitch. Unless, of course, it's necessary; better a living grovel than a dead defiance.

Mark slaps the edge of the cassette recorder almost casually against Koo's shin. It hurts, like bumping into something in the dark. Koo winces, and Mark says, "Did you hear what I said?"

"Yes. No mistakes."

"That's right." Mark seems to consider more physical stuff, then changes his mind. Instead, he puts the recorder on his lap and takes from his pocket a folded sheet of paper. "Your new script," he says, opening it and extending it toward Koo.

"I'm sorry—I can't hold it."

Mark looks annoyed, but makes no comment. Instead, he holds it up where Koo can look at it.

This one is shorter, typewritten like the last one, and again with the heavy editing and alterations done by several hands. Apparently, script conferences with this crowd are even hairier experiences than in the television industry. Koo reads it over, knowing he isn't going to like what it says, and not liking it. "Terrific," he whispers, at the end.

"I'm glad you approve." Mark unlimbers the microphone, raises the recorder, then puts a small pillow on Koo's chest and props the sheet of paper against it. "This time," he says, "you read the script the way it's written. You don't add any lines or crack any jokes. If you do, I'll make you regret it. You follow me?"

"I follow you."

"That's good. Are you ready?"

"Do you want me—to, uh—start with personal—things again?"

Mark considers that, then says, "That's a good idea. You don't sound much like yourself."

"I been off my feed." Koo closes his eyes once more, gathering his thoughts, then opens his eyes and says, "Okay." Mark switches on the machine, and Koo says, "This is—what's left of—Koo Davis—speaking to you—from inside the whale—I wanna say hello—to Lily and my sons—Barry and Frank—and especially— Gilbert Freeman—my favorite host—in all the world—and now I got—a script to read."

Koo drops his head back onto the pillow, gasping for breath, and Mark switches off the machine, saying, "What's the problem?"

"Wore myself—out—gimme a minute."

"All right. One minute."

His eyes again closed, Koo breathes hard, struggling for strength and hoping somebody will pick up that message. Surely Lynsey will get it, won't she? Jesus, *somebody* better get it.

"Don't go to sleep."

"I'm not asleep." Koo opens his weary eyes, focuses with difficulty on the messy script. "All right—let's put it—in the can."

Mark starts the machine and Koo reads, slowly and painfully, his voice a grating whisper. "It is now—noon—and I have been—given my medicine—the twenty-four hours—will be up—at six o'clock—if the ten—aren't released—by then—my medicine will be—taken away from me—again—until the demands—have been met—announcements—on the radio—will reach the people—who are holding me."

That's all. Koo lies back against the pillows, watching as Mark rewinds and then listens to the tape, making sure it's all right. There's no expression on Mark's face as he removes the script and pillow from Koo's chest, and when he stands to leave Koo whispers to him, "They won't, you know—they can't—you *are*—gonna kill me."

Mark shrugs. "Either way. It doesn't much matter to me."

"But *why*? Jesus Christ, man—you act as though—you got a grudge—against *me*."

"Not at all," Mark says. "It's the system I hate. It has nothing to do with you."

"But it *does*," Koo insists, fired now by an irrational conviction. "It *is* me—what did I—ever do to *you*?"

Mark gives him a look of contempt and walks away toward the door, out of Koo's sight. But there's no sound of the door opening and Koo listens, wondering what's coming next. After about ten seconds, while the hairs have been rising on the back of Koo's neck, with the silence behind him unnatural and eerie, Mark suddenly reappears, transformed. The cold white face is now hot and red, the hands and arms are trembling, the lips are actually writhing with hatred. *This* is the rage, out on the surface now, and Koo is utterly terrified of it. This is no fooling, this kid really is death on its way to happen to somebody.

Even Mark's voice is different, a strangled snarl. "You want to know what you ever did to me? All right, I'll tell you. You *fathered* me."

Koo has no idea what he means; terror keeps him from understanding much of anything. All he can do is stare at the kid and shake his head, mute with fear and ignorance.

Mark leans down over him, controlling himself, managing to speak more calmly. "I'm your son," he says. Then he straightens, gradually becoming again the restrained cold hater. Hefting the cassette in his palm, he says, "I'll go deliver your message to the folks." And this time, he does leave the room.

## 14

When Lynsey, who had slept for a few hours but was not refreshed, arrived at Police Headquarters a little after two P.M. to hear the latest tape—which had been delivered by a small boy to a local black-community radio station—Jock Cayzer met her at the office door and shook her hand, saying, "I want to apologize, Ms. Rayne, for that business with the tracking device."

"I don't blame *you*, Inspector Cayzer," she said, which was perfectly true. The bluntness of the action, its immorality, its hypocrisy and its assumption that everybody *else* is stupid; she recognized those hallmarks and knew where to place the blame. It was exactly the kind of thing she'd feared from a Watergate tough guy like Mike Wiskiel. Casting that to one side, as not worth discussing, she said, "You told me there was a new tape."

"Let's wait for Mike Wiskiel to get here," he said, "and all listen to it together."

"Wiskiel!" She felt her face tighten, in shock and distaste. "Why on earth would *he* be here?"

"That's on the new tape," Cayzer said, and she was surprised to see that he was grinning; he was *enjoying* this. "Seems our kidnappers like working with an old established firm," he said. "One of their demands is, Mike get put back on the case."

"As the devil they know?"

"Could be that's it," Cayzer said, and glanced over as the door opened. "Here's Mike now."

She turned toward him with a frozen expression, and was surprised to see in him a kind of boyish awkwardness and sheepishness. Moving quickly toward her, he said, "Ms. Rayne, I owe you an apology."

The directness of his capitulation startled her, but she wasn't about to let him off that easily. She said, "You owe Koo a lot more than that."

"I hope to make it up to him. And to you."

"But not with more shabby tricks."

He shook his head, obviously becoming more sure of himself. "Ms. Rayne, please," he said. "Just a minute. Let me make it clear what I'm apologizing *for*. You were right about the other side, and I was wrong. You had them pegged for how smart and tough they really were, and I underestimated them."

"You were dishonorable," she said, both surprised and re-angered that he didn't yet understand the problem. "It doesn't matter that you lied to *me*," she went on, though in fact it did, "the point is you gave your word to those people and you went back on it. If Koo is going to be safe at all in their hands, they have to feel they can trust us."

"No, ma'am," he said, stubbornly shaking his head. "That isn't the case at all. The legal principle is, a promise made under duress carries no force. It's my job to get Koo Davis back and bring his kidnappers to justice. If I'm forced to promise I won't give the job my best efforts—if my choice is either make the promise or risk harm to the victim—I'll promise on a stack of Bibles if they want, but I won't live up to that promise for a second, not if I get a good shot at them."

She couldn't believe what she was hearing. Staring at him, she said, "So you're still just as dangerous for Koo as ever."

"No, I don't believe I am. I told you, I was wrong before, and to be honest I hate being wrong. I'll be a lot more cautious in the future." He essayed a very tentative, very small, somewhat apologetic smile. "And I'll give a lot more weight to your opinions from now on, too."

"Not as to whether you're more honest than they are," she said, "but only if you're more clever."

He was insulted and it showed. "If I have questions about my honesty, Ms. Rayne," he said, "I'll inquire of my own conscience."

Startled, she looked at him wide-eyed for a few seconds, then abruptly said, "I'm sorry. You're right, that was impertinent of me."

Wiskiel seemed surprised by her apology, but then he relaxed into a grin, saying, "The funny thing is, Ms. Rayne, at bottom we're both on the same side."

"I'll try and remember that," she promised, and finally her own face softened into a faint smile of acceptance. She would never see eye to eye with this man, but in fact they were both interested in the same result, and he was doing the best he could within his preconceptions. There was no point prolonging the squabble with him.

He stuck out his hand. "Truce?"

"Truce." His handshake was firm, as it had been yesterday.

Jock Cayzer, who had watched the scene with undisguised amusement, now said, "You two ready to listen to this tape?"

"Let's," Lynsey said. "I'm looking forward to hearing *why* they want to go on dealing with Mr. Wiskiel."

"So am I," Wiskiel said.

The three of them trooped into the workroom, where the technician had the tape already in position on the machine. He started it, and a sudden stir of unease and shock touched them all at Koo's first words: "This is—what's left of—Koo Davis—speaking to you—from inside the whale—"

That was not the famous Koo Davis voice. This tattered croak was barely above a whisper, the panted breath rapid and harsh, the sound altogether that of utter exhaustion and illness.

Looking across at Mike Wiskiel, Lynsey saw that he too was shocked by it, jolted out of ignorant complacency.

From the machine, the pain-wracked voice went on: "I wanna say hello—to Lily and my sons—Barry and Frank—and especially—Gilbert Freeman—my favorite host—in all the world—and now I got—a script to read."

A pause. Clicks on the tape. The voice again:

"It is now—noon—and I have been—given my medicine—the twenty-four hours—will be up—at six o'clock—if the ten—aren't released—by then—my medicine will be—taken away from me—again—until the demands—have been met—announcements—on the radio—will reach the people—who are holding me."

There followed a brief rustling silence, and more clicks, and then the familiar harsh voice spoke out, startlingly loud and aggressive after Koo's labored faintness:

"Put Mike Wiskiel back in charge. We'll negotiate with no one else. He understands us now, he won't make the same mistake again. We don't want to have to train any more FBI men. And Wiskiel knows we're serious. Six o'clock is the deadline."

The voice stopped, the technician shut off the tape, and there was a brief awkward silence, in which everyone moved slightly, shuffling their feet or clearing their throats. Mike Wiskiel sat forward on the folding chair, elbows on knees, continuing to gaze at the black composition floor, and Lynsey found herself feeling sorry for the man. His nose was really being rubbed in it. Not that he didn't deserve it.

But there was something else, something tugging at her mind, taking her attention away from the question of whether or not FBI Agent Wiskiel had learned anything about humility. Turning to Jock Cayzer, she said, "May I hear it again?"

"Well, sure," he said. "If you want."

"Yes, please." Then she became aware that Wiskiel was giving her an aggrieved look; did the man think she was just trying to make him feel worse? She explained, "There was something wrong with it. In the first part, before he was reading."

Wiskiel frowned. "Wrong? What do you mean, wrong?"

"Just let me hear it again."

So the technician ran the tape back to the beginning, and once again they heard Koo say, "This is—what's left of—Koo Davis—speaking to you—from inside the whale—I wanna say hello—to Lily and my sons—Barry and Frank—and especially—Gilbert Freeman—my favorite host—in all the world—and now I—"

"Stop," she said, and the technician hit the button, and the grainy voice broke off.

Jock Cayzer said, "Did you get it?"

"Gilbert Freeman," she said. "Why would Koo talk about Gilbert Freeman?"

"Who is he?"

Lynsey was astonished; you didn't have to get very far from your own field to discover that fame was relative. "Gilbert?" she said. "He's one of the most famous directors in the world. He did *Chattanooga Chop*."

Wiskiel said, "A movie director. So what's the problem?"

"Koo scarcely knows the man," she explained. "They've met three or four times, at parties or dinners, but that's all. Why would Koo talk about him now?"

Jock Cayzer said, "Koo Davis has been in a lot of movies. This fellow Freeman ever direct any of them?"

"Oh, no. Gilbert is an entirely different sort from Koo, very trendy and hip-artistic. Improvisational. Tricky sound tracks, indirect story lines. Pauline Kael loves him."

It was clear that Pauline Kael was another name that rang no bells with either man. Nevertheless, Wiskiel said, "So you're saying there's no real link."

Lynsey said, "He might as well have talked about the weekend in Reno he spent with Simone de Beauvoir."

Wiskiel said, "Okay, I've got the idea. Now, what does he say about this fellow?"

She quoted from memory. "Gilbert Freeman, my favorite host in all the world."

"Favorite host."

Jock Cayzer said, "Let me see do I follow this. Gilbert Freeman never *was* Koo Davis' host."

"That's right," Lynsey said.

Cayzer scratched his head with big-knuckled fingers. "I don't get it. Does he mean *Gilbert Freeman* is one of the kidnappers?"

"Oh, he can't," Lynsey said. "No, that's just too silly."

"He means *something*," Mike Wiskiel said, "that's for sure. And let me say, that's beautiful work he did there. He's sick and he's hurt, and still he threw a curve ball right past them."

"That's right," Lynsey said. "And it's up to us to be up to him, to be as good as he is. He got that out to us, and now we have to do the rest."

## 15

Koo is listening to a talk on tribal problems in Africa. *I don't believe this*, says his internal monologue. *I don't believe this is happening*.

It's been an hour since Mark dropped his bombshell statement and walked out of here, and Koo's mind is still reeling. On the other hand, his physical condition has improved steadily, leaving now only a residue of deep weariness, a drained feeling as though the knots of all his muscles have been untied. What he mostly feels like is a flat tire.

Earnest Larry is saying, "So you see, Koo, the national boundaries are all wrong. Here's the Luanda tribe, they're spread over parts of Zaire and Zambia and Angola, and their loyalty isn't to any of those nations, it's to their own tribe. Is there any greater proof of the continuing dominance of the imperial powers? The African nations have boundary lines drawn according to which European nation colonized where, when the lines *ought* to be drawn according to tribal and linguistic groupings. Every single war and revolution in Africa in the last twenty years has been inter-tribal: tribes with no sensible relationship jammed willy-nilly into the same so-called nation. Who profits from that, Koo? Well, let's look at it."

But what Koo is looking at is his memory of Mark's face, in those climactic few seconds before he left the room; all those emotions crowding by, furious and bitter and speciously calm, ironical. What in Christ's name did Mark *mean*? "You fathered me. I'm your son." Then he ran out, while Koo was still too stunned to ask him anything, and now the question grows with every second. Is it some lamebrain political credo? Larry here might build some idiotic family-of-man allegory into that ultimate statement—"You fathered me. I'm your son."—but is that Mark's style? What *is* Mark's style anyway, other than simple brutality?

Does Larry know what Mark had in mind? If Koo could develop some sort of conversation with Larry, he might be able to ask the question in some indirect way, but the problem is, he can't think of anything to *say*. Even without the enigma of Mark distracting his brain it'd be tough chatting with Larry; how do you *respond* to such half-baked bullshit? Larry knows all these facts and figures, he's got these set-pieces about African tribes, value-for-labor, child mortality, community responsibility, you name it, but the connections he makes and the conclusions he draws are completely weird. He obviously possesses great sincerity and a strong moral sense, but he's trying to make virtue take the place of brains. What Larry's doing, he's making a pearl necklace using some real pearls, some fake pearls, and imaginary string.

Jesus Christ, it suddenly comes to him; ever since Larry started talking to him, in the back of Koo's mind there's been this feeling, this sense of familiarity, of being reminded of something out of the past, but he's been ignoring it because it's ridiculous. How could there have been anything like *this* before?

Well, there was something, and the memory has just popped into Koo's mind, complete and entire, and he's astounded by it. How long ago did that happen? Jesus, it's over twenty years, it's almost a quarter of a century ago. Jesus...

The place was Korea, January of '53, Koo's annual Christmas tour. Korea: that was the good war, maybe the best. For one thing, you could tell the good guys from the bad; also, there was never any chance of the American mainland being involved (Koo still remembers the ongoing silent panic along the Pacific Coast during World War Two, expecting the little yellow men to land at any moment); and besides that the whole damn war was taking place along the same small peninsula. Little danger, no ambiguity and only minor travel; *that's* the way to run a war.

Or almost. Nothing in life is perfect, and in Korea the imperfection was that nobody was supposed to go all-out. America wasn't used to pulling its punches in a war—who is?—so there was a certain amount of frustration, particularly after American defeats. Inchon Reservoir, for instance. That was where the rule-changes started; fighting a war without giving it your total effort, and in fact never even admitting it *was* a war: a *police action*, that was what everybody was supposed to call it. "I didn't raise my boy to be a policeman." You could still joke about such things then; nobody knew they were serious.

But that was where everything started, and now Koo remembers seeing a bit of it: the beginning. The place was called Campok, a crossroads village in a fold among low steep hills. Damn little of the village was left, and for that matter damn little of the roads; everything in the area had been bombed, shelled, mined and fought over for three years. The hills were like the unshaven cheeks of giants, pocked with shellholes and stubbled with tree trunks and bits of underbrush, all smeared with a scum of wet cold snow. The world was in black and white and olive drab, with the shit-brown herringbone lines of jeep tracks quickly obscured by more of that same endless, wet, drifting, cold, goddamn unpleasant snow. It wasn't like Christmas snow, deep and soft and somehow friendly and comfortable. It was war snow, tiny glittering wet flakes like bits of ground glass swirling among the low steep hills in the never-ending wet wind, ramming snowflakes in your ears and down your neck, giving

the skin of your face the look and texture of dead fish. Your
bones ached from it, and for the first time you could actually
feel your skeleton, this twisted clumsy trestle inside your skin.

Carrie Carroll was the blonde that year, a hard-faced broad
with a mammoth ass and sexual preferences that tended toward
the violent; she liked to be forced a little. Already Koo was too
old for all that crap, so by the time they reached Campok he
and Carrie were just touring together, doing the shows, traveling in the same helicopters and jeeps, and otherwise leaving
one another strictly alone. If Carrie was being forced onto her
back by the occasional jeep driver or PIO officer, that was her
business—and good for general troop morale as well.

There was a routine to these tours. Koo and his current
leading lady and one or two special-material writers traveled by
helicopter, while the rest of the troupe came on in a bus-and-
truck convoy: musicians, dancers, technical crew, sound and
light equipment, cameras and film crew, musical instruments,
props and sets and a portable stage. Also portable toilets, dressing
rooms for the stars, and half a truck of costume changes. The
next camp on the tour was never very far away, so while Koo
and Carrie dawdled over a late breakfast the convoy would start
out, groaning and jouncing along the mud-tracks, the technical
crew playing poker while the musicians read *Downbeat* and
*Esquire*. (*Playboy* wasn't around yet, though the first thin issue
did appear later that year.) Some time later, Koo and Carrie
would take the chopper flight, being seen off by the local brass
(unit commanders, PIO officers, chaplains, one or two favored
adjutants) and within an hour being greeted in an identical
frozen hellhole by an identical set of brass, who would lay on as
lavish a lunch as possible before Koo's first show—usually at
one o'clock.

The area commander at Campok was a Colonel Boomer, a

round-faced retread, insurance company executive in civilian life, who was obviously still trying to remember just how he'd managed to behave like a soldier a decade earlier during World War Two. (Mel Wolfe, the special-material writer that tour, stuttered out a thousand one-liners on Colonel Boomer's name, like a jammed machinegun helplessly producing bullets, but Koo couldn't use any of them. He would joke about vague faceless Authority for the troops' enjoyment, but he wouldn't put down individuals. Still, some of Mel's lines were pretty funny; at least, at the time.)

It was during lunch that Colonel Boomer mentioned the deserter. Two days before, a minor skirmish had unexpectedly turned into a quickly advancing thrust into gook territory, a town used by the Other Side as a command post was encircled, and among those captured was an American, one PFC Bramlett. He'd been broadcasting propaganda by loudspeaker toward the American positions. He was being held awaiting transport south, and Colonel Boomer with his round soft face and his earnest insurance man's eyes told Koo about the boy over lunch: "I just don't understand him, Koo," he kept saying, repeating the same words and shaking his head. "I can't understand a boy like that."

And Koo's reaction was immediate: "Why don't I have a word with him?"

Colonel Boomer looked startled, then doubtful. "What good would that do?"

At that time Koo still believed that he understood all Americans, and that all Americans understood him. It was arrogance, it was the simple belief (which he shared with most people then) that the United States was an uncomplicated straightforward upright nation and that he himself was completely, quintessentially, an American. Which was why it was so easy for him to say, "Who knows? Maybe I could help the boy."

The Colonel remained doubtful, but Koo was insistent, and inevitably he got his own way; he did have weight to throw around, when he wanted. That evening, therefore, after his second and final show and before dinner at the officers' mess, he was taken to see Private Bramlett.

The setting was an eight-foot cube dug into the side of a hill. Three of the walls were packed with earth, exuding cold and damp, and the curving wooden outside wall contained only a windowless door. On the plank floor stood a cot, a metal folding chair and a small square wooden table. A bare electric bulb on the wall over the door was the only source of light. The room was small, dark, cold, wet and uncomfortable, but it had one great advantage over every other accommodation in the vicinity; it was safe. Built into the southern slope of a steep hill, it was proof against mortars, grenades, bombs, snipers or anything else the gooks might toss this way. Private Bramlett was going to be returned undamaged from his war.

Bramlett had been told that Koo Davis wanted to see him, and had readily agreed to the meeting, but still it was something of a shock to walk into that dank room and have the emaciated boy step forward with such bashful polite eagerness, bony hand tentatively extended for a shake (but ready to be withdrawn at once, without offense, if Koo chose to ignore it), and to have the boy say, "Mr. Davis, it's terrific to meet you. I'm a big fan of yours."

Koo automatically took the hand, which felt like a paper bag filled with jumbled nails and twine, and automatically smiled in response to the compliment. But before he could mouth the automatic *thank you* and one of the stock gaglines for meeting a fan ("You've got a funny sense of humor") he caught up with himself, and quickly frowned. Clutching harder to the boy's

hand—not a handshake now, but a grip expressing concern—
he said, with spontaneous anxiety, "Jesus, guy, what happened
to you?"

"Oh, well…" The boy's eyes slid away, he seemed both saddened and amused, lost briefly in memory; then, easing his
hand out of Koo's grasp, he faced Koo directly again, as though
wanting to be very explicit and very clear; but all he said was, "I
guess, a lot of things."

"Jesus, I'll say. Let's sit down, let's talk about it."

So they sat together. The boy insisted on Koo taking the cot,
on which the blankets had been carefully smoothed—"It's more
comfortable, sir, it really is"—while he himself sat on the
folding chair. (A part of the arrangement had been that a guard
would remain in the room during Koo's visit, so a GI stood
leaning against the door through the whole conversation, but
neither Koo nor Private Bramlett paid him any attention.)

Koo had planned an opening question, though nothing else:
"You're in a lot of trouble, aren't you?"

"Oh, well. I'll be all right." The boy's manner was strange, so
much so that Koo wondered from time to time if he were
drugged, despite the battalion doctor's earlier statement to the
contrary. Bramlett seemed completely aware of his situation,
but instead of being frightened, or angry, or aggressive, or cun-
ning, he was simply passive, his expression alternating between
earnestness (when trying to explain himself) and a kind of
mournful humorousness (when reminded of his current fix).
He was like someone who knows the joke is on him and who
can see no way to handle it except to try to act like a good sport.

In the boy's presence, in the face of this odd self-containment,
Koo's earlier assurance drained away, and he no longer knew
what he wanted to tell the boy, what he wanted to ask, what
he'd thought he might accomplish here. (Rescue; it was as simple

as that: he'd seen himself as a personification of America, rescuing this strayed lamb, this prodigal son, bringing him back to the safety of American truth.) Looking at the boy now, seeing how foreign Private Bramlett had become—foreign, alien, unearthly, almost unhuman—Koo was abashed, an emotion he rarely felt and had difficulty recognizing. All he understood was that the boy made him uncomfortable, and he struggled against an instinctive sense of dislike.

Hiding that dislike, from himself as much as from the boy, and struggling for a footing in this conversation, Koo fell back on small talk, that inevitable first question to any casually met GI: "Where you from?"

But the boy had *none* of the usual answers. "America," he said, and let it go at that.

"You have to be from somewhere, you can't—" But then it occurred to Koo (wrongly, he later thought) that the boy might be embarrassed at the reminder of his home and parents, and was evading the question for that reason; so he switched to another standard conversation filler, extending his cigarettes toward the boy, saying, "Smoke?"

"Thank you." The boy took a cigarette, but at first merely held it between the fingers of both hands, smiling wistfully at it, rolling it back and forth as though to study it from all sides. Glancing almost playfully at Koo, he said, "America has the best cigarettes."

"America has the best everything," Koo told him, and extended his Zippo lighter with the logo sketch of himself outlined on its chrome side.

"I used to think that." The boy puffed, leaning forward over the Zippo flame, having trouble making the cigarette catch fire. His lips and eyelids were trembling; Koo watched them in shock and disgust. He couldn't help himself, he found the boy unlikeable, unappetizing; like a leper, a child molester. The illness had become the person.

The cigarette finally smoldering, the boy leaned back, the metal chair squeaking under him. "Thank you," he said.

It was wrong to dislike the boy, wrong and surprising and useless. Before entering the room Koo had felt both curiosity and pity, without that automatic hatred for the Traitor which seemed so inappropriate toward someone who had been *brainwashed*, who had been *subjected to techniques*; but in person the boy was physically repellent, grublike, pale and anemic, almost boneless.

Struggling against the revulsion, Koo pushed himself to an exaggerated display of concern, leaning toward the boy, saying, "How'd this happen, son? How'd you get into this?"

The weak smile tinged the boy's face again: "Well, I saw the truth."

"You were brainwashed, huh?" Koo was eager to have the boy *explained*, to excuse his unloveliness. "Wha'd they do to you? Do you want to talk about it?"

Looking troubled, ineffectual, the boy said, "They didn't *do* anything to me, they just showed me the truth." Then, more strongly, more earnestly, he said, "Mr. Davis, I never knew the truth about America before."

There was no way any longer for Koo completely to hide his dislike; it emerged as impatience. "Oh, come on, boy. Do you think I don't know the truth about America?"

"No, sir, I don't think you do." The boy spoke calmly, not argumentatively, as though stating an obvious fact.

Koo leaned back, looking challengingly at the boy, saying, "Tell me this truth of yours."

"Yes, sir." The boy was polite but unflinching, weak but determined. "America's a rich country," he said. "The richest country in the world. But we stay rich by exploiting other countries, poor countries. We're an imperial power, and the thing is, under the present system we don't have any choice. You see, capitalism requires aggression to maintain itself."

All of which was said with as much sincerity as though it meant something. Koo, regretting having initiated this interview, impatient to get it done with, no longer even trying to hide his dislike, said, "Don't gobbledygook at me, boy."

"It's not gobbledygook, sir. You see, the capitalist system—"

"And don't talk to me about capitalist systems. America's no capitalist system, America's a *democracy*."

"No, sir, I'm sorry, it isn't." The smile Koo had thought of as weak now returned to the boy's face, and Koo saw that it was actually mocking. "What do you think we're doing *here*?" the boy asked. "In Korea?"

"Resisting Communist aggression," Koo snapped. Even while he was saying the words, he knew they were his own form of gobbledygook, stock phrases from government announcements or newspaper editorials, but he couldn't help himself. "Coming to the assistance," he went on, "of one of our partner nations in the free world."

The smile was openly mocking now; or at least it seemed so to Koo. The boy said, "Mr. Davis, you've been in Korea a lot. Do *you* think this is a free country?"

Koo hadn't thought about it at all, and he didn't now. He was embarrassed at the banality of the things he'd just said, and he struggled toward another mode of argument, saying, "Son, all of Korea I've ever seen is Army bases and helicopters, but I can guarantee you this much: The people of South Korea are a hell of a lot more free than the Communist slaves in *North* Korea."

"But that isn't true." The boy's smile had gone again, replaced by his earnest-and-sincere expression. "North Korea is a People's

Republic," he said, solemnly, as though the words were magic. "The people rule themselves. In South Korea, there's nothing but a puppet government set up by the Americans. *America* rules South Korea."

Koo shook his head, frowning at the wrongness of this boy. He was caught up now simply in the argument, no longer trying to understand or make contact with the boy himself, but only to pursue the difference of opinion. (Another linkage; this was the first time in his life that Koo ever tried to enunciate his political assumptions. Everything *did* start there, a quarter century ago, in Korea, and nobody even noticed.) Speaking out of his own conviction, but choosing his words as a debater would, for their value in the argument rather than their usefulness in clarifying his thoughts, he said, "Son, you've turned everything upside down. The United States isn't like that. We don't run any country except our own. Look around you. Who controls every Communist nation in the world? Russia! They've just been filling your head with a lot of crap up there." Then, still wanting somehow to champion the boy despite his unlikeableness, to rescue him if it was at all possible, Koo said, "They starved you, right? And they don't let you sleep. Then, when they've got you worn down, they fill your mind with all this garbage."

But the boy was suffering some sort of political equivalent of rapture of the deep; he didn't want to be rescued, he wanted to drown. "Mr. Davis," he said, with all his pale fervor, "it isn't like that at all. We had classes, we learned things. We could ask all the questions we wanted. They showed us facts, history, things our own leaders had said."

"That we run South Korea?"

"That the Western nations, Europe and America, only survive by exploiting the colonial nations."

His irritation growing, Koo said, "This is utter crap. Let me put you straight, once and for all. America is a rich country, and you know why? Any kid in school can tell you this. One, we're rich in raw materials, coal and oil and metal and wood and water and whatever we want. Two, we're a goddamn bright people. Henry Ford, Thomas Edison—Americans *invented* America. What've these Koreans got? What did they ever do for themselves? America is the first and only absolutely free country in the world, even more than England and France and anybody, and all we're interested in in the world is democracy and freedom. Do you think we fought the Second World War for *colonies*? What colonies? Americans are *idealistic*, son, that's the only reason we're here. For an ideal. For freedom."

"I know you believe that, Mr. Davis—"

"Of *course* I believe it, because it's true! *Every* American believes it, for the same reason. What's the *matter* with you?"

"American aggression," the boy said, calm, dogged, hearing nothing, pushing his own parroted lessons into every silence, "robs the Korean people of self-determination. It is the historical reality that the capitalist aggressor must always widen the area of—"

"Jesus *Christ*! Listen to yourself! Do you even know what those words *mean*?"

"Yes, sir, I do. I'll tell you what they mean, sir, every—"

"You will not," Koo said, getting to his feet. "You already told me too much. And now I'll tell *you* something, boy. You aren't even a person anymore. I don't know what you were before they captured you, but all you are now is some sort of stupid machine, you just jabber these words and they don't make any *sense*." Koo had worked himself up, he was almost visualizing himself as America personified, facing down Communism personified in this pitiful boy, as James Cagney used to personify America facing down the Gestapo in World War Two movies;

but that was too ridiculous, too melodramatic for the true situation, and Koo's reaction to his own excess was immediate embarrassment, and a turning down of the rhetoric. "I hope you come out of it all right," he said, grudgingly. "I hope you get back to your right mind."

"I'm not crazy, Mr. Davis. I just know more than I used to, that's all."

"Yeah, well—" But Koo shrugged and shook his head, seeing it was hopeless. No rescue was possible, no human contact was possible; there was nothing to do but leave. "Good luck to you," he said, curt and impersonal.

"Thank you, Mr. Davis." Some pale green flame burned within the boy, gave him his sustenance, provided him with the solemnity for what he said next: "But I won't need luck. I have Truth, and History, on my side." The capital letters were clearly sounded, brave flourishes in his gray speech.

"Oh, yeah?" Koo's jokes were rarely sour, but this one was: "Well, one of them's picking your pocket," he said, which was an exit line, on which he left, and later over dinner with Colonel Boomer he agreed that he too couldn't understand a boy like that. "How does it happen?" The officers around the table shook their heads.

By morning, with the familiar but still exhausting routine of the next move and the farewell and the chopper flight and the next hello, Private Bramlett slipped out of Koo's memory all but completely, and he hasn't actually thought about the boy from that day till this. Now Koo wonders what did finally happen. Did he go to jail? Did he smarten up, did he recover from his brainwashing? Where is he now, Private Bramlett, a man nearing fifty by this time; does he still believe the things he said to Koo all those years ago?

And does Koo still believe the things *he* said to Bramlett?

And *is* there a connection between Bramlett and this fellow Larry, droning away about his African tribes and his Power Elites? Does Bramlett, alone and weak and hopeless and incomprehensible, nevertheless lead to all the Larrys of the Vietnam anti-war movement, in their infuriating thousands?

There's another pause in Larry's monologue, the kind of pause in which Koo has been able to offer nothing more encouraging than a smile or a nod—hopeless conversational gaps—but this time he fills the silence with one word: "Korea."

And Larry brightens like a proud mother when the baby says Mama. "That's *right*! Korea's a *perfect* example. You do begin to see it, don't you?"

"I think I do," Koo says. "Tell me, uh… Do you know somebody named Bramlett?"

Larry is confused. "Bramlett?"

"He'd be—I guess he'd be forty-five by now, something like that."

"Who is he?"

"A boy I met in Korea. Defector." Then Koo frowns, trying to think. "Is that what we called them then? Brainwashed. They went to the Other Side."

"They were martyrs, Koo," Larry tells him, with that po-faced earnestness of his. "They were martyrs to History and Truth."

"Jesus." The old punch lines are losing their zing. Koo feels a sudden nervousness, like a man stepping incautiously, suspecting too late that beneath these dead leaves quicksand waits. "Maybe you're brainwashing *me*," he said. "Get me weak, get me sick…"

"Koo, *we* didn't get you sick," Larry objects reasonably. "And I'm not lying to you. Everything I've told you is facts, you can verify them yourself, look them up, you'll see—"

"Mark," Koo says.

Larry bewilders often. "What?"

"I want Mark, I'll talk to Mark."

"You mean—you mean *Mark*?"

"Now he's giving me doubletakes," Koo mutters. "I'll talk to Mark," he repeats, with emphasis. "Nobody else. Not you, nobody, just Mark. The king of beasts himself."

"Koo, I don't understand. Why on earth would you—?"

But Koo has turned his face away, has clenched his jaw, is staring mulishly at the opposite wall. He has said he will talk to nobody but Mark, and he will talk to nobody but Mark. Period.

The silence stretches between them, Koo determined, Larry dumbfounded, until finally Larry says, tentatively, "Koo, Mark isn't— Mark isn't *pleasant*."

*You're telling me*. But Koo remains silent, unmoving.

"Also," Larry says, then stops, then starts again: "Also, Mark isn't…well, he isn't very strong on the dialectics. I mean, if you have questions, it's more likely I could answer them. At least, I could try. Mark is more…pragmatic."

Nevertheless, if there's any kind of sense in all this, Koo is convinced that Mark is the one with the answers. Larry clearly doesn't even know what the questions are. Koo will not budge.

And at last Larry gives up, getting to his feet, shrugging in wimpish resignation, saying, "But if that's what you want—I just don't think he'll be very useful, Koo, but all right. And I tell you what, I'll make a deal with you."

Koo turns his head, watches Larry's good-guy face, waits.

"You talk to Mark," Larry says. "*Then* you talk to me again. But instead of me telling you things, you ask questions, and I'll do my best to answer them. All right?"

"Sure," Koo says. Because it doesn't matter what happens afterward, not if first he can talk to Mark.

"I'll go get him." But Larry still hesitates, frowning, and says, "What was that name you asked me about?"

"Bramlett."

"And he was a Korean War defector."

"Right."

"Bramlett. What made you think of him?"

Koo struggles to a more comfortable position in the bed. His arms and legs feel like too-thick bread dough. "He was sick, too," he says.

## 16

It was years since Peter had slept a normal eight-hour night. The tensions of his life never permitted him more than three or four hours' sleep at a time, so that he usually had to supplement his night's rest with one or two naps during the day; short uncomfortable naps in which he remained very close to the surface of consciousness, still aware of the world around him, and fully dressed except for his shoes.

Now, at the first noise from the living room, he flung aside the blanket, bounded off the bed, stepped quickly into his shoes and hurried down the hall to find Larry sprawled on the living room floor while Mark, fists clenched, loomed over him, and Joyce was just running in, screaming, from the deck. Larry too was screaming, hoarsely, both hands clutching the side of his neck; as Peter entered the room, Mark deliberately kicked Larry in the stomach, and Larry's screams dissolved into agonized gurgling as he doubled over around the pain.

But Mark wasn't finished. He was reaching for Larry's head, apparently planning to drag him up by the hair, when Joyce got to him and grabbed at his arm, yelling *don't-don't-don't!* Unthinking, Peter crossed the room and slapped Mark hard across the face.

Mark, as though insulted, stared at Peter over Joyce's bobbing head. "Don't you do that," he said.

Peter glared back, trying not to show his uncertainty: "Are you calm now?"

"I've been calm all along," Mark said, then looked down at Joyce, still clutching at him like an exhausted marathon dancer. "Let go of me, Joyce."

But she obviously couldn't. She seemed too terrified to think; all she could do was go on clinging to Mark, panting, staring up at his face.

Mark looked beyond her again at Peter, saying, "Get her off me."

Peter was troubled, cautious, watching Mark as though he were some dangerous dog whose chain had snapped. Reaching tentatively forward, he tugged at Joyce's elbow, at the same time continuing to watch Mark's face. "All right, Joyce," he said. "All right."

Joyce finally did release her grip, moving back with Peter but staring constantly at Mark, who stepped back a pace and glared at them in apparent outrage. Larry, both forearms pressed to his stomach, was sitting on the floor now, hunched forward, wheezing hoarsely in his throat. Pointing at him, Mark said, "I won't have that sniveling moron pestering me."

Larry was trying to talk through his wheezes, but couldn't. Even in pain, in panic, on the floor, unable to breathe, Larry went right on talking. Incorrigible.

Peter said, "For God's sake, Mark, what's this all about?"

"I won't be part of Larry's plans," Mark said; then, obscurely challenging, he added, "And I'm not sure I'll be part of yours."

"Take it easy," Peter said. "We're still one group."

Mark's lips twisted in scorn, but all he said was, "Keep them away from me, Peter. All I need is to be left alone." And he turned away, crossing the living room in quick nervous paces, leaving the house, slamming the door behind himself.

Joyce had now dropped to her knees beside Larry, was murmuring and cooing at him, touching his hair and his shoulder and his arms. Peter, exhausted and raw-nerved, seated himself on the edge of the nearest armchair, elbows on knees as he leaned forward and down toward Larry, trying to hide annoyance and uncertainty with an expression of concern as he said, "Larry, for God's sake what was that all about?"

Larry shook his head. Joyce kept dabbing at his face, saying things.

Peter said, sharply, "Joyce, leave him alone. Larry, tell me what happened."

"Mark is an *animal!*" Joyce said, indignantly, glaring at Peter.

"No, he isn't," Peter told her. "He's a very disturbed and explosive human being, and I'd like to know from Larry what set him off."

"I don't know," Larry said, voice rasping. "He's always so— I only—" He shook his head.

"All right, Larry, from the beginning. What happened?"

Larry rested his forehead on his palm. An occasional shudder rippled through him as gradually he calmed. "I was talking with Koo," he said. "Then Koo said he wanted to speak with Mark. I pointed out—"

"Wait a minute," Peter said. "Koo Davis *asked* for Mark?"

"It surprised me, too," Larry said, lifting his head, looking up at Peter. "But he insisted. We made a deal; first he'd talk with Mark, then again with me. He was getting interested, Peter. He brought up the subject of Korea himself, he's beginning to see how the pieces fit."

Peter was skeptical, but he said, "All right. So you came to Mark."

"I told him about Koo," Larry said, petulance creeping into his voice. "He refused, he just flat refused. No explanation, nothing. Then all at once he started hitting me."

"He's a beast," Joyce declared. She was seated now on the

sofa, shredding damp tissues nervously between her hands.

Peter shook his head. "Larry, no. There had to be more to it than that."

"But there wasn't. I asked him, he refused, he started hitting me."

"How many times did you ask him?"

"Two or three," Larry said, obviously grudging any piece of information that might complicate his story.

But Peter was insistent: "What did he say the first time you asked him?"

"He said no! He never said anything but no, and then he started using his fists."

Shaking his head, Peter said, "There's something more in all this. There's something I don't understand."

"Oh, is there? Well, I'll be happy to tell you what it is." Larry struggled to his feet, pushing away Joyce's eager attempts to help. "What you don't understand, Peter, is that Mark is taking over!"

"Oh, now," Peter said, with a little sardonic smile, "don't get carried away, Larry. Mark is not exactly what we call leadership material."

"That's right," Larry said. "When Mark's in charge, everything is going to blow up. And it's happening, he's taking over. Only because *you* won't stop him. Like that business with Davis' medicine."

"Stop right there," Peter said, defensively becoming angry himself, getting to his feet and pointing at Larry with a jabbing forefinger. "It so happens Mark was right about that. They needed a lesson. And they apologized in plenty of time, just as Mark said they would."

"And demanding that Wiskiel be put back in charge?"

"Mark was right again. You didn't argue against it. Larry,

sometimes you're right, and I listen to you. And sometimes Mark is right, believe it or not."

"This time *I'm* right," Larry insisted. "You're losing control, and Mark is moving into the vacuum, and that's disastrous. You've always been very good, Peter, but before this we've always been hit-and-run. None of us is right for this kind of long-term operation."

Peter's cheeks burned and stung. "Everything is working," he said. "The only problems are among ourselves. The operation is doing fine."

"Problems among ourselves? Peter, that's what'll kill us. You have to take charge, you have to be in command. You absolutely have to run things."

"All right," Peter said, cold and angry. "Then I'll give you a direct order. Stay away from Mark."

"And him? Mark? What about him?"

"He's none of your business. *I'll* take care of Mark."

"But you won't."

Peter was about to say something even angrier when Joyce suddenly cried, "Oh, my gosh." Turning, he saw Liz on her feet out by the pool, walking in slow circles, patting the air in front of her as though it contained an invisible wall. Joyce hurried out there, and Peter watched her take Liz by the arm, walk her back to the yellow chaise longue.

Speaking quietly, Larry said, "We're breaking down, Peter. We're *all* the weakest link."

"We'll hold together," Peter told him; firmly, making it true by the sheer determination of his manner. Then, unable to hear any more dispute, he turned away, hesitated, unsure for a second where he intended to go, and then crossed the room and went out the front door, following Mark.

Who was gone; and so was the Impala. Not good. Mark was

too unpredictable. He might merely go for a drive until he'd cooled off, or he could start a fight in some bar and get himself in trouble, or he might even leave entirely, deciding again to break with the group. Mark had disappeared more than once over the years, each time returning a few days later or phoning from some distant place; it was never convenient when he pulled such stunts, and this time it could be a disaster. Aside from anything else, he had their only transportation, since the van had been dumped last night in the Burbank Airport long-term parking lot.

It was difficult for Peter not to show his increasing hostility toward the group. He'd known them all a long time, too long and too well. They were the only soldiers available to him now, here in the Valley Forge of the New Revolution, but after this operation he would never see them again. Only this operation was needed, the freeing of the ten, himself as an instrument, and the corner would be turned. Peter Dinely would be established.

He knew he was the only one in the group who thought historically. None of the others could project beyond the immediate results of action, but at least they were prepared to follow where they themselves could not see the path. Did they know *why* it was so vital to free the ten? No, and if he were to waste his breath in explanations they still wouldn't understand. But they acknowledged *his* capacity and followed his orders, which made them both essential and unbearable. Soon I must have equals about me, Peter thought, or I shall wither.

Everything was pressing in. Peter wouldn't admit it out loud, but Larry was to a degree right; the pressure was becoming too great. That was why the deadline had to be met, why they didn't dare let this thing drag on any longer. Six P.M. today; four hours from now. There had to be an answer by then, period.

And if the answer was no?

"We'll kill him," Peter muttered aloud. "And start all over."
And next time, if Davis were dead, they'd be treated more seriously by the other side.

Oh, God, how his cheeks hurt! How he wished he could stop the chewing, chewing, chewing. Sometimes he'd hold a knuckle in his mouth and bite down on that, but with his lips parted the air could touch his wounds, causing them to sting and burn even more. Rubbing his cheeks with both hands, moaning in his throat at the pain, Peter stood just outside the front door and tried to think what to do next.

Not go back inside; he couldn't deal with another Larry scene, not now. And God alone knew what was happening with Liz. No, not back into the house.

In front of him, the hill sloped steeply upward, clothed in a ground cover of dark green ivy. A red brick path meandered up through the ivy, slanting along the hill face, here and there becoming shallow brick steps. At the top, he knew, was an untended garden, where remnants of asparagus and strawberries struggled amid choking thick weeds. Some previous owner had planted that garden, which had not been cared for in at least three years. Having no other possible destination, Peter climbed the path, moving slowly, holding his jaw clamped shut.

At the top, the land leveled somewhat and the brick path widened into a kind of small patio, with a stone bench facing the view of the valley over the roof of the house. At one end of the patio was a small weathered plywood toolshed, barely four feet high. The garden was beyond the patio on the level width of land, and beyond that, just before the hillside rose steeply upward again, was the fence marking the property line, with a small locked gate leading out to a blacktop driveway, a common road shared by several of the neighbors farther up the hill. Peter, reaching the level part, glanced without interest at the tangle of plants in the garden, then stood looking out at the Valley, trying not to think, trying not to chew.

After a few minutes, he sighed and turned to sit on the stone bench, and that was when he saw the trousered legs jutting out from behind the toolshed. He cried out, reflexively, as though he'd been punched in the throat, and actually felt his heart bulge inside his chest. Icy terror drenched him, and all he could do was stand there, strangling, his eyes fixed on those legs. Who? For the love of God, *who*?

But then the person, who had been sitting back there with his legs stretched out, leaned forward, his grinning monkey face coming into view, and Peter gasped, "Oh! Oh, it's *you*! Jee-sus! Son of a *bitch*, you scared the hell out of me!"

"Why, Peter," said the sly monkey face. "What an effect I have on you."

"Jesus God." Peter was sure he would fall, he was that weak and dizzy. Clutching the stone bench, he lowered himself onto it and sat there panting. "Oh, Ginger," he said. "For God's sake, Ginger, don't ever do that."

Laughing, enjoying himself hugely, Ginger Merville clambered to his feet and came over to sit beside Peter. "If you could see your face—!"

"What—what are you *doing* here? You're supposed to be in Paris."

"I came back." Ginger shrugged, still delighted with himself. "We're off to Tokyo, actually, but I thought it'd be fun to come back *en route*, see how the old plantation's getting along without me."

"But where's Flavia?"

"Still in Paris. She's flying direct. Over the po-o-o-ole," Ginger said, sweeping one arm over his head, languidly wiggling callous-tipped fingers.

Peter was catching his breath now, calming down. He said, "What's the matter with you, Ginger? Do you *want* to get involved? The whole idea was, you're in Paris, we broke into your house, you didn't know a thing about it."

"Well, I *don't* know a thing about it. I'm staying at a beach place in Malibu. *You* know; Kenny's place. He still has it, after all these years." Then Ginger smiled in a sympathetic way, giving Peter a consoling pat on the knee. "Don't worry, my dear," he said, "I've explained it to just *everybody*. Since the house is for rent, and I'm only here two or three days, I didn't want to open the place and mess it all up. *Ergo*, the beach house."

"Ginger, you're crazy," Peter said. But then, since in fact that was true, he awkwardly added, "You're risking your position. And what for? There's no *point* coming here."

Ginger leaned closer, smirking as though he were about to confide a dirty secret. "I want to see him," he whispered.

Peter stared in shock; this *was* a dirty secret. "See him!"

"Through the window. I'll slip into the pool—"

"No! For God's sake, Ginger!" Peter's repugnance showed on his face. "If you want to see him, watch television, they have all his movies on."

"I know," Ginger said. "Just as though he were dead. But I want to *see* him, Peter, in my little hideaway room."

"And he'll see you."

"I'll wait till after dark."

"It'll all be over by then," Peter said confidently. "The deadline's six o'clock."

Ginger's smile turned mock-pitying. "Oh, come off it," he said. "*You* know they can't gear up by then. Twenty-four hours? You must be joking."

Twenty-four hours. It was true, they'd captured Davis only

yesterday afternoon. Emotions create their own time, and it seemed to Peter now as though he and Davis and Mark and Larry and Liz and Joyce had been imprisoned together for months. He said, mulishly, "It has to end."

"But not by six o'clock, not *today*."

"We'll kill him," Peter said, glowering as though Ginger were on the other side, as though this were the negotiation.

Ginger's monkey face at last forgot to smile. "Peter," he said, looking and sounding worried. "Don't lose your cool, Peter. Killing Koo Davis isn't the object of the exercise."

"I know that. You don't have to remind me."

"But I'm awfully afraid I do," Ginger said. Squeezing Peter's knee, he said, "Forgive me for being a schoolmarm, but you do *remember* the object of the exercise, don't you?"

"Ginger, stop it."

"I'm just terribly afraid you've become caught in the drama of it all. Don't become a Dillinger manqué, my dear."

"I won't," Peter said sullenly. He didn't like being lectured, and particularly not by a shallow creature like Ginger.

"Ease my mind, Peter," Ginger said. "Tell me again the object of the exercise."

Peter pressed the heels of both hands to his cheeks, squinting against the pain. "Not now, Ginger."

"Then I'll tell you," Ginger said. "America today is very very roughly analogous to Russia between 1905 and 1917; between the revolution that failed and the revolution that succeeded. The revolution of the sixties failed, the cadres are dispersed, the militants have faded back into normal life, the threat to *this* society is ended. For now."

"All right," Peter said.

"Your task in this period," Ginger persisted, "is to maintain yourself and prepare for the next round, the successful round. And *I* am backing you to be one of the new leaders."

"Yes."

"You may not be the Lenin of the New American Revolution, but you'll be one of those with him in the sealed train."

"Yes." Peter lowered his hands from his face, and sat up a bit straighter. Hearing his own ideas recited back to him, in all seriousness, was bringing him out of his funk, reminding him that all this had a reason.

"Brownie points," Ginger said, with his elfin grin. "Brownie points with the remaining revolutionaries. *That's* the object of this exercise. *You* will be the man who freed so many of them from prison."

"That's right," Peter said. "That's the whole task now, to keep as much of it alive and whole as possible, and wait for the next opportunity."

"Koo Davis is not germane, Peter. He is a tool, a small wedge you're using to open some doors. His death does nothing for anybody."

"We can't lose our credibility," Peter said, thinking of Mark.

"But you can negotiate. You can be flexible."

"Within limits."

"Twenty-four hours isn't enough time. You know that yourself."

Peter did. But he also knew that the group in the house was fragmenting. Their stability was gone, they were breaking down. But not yet, they couldn't collapse yet; Peter had to somehow hold them together just a little longer. *After* the operation was finished, after Peter had made his way out of the country—in his mind's eye he saw himself at the airport in Algiers, smiling, shaking hands with the men and women he'd rescued—after this task was done, the others could destroy themselves in any way they chose; they wouldn't matter anymore. Joyce would undoubtedly surrender to the authorities, for instance, something she'd been wanting to do for a long time. Suicide was the likeliest end for Liz, some sort of violent murder for Mark. Larry would probably be caught by the police while trying to rob from the rich to give to the poor. This idea amused Peter, who smiled. Ginger said, "Something funny?"

"A stray thought."

Ginger shrugged, then sat back on the stone bench, considering Peter in a thoughtful manner. "I do have one little question, Peter," he said.

"Yes?"

"That list of people, the ten you want freed. There are some very odd names on that list, my dear."

"I wanted a spectrum," Peter explained. "Not just this group or that group, but as wide a range as possible."

"They look like names picked at random."

"They almost are. The fact is, there really aren't that many political prisoners left in this country. We needed a big enough number to make it worthwhile, and I wanted them to represent the whole broad range of resistance and rebellion."

"Well, try not to turn your back on some of them," Ginger said.

"I'll watch myself," Peter promised. "And you watch yourself, Ginger. *Stay* in that house in Malibu."

"Some of the time," Ginger said, then leaned close again, with his confidential smirk. "But if you hear a little wee splash in the pool tonight, my dear, it isn't dolphins."

"Ginger, don't do it."

"I'm off, darling," Ginger said, getting to his feet, patting Peter on the cheek. (Peter winced, trying not to betray the pain.) "Don't worry about your little Ginger."

Standing, Peter said, "But I do. You've got to keep your cover, Ginger, you wouldn't be any good at all underground."

Ginger giggled as though the idea appealed to him. "On the run?" he asked. "With my famous Fender?" And he took an exaggerated macho stance, strumming an imaginary guitar.

"You wouldn't like it, Ginger," Peter warned him. "You enjoy first class too much."

"Oh, but my heart is with the Movement," Ginger declared theatrically. "What is it to live dangerously? I shall tell you, my dear. To live dangerously is to live in two opposite directions at once. Like the adulterous wife, easing the lover out the back door while the kiddies home from school are entering via the front. *You* don't live a lie, my dear, you live a simple one-dimensional life." Ginger took another dramatic stance: "The Revolutionary! When you get up in the morning, you know precisely who you are, and you never deviate all day long. My dear, I never know who I am. It's such a wonderful party being me!"

"Don't spoil it, Ginger. Don't take too many chances."

Ginger laughed, clapping his hands together, then winked and said, in a conspiratorial half-whisper, "Splish splash, I was takin' a bath."

"Ginger, don't."

"Bye-eye." Ginger wiggled all his fingers at Peter, then danced away toward the upper gate, like a figure from *The Wizard of Oz*. Peter watched him, worrying, frustrated, helpless to avoid these unnecessary dangers. There was no escape; when Ginger was at last out of sight, Peter turned and walked back down the brick path to the house.

As he neared the house, he saw a pale blue van just driving away down the hill. Joyce was out by the garage, obviously just having seen the person off, whoever he was. Frowning, Peter finished his descent as Joyce walked back toward the house, and they met by the front door. Peter called, "Joyce!"

She glanced at him, weariness in her every feature. "I have to get back to Liz. She still hasn't grounded."

"What was that truck?"

"The gas company. A man was looking for a gas leak."

"He was? Did he find it?"

"No, he said it must be farther up the hill."

Peter looked away down the drive, as a cold breeze touched his spine. "He did, did he?"

## 17

Koo awakes. At first he doesn't understand where he is or what's going on, but as his eyes focus on the large window with all that water behind it memory returns, frightening and depressing. "So this is Baltimore," he mutters, but his heart isn't in it. He shifts position on the couch, then remembers in more detail: He'd been waiting for Mark, half-dreading and half-needing the confrontation, and at some fuzzy time along in there, incredibly, he'd faded away into sleep.

What time is it? His watch isn't on his wrist, it's— Where the hell is it? Fear and depression are making him cranky with himself.

The watch is on the end table near his head, reading a little after three-thirty. He'd been asleep nearly an hour; so where's Mark?

Koo sits up, noticing with surprise how much stronger he feels. He's been using his pills again for six hours now, and while he's still weak and nervy he's in much better shape even than when he'd dozed off.

He's in such good shape, in fact, that he now has leisure to notice he stinks. All that old perspiration is still stickily on his body, beneath his filthy clothes. He's also very grizzled, this being his second day without a shave. "I feel like King Kong's socks," he says, and gets to his feet.

Whoops; too fast. Rocking briefly under the wave of dizziness, he sits down again, hard. He's not *that* healthy, not yet. For the next try he moves more cautiously, pausing to rest after he makes it to his feet. "Wal, sonny," he says, in an exaggerated old man's cracked voice, "I may be stupid, but I ain't the one who's lost." Then, in his own voice, he says, "Oh, yes, I am," and depression settles deeper.

The bathroom is tiny, but it contains a stall shower. Koo scrubs himself briefly, then dons a pale blue terrycloth robe hanging behind the door. In a storage cabinet beside the sink he finds a Norelco electric razor and a half-full bottle of Lectric Shave. He's feeling chilly, so he shuts the bathroom door while shaving.

These ordinary acts lift his spirits a great deal. The reason he became a comic in the first place is that he has a naturally cheerful view of life. It's true he's so weak while shaving that he has to support most of his weight by leaning forward against the rim of the sink, and his hands contain a tremble that was never there before, but by God he's still alive, and he's clean, and his health is improving by the second.

Finishing the shave, looking at his clean face in the mirror (ignoring the red eyes in the pockets of gray flesh), Koo says, "Okay, kid, we've worked in worse toilets than this. Don't get all flushed about it." Then, touching the walls for support, he moves slowly out to the main room and there's the mean blonde seated in the swivel chair down by the window. She's wearing dark-lensed sunglasses and a yellow dashiki, and she's swiveling the chair left and right in short bad-tempered jolts. "Shit," Koo says, and totters over to sink down onto the studio couch, where he sits gasping for breath—the exertion has used him up— while he watches her warily from the corner of his eye.

Liz—he remembers somebody referring to her as Liz— studies him for a long silent moment from behind her impenetrable sunglasses, then says, in tones of exaggerated contempt, "Old men are disgusting."

Koo is cautious, but he didn't come here to be insulted. "You look better with your clothes on," he says.

Her scornful expression is oddly imperfect, like a poor imitation of the real thing; what Koo thinks of as Producer's-Girlfriend level of acting. She says, "You don't know how to treat a woman who isn't a sex object, do you?"

"You've been spayed? Good."

Is that surprise she's showing? Something is happening on those parts of the face that he can see; her mouth twists into unusual shapes, her forehead furrows, her head nods in tiny random non-rhythmic movements. Then, speaking at first with exaggerated precision, like talking computers in the movies, but with the words becoming more and more rapid and jumbled, she says, "I haven't run run run-run-run-runrunrunrunrun-rurururururururu—" and turns her head at last away, muttering and mumbling down toward her shoulder, and finally grinds into silence.

*Jesus*, Koo thinks, *she's coked up to the eyeballs*. He watches her, warily, to see what she'll do next.

Talk. Her face still half-turned away, her expression still impossible to read behind those round nearly black sunglass lenses, but her voice more neutral, more natural—more human, really—than Koo has ever heard it before, she starts to talk.

"In the explosion, Paul's arm was blown off. He was using—" a hand gesture, half bewildered and half impatient "—paraffin, something—" the hand drops lifeless to her lap "—it stuck to me. His arm, it stuck to my back, I couldn't get it off. It was burning. His hand—" She makes a shivering recoil movement, writhing her shoulders like someone who has backed naked into a spider web, but her voice remains flat, calm, uninvolved: "I can feel his fingers sometimes, spread out between my shoulder blades."

Koo winces, but she doesn't seem to be looking at him or to care in particular what his reaction is. She holds her left hand out away from her body, fingers splayed as those other fingers must have been splayed against her back, but she doesn't look at her hand either, or seem aware of her gesture. "I couldn't get it off," she says, her narration increasingly choppy. "I was burning, all my clothes burned off—my hair burning, everything burning—Frances grabbed me by the face, she held my chin and led me—she knew the house, how to get out—and the arm on my back, burning."

She stops, and Koo looks at her in silence. His mind is full of questions—what explosion, where, who was Paul, how did she escape—but her manner is too crazy, he's afraid to poke at her with words. So he sits watching her while the silence lengthens. The outstretched tense hand gradually settles to her side, rigidity leaving the long bony fingers. Her head twitches or nods from time to time, reminding Koo of a sleeping dog agitated by dreams of hunting, and he's wondering if he should say something after all when suddenly she begins again:

"The kitchen, the wall was—they'd taken it down, all the plaster and paint—down to the brick, just the one wall—it was supposed to look nice, brick—Frances took me through the kitchen, but my back—the arm—I scraped my back against the brick—even the brick was hot, everything—it was the only way, the arm—I scraped it off against the brick."

"Jesus," Koo whispers, staring at her.

She doesn't seem to notice. With only the slightest pause, she goes on: "Frances waited for me—I scraped and scraped, everything burning, and the ceiling fell in and hit her—under the wood, down on the floor—I pulled her out, and we ran away."

A deep breath and now she nods, almost in satisfaction, as though approving of her own report, and her next sentence is more coherent, more normal in tone and phrasing: "Grace was just around the corner, so we went there and she gave us clothes, and then we ran away."

"What happened to Frances?" The question pops out, unplanned.

A vague hand gesture. "She died, from the ceiling. We all died."

"When was this?"

"Yesterday."

"Ah," Koo says, and knows better than to ask any more. Maybe this girl is hopped up, as he'd originally thought, and maybe she's merely crazy, but it's clear enough there's one central real-life event in her mind—an explosion, a fire, a burning arm stuck to her back—surrounded by layers of weirdness. This creature shouldn't be walking around loose.

Koo's watch is now on his wrist, and it tells him the time is shortly after four; shouldn't he be taking more of his pills? (He's always thought of them as his "pills," but maybe from now on he should think of them as his "medicine." Grim thought.) Doctor Answin's letter of instructions is on the table near Koo's left hand; still cautiously watching Liz, he picks up the letter, glances at it, and sees the answer is yes.

Will she mind if he gets up, moves around? "I have to take some pills," he says, but she doesn't seem to notice, to see him or hear him or be aware of anything except the drifting phantoms in her mind. He gets to his feet, crosses to the pill case on a side table, assembles the right dosage, and goes off to the bathroom for a glass of water. And when he returns she's changed again, she's removed her sunglasses to show the cold small eyes, and she's smiling at him, a hostile nasty smile; back to the good old Liz of yesteryear. Under her icy gaze he returns to the couch and lies down, adjusts the tails of the robe over his knees.

"So you like women," she says.

"They're better than tuna on toast."

She glares at him, rage distorting the attempted superiority of the smile. "You *hate* women."

"Oh, goody," he says. "Psychology."

"You don't know how to deal with women, so you fuck them and then run off."

"It doesn't work the other way around."

"You think *we* need *you*?"

"I don't know what you need, honey," Koo tells her, in utter sincerity, "but if it's me, you're outa luck."

"I'll show you how much we need you," she says. "Watch."

Koo doesn't know what to expect—he's actually braced to duck a thrown knife, something like that—but what happens is, she slides lower in the upholstered swivel chair so that she's sitting on the base of her spine, then pulls up the skirt of the dashiki over onto her stomach and spreads her knees far apart, showing that she's naked beneath, her cunt a beginner's origami within its shawl of hair. Astonished, now believing she has some sort of seduction in mind—with a last-second refusal, no doubt— Koo watches her angry eyes, wondering how far he dare go in letting her see just how little she turns him on. But next she slips the middle finger of her right hand into her mouth, smiling around it like some evil child, then lowers the moistened finger between her legs, touching herself, finding the clitoris, manipulating it, her finger and hand moving in a small quick repeated circle, like a piece of machinery in a model railroad set.

So it's craziness, simple craziness. Koo refuses to turn away, but also refuses to watch directly what she's doing; he stares at her eyes instead. His feelings shift from alarm to annoyance and outrage—kidnapping is one thing, but *this* is too much— but as her eyes become less focused, as the artificial scorn fades from her face and color begins to flush her cheeks, he thinks, *She's going to make herself come,* and what he feels is embarrassment—for them both.

It doesn't take long. Her leg muscles are rigid beneath the tanned flesh, her face is increasingly swollen and red, her gaze slides away to stare at the ceiling, her mouth sags open, she breathes in tiny desperate gasps, her finger spins and spins, and from her throat come two quick guttural coughs. Mouth straining wide, she suddenly thrusts the finger into herself, jabbing and jabbing, the side of her thumb jolting against her clitoris at every plunge of the finger. Bending forward, her other hand reaching almost protectively between her legs, she prods and batters at herself in semi-privacy a few instants more, then sags over her drawn-up knees, her head lowering so he can no longer see her distorted face.

Koo also is released; he turns away, staring at the furniture, the wall, the closed bathroom door, anything at all. That was the least sane thing anybody, man or woman, ever did in his presence, and his mind is a jumble of response; pity, outrage, embarrassment, humiliation, fear. Everything, in fact, but lust: *You're a great argument for monasteries, baby*, he thinks, but he doesn't say it out loud.

Liz, in fact, is the first to speak, three or four minutes later, saying, "Well?"

He looks at her, and she's back to her old self, angry, hostile and scornful. She's also sitting up straight now, the sunglasses hiding her face and the dashiki down over her legs. Koo has nothing to say, but he watches her, waiting for whatever will happen next.

The drug or madness or whatever it was seems gone now. She's merely a nasty woman; nastier than most. With more belligerence than challenge she says, "Do you think you could make me come like that? You couldn't. Not even close."

Koo answers without the slightest overtone of comic manner: "For the first time in my life," he says, "I know why they call it self-abuse."

"Funny man," she says, as mirthlessly as he. Then she shakes her head, saying, "Do you really expect to live through this?"

"I don't think about it," he says, while a lump of dread forms in his stomach.

What a lot of different sneers she owns! Using a brand new one, she says, "Afraid?"

"Very. Aren't you?"

"We having nothing to fear but fear itself," she tells him. "And that big guy over there with the sword."

Koo gapes at her; does she realize she's quoting an ancient line of his?

Yes. With an ironic smile she explains, "They're showing your old movies on television. Because of all this."

"Oh. Is that the silver lining, or the cloud?" And, astonishingly, he senses the beginning of human contact between them.

But she won't let it happen. Souring again, lips turning down, she says, "*I'm* not your fan. We're not chums."

"That's the silver lining."

"Shut up for a minute. You're a boring person."

"Send me home."

She looks at him, stolidly. "You'll never see home again. Now shut your face."

He says nothing. She wants the last word? Fine, she's got the last word.

And some last word it is. While the silence goes on and on in the small room—she's brooding about something, over there behind her sunglasses—her last statement keeps circling in Koo's head. "You'll never see home again." That's the fear, tucked down into a capsule and neatly answered, the fear that there *is* no way out, that kidnapping isn't really what's happened to Koo Davis. *Death* is happening to him, that's what, Death, in easy stages. He's on the chute, the long slippery chute, sliding down into the black.

It must be five minutes they sit there in jagged silence when the door behind Koo opens again and Joyce enters, looking hopeful and almost happy—and then surprised, when she sees Liz: "So there you are!"

"Maybe," Liz says, unmoving.

"Did you hear the announcement?"

Liz shrugs.

"On the radio," Joyce says, as though a piling on of detail will encourage Liz to respond.

Koo says, "Something about me? Excuse me butting in, I take an interest in my well-being."

"Yes, of course," Joyce says. "It was from the man Wiskiel. He said the kidnappers should watch a special program tonight at seven-thirty on Channel 11, we'll have an answer from Washington then."

"A special? They can't just say yes or no, they have to bring on the June Taylor Dancers?"

"They apologized for not making the six o'clock deadline," Joyce goes on, oblivious, "but they said seven-thirty was the absolute earliest they could have the answer ready. Doesn't that sound hopeful to you?"

She's asking Koo, having obviously decided not to waste her high spirits on Liz, but Koo isn't feeling particularly perky himself at the moment, and he says, "What's so hopeful about it? It can still be yes or no."

"Oh, it's *much* more likely to be yes. If it was no, they could just say so, but if it's yes they have to get everybody ready, get them out of their jails and all, and that takes time."

"I hope you're right," Koo tells her. "In fact, I'm positive you're right."

"I know I am." Joyce takes everything literally. Now she actually smiles fondly at Koo, and says, "It really hasn't been that bad, has it?"

Can she be serious? Koo studies her earnest face, and decides she can. He says, "You know how, sometimes, there's a thing that somebody doesn't like, and he'll say, 'Well, it's not as bad as a poke in the eye with a sharp stick'? You ever hear anybody use that remark?"

"I think so," she says, doubtfully.

"Well, *this*," Koo tells her, "is *exactly* as bad as a poke in the eye with a sharp stick. In fact, worse. In fact, two pokes, two eyes, two sharp sticks."

"Oh, it isn't *that* bad," she says, with a laugh, as though he's joking.

Koo frowns. He will not do Burns and Allen with this nitwit. "Okay," he says. "So it isn't that bad."

Abruptly Liz yanks herself to her feet, saying to Joyce, "He's an insect. He'll be squashed, that's all, sooner or later. Don't smile at him, he's dead already." And she strides from the room, closing the door hard behind her.

Joyce looks pained, like a punctilious hostess. "Don't mind Liz. Really. She's been…upset today."

"You don't know the half of it."

"I'll have to—" Joyce is edging, in tentative muddled movements, toward the door, drawn by Liz' wake. "Things will be all right now," she says, but her smile is panicky.

*Will* things be all right? One of these people is talking death, one is talking release, one is talking father-son, one is talking African tribes, and Count Dracula isn't talking at all. And Koo is not at all as heartened as Joyce at the prospect of this seven-thirty television spectacular; it sounds more like a negotiating phase than a final step, and so far Koo doesn't much like the way these people negotiate. Making a sudden decision, surprising himself, he says, "Wait."

"Yes?"

Is this the right move? Who knows; it's what he's going to do. "I want you to take a message to Mark."

"Mark?" She frowns at him, her manner more keen than

usual. "Is this the same thing that Larry talked to him about?"

"That's right. Why?"

"They had a fight about it. Mark and Larry."

Koo can't quite contain a sudden triumphant grin. So his instinct *is* right; Mark went too far with that father-son line, he scared himself. Mark is on the run now, Koo has the edge, and by God he's determined to find some useful advantage in it. With all these crazy people on the loose around here negotiations with Washington are less useful to Koo than his own initiative; somehow, somehow, he has to get himself *out* of here. (Was his message received, in that last tape? Was it understood? Is the house being surrounded at this very moment? No, he can't count on that either; wishing won't make it so.) "You tell Mark," he says, "that if he won't answer my questions I'll ask them of you."

"Well, what are they? Why not just ask me to begin with?"

"Tell Mark," Koo insists. "Then either he comes down or you do."

She hesitates, then slowly nods: "All right. But I don't want him to fight with *me*. I'll ask him once."

"That's fine."

She leaves, and Koo lies back on the studio couch, staring at the ceiling. Now that it's too late, he's no longer so absolutely sure he has the upper hand with Mark. That's a brutal boy, after all; swift violent action is his specialty.

Although he's still very weak, nervousness soon drives Koo up onto his feet. He treads slowly the length of the room, door to window, and then back, pausing at the door; with all this traffic in and out, would somebody have forgotten to lock that?

No. He tests it, and it's still solidly sealed against him. And the next time it opens, will Mark be coming in? With balled fists and enraged eyes? The thought pushes Koo away from the door, and he moves shakily down the room again to the far end, to the window and all that heavy viscous weight of translucent water. With his back to the water, Koo stands with his hands in the pockets of the terrycloth robe, and waits.

One minute; two minutes; and the door swings open and Mark walks in.

Koo presses his back against the window glass, ashamed of his fear and hating his physical weakness, watching Mark push the door shut behind himself and advance into the room. And into Koo's mind comes a scene from one of those early movies, *Ghost to Ghost*: Fleeing the villains, the character he played backs through a doorway, unaware it leads to a tiger's cage containing a tiger. Shutting the door, inadvertently locking it, he turns, sees the tiger, and freezes. The emotions Koo portrayed in that long-ago scene he now feels, almost literally; he is locked in a cage with a tiger, with a ferocious beast.

The ferocious beast paces to the middle of the room, his expression a deeply sullen glare. "All right," he says. "Get it over with."

Koo's mouth and throat are dry. He has trouble breathing, making sounds, forming words. Hoarse, he finally says, "Is it true?"

"Is what true? Say the words."

Koo nods. He knows the answer now, but he understands he does have to say the words: "Are you my son?"

"Yes." There's nothing in the word but Mark's usual flat bluntness.

"You mean it—you meant physically, actually."

"Flesh of your flesh." Mark's lips writhe in loathing over his teeth as he says the words. "Bone of your bone."

"I—" Koo shakes his head. "I don't understand." Could Lily have had another child after they'd separated? But there wouldn't have been any reason to keep it secret.

"You paid five hundred dollars to have me killed," Mark says, without particular emotional force. "My mother spent the money to have me born instead."

"Five hundred...an abortion."

Mark's smile is terrifying, and so is his low voice: "Did somebody call my name?"

"Jesus," Koo says, barely above a whisper. "I don't—I'm sorry, I don't—" He gestures helplessly with both hands, his weight sagging back against the window.

"You don't remember?" Anger, mockery, hatred; Mark leans toward Koo, but doesn't step closer. "I was worth five hundred dollars to you not to exist, and now you don't even remember?"

"It's been—I don't know how—"

"You don't know *which*!" Mark stares at him in a kind of triumphal horror. "You filthy monster, you don't even know which of your little murders I am!"

Ahhh, God, that's true. There were three over the years, all of them decades ago; all, in fact, in the right era to be this fellow standing here. How old is he; thirty, thirty-two? Grown from a hasty error, all the way up to this. "I'm sorry," Koo says, fighting down a sudden tidal wave compulsion to shed tears. "I'm sorry."

"Sorry." Mark becomes calmer as Koo's agitation increases. "Sorry for what?"

"For everything. Everything."

"Sorry you don't know which one I am. Sorry you didn't get what you paid for."

"No! Jesus, I'm not—" But of course he is. Five hundred dollars thirty years ago to not be in this room with this savage? There's no way Koo can keep his reaction to that idea out of his mind.

And apparently no way he can keep it off his face; Mark emits an angry bark of laughter, saying, "That's right. If only my mother had obeyed orders, you wouldn't have *me* to worry about, would you?"

"Is that—is that why I'm here? Is that why you picked me?"

Rage flares in Mark at the question. His hand, clawlike, shoots out as though to clutch Koo's throat, but then merely stays in the air, trembling. "*I* didn't pick you! *They* picked you." With a hand-wave to indicate the others in the gang. "All I did was…" the enraged face permits again a suggestion of the terrifying smile, "*hint* a little."

"You mean the others don't know. Is that it? They don't know?"

"If you tell them, I'll kill you."

"But if they don't know, if that isn't the reason, then why me? Why *me*?"

"Because you were the hawks' jester. You're here because you are who you are. *I'm* here because you are who you are. It all comes together."

"Who—who was—" But Koo can't ask the question, even though he craves the answer. He stares at the boy's face, trying to see some other face in it, some face he can recognize.

Mark understands the unasked question, and it makes him laugh, not pleasantly. "Who is my mother? That's up to you."

No familiar feature can show through that mask of rage. Koo stares and stares, but it's impossible. And if he knew, would it make anything better? Cozier, more familiar? Familiar; family. He gestures helplessly: "I never knew."

"You have cockroaches," Mark whispers at him, gloating, intimate. "Cockroaches in the walls. *Me*."

"Don't. Please."

But Mark is no longer under control. The break that Koo feared has occurred; suddenly everything is different: "*I'm* the cockroach in the wall," Mark says. His eyes are bright and lifeless, pieces of quartz. "Call the exterminator, Koo, call him back. *I'm still here*."

"Wait."

"You shouldn't have asked, Koo. You really shouldn't have asked."

Mark's face is closer, larger, filling Koo's vision; a stone face, not human. Mark's hand reaches out again, this time rests on Koo's shoulder, a neutral weight like a board or a hangman's rope. Everything drains from Mark's stone face, and Koo closes his eyes. *He's going to kill me now.* There's no evasion, no salvation.

The other hand touches Koo's trembling throat at the same instant that Peter's voice says, "Well, now what?"

The hands lift from Koo's body. He opens his eyes, seeing the expressionless face receding, Peter in the open doorway at the other end of the room. Koo droops against the window and Peter comes deeper into the room, saying, "Mark? What are you doing?"

"A discussion," Mark says, and gives Koo a flat look. "Isn't that right?"

"Yes," Koo says.

"Discussion?" Peter looks from face to face. "About what?"

"A private discussion." Mark looks again at Koo, again says, "Isn't that right?"

"Yes," Koo says.

Peter continues to frown at them both, then shrugs, giving it up. "Get dressed, Koo," he says. "There's been a change of plan."

# 18

At ten past four, Mike Wiskiel was in the Butler Aviation waiting room at Los Angeles International Airport, awkwardly shaking hands with Lily Davis, wife of the kidnapped man, who had flown with her two sons out from New York in a private plane owned by one of the companies that sponsored her husband's TV specials. Mike was awkward because he knew Lily Davis had a lot of friends back in Washington, and he didn't know how severely the fuck-up with the transmitter had hurt his chances for getting back there himself. It could be he smelled too bad now for *any* recovery, no matter how brilliantly he handled the Koo Davis case from this point forward, but if there was even the slightest chance he could recoup his losses he wanted to be sure he had no unnecessary enemies with D.C. strings to pull. Lily Davis, a powerful figure in her own right as well as Koo Davis' wife, could help or hurt Mike's comeback with a casual lift of the eyebrow.

Meeting the problem head-on, Mike said, "Mrs. Davis, I'm the man who did it wrong last night. I hope very soon to be able to apologize to your husband; in the meantime, let me assure you just how sorry I am for what happened."

"Mr. Wiskiel," Lily Davis said, her manner calm and her handshake strong, "there's no apology needed. You have an excellent reputation, and you did what you thought best under the circumstances."

The word for Lily Davis was *magisterial*. A stocky, compact woman of not quite sixty, she carried herself with a patrician grace; a matron of ancient Rome, shopping at the slave market. (There was in her no remnant of that timid hausfrau abandoned all those years ago by her husband.) A committeewoman, active in any number of worthy organizations, she possessed the rather forbidding calm of a person who has learned how to control people in groups. Her assurances to Mike seemed sincere but impersonal, as though at bottom she didn't really give a damn, not about Mike and not about her husband. Mike said, "Thank you, Mrs. Davis. It was still a mistake, and a bad one. I hope to make up for it."

"I'm sure you will." Calmly dismissing that subject, she said, "May I introduce my sons. Barry, and Frank."

Both men were probably under forty. Barry, fastidious in blue suit with vest, white shirt and narrow striped tie, was the one who lived in London as part-owner of an antique business; there were odd traces of English accent in his voice, and his manner seemed to Mike obviously homosexual. Frank, on the other hand, the television network executive from New York, less formal in tweed jacket and open-collared blue shirt and slacks, showed a hearty easygoing masculinity that mostly suggested some kind of salesman; anything from insurance to used cars. Both men had, in their very different ways, firm handshakes, and neither seemed particularly broken up by what had happened to their father.

After the introductions, Lily Davis said, "Mr. Wiskiel, would you ride along in our car and tell us the current situation?"

"My own car is here."

Lily Davis was a long-time professional organizer: "Frank can follow us in your car."

But wouldn't Frank also like to be told the current situation? Apparently not; a willing smile on his amiable salesman's face, Frank said, "Good idea, Mom. You can fill me in at the house."

"Okay, then," Mike said.

As they moved toward the exit Lily Davis said, "You've managed to keep us free of reporters. Thank you."

"Part of our job, Mrs. Davis."

A black Cadillac limousine was waiting just outside. While Lily and Barry were handed into the back seat by the chauffeur, Mike gave his car keys to Frank and pointed out his Buick Riviera parked just across the way. "I'll take good care of it, Mike," Frank said cheerfully, and trotted off.

Didn't any of these people *care*? Taking the limousine's fur-covered jump seat, just ahead of Lily and Barry Davis' knees, it occurred to Mike that neither son looked very much like the father. In fact, not at all. Koo Davis' rubbery face was so well known that surely any trace of it in these men would be immediately obvious. Salesman Frank had some of his mother's square-jawed heavy-boned look, but exquisite Barry's face was a series of delicate ovals, reminiscent of neither parent.

The glass partition was up between the chauffeur and the passenger compartment; but apparently the man knew the way, and required no instructions. As the limousine moved out, Mike half-turned in the jump seat (seeing his own Buick obediently following) and said, "As a matter of fact, we have a hopeful clue that Koo Davis himself gave us."

"*Koo* gave it?" Even her surprise was even-tempered. "How did he manage that?"

Mike told her about the reference to Gilbert Freeman in the second tape. "We've checked Freeman and there's just no way he can be involved. So the thinking is, maybe your husband meant he's being held in a house that *used* to be owned by Freeman. Unfortunately, Freeman moves a lot; we've got seven houses to check."

"That's being done now?"

"Right. So it's possible we'll end this thing any minute. On the other hand, most of life isn't that easy." And he went on to tell them about the four o'clock radio announcement, which he himself had taped at three-thirty and then heard over the car radio as he was arriving at the airport.

It was Barry who asked the obvious question: "What will this seven-thirty program have to say?"

"I have no idea," Mike told him. "Deputy Director St. Clair is on the way out now, bringing it with him. At this moment, nobody in Los Angeles even knows if the answer's yes or no."

"If it's no," Lily said, "will they murder my husband?"

It was a very coolly phrased question. Mike tried to see behind or beneath the composed manner to some sort of emotion; surely the woman was feeling *something*. Simply asking the question showed she wasn't as calm as she behaved. On the other hand, she didn't act like someone on tranquilizers. Was she thinking only of the inconvenience? Mike said, "We don't know what they'll do. My guess is, they'll keep him alive at least a while longer, trying to pressure us to change our mind."

"So this could go on—indefinitely."

"I hope not," Mike said.

Barry said, "We all hope not, Mr. Wiskiel, but it does happen. In Europe we've had kidnap victims held for *months*. In Italy, for instance, and Germany."

"These people seem more impatient than that," Mike said. Then the other implications of the remark struck him, and he very much regretted having said it.

Not that it made any evident difference to the family. Their manner remained serene, imperturbable, as the limousine bore them north on the San Diego Freeway. The discussion continued, placid, speculative, considering the possibilities with a minimum—no, an absolute absence—of emotion. It was partly to try to force *some* response from them that Mike said, as the chauffeur angled the limousine down the exit ramp at Sunset

Boulevard, "This is where the car carrying your husband's medicines got on the Freeway."

"And the tracking device," Barry Davis mentioned casually. There seemed no particular meaning in the words, no particular expression on the man's face. The eyes, when Mike peered at them, seemed merely bored.

"That's right," Mike said.

The limousine, with Mike's Buick trailing, followed the hilly curve of Sunset eastward to Beverly Glen Boulevard, and there turned north once more, into Bel Air. The houses became more and more grand, the individual pieces of property larger and more elaborately landscaped, the fences and other security measures more common, and the limousine purring up into these hills evidently felt very much at home.

In Los Angeles, Beverly Hills is the well-known seat of luxury, but Bel Air to its west is as much more sumptuous as it is less recognized. And north of Bel Air, higher in the Santa Monica Mountains, is Beverly Glen, which is to Bel Air as Bel Air is to Beverly Hills. It was toward Beverly Glen that the limousine was directing itself, as though General Motors had built into the car some sort of electronic racial memory. This sleek black vehicle belonged in these hills the way elephants belong on the African veldt.

Here the glimpses of habitation were rare, particularly after they turned off Beverly Glen Boulevard itself onto curving climbing streets named for flowers and women. Tall fences guarding tangled lush foliage gave way to high blank stucco-faced walls of coral or peach, with here and there a Spanish-motif broad wooden garage door. It was at one of these windowless garage doors that the limousine came to an eventual stop, and the chauffeur got out to identify himself via the speaker grid beside the door.

In the car, Lily Davis extended her hand to Mike in a dismissing handshake, saying, "I do appreciate your giving us your time, Mr. Wiskiel. Do keep us informed of developments, won't you?" Not waiting for an answer, she turned to her son: "Barry, give Mr. Wiskiel our phone number here."

"Certainly." Barry withdrew from his inside pocket a gold pen and a small notebook in a gold case.

Mike released Lily Davis' cool dry non-trembling hand as soon as it was polite to do so, and took from Barry the square of paper on which a phone number had been jotted in a tiny precise hand. "I'll let you know what happens," he promised, and climbed from the car.

The wide garage door in the eight foot high stucco wall had now opened, revealing not the interior of a garage but a sunny jungle; crowded tropical trees and shrubbery through which a blacktop drive meandered, disappearing toward unimaginable splendor. It was like a scene in a children's book—*Alice in Wonderland*, perhaps—in which the opening in the wall leads to a completely different world.

Frank Davis came cheerfully forward, having parked Mike's car just behind the limousine. "Nice car you've got there, Mike," he said.

Frank seemed somehow a bit more human than his mother and brother, but should he be quite this cheerful under the circumstances? "Yours is okay, too," Mike said.

Frank laughed. "Keep in touch," he said, and got into the limousine. Not on the jumpseat; his mother made room for him beside her.

Frank had left the Buick's engine running, the shift lever in Park. As Mike got behind the wheel the chauffeur also re-entered the limousine, which rolled serenely through the open doorway. As Mike watched, the limousine nosed along the drive into the jungle lushness, and the broad wooden door slid downward again, snicking shut. "Drink me," Mike muttered.

As a matter of fact, after the Davis family that was a very good idea. If he were to return to Beverly Glen Boulevard and continue north, over the hills, he would come down on the other side of Sherman Oaks. And just to the west of Sherman Oaks was Encino, home of the El Sueno de Suerte Country Club. It wasn't yet five o'clock, and Mike didn't have to be in the Metromedia Studios in Hollywood until quarter after seven. "Drink," he repeated, and swung the Buick in a tight U-turn.

Jerry Lawson, Mike's realtor friend, was just getting into his car when Mike steered into the country club parking lot. Mike honked to get his attention, waved, and yelled out the window, "Stick around, I'll buy you a drink!"

Jerry waved in agreement. Mike parked the Buick and walked over to Jerry, who said, "How you doing?"

This was the first time Mike had seen his friend since the tracking device disaster and his later reinstatement. "Rolling with the punches," Mike said. "Some of them, anyway."

"That was rough, what you went through. I felt for you, Mike, I didn't know this morning if I should phone or not. I figured you wanted to be left alone."

"Thanks, Jerry, you're a good friend." Mike was truly touched, and he patted the other man's arm as they walked toward the clubhouse. "I was really low this morning, I don't think I could have talked to anybody."

"It was just rotten luck."

"Well, I've got another chance." Mike held the door, then followed Jerry into the cooler, dimmer interior. "Just so I don't screw up again."

"You won't, Mike."

They went down the broad hallway together to the bar, their shoes squeaking on the composition floor. The bar was nearly empty, standard for this time of day, though in half an hour or so it would begin to fill up. Mike and Jerry took their usual table, ordered drinks, and Mike talked for a while about the Davis family and the dislike he'd taken to them. "They just think the whole thing's a pain in the ass," he said.

Eventually that topic ran down, and Jerry said, "There's nothing new at all, huh?"

"Actually, there is something." Mike leaned closer over the table. "Keep this under your hat, Jerry, it isn't public knowledge, and you'll see why when I tell you."

"You know me, Mike."

So Mike told him about the Gilbert Freeman message in the second tape—if in fact the reference to Freeman *was* a message. On the way here, Mike had stopped at a phone booth in Sherman Oaks to call the office and Jock Cayzer had told him all seven houses had checked out negative. "Still," he told Jerry, "there seems to be something in it. We're trying to figure out what other location Gilbert Freeman might be connected with."

"Gee, that's a strange one," Jerry said. "Seems as though it *ought* to mean something."

"We've been figuring it the same way." Mike shook his head. "I don't know, maybe it's something from one of his movies."

"You know," Jerry said, casually, anecdotally, "I sold a house of Freeman's once, up here in Woodland Hills. The one with the underground room."

"Oh, yeah?" Then Mike did a doubletake: "The what?"

"Room under the house."

"You mean a basement?"

"No, it extended out from the house to the swimming pool. Window at the end, you could look right out at the pool. Underwater, you know. People in the pool could dive and look through the window into the room." Jerry laughed, lasciviously. "You'd be amazed how many dirty thoughts a setup like that can put in a person's mind. Added eight or ten thousand to the purchase price, let me tell you."

But Mike's mind was on neither sex nor money. His eyes intent on Jerry's amiable face, he said, "This room. How obvious is it?"

"Obvious? It's underground!"

"I mean, from inside the house. It's a regular room, right?"

"Well, not exactly. In fact, from a sales point of view that was the only drawback. You got to it through the utility room; not exactly a romantic or an elegant approach."

"Jesus," Mike breathed, and quoted from memory: "This is what's left of Koo Davis, speaking to you from inside the whale." He punched the table with the side of his fist, angrily saying, "God damn it, he *told* us! Inside the whale! Underground! Under *water*!"

Jerry gaped at him. "Mike?"

But Mike had turned his head, "Rick! A phone!"

## 19

Blindfolded, Koo stumbles up the stairs, urged on by nervous hands. *Their* nervousness is the only thing he finds reassuring about all this; it suggests circumstances aren't quite as hopeless for Koo as they seem. On the other hand, maybe the nervousness simply means they're taking him away now to kill him; after all, it's easier to dispose of a body if you can keep it alive long enough to walk to the disposal site.

Koo wishes he could get his mind off such things, but death is in his thoughts at the moment, what with one thing and another. The "one thing" being the fact, the indubitable fact, that Peter's arrival in the underground room interrupted a murder; Mark was going to strangle Koo at that moment, there's no question. And "another" being the additional fact that he is still a kidnap victim in the hands—nervous or not—of crazies.

Head of the stairs. As well as being blindfolded, Koo has his hands tied behind his back, so that when his shoulder bumps painfully into a doorpost he very nearly falls backwards down the stairs; but impatient hands shove at him from behind, he brushes through the doorway, and now he's marched for the second time through this house he's never seen, and out to warm, somewhat moist air, and over a path that has the unevenness of brick. The hands stop him, and Peter's voice says, close to his ear, "You'll be traveling in the trunk of the car now, Koo. We're going to lift you into it, so just relax."

"Oh, *I'm* relaxed. It's the suit that's tense."

"That's right, Koo."

Hands grasp him, shoulders and legs and waist, lifting him

off the ground. His knee hits something metal, the top of his head grazes something else, and then he feels the rough hardness below him as they deposit him on his left side, knees bent. "Don't move, Koo," Peter's voice says, from farther away, and the trunk lid slams, with a disagreeable implosion feeling in Koo's ears and eyes. And in his nostrils there's a rank oil-and-rubber odor. "I never was a rubber freak," Koo mutters, and sings quietly to himself, "I was stuffed in a trunk, in Pocatello, *I*-daho." But then he stops, and his mouth corners turn down, and he mumbles, "I may be losing my sense of humor."

His clever message to the FBI; useless. Obviously nobody caught it, or they'd have been here by now, and if they ever do notice it'll be too late.

The others are getting into the car; back here, the jounce as the weight of each body is added to the car is very pronounced. Bunk-bunk-bunk-bunk-bunk; all five of them coming along for the ride. And the slamming of four doors, and then the surprisingly loud sound of the engine starting up, followed by the heavy-seas motion as the car first backs in a half-circle and then moves forward.

Carbon monoxide? Death has so *many* threads tied to Koo, it's positively discouraging. All roads lead to death.

God, but this trunk is uncomfortable! Doubled up in here like a shrimp, bouncing and bumping with every move of the car, Koo is beginning to feel like a potato in an automatic peeler, and when he starts picking at the cord holding his wrists it's initially only in an effort to get into a more comfortable position.

It takes forever. The fingers of his right hand can just about reach the knot, or one of the knots, but the way the car flings him around he keeps losing the damn thing. Fortunately there are fairly frequent stops, apparently for traffic lights—with this cargo in the trunk, the gang has apparently decided to avoid the freeways, where police spot-checks are not an unknown occurrence—and at each stop Koo loosens the knot a bit more, until all at once it becomes easy, it unravels and unravels, and his hands are free!

Oh, thank God for that. Koo rolls onto his back, his bent knees still forced over to the left by the nearness of the trunk lid, and reaches up both hands to shove the blindfold away onto his forehead. Then he blinks, in total darkness, and for a few minutes simply lies there, resting from his exertions and enjoying the change of position.

The next time he moves, his right elbow smacks into something unyielding. "Ouch!" He reaches over with his left hand to massage the elbow, and his knuckles graze the same thing; he pats it, explores it with his fingers, and realizes it's the latch for the trunk lid.

Oh ho. Is it possible that—? "Just let me do this, God," Koo whispers, "and I'll never say a fucking bad word again."

The first thing is to roll over on his right side, so he'll be facing the latch and can put both hands to work on it. The problem is, this trunk is both too narrow *and* too low; in order to get his legs from the left to the right he had to double them up like one of those exercise mavens on TV, bring them across his chest with knees and shoes both scraping the lid, and then discover that the lid slants down and he just can't wedge his legs in there. He tries, gives up, tries to move the legs back to the left, and finds he can't do that either. "Jesus Christ, I'm stuck. And what a position. Next thing, some crazed rapist will come along."

This is ridiculous. The trunk lid presses down on his legs, his thighs press down on his stomach and chest, and he can feel the first twinges of cramp in both hip joints. "And that, children, is how the pretzel was invented."

Got to— Got to get *out* of this fix! Koo's flailing left hand finds the curving metal hinge piece and he clutches at it, pulling hard, at the same time pushing at the metal wall to his right. Slowly, very slowly, his body scrapes leftward across the rough pebbled surface of the trunk, gradually becoming easier, then all at once absolutely simple. He rolls to his right, his legs unfold as much as the narrow space will permit, and his hands reach out to touch that blessed latch.

If only there was some light in this goddamn place, but the rubber grommet around the lid makes a perfect seal. "I feel like I'm in a clam," Koo mutters. If he still smoked, he'd have his old Zippo lighter with his profile-logo, and he could give himself some illumination with that. "Yeah, and if I was in Turkestan I wouldn't be in this Christmas package here at all."

His fingertips are working out the details of the latch; a metal piece shaped like a crook'd finger, chunked from below tight against two metal bars about an inch apart. What's at the other end of the metal finger? A circular thing, some counter-sunk screw heads— Ow! Something sharp. This must be the lock mechanism, where the key is put in from outside. How does it work on the inside? *Pushing* at the metal finger doesn't do any good. The circular thing won't turn. In fact, none of the parts seem prepared to move.

While the car continues to jounce along Koo tugs and pokes, his fingers losing their sensitivity from hitting too hard too often against unyielding metal. And that sharp thing— What *is* that? The lip of something, he can't quite figure it out— Goddamn it, the thing moves! It's a lever or something, the only part of the whole gizmo that moves, and the only way to make it move is to push directly against the sharp cutting lip with the ball of the thumb—no, with the flat part of the thumbnail—and there's no way to tell while he's cutting himself to pieces here if he's even doing any good, pushing this sharp lever bit by bit to the right. It won't stay where he pushes it, but springs right back every time he lets go. Okay; goodbye, thumbnail. Gritting his teeth, pressing with the heel of his other hand against the ball of his braced thumb, Koo *puuuuuuuussssssshhhhhheeeesss*.

Snap!

Light, daylight, the trunklid lifts an inch, two inches—

It stops. Koo, now squinting against the unexpected daylight, sees the metal finger hooked against just one of the two metal bars. So that's the way it works. He can see it now, a safety mechanism, it locks at one level and then at another level, it—

The car hits a bump. The lid snaps down. Darkness.

"Oh, *shit*!" The fucker's locked itself again!

Koo pauses to regroup, his cut thumb in his mouth, sucking thoughtfully. The car stops briefly, then starts again. Jounce jounce.

Okay. It opened once, it'll open again. This time, Koo can hold it up in the safety-lock position by wedging his knees against the lid, giving him light to examine the lock more closely. Then, the next time the car comes to a stop, he'll spring the second lock and get the hell *out* of here.

Jesus, is it possible? Home again, I'm going home again. I'll call Jill, she can spend the whole night. I don't care if I get it up or not. Just to see a friendly face, sleep nestled on a soft tit, wake up safe and happy in a bed full of warm and willing woman. Oh, boy. Oh, boy.

Gingerly, he reaches out to the lock again, presses, moves the sharp-edged lever to the right, farther, farther, farther...

Snap. Light, the slit widening, narrowing, widening, the car jouncing on rough pavement, Koo pushing *up* with his knees, in a desperate hurry because the slit is closing again, the lid is slamming down, it *whacks* his right kneecap, he pushes *up*, digs his heel in against the bottom of the trunk—and the lid stays up.

Now. Just stop, fellas. Just a brief little halt for a traffic light or a pedestrian crossing or a red stop sign or any damn thing you want. Just pause, and old Koo will be out of this trunk like Venus out of the sea, like toothpaste out of the tube, like the human cannonball—

Slowing. The car is slowing. "Ohhhhhh, Jesus," Koo whispers. "Oh, I'm scared."

Nothing to be afraid of. When the car stops, he'll be up and out, into the nearest house or store depending on neighborhood, or maybe into the next car back. Something like that. The point is, he has a known face, people will recognize him, they'll know him and help him. All Koo has to do is get out of the car *fast*, and everything will be all right.

"Feet, don't fail me now." Oh, shit, what if he's too scared to move? What if his legs give out?

Well, it won't happen, that's all.

Slowing, slowing. Will you *stop*?

Yes. The car stops.

"Oh, boy. Oh, boy." Teeth chattering, gibbering words without knowing it, Koo claws at the lock, forces himself to lower his knees so the lid descends, descends, just enough so he can shove that metal finger *back*. Snap, it flips away, the trunk lid yawns upward and Koo, eyes staring, mouth strained wide open, lunges up onto his elbows, kicks his feet over the rim of the trunk, shoves himself up, slips, falls back, shoves up again, lunges, gasps, groans, grabs the rear bumper and *pulls* himself out of the trunk; losing his balance, toppling forward onto blacktop.

Up. *Up*. Koo rises, staring around for houses, cars, people, rescue, civilization, assistance, succor, aid, help—

Nothing. Where in holy hell is *this*?

It's a fucking desert. Scrubland on all sides, no houses, no traffic, just this intersection with the stop sign. And the other sign: Mulholland Drive.

Oh, no. Mulholland Drive, that's the road running east and west along the ridge line of the hills, with Los Angeles to the south and the Valley to the north. Some parts of Mulholland, particularly the eastern end near Hollywood, are as built up as any residential section anywhere, but much of the Drive is virtually unpopulated and parts of it are still dirt, not even paved.

What a fucking asshole way to build a major city, with a deserted mountaintop desert right smack in the middle of it! Peter and his pals, to be absolutely safe, have been taking back roads toward where their destination is, and that's why there's been so much jouncing. And here they come, boiling out of the car, all four doors flaring open. They have seen the trunk lid in the rearview mirror.

Terrified, Koo looks around in all directions. The road they've just come up angles away steeply downhill through pines and shrubbery back toward the Valley. To left and right Mulholland Drive meanders along the ridgeline; way to hell and gone that way, east, he can see a couple of houses, but he'd never get that far. He can't outrun these people.

Hide; it's the only chance. While the gang is still clambering out of the car, Koo makes his dash, across the road and out over dusty tan earth, low shrubbery, stunted low trees, then a steep stony slope, his feet scrabbling for purchase, dust rising, half the goddamn San Fernando Valley visible out there far below, and nobody to help. Voices shout behind him, he clutches at the rough trunks and branches of stunted pine trees, not quite falling, tottering, careening and blundering down the hill, directly into a tangled mass of prickly shrubs, knee-high, waist-high, covered with thorns, all too thick to force his way through, so that he wades at an angle to the left, stumbles into a tiny rain-formed gully making a deep narrow wedge-shaped cut into the shrubbery, drops to hands and knees, crawls down the gully under the thorny branches, deeper into the brush, finally turning, gasping, staring, peering out past branches and leaves and thorns, his mouth dry with dust and fear, the dust-stained sweat pouring down his face as he stops, and waits, and listens:

"He came this way!"

"He's hiding someplace! In the bushes!"

"He can't get far! He can't get away!"

"Circle to the left!"

"Koo! Koo!" That's Peter's voice, uncomfortably close. "Don't make it tougher on yourself, Koo, we're going to find you anyway! Don't waste our time, Koo!"

Screw you, Mac. Koo knows it's no good, his luck is rotten, he isn't going to get away, but he's damned if he'll make it easy for them. "Do your own work," he mutters, and closes his eyes, and waits with his face turned away.

"Here he is!" Larry's voice, the son of a bitch. "I see his legs."

"Come out of there, you old bastard!" That's Peter, sounding shrill and angry. "Larry, Mark, drag him out of there!"

Hands grab at his ankles, tugging at him, and he says, "All right, all right, I'll come out." But they won't let him do it himself; they insist on dragging him out, back bumping on the stones, branches and thorns picking at the arms he holds protectively over his face.

They're all clustered there, panting, on the steep slope. Larry and Mark pick Koo up, get him on his feet, and angry-faced Peter comes over, glares briefly, then deliberately punches Koo hard on the left cheek. Koo staggers, and would fall backward into the bushes if Larry weren't still holding his arm. "Peter!" Larry cries, reproach in his voice. "You don't have to do that!"

"I'm sick of this old man," Peter says, and comes close to Koo again, glowering into Koo's eyes, saying, "Don't try anything else. I'm not feeling patient today."

"You're a nasty son of a bitch," Koo tells him. His mouth is too dry with dust and fear, or he'd spit in the bastard's lousy face.

And Peter knows it; look at him withdraw a pace, a fake superior smile on his lips. "That's right, Koo," he says. "I am a nasty son of a bitch. You remember that, and watch your step." To the others he says, "Bring him back to the car," and turns away.

# 20

Mike walked into the underground room where Jock Cayzer stood with hands on hips, cowboy hat pushed back from his forehead, disgusted expression on his large face. "Flown," he said. "But he was here, all right."

"That's what they said upstairs."

Jock sniffed. "You can smell how sick he was."

Mike could, but he'd rather not. "Who ran the check on this place?"

"One of your boys, I'm happy to say. Dave Kerman." Jock's smile was sympathetic, not malicious. "According to him, he did enter that utility room out there, and this door was hidden behind a stack of wine cartons. You can see them in that corner there, all tossed behind the water heater."

"We haven't been running in luck."

"The worst of it is, I should think our man's visit is what spooked them. But there is one hopeful item."

"Tell me quick."

"They didn't *plan* to move. This was their base, but now they're scrambling, improvising, it'll be easier for them to make mistakes and attract attention."

"And harder to keep Koo Davis alive."

"Ah, Mike, take comfort where you can."

"There's no comfort until we've got him back," Mike said. "Do you realize he was in this room less than an hour ago?"

"I do."

"And he *told* us!" Moving toward the window, gesturing at it, he quoted, "Inside the whale."

"I've been remembering that statement myself," Jock said.

Mike stood at the window, gazing through his own faint reflection at the heavy wobbling oily translucent water; it seemed a less friendly element from this vantage. He wished he'd had time for another drink at the club, or that he'd taken a snort from the pint in the glove compartment. He would when he left here.

This thing was taking too long. It would be *better* if the bastards killed him. Let Davis be found murdered and the heat wouldn't be so heavy on Mike Wiskiel anymore. Everybody would agree he'd done his best, and the incident with the transmitter would merely have been an example of over-eagerness. He could still come out of it clean, he could still have that shot at getting back to D.C.

Or, if the sons of bitches *weren't* going to kill Davis, then Mike and Jock and everybody else better get on their horses and *find* the guy, while there was still some glory left to reap.

Turning away from the window, Mike said, "Do we know whose house this is?"

"Some musician named Ginger Merville. He's away in Europe, we're trying now to get in touch with him. The house is for rent."

"Something wrong there," Mike said.

"Yes, there is," Jock said gravely. "It's been sticking in my own craw, I must admit. But I don't quite see what it is."

"Was this house supposed to be empty? Would they *all* hide in here if the realtor brought around a prospective tenant? And wouldn't the realtor know about this room, even make a point of showing it?"

"Those are all good questions," Jock said.

"I'll talk to the realtor," Mike decided. "Do you have the name?"

"Calvin Freiberg. He's got an office on Ventura Boulevard in Tarzana."

"I'll go see him now, on my way to the TV studio. You'll run things here?"

"Your people and mine are upstairs now," Jock said, "poking and prying."

"Good luck to them. Where's Dave Kerman?"

"He went back to the office, he said to beat his head against the wall." Jock's ruefully sympathetic smile appeared again. "He says he now believes the woman who showed him through the house is the one we have in the sketch."

"No shit." Mike shook his head. "When *Dave* gets done beating his head against the wall, *I'll* beat his head against the wall. See you later."

"Happy hunting," Jock said.


"Calvin Freiberg?"

The realtor, a narrow bald man whose polyester leisure suit, huge sunglasses and deep regular tan all looked like the parts of some masquerade costume, rose from his desk to blink mildly at Mike and say, "Yes?"

"FBI, Mr. Freiberg." Mike held open his ID. "My name is Michael Wiskiel."

"Oh, my goodness, I've seen you on television. Sit down, sit down."

This paneled and vinyled office was actually a small storefront on Ventura Boulevard, its street wall a sheet of yellow-tinted glass, its interior neat, cheap and impersonal. There were three desks spaced around on the functional tan carpet, but Freiberg was the only one actually present. Taking the client's chair as Freiberg reseated himself behind his desk, Mike said, "You handle the rental on a house in Woodland Hills owned by a musician named Ginger Merville."

"That's right!" Freiberg seemed surprised to hear this information. "That's right, I do."

"I've just come from there, Mr. Freiberg, and until an hour ago that was where the kidnappers were hiding out with Koo Davis."

"Kid—! Koo—! Oh, my *God*!"

Such astonishment could not be faked. Mike watched the flush glow pink through that artificial tan, watched Freiberg sit there open-mouthed and blinking, and waited for the man to recover himself. Finally Freiberg swallowed, shook his head, and said, "That's incredible. My God, it's lucky I didn't try to *show* the place with those people in it."

"*Was* that luck?" Mike said. "I mean, was the house available for rent or not?"

"Well, yes and no." The realtor frowned, as though he'd confused himself with that answer, then said, "I take it you know who Ginger Merville is."

"A musician."

"A rock star," Freiberg said, then corrected himself again: "Well, not a *star*, precisely. A sideman with stars, I suppose you'd say. In any event, he has a good deal of money, and he travels a great deal, so from time to time we rent his house for him. If he's going to be away for an extended period." Turning to a nearby filing cabinet, he fingered rapidly through the three-by-five cards, withdrew one, and handed it to Mike. "That's the record of our rentals over the last several years."

Mike glanced at the card without much interest, and said, "Why isn't it rented this time?"

"He wanted too much money." Freiberg pointed at the card in Mike's hand, saying, "You see the prices there, gradually going up. A thousand a month, twelve hundred, fourteen hundred. At the moment, we could surely get fifteen or sixteen for the place; perhaps a bit more if we were willing to wait. Ginger for reasons best known to himself, insisted we market the property at *three* thousand a month!"

"Ah," said Mike. "Did he give a reason?"

That Freiberg's professional advice had been ignored had obviously left in the man a residue of resentment, so that a kind of petulant irony came into his voice as he passed on Merville's reasoning: "Well, he would only be gone two months, and he found subtenants more trouble than they were worth anyway, and really he'd prefer the place empty if he couldn't get his price. I *told* him it was hopeless, but he wouldn't take my advice, and the result is, the house is *technically* for rent, but we haven't seen any point in showing it. I mean, three thousand a month. There isn't even a tennis court. And it's still the Valley, it isn't Brentwood or Beverly Hills."

"How long would the place be available?"

"Till the end of next month."

"So by this time you probably wouldn't show it anyway, at any price."

"Weekly rentals." Delicately the realtor shivered. "Not a good type of tenant, usually. Not *careful*, as a general rule."

"Thank you, Mr. Freiberg," Mike said. "Thank you very much."

Metromedia, Channel 11, in addition to airtime, was providing the FBI with office space in its Sunset Boulevard studio, and even a receptionist. On arrival, Mike identified himself to this girl and said, "Is Mr. St. Clair here yet?"

"Is he the gentleman expected from Washington? No, sir, not yet. We received a call about an hour ago that he'd landed at March Air Force Base in Riverside. He'll be traveling by helicopter to Burbank Airport, and then a car will bring him here, so he should be arriving any time now."

"Fine."

"Agent Kerman is in that office there, sir. He asked me to let you know about him when you came in. He's on the phone with St. Louis."

"Dave Kerman?" Frowning, Mike crossed to the office she'd indicated. What was Dave Kerman doing *here*? When last heard from, according to Jock Cayzer, Dave Kerman had been in Burbank, beating his head against the office wall next to the sketch of the woman he hadn't recognized. Secondly, and even more bewilderingly, what was he doing on the phone to *St. Louis*?

Waiting. When Mike entered the office—smallish, square, neatly but anonymously furnished, with windows overlooking the buzz of traffic on the Hollywood Freeway, half-screened by trees and shrubbery—Dave Kerman was seated at the desk with a telephone receiver hooked between ear and shoulder, and with the semi-doped facial expression of a person who's been on hold for a long long time. He grabbed the receiver away from his ear and hopped to his feet at Mike's entrance, his manner showing a combination of pleasure and embarrassment. "Mike! Hello!"

"What's happened, Dave?"

Kerman became sober, apologetic. "I'm really sorry about the fuck-up, you know. I could kick myself."

"I've seen the house, Dave. Nobody could have guessed that room was there." If you want the troops on your side, you've got to be on their side; even if you'd love to kick their ass.

"But the *girl*! She was right in front of me and I didn't connect it for a *second*."

"Dave, tell me the truth. How close was the sketch?"

Kerman nodded, as though reluctantly. "In my own defense," he said, "I must say it isn't that damn close." Continuing to stand, he had again propped the phone between ear and shoulder, and as a result was slightly bent to the left.

"That's often a problem with those sketches," Mike said. "If you already know who it is, you can see the resemblance, you can connect from person to sketch, but it's a lot tougher the other way, from sketch to person."

"Still," Kerman said. "Still and all, I should have seen it. She was right *there*."

"Remember all those sketches the New York cops did in the Son of Sam case? None of them looked like each other, and none of them looked like the guy when they finally grabbed him."

"The goddamn thing is—" Kerman started, then paused and listened to something on the phone. "Sure," he said into it. "I'm still here. Yeah, I'll wait, I told you I'd wait. You just find him. Terrific."

Mike, gesturing at the phone, said, "St. Louis?"

"That's right. That's the other bit of news." Kerman gestured at the low sofa against the other wall. "Take a load off while I tell you."

Mike sat on the sofa and Kerman returned to his seat at the desk. While he talked he gestured with both hands, the phone remaining wedged beside his neck. "Once I took another look at the sketch," he said, "I knew for sure that was her. There were two women in the house, that's all I saw there and I haven't been able to identify the other one, but this one I've got. You know we had all those photos out already on likely radical types, so I went through them again, and bingo. Her name is Joyce Griffith, she's been a known radical ten years or more, and she's wanted for a whole lot of stuff: damaging government property, attempted murder, interstate flight, you name it."

"Good work."

"But that isn't the kicker," Kerman said, as the door opened and Maurice St. Clair entered, followed by a tall slender neatly dressed young man carrying what looked to be a shipping case for reels of film.

Mike jumped to his feet. "Murray!" Maurice St. Clair was an old friend and a good one; in Mike's campaign to get back to Washington, St. Clair was definitely on his side.

St. Clair came forward to give Mike a hard massive handshake, saying, "Good to see you, Mike. *Good* to see you."

"You're looking trim, Murray." Which wasn't at all true; St. Clair was a big heavy man who took too much pleasure from his food and drink. Still, Mike knew that St. Clair worried about his appearance and health, and it was only the act of a friend to reassure him.

"I felt for you this morning, Mike." St. Clair continued to grip Mike's hand. "I'm glad you got this second chance."

Mike's grin was rueful. "Apparently they don't think I'm much of a threat."

"They'll learn better," St. Clair said, and with one last squeeze finally released Mike's hand.

At the desk, Kerman suddenly said, "Douglas? Tom Douglas? Dave Kerman here, from the L.A. station, working on the Koo Davis case."

Mike said to St. Clair, "Hold it, Murray," then turned to Kerman. "Finish your story."

"Hold on, Tom, will you? Just ten seconds." And Kerman, grinning with accomplishment, put his hand over the mouthpiece and said to Mike, "The kicker is, this Griffith girl is one of ours!"

"She's what?"

"A double agent. From sixty-eight to seventy-three she was on *our* payroll, reported every place she went, everybody she met, everything she did." Gesturing to the phone, he said, "This fellow, Douglas, he was the one she reported to, in Chicago. He's in the St. Louis station now."

"Jesus Christ," Mike said. "Can he still get in touch with her?"

"Let's find out." Kerman spoke into the phone again. "Tom? I want to talk with you about a one-time informer of yours named Joyce Griffith. Yes, that's the one."

St. Clair, speaking quietly, said, "What's going on?"

While Kerman carried on his telephone conversation, Mike briefly explained the situation, including the belated discovery of the gang's original hideout, and finishing, "Maybe this Griffith thing can help."

"Let's hope so." St. Clair looked troubled. "I'm afraid we're all going to *need* some help."

"You mean—the answer's no?"

"It's more complicated than that," St. Clair told him. "But not very good." Gesturing at his assistant's film case, he said, "Let's just say we have here an unpleasant surprise for our friends on the other side."

# 21

In this stupid room full of mirrors, Koo is trying to save his life. "Larry," he says, holding tight to the young man's wrist, "Larry, help me."

"I want to," Larry says. "But I can't help if I don't understand what's going on."

"Just get me out of here."

"No, Koo." And Larry sighs, as though *he's* the one who can't get the message across. "We're talking at cross-purposes," he says. "I'm not offering to help you get away, I want to help you comprehend the *reality* of the world."

"The reality is," Koo says, "if I stay here I'll die."

"I know you believe that, Koo," Larry says, "but I promise it won't happen. Now, I accept the fact that this television program is undoubtedly just a stall, just an attempt to string out the negotiations, but Koo, don't you see? We already *know* that. We're prepared for it, we're prepared to wait them out. No matter what they say on that program, nothing bad will happen to you. I promise."

"Listen, Larry," Koo says, "that isn't the point. Believe me, there are other things here, there's—" He shakes his head, releasing Larry's wrist to wave his arms vaguely as he says, "It isn't as simple as that."

"If you could explain it, Koo. What was it you thought Mark could tell you that I can't? What's the *subject*, Koo?"

"Ahhhh, Jesus." That's the crux of it; does he dare tell Larry about Mark's paternity? Sinking back on the purple bedspread, releasing pent-up breath, he says, "Comics are supposed to want to do Hamlet, not King Lear."

"I don't understand."

Koo makes a negative hand-wave. "Lemme think a minute."

"Sure, Koo. Take all the time you want."

All the time he wants. But since the move—after his failed escape attempt he'd traveled the rest of the way reblindfolded, on the floor in back, among their legs—Koo has felt time running out, the pressures closing in. He can't forget that Mark was just about to kill him with his bare hands when Peter walked in to announce the move.

And this new room doesn't help. It's a bedroom, but it isn't precisely restful. Small, windowless, its walls and low ceiling are covered in mirrors with a faint bluish tinge. A white deep-shag carpet covers the floor, on which most of the available space is filled by a large round purple bed. Two white fur armchairs and a pair of mirrored bedside tables complete the furnishings. Illumination is provided by pinlights in the ceiling corners, plus a pair of imitation Old West wall sconces above the bedside tables. Whenever Koo looks away from Larry, he sees instead a tableau of the two of them endlessly repeated in the mirrors, the younger man seated on the edge of the bed, looking uneasy but sincere, and the older man sprawled back on the heart-shaped purple pillows, shaking his head in weakness and despair.

The problem is, if he tells Larry the truth, that Mark wants to kill him because Mark is his son, will Larry make the right response? There are so many ways Larry can do the wrong thing with that information. For instance, he could disbelieve Koo, and out of his disbelief he could go tell Mark what Koo had said, and *immediately* Mark would come raging in here to finish the job; no question. Or, Larry being Larry, he could believe Koo and *still* go tell Mark; it would fit right in with that unquenchable belief of his in the power of discussion to resolve all problems. The only reason Koo would tell Larry the truth is if it would encourage Larry to help him get away from here, and he's just too afraid that isn't what would happen.

Rousing himself, Koo says, "What time is it?"

"Twenty past."

Ten minutes before showtime. "You're sure there's a TV in here?"

"That's what I was told. Let's see."

Getting to his feet, Larry begins to open mirrored doors. Cupboards, closets, a small lavatory, a separate shower, all are behind the mirrors. "This is some place, isn't it?" Larry says.

"A three-year-old's idea of a whorehouse."

"Here it is." Larry has found the TV, behind a mirror facing the foot of the bed; he turns it on to Channel 11 but leaves the sound down. Jackie Gleason and Art Carney, in an old black-and-white *Honeymooners,* mouth disconsolately at one another and take long, slow, stagy steps.

Returning to the bed, Larry says, "With any luck, you won't be here long."

"With the wrong kind of luck I won't be *anywhere* long."

"Don't talk that way, Koo. It won't happen."

"You don't know what can happen, my friend."

"Then tell me," Larry says. "Koo, I swear to God I'm your friend. *Tell* me."

Koo frowns at him, thinking it over. What's the alternative? And what, after all, does he have to lose? He says, "Will you stay in this room?"

"Stay here? Do you want me to?"

"Yes. Until I'm set free."

"I will." Larry looks very solemn, as though he's just been ordained.

"We'll watch this special," Koo tells him. "We'll see what they have to say, and after that we'll talk."

# 22

The TV set was switched on half an hour early, by Joyce, but no one watched it, though it was one of those monsters with the huge six-foot screen, like a movie screen, dominating the living room. But they were all too involved with their own problems to watch non-essential television. Mark could be seen through the glass doors, prowling back and forth out there on the beach, brooding at the sand and ignoring the Pacific's huge sunset. Liz did her brooding curled up in an Eames chair near the fireplace, her back to both the view and the TV. Larry had locked himself into the bedroom with Koo, Joyce was in the kitchen fretfully and compulsively preparing food no one wanted—cups of coffee, pots of soup, plates of sandwiches cut into triangles with the crusts meticulously removed—and Peter and Ginger were bickering together. "This is very bad of you," Ginger kept saying. "Very bad. Very bad." His monkey cheerfulness was gone, as though it had never been, replaced by a fidgety snapping, like a neurotic lapdog. Even his face was now the pinched countenance of a Lhasa Apso or Yorkie. "It's just too bad of you, Peter."

"There wasn't any choice," Peter said, for the hundredth time. He knew he had to placate Ginger somehow, but it was all so difficult. His cheeks burned and stabbed, he kept swallowing blood, and for the first time in years he was *blinking*. The very symptom he had so long ago conquered by gnawing his cheeks had now returned, completely out of his control. Following Ginger from room to room, prowling with him, trying to smooth things over, he ground his cheeks while his eyelids blink-blink-blinked, and through it all he just kept talking: "I knew they'd be back, and I was right. We got Davis out of there just in time."

"To bring him *here*. Oh, Peter, this is so bad of you. After all you said, about keeping me out."

"What else could I do? We can't drive the goddamn man around in the car forever. Did you want me to kill him?"

Ginger, walking down the hallway toward the kitchen with Peter in his wake, abruptly stopped and turned back, so that Peter nearly bumped into him. "Don't talk to me about killing," Ginger said. "Don't talk to *me* about killing."

"That's what Mark wanted to do," Peter said, bitterness in his voice. Things weren't working out. If he'd only walked in on Mark and Davis a few minutes later the problem would have been solved, taken out of Peter's hands. That Mark had been about to murder Davis Peter had no doubt, though he hadn't talked about it with either of them, nor did he intend to. He could not himself have ordered Davis killed simply for the convenience of it, but he would have been very pleased—among other reactions—if the decision had been made for him. As to why Mark was so determined to murder Davis, or why Davis on his side was so determined to have conversations with the man thirsting for his death, Peter had no idea what either of them was about, and in truth he felt scant curiosity. His main interest was in himself, and his attention to the outside world waxed or waned as the world impinged on his own desires or needs.

Ginger, with his discontented lapdog face, turned away and continued on to the kitchen, Peter trailing. In the kitchen, Joyce turned from stirring a pot of soup to say, with a chipper kind of lunatic normalcy, "You ought to eat. Both of you."

"Save *some*thing for tomorrow," Ginger told her irritably, then turned to Peter again, saying, "Or will you be *out* of here by tomorrow?"

"To go where? Ginger, where else is there?"

"Oh, it'll all be over by tomorrow," Joyce said brightly. "You wait and see."

"We'll wait," Ginger said meaningfully, with a glance up at the kitchen clock: seven oh five. "And after we hear what the FBI has to say, then we *will* see. In the meantime, young woman, kindly stop treating *my* kitchen as your personal chuck wagon. No one wants all those ditzy little sandwiches. What's in that pot?"

"Scotch broth."

"No no, the one behind it, with the lid."

"Pea soup," Joyce said, with a first hint of defensiveness. She and the others—except Peter, of course—were all meeting Ginger for the first time. She added, "Not everybody likes Scotch broth."

"Not everybody likes their larder wasted by a hysterical female," Ginger told her. "Are you menstruating?"

"What? No, I— No."

"Then you have no excuse." Turning to Peter, Ginger said, "Have you control over no one? Nothing?" Then he shrugged with nervous anger and left the room.

Peter tarried long enough to grate at Joyce, in a harsh whisper, "No more food! Stop it now!" Then, ignoring her wide-eyed uncomprehending gaze, he hurried after Ginger, back toward the living room.

Mark had disintegrated, he was nothing and nobody. All his thoughts splintered into shards and disconnected fragments, like those waves out there breaking on the black rocks. He was the junked remains of himself, a disposable artifact used up and thrown away, a shell, drained and purposeless. Years and years ago the key had been inserted, twisted and twisted, winding him tight and ever tighter, setting him to march forward through life, a robot patricide with but one function, one milli-second of true blazing purpose; when he would hold his father's life between his hands, and end it.

The moment had come, he had activated himself, he had shone like the sun in his flash of life, and now he was burned out, his potential all in the past; he had nothing, he was nothing. He was as incapable of murdering the same victim a second time as if he had not been interrupted. He *was* a patricide, the decision had been all, the performance merely its outward effect. That Mark continued to breathe, to move through life, to experience time, was a frustrating anomaly. Certainly he could no longer react, not to events nor to other human beings. The makework of existence was finished; nothing touched him now.

"Maa-ark! Maa-ark!"

On the cantilevered deck of the house, silhouetted by the glowing stonewalled living room behind her, Joyce was waving, bobbing up on tiptoe. Mark saw her without curiosity, and con-tinued his plodding walk through the sand.

"Mark! It's about to begin! The show's coming on!"

His left hand made a full-armed broad down-sweeping gesture of rejection: *Go away. Leave me alone.* He did not look up again.

Someone swiveled the Eames chair to face the huge television screen. Liz frowned, grabbing the rudimentary chair-arms as it swung, but said nothing. From above and behind her, Peter's voice said, "Watch the program, Liz. Take an interest."

But she *didn't* take an interest, that was just it. Tripping had been a disaster, a terrible mistake. She'd had great difficulty coming back, and even now was still subject to brief visual phenomena, light flashes, shifts in the color spectrum, quick dissolving and immediate reconstructions of solid objects like that stone wall behind the free-standing television screen.

Otherwise her mind no longer floated, but she had returned freighted with the cruel discoveries of the journey; though not discoveries exactly, having existed in her mind all along, kept out of sight because they were both true and unbearable.

That she had gone too far, that's what it came down to. Not in this trip alone, but always, completely in her life. For the sake of passions of the moment—political, personal, social passions—she had acted in ways that kept her from *ever* coming back. America had calmed from the excesses of the sixties, was putting its house in order, returning to normal life; but for Liz there was no return, there would never again *be* a normal life. She had gone too far, back when it had seemed that the sixties would last forever. To this degree she had been right: for *her*, the sixties were forever. She was imprisoned in that time more securely than the government, if it ever did get its hands on her, could possibly imprison her.

Sometimes she almost envied Frances, six years dead, out of it when it was still fresh. Let federal warrants be out for Frances Steffalo; after six years in Lake Erie water, weighted and silent and sinking into the scum, she would not be found, would not be paraded before the shallow giggling media as Eric had been, as so many had been. "Not me," she said, not aloud, merely mouthing the words, staring sightless at the TV screen.

*Eric* had been everything. Eric had taught her what her body was for, what her brain was for, what the world was for. "It isn't hard to change society," he used to say, with his easy bright *intelligent* grin. "Society changes all the time, whether we help it along or not. Capitalism is an aberration, a mistaken turn away from feudalism—it would have been so much easier to go directly to collectivism then, simply remove the landlord class and permit the masses to absorb the land they already occupied. All right, an aberration. But it's coming to an end, and unless somebody gives the whole rolling mass a shove in a new direction we'll simply go right back to feudalism under another name, with General Motors and Chase Manhattan instead of the kingdom of this and the duchy of that. We have to push on it, that's all, deflect it a little. We may not even see the effect in our lifetime. Not everybody can be Martin Luther. Columbus died having no idea how much he'd changed the world."

Change the world. Eric changed *me*, and then he went away, his work unfinished. If he'd even been killed, if he'd died along with Paul and the others, it would be easier to forgive. What did it matter that he had abandoned her unwillingly, only because he'd been captured and put in jail? He had swept her beyond the point of no return, that was all that mattered, and then he had gone away.

Take an interest? Yes. She did have an interest after all. She raised her eyes, finally, to gaze at the giant television screen, where the program was about to begin, where the government was about to announce whether or not they would release Eric Mallock. *Let him go, you bastards*, she willed at the screen. *Let him go so I can kill him. And then myself.* That last journey they would take together.

After the usual station identification the screen abruptly went black, and a male voice spoke: "Ladies and gentleman, the following is a special news event program for which Channel 11, Metromedia, has donated its time and facilities to the Federal Bureau of Investigation. Channel 11 is honored by this opportunity for public service."

The black screen then gave way to a view of the FBI man, Wiskiel, standing in front of a pale blue curtain; on the huge screen of the living room he was a powerful, intimidating presence. He stood silent and blinking a few seconds, apparently waiting for something, then all at once started to speak:

"I am Michael Wiskiel, Deputy Chief of Station, Los Angeles

office of the FBI. I have been in charge of the Koo Davis investigation, and I am now addressing myself to his captors. You have demanded that I remain in charge, so I'm here, but I'm not the man who can answer your other demands. Deputy FBI Director Maurice St. Clair has flown out from Washington with the government response. I assure you I'm still in charge of the investigation even though Director St. Clair is the man who will talk to you in the course of this program."

Having finished, Wiskiel stood where he was, gazing solemnly at the camera. Peter, laughing, said, "A television star is born." But the evident tremble in his voice foiled his attempt to dispel the nervous gloom created by that overwhelming presence.

"I don't like that TV," Joyce said. "The picture's too big." Which was true.

"Quiet," Peter said. He and Ginger were seated at opposite ends of the long beige suede sofa, while Joyce was curled on the fur rug at Peter's feet.

On the screen, Wiskiel had been replaced at first by more blackness and now by a picture of a man seated at a desk. This was evidently a set, a suitable location already existent in some corner of Channel 11's studios and employed now not for effect but convenience. The desk was wood and fairly ornate; the man behind it was seated on a padded swivel chair, and in the background were shelves filled with old-fashioned books, in sets. The man himself was probably in his late fifties, heavyset, with a red-complexioned rugged face gone to jowly fat. Sheets of typing paper, evidently a script, lay neatly squared on the green blotter before him, held at their edges by his blunt thick fingers. Looking up at the camera from time to time with small angry eyes, but speaking in a gravelly voice devoid of emotion, the man read the script:

"I am Deputy Director Maurice St. Clair of the Federal Bureau of Investigation. The terms you have given us for the release of Koo Davis call for *our* release of ten so-called political prisoners. Let me say right now, at the outset, that Koo Davis is an American institution of whom all Americans are proud, and that the government of the United States and the Federal Bureau of Investigation will do anything within our power to see that no harm comes to Koo Davis, up to and including the agreement to any *reasonable* or *possible* ransom demands. We are not slamming the door. But I must also say that this initial demand is neither reasonable nor possible, and that we simply can't meet it."

There was a stir in the living room, but no one spoke. Joyce's expression was shocked, Liz was taut, Ginger pained, and Peter affronted. But none of them made a sound.

"I promise you this is not a trick, or a ploy. We are prepared to negotiate in good faith. But, in order to do so, we'll have to prove to you that our inability to meet this demand is not our fault, and we'll have to make it clear to you what we can and cannot do. For this reason, I'm going to have to speak to you specifically about each of the ten individuals you have named. Even though you presumably already know these individuals, I will have to describe each one briefly; you will soon see why."

"For the wider audience," Ginger said; a kind of fatalistic humor in his voice. "Something very bad is about to happen, Peter."

"Shut up," Peter said.

On the screen, Deputy Director St. Clair had been replaced by a black-and-white photograph of a scruffy young man in a jacket. The picture was apparently a blow-up from an ordinary snapshot, with the graininess and grayness of such blow-ups. The young man, whose otherwise bland face was decorated by a wispy dark beard, squinted in sunlight; behind him farm buildings could be seen.

"Norm Cobberton," said Joyce, at the same instant that

Deputy Director St. Clair's voice sounded again, speaking while the screen still showed the photograph:

"This is Norman Cobberton, thirty-four, currently serving twenty years to life at the Federal Correctional Facility at Danbury, Connecticut. Cobberton, in the late nineteen-sixties, engaged in union organizing activities among migrant farm workers in the plains states and the American southwest. His activities included such crimes as arson and other destruction of property, as well as the organizing of so-called goon squads to attack and intimidate non-striking workers."

St. Clair himself reappeared on the screen, still reading his script: "Early this afternoon, Cobberton was interviewed at Danbury. This is his response." St. Clair looked up at the screen, his stubborn eyes gazing without forgiveness at the audience for two or three seconds before the scene switched.

This setting was clearly institutional. In the background was a pale green wall with a barred window, through which rain obscured the outside world. At a wooden table, on an armless wooden chair, sat a man identifiable as the one in the photograph; but older, and clean shaven, and wearing wire-rimmed glasses. His left forearm rested on the table, his fingers poking and pulling at something invisible, and while he spoke his sad and rather tired eyes watched his moving fingers:

"I don't know who those people are who kidnapped Koo Davis." The echo of the hard-walled room made his words rather hard to understand. "I don't say they're wrong. *Or* right. Everybody does what they think best." He looked up at the camera, then quickly down again. "What's best for me is not to go. Even if it's offered, I mean. I expect to be released in three years, I think I've learned a lot, and Americans have learned a lot, too. I intend to go back to the work I was doing before, but I believe this time it'll be possible to work within the law. Within the system. Cesar Chavez, others, have shown us it can be done."

An off-camera voice said, "You don't want to go to Algeria?"

"I don't want to leave the country, no." Again Cobberton looked at the camera, his expression troubled but determined. "I don't want to give up."

"Traitor!" The word burst out of Peter, as though not of his own volition. "Toady! Coward! Traitor!"

Ginger slapped the sofa seat between them: "Be quiet."

Another black-and-white photograph had appeared on the giant screen, this time showing a fat-faced young woman in her late twenties, with wildly unkempt hair and heavy dark-framed spectacles. The background was indistinct. St. Clair's voice said, "This is Mary Martha DeLang, thirty-eight, currently serving an indeterminate sentence in a California state prison. A radical theorist, author of several books on left-wing social theory and revolutionary practice, she was convicted in 1971 of smuggling guns to revolutionary friends in a California prison. The friends, and two prison guards, were killed in the subsequent escape attempt. Miss DeLang was interviewed this afternoon."

She appeared on the screen, older than the photo but still fat and still with the same unmanageable wild hair. Gazing intently to the right of the screen, apparently at her interviewer, she said, "I can work here. The book I've *wanted* to write all my life. I'm not an activist, that was an—aberration. Eventually I'll be released, but certainly not before the book is *finished*. Nowhere else would I have the—opportunity—I have here. I won't go."

"They bribed her," Peter said. "They paid her off." But the others watched the screen, as though he hadn't spoken.

St. Clair again, glancing up at the camera then down at his script: "Also on the list is Hugh Pendry, thirty-seven, in the Federal Penitentiary at Leavenworth, Kansas. Pendry's activities included skyjacking, the planting of bombs in such public places as the American Express office in Mexico City, and direct involvement with guerilla groups in South and Central America. He was briefly with Che Guevara in Bolivia, but returned to Cuba before Guevara's death. He is serving concurrent life sentences for attempted murder and other crimes. When informed this morning of the kidnappers' demand for his release, he expressed the hope that the demand would be met. Hugh Pendry wishes to leave the United States for Algeria."

"All *right*," Peter said, rubbing his palms together, looking left and right. "All *right*."

A picture of a thin-faced frightened-eyed black man flashed on the screen. St. Clair: "This is Fred Walpole, thirty-five, originally a leader in student demonstrations in the New York City area, later responsible for the fire-bombing of several banks in New York and other northeastern states, currently serving twenty years to life in the Green Haven Correctional Facility in upstate New York. Walpole refused to be filmed, but this afternoon he gave the following recorded statement."

The picture on the screen remained the same. An anonymous voice, baritone with falsetto overlays, spoke: "I don't wanna go anywhere. I come up for parole in four, four and a half years. When I get outa here, that's it for me. From now on, I worry about *me*. I don't know those people, I don't want to know them, I got no connection with them. And I never had anything against Koo Davis."

"That could be anybody," Peter said. "It's a fake."

Joyce, her voice and expression miserable, said, "No, it isn't, Peter. I'm sorry, I'm dreadfully sorry, but you know it isn't."

"Shut your nasty little faces," Ginger said, "or leave my house."

The picture of Fred Walpole had now been replaced by a color photograph of a priest in front of a church; the priest, a slender black-haired youngish man in black gown and black-rimmed glasses, looked serious, sincere and not particularly intelligent. St. Clair's voice was saying, "Louis Golding, forty-two, an ex-priest currently serving an indeterminate sentence in a Federal Correctional Facility in Pennsylvania for destruction of government property, was interviewed earlier today."

Another institutional setting, another nervous man sitting at a wooden table with a barred window behind him. This man, however, looked almost nothing like the photograph of the priest; his dark hair was much thinner, his face was more drawn and lined, and his plain-rimmed glasses made it easier to see his level intelligent eyes. "I would certainly never leave the United States of America," he said, with a passionate intensity only increased by the weakness of his voice. "I consider myself a missionary to America, as much as Pere Marquette or any of the other priests who came here three hundred years ago. This is still a *barbarous* nation. My work is *here*. When I am released, whenever that may be, it is in America that I must continue my mission."

"Well, he's stir crazy," Peter said. "You can see that. Can't you?" Needing a response, he reached out to pat Joyce's head where she sat on the floor in front of him. "Can't you?"

"Yes," she said.

St. Clair was on the screen again, looking at his audience. He said, "It was two-thirteen Van Dyke."

Joyce started, a sudden tremor through her entire body as though an electric charge had just thrummed through her. Peter, his hand still resting on her hair, frowned down at the top of her head, saying, "What's wrong?"

"Nothing. Ssshh, listen."

St. Clair was reading his script, "The next person on the list, Abby Lancaster, thirty-three, a leader of rent strikes and anti-landlord demonstrations in New York City, also leader of a movement for free subways in New York City, now in a New York State Correctional Facility, convicted of arson, assault, destruction of public property, and other crimes. Miss Lancaster also refused to be filmed, and refused as well to allow a re-cording of her voice. Following our agreement not to show *any* picture of her on this broadcast, she made the following signed statement, in the presence of two witnesses who have personal knowledge of her identity. This is the statement: 'I, Abby Lan-caster, no longer believe violence can ever produce lasting good. I will become eligible for parole in ten months' time. It is my hope to receive parole, and to continue the career in social work I misguidedly deviated from several years ago. I have no desire for further notoriety.' That's Miss Lancaster's statement."

Peter closed his eyes. The hand that had patted Joyce's head rubbed his cheeks. Ginger watched him, eyes glinting.

Another photo appeared on the screen, a serious-looking young black man with an exaggerated afro. This seemed to have been cropped from some larger group photo, a graduation or team picture or some such thing. St. Clair's voice said, "This is William Brown, thirty-three, currently serving a life sentence in the New Jersey State Prison at Rahway for murder in the first degree. Brown, originally a Black Panther, later joined one of the more militant offshoots of the Panthers and was convicted of murdering two Black Panther leaders in 1969. Other black militants had tried him in absentia in their own kangaroo court, found him guilty of murder and sentenced him to death. He turned himself in to the authorities for his own protection. When informed this afternoon of the prospect of leaving prison and going to Algeria, Brown stated that he would be agreeable."

"All right," Peter whispered, but he went on rubbing his cheeks.

Liz gasped as the next photograph appeared on the screen: a dark-haired, recklessly grinning, handsome young man. St. Clair's voice said, "This is Eric Mallock, thirty-three, serving an in-determinate sentence in the Federal Penitentiary at Lewisburg,

Kentucky. He was captured in 1972 when his bomb factory in Chicago exploded. He has been convicted of second-degree murder, manslaughter, attempted murder, assault, arson and other crimes. He was interviewed this afternoon at Lewisburg."

Liz covered her eyes with a rigid hand, but at the sound of Mallock's voice she lowered the hand and gazed unblinking at the screen.

Another institutional setting, but this time the man was seated on a metal folding chair in front of a tan tile wall. He sat bent forward, elbows on knees, eyes looking at a presumed interviewer to the camera's left, hands gesturing between his knees as he spoke. His was recognizably the same face as before, but blurred by a smoothness of flesh; he'd apparently put on thirty or forty pounds since that earlier picture had been taken. The recklessness was gone from his mouth and eyes, and his hair was neater, more controlled. He said, "It's hard for me now to understand myself as of several years ago. I made mistakes, criminal mistakes. The cause I was working for was not wrong, I think most Americans realize that now, but my *methods* were wrong. The desperation I felt, some of my friends felt, I don't know if we were right, if change would have come about no matter what we did. All I know is, we all claimed we were prepared to pay the consequences; as for me, when the time came I found I *wasn't* prepared to pay the consequences. My first few years here were very difficult. Now I feel differently. I don't know what the future holds, I'm just living day by day. I've been very active in forming various prisoner programs here, I started a very successful bookkeeping course, I work on the prison newspaper. There's still a lot to be done here, every-where—I suppose in Algeria, too. But not for me. If those are my friends out there—" and for the only time he glanced directly at the camera, his eyes and here-and-gone grin a quick faint echo of that former recklessness "—and I suppose they are—" he returned his gaze to the interviewer, the somber mask again firmly in place "—I appreciate their intentions, I wouldn't presume to say whether they're right or wrong, but I think they ought to go on without me."

Liz closed her eyes and lowered her head, covering her face with her hand.

Mallock was followed by a black-and-white news photograph of an angry demonstration scene. The focus was on two uniformed policemen struggling with a stocky bushy-haired moustached man flailing about himself with a sign on a long stick. St. Clair's voice said, "This is Howard Fenton, thirty-nine, convicted of tax evasion and related offenses. He is currently in the Federal Correctional Facility at Danbury Connecticut, where he was interviewed this afternoon."

They were shown again the same room where the first prisoner, Cobberton, had been interviewed. The man sitting at the table this time was a somewhat older and thinner version of the man in the news photograph. His speech was rapid, the words jumbling together, his hands jittering in the air as he spoke: "I don't know who these people are. They're nothing to do with *me*. I'm non-violent, that's my whole *point*. The whole military establishment has to be dismantled. I will not pay taxes or obey any other federal law while this government continues to support a huge military machine. And I *certainly* won't be tricked into *leaving* this country. I wouldn't be surprised if this whole thing isn't a scenario dreamed up by Army Intelligence. It would go right along with their paranoid view of life."

Ginger laughed aloud. "Oh, what a cadre! What a formidable regiment of revolution!"

Now on the screen was a police mugshot, front and side views of a very tough-looking man. "Finally," St. Clair's voice said, "this is George Toll, forty-one, currently serving twenty years to life in the Texas State Prison at Huntsville, convicted of armed robbery and associated crimes. This is his third prison term for felony convictions."

The screen showed St. Clair again, doggedly reading his script, sliding pages away off the blotter as he finished them: "When Toll was arrested for the crimes for which he is now serving his sentence, he claimed to be a Black Panther and to have robbed banks and other places to obtain money for the Panthers' legitimate activities, such as their free lunch program in some ghetto schools. The Panthers, however, have consistently denied that Toll has ever had any relationship with them or that Toll has ever donated money to them. His previous felony convictions, also for armed robbery, did not include any claims to have been politically motivated. When informed of the present situation, Toll at once stated that he would be desirous of leaving prison and going to Algeria. However, forty-five minutes before this program began, the Algerian mission in Washington announced that, of the ten names on the original list, Algeria would accept nine, excluding George Toll."

St. Clair lifted his head to gaze briefly and expressionlessly at the camera, then looked down again at his script: "Of the ten names on the list, only three are willing to accept the arrangement, and of the three only two are acceptable to the Algerian government. Given these realities, we are at a loss to know how to negotiate with you. You can't want us to force these individuals out of the country if they don't want to go. You have my personal word for it that none of these individuals has been pressured in any way. What you have seen and heard is their own honest response to the offer that was made them. We ask you not to blame us for this situation, and not to blame Koo Davis. You have our phone number. We are available at any time, day or night, for further discussion. We do not consider this a closed issue. We want Koo Davis back, and we want to emphasize that we are at all times willing to discuss terms."

St. Clair's heavy, bleak, angry face remained a few seconds longer on the screen, gazing out at the audience; on the screen in this room it was a huge brooding ominous presence. Then the picture faded to black and the announcer's voice was heard: "This has been…"

# 23

Koo stares at the TV screen. "That's not funny," he says. The screen is black, but then the Channel 11 identifying logo appears, with the ID jingle. It contains a repetition of the channel numeral, sung by a chorus with an echo effect: "E-*lev*-en, E-*lev*-en, E-*lev*-en." The echo reverberates and reverberates in Koo's head, as though the brain has been removed and it's all empty space in there now. Space Available—Will Divide to Suit.

When a Pampers commercial comes on—"I don't use Pampers anymore, I use *new* Pampers"—Larry at last gets up and goes across the room to switch off the set. When he turns back, his movement visually reverberating in all the mirrors, his face looks as agonized as Koo feels; and at least he has the sense not to make any Mickey Mouse hopeful statement. "I can't understand that," he says. "Koo, I'm as astonished as you are."

"I'm done for," Koo says.

"How could they have turned their *backs* that way? What's *happened* to them in jail?" Larry seems to have latched on to a different aspect of the problem.

Koo's aspect of the problem is that now he's a dead man. Any minute now, somebody's going to come through that door, and it's going to be all over. If *only* there'd been a house, a store, even another automobile, when he'd gotten himself out of that goddamn trunk. That was his moment, and he blew it, and now it's finished.

And it won't even necessarily be Mark who does the job. Koo has known all along that these people are assholes—granted they're dangerous assholes, they're still assholes—but now the whole *world* knows it. Rage, humiliation, revenge for their defeat; Peter, for example, would kill for much less reason. Liz would kill out of general irritation, and surely there was enough general irritation in that program for anybody's taste. Larry here might spend the aftermath in a moony post-mortem about whatever happened to the old bunch, but in this house there are *killers*. And a victim. "I'm done for now," Koo says.

"No, Koo. *You* didn't do anything wrong."

Koo points at the door. "They'll be coming in."

"No, they won't. I promise. I'll stay right here." Eager, questing, Larry sits on the bed near Koo, gazing into his face. "Talk to me now, Koo. About you and Mark."

"No."

"You said, after the show, you said—"

"No." Koo can't talk about all that, his own distress. "There's no point in it now," he says. "I'm done for. I'm dead."

"*No*, Koo."

"I'm *dead*," Koo says.

# 24

Lily Davis pushed the Off button in the controls built into her chair arm, and across the room the television image collapsed inward to a descending point, then snuffed out. "They'll kill him now," she said, and pushed another button, which caused the wall panel to descend, hiding the built-in TV set.

In this sitting room in the house in Beverly Glen were four people: Lily, her two sons, and Lynsey Rayne. When the drift of the program had become obvious, Lynsey had gotten to her feet and spent the rest of the time pacing up and down the long room, from its broad arched entranceway to the sliding glass doors closing out the flagstone patio and the floodlit lush jungle greenery on the slope beyond. Now she paused in lighting a new cigarette from the last, coming deeper into the room to exclaim, "Lily, how can you say that? How can you say such a thing?"

"Because it's true." Lily gave her a calm look.

Frank and Barry had been seated, not very close together, on the long gray sofa. Now Frank hopped to his feet, with that inanely cheerful smile he seemed unable to turn off, and as he rubbed his hands together like a fly grooming itself he beamed around at them all, saying, "I for one could use a drink. Barry?"

"I think not," Barry said coolly, that evanescent trace of English accent clicking in his words. "It's four in the morning, my time. Tomorrow morning. I'm afraid a drink would slaughter me."

"The *reason* it's true," Lily went on, calm and indomitable, "is because they have been humiliated now. No one can bear to be humiliated; believe me, I know."

The last phrase made no sense to Lynsey, who therefore first disbelieved and then forgot it, concentrating on Lily's stated *reason*. "That isn't necessarily true. When Patty—"

Frank called, "Mom? Drink?"

"A sherry might be nice, dear."

"Lynsey?"

"No," Lynsey said, irritably, annoyed at the distraction and enraged with them all for not being able to concentrate on what was happening to Koo. Then she said, "Wait, yes. Scotch, I suppose. And soda."

"One Scotch and soda, one sherry." Frank frisked up the two marble steps and through the archway.

Lynsey struggled back to her sentence: "Patty Hearst's kidnappers were humiliated, too. That business with the free food program they demanded, it turned into a joke. They didn't kill Patty Hearst."

Lily shrugged. "She was one of them."

"Oh, not really. Besides, this man said the government was still open to negotiation."

"He could hardly say anything else."

Yawning, Barry rose gracefully to his feet, saying, "I am exhausted. If there are further developments, do let me know."

"Of course, dear," Lily said. "Have a good rest."

"I shall. Good night, Lynsey. Don't fret; there's nothing to be done anyway."

"That's the worst of it," Lynsey told him. She found herself for some reason less irritated by Barry than the other two. "I keep *needing* to do something."

"Thus, one frets. Yes, I see. Well, try not to overfret yourself, then," Barry said, with a faint hint of grin which made him look for an absurd instant like Boris Karloff; then he nodded to his mother and Lynsey, no longer Karloff at all, and departed.

Lynsey had no choice; she *had* to fret too much. She said to

Lily, "Even if what you say were true, and I don't believe it for an instant, but even if it were, what's the point *saying* such things?"

With another shrug, Lily said, "For that matter, what's the point saying most things? Communication is almost always an option, Lynsey."

Lynsey studied the older woman. "Are you suggesting I shut up, Lily?"

"Not at all. But you probably ought to give more consideration to the difference between us. I mean, the differences in our relationship with Koo."

"You're his wife and I'm his agent."

"Oh, those words don't mean anything, Lynsey, *you* know that. The difference is, you love him and I don't."

Lynsey found herself blushing to the roots of her hair. Displeased by such a reaction at her age—she was not, after all, some tremulous teenager—she said, angrily, "And did you *never* love him?"

"I don't remember," Lily said, cool as ever. "Someone who once wore my name loved someone who once wore his. But it was unrequited and died, as such loves do. Except Dante, of course, but I've never been that sort of masochist. Or any sort of masochist. That was probably what went wrong with the marriage. But I shall not," she went on, as Frank returned to the room with a tray containing three drinks, "give you the sordid details of my marriage in its active phase, even if I remembered them. You may merely assume that Koo and I had adequate reasons for living apart these last forty years."

"Not quite that long, Mom," Frank said, as though gallantly, giving her the flute glass of sherry.

"I can't be bothered to keep track of such an anniversary," Lily said, with evident disgust.

"You came out here to see him die," Lynsey accused, looking

at Lily past Frank, who was offering her the Scotch and soda. "You hate him and you *want* him to die." Distracted, she took the drink from Frank's hand.

"I don't *want* anything, where Koo is concerned," Lily said. "Desire ceased a long long time ago."

Frank having distributed the glasses raised his own, said, "Salud," and drank. Then, smiling at Lynsey, he said, "Mom won't defend herself, but believe me Lynsey, this thing was as much a shock to her as to anybody else."

"Where Koo Davis is concerned," Lily said, "I am one with the public. I would be distressed if he were killed. Surely you don't expect from me anything more intimate than that? My relationship with the man is hardly as personal as yours."

Which was the second reference to that subject; this time Lynsey answered it: "I'm not Koo's mistress, if that's what you mean. You know I'm not his type."

"You mean those overblown blondes," Lily said, with a faint smile. "Oddly enough, I was rather the type myself as a girl; without the cheapness, of course. But don't tell me Koo *never* took you to bed; it's not like him to pass up an opportunity."

This time Lynsey managed to keep from reddening only by threatening her body with immediate self-destruction. Nevertheless, the three times—early in their business relationship, when she was still Max Berry's assistant and Max was Koo's agent—that she had spent the night with Koo still burned behind her eyes. Could Lily gaze at her with her own cool eyes and see the flames? Lynsey blinked, turning her face away, sipping in confusion at her Scotch and soda, only too late realizing that these gestures too admitted the truth.

Frank said, cheerfully, "Oh, there's so much fuss all the time about who's going to bed with whom. What does it matter? It plagues us in television, let me tell you, on *and* off the screen. After a while you just don't care anymore."

Lynsey understood that Frank was trying to ease her past this awkward moment, but though she was grateful she also knew that his assistance was really automatic; Frank went through life making the best of things, easing the rough spots for everybody else because he wanted no rough spots for himself. Television was the ideal arena for his talents, his capacity to take the blandest route to any goal. She said, looking at Frank but actually speaking to Lily, "The important thing now is that we care what happens to Koo. It doesn't matter if we can *do* anything or not, it doesn't even matter what Koo might have done wrong in the past. The point is that we *care* about him *now*."

Lily, with a kind of amused wonder, said, "Lynsey, I've always admired you, I think you know that. If Koo can arouse such tremendous loyalty from a person like you, there must be more to the man than I've given him credit for. I suppose my vision is still colored, even after all these years."

This combination of sincerity, condescension and naked self-analysis was too complex for Lynsey to encompass. She could only fall back to a safe position: "Whatever he's done, Koo doesn't deserve what's happening to him now."

With only the slightest hesitation Lily nodded, saying, "I agree."

"The poor guy," Frank said, and for once his smile seemed actually clouded. "It must be rough on him. All we can do is hope the FBI can get him out of there."

Looking at Frank, Lynsey thought with some surprise, *Koo never was his father, his or Barry's. The marriage broke up too early. Naturally the boys aren't responding the way I'd expect. How complicated and melancholy this must be for them, having to hope for the return of a father who had never been there in the first place.* Turning her head to glance at Lily, she wondered who had taken the father's role with these boys. *Was* there a father? Had this straitjacketed woman ever taken lovers?

Lily heaved herself out of the chair, saying, "We should dine. I come from a background where even at funerals one eats." With a meaningful look at Lynsey she added, "And this isn't a funeral."

## 25

The knocking at the door woke Larry from a light doze; when he opened his eyes in the mirrored room he thought he was still asleep, in a dream, and that he had nothing to do but passively observe. But the knock was repeated, more insistently, and he sat up, groaning. He'd fallen asleep in one of the armchairs, in an awkward position, and was now stiff and sore.

He looked over at the bed, where Koo slept on, under the fur throw with which Larry had covered him. Poor man, he was still weak from his illness and kept nodding off. Larry pushed himself out of the chair and crossed the room to unlock the door, wanting to get it open before the knocking disturbed Koo's rest. But then, remembering Koo's terror, he hesitated with his hand on the knob, and when he did open the door, just a few inches, he kept both hands on it and his left foot braced against it, so he could slam it again if the person outside were Mark.

But it was Joyce's worried face that peered at him through the crack. "Larry," she said. "I have to talk to you. Come out of there. Why are you staying in there all the time?"

"Ssshhh. Koo's asleep."

"Come *out*."

So he stepped through, closing the door behind himself, standing close with Joyce in the small areaway at the head of the stairs. The house was designed with most of the living quarters downstairs, at the rear for the ocean view, leaving the double garage and the utility room at the featureless windowless front, facing the Pacific Coast Highway. The bedroom in which they'd put Koo was over the garage, with another suite of rooms behind it, facing the ocean, opening onto a large deck built on the roof over the living room.

Her voice low and hurried, Joyce said, "Did you watch it?"

"I don't understand," Larry said. "How could they all…give up like that?"

"You should talk with Peter. He's closed himself in downstairs with that man Ginger, I don't know what's going to happen." Looking over her shoulder at the stairs extending downward, she said, "I don't like Ginger. I don't trust him."

"He's all right. He just didn't expect to be dragged into this, that's all."

"Go talk to Peter, Larry. Find out what he wants to do."

"I can't," he said. "I promised Koo I'd stay with him."

"For heaven's sake, why?"

"He's afraid of Mark, and I think he's right."

"Mark's outside somewhere," she said. "He didn't even come in to watch the program."

"He's going crazy; Koo's right. Also, I think there's something else between them, some problem Koo won't tell me about. He was going to tell me, but then that program came on and all he'd say was, 'I'm done for now.' "

Joyce reached out to hold his forearm in both hands, looking up at him with an intensity he found disquieting. She said, "Larry, what's going to happen?"

"I don't know."

"It's all gone wrong. Mark's gone crazy, Liz just stays inside her shell down there—"

"The Eric Mallock thing; that must have been hard for her to take."

"I'm afraid of what Peter and Ginger might decide together. That's why I want you to go down there."

"I can't leave Koo."

"Oh, it's getting so hopeless. Maybe we should just let him go."

"Peter wouldn't agree, that's one thing certain."

She sagged forward against his chest, putting her arms around him, sighing, "Nothing's going the way we thought."

He stroked her hair, remembering this feel and smell of Joyce, surprised to realize how long it had been since they'd physically touched. "I know," he said. "I know."

"We aren't a family anymore." She was holding him tighter and tighter, burying her face in his chest, her words muffled. He felt the trembling of her shoulders beneath his hand. "We aren't together anymore."

"After this is over—" But there was no way to end that sentence; it had become impossible to think about life after this was over.

She raised her head, and he saw tears on her cheeks. "Make love to me," she whispered.

He wanted to, suddenly, overpoweringly; she had to be aware of the physical manifestation. But he turned his head toward the closed door to Koo's bedroom: "Where—"

"In here," she whispered, leading him by the hand to the bedroom on the opposite side of the landing. "We'll leave the door open, you'll be able to see that door."

The bedroom was in darkness, with the view of the ocean a kind of unfinished empty diorama seen through the wall of glass doors on the opposite side. Low massive furniture, indistinguishable in the dark, hulked like sleeping beasts on the wall-to-wall carpet. The room was large, muffled, quiet.

Larry wanted her achingly, demandingly, in waves of concupiscence; his hands trembled with the need of her. He'd been away from active thoughts of sex for such a long long time, and now sexual desire was like a revelation. He touched her breasts through her clothing, the shape of her body exciting him further. "Take everything off."

"Yes. Yes."

They pulled off their clothing with great haste, but then stopped and looked at one another, smiling slowly together, like old acquaintances unexpectedly meeting, who learn they can still be friends. Joyce was surprisingly voluptuous naked, with a long-torsoed body and full breasts, mysterious in the dim indirect illumination from the small chandelier at the head of the stairs. Larry cupped the side of her right breast with his hand, touching the hard berry of nipple with the ball of his thumb. Her face was wide-eyed and solemn in the shadows. He pulled her close, kissing her, rubbing himself against her.

"Yes. Oh. Don't hurt me."

"Down," he whispered.

He held her hand, helped her lower herself to the carpeted floor, then knelt between her legs. Memory now only increased the novelty of this desire; had she always been so serious, so grave, and yet so open and warm and pliant in her lovemaking? Penetrating her, he would have lowered onto her breast but she held him up with her forearms under his shoulders, whispering, "I want to see you."

"Yes. Good." The posture was awkward for him, hands splayed on the floor, but he maintained it. Below, their bodies moved together, rolling in the tidal motion, while their somber faces remained still. He watched her in wonder, the shadowed eyes, the soft smooth skin of her face, the parted lips, stray shards of light glinting from her moist teeth, her hair fanned on the carpet beneath her head and curling around her small ears. A door was opened in his mind, and he saw that for all these years he had been in love with Joyce. In personal exclusive demanding love with one individual human being; as though nobody else existed. He had spent years denying it, refusing to distract himself from his concern with all of humanity, refusing to recognize the awful jealousy in the early days when she would go to bed with Peter or Mark or any of the others who were still with them then; and all this time had successfully hidden from himself the truth.

Years ago, in college, he had memorized a portion of Pope's *An Essay on Man*, thinking it expressed his own beliefs better than he ever could, and only now understanding he had always misunderstood it. In a murmuring voice, slowly, in time with their lovemaking, he recited:

*"Know then thyself, presume not God to scan, the proper study of mankind is man. Placed on this isthmus of a middle state, a being darkly wise, and rudely great: with too much knowledge for the skeptic side, with too much weakness for the stoic's pride, he hangs between; in doubt to act or rest; in doubt to deem himself a god or beast; in doubt his mind or body to prefer; born but to die, and reasoning but to err; alike in ignorance, his reason such, whether he thinks too little or too much."*

"Don't think," she whispered, and the hint of a smile touched her lips in the semi-dark. "Larry, don't think at all."

"I love you."

"Oh, don't say that. Not now." Then, her expression fierce, she clamped his face between her hands. "Come in me."

Yes. Still holding him so she could see his face, her own face suffusing, the eyes losing focus, she strained and pulsed beneath him, and he could feel the surge of her body just before his own final, demanding, insistent thrust. "For*ever*," he cried, forgetting silence and noise, and collapsed atop her.

The darkness was comforting. Their bodies were warm together, her hands and arms were soothing as she stroked his back, the warm suspiration of her breath beside his ear was reassuring. His lower body trembled, spending itself, the aftershocks of orgasm rippling through him, but his head at least was at peace, drooping downward, forehead touching the friendly roughness of the carpet. A long stretch of Nontime went by, and then Joyce sighed, shifting beneath him, and he knew they had to go forward again. Lurch forward, into the impossible. He echoed her sigh, and lifted himself onto his elbows, feeling the sudden chill air on his chest.

"Larry."

"What are we going to do?"

"Let him go."

Larry closed his eyes. It was the other impossible goal; first to love Joyce, second to be finished with Koo Davis. "We can't," he whispered. "Peter would never allow it. Not now, not when he's been humiliated."

"Will he kill him?"

"No." Larry was certain of that part, he'd thought it out before. "That's just another way to admit defeat. Peter will want to make up for it now, to get his dignity back."

"The longer we go on, the worse it is for us. For us."

"It's already too long," Larry said, and kissed her, and rolled off onto the floor.

This bedroom had its own lavatory; Larry used it, then returned to find Joyce already dressed and standing in the bedroom doorway, frowning across the landing at the door of Koo's room. She said, "I'll watch him. You go talk to Peter."

"I promised Koo."

"Larry, it's all right." Something had made her stronger, more sure of herself. "I can deal with Mark just as well as you can. Besides, I think he's gone, this time I think he's finally run away for good."

"None of us will get away for good," Larry said, but he didn't argue anymore. He shivered, all the warmth out of his body now, and began to dress.

°

It was the worst day of Peter's life. He had gone through defeats before, and had his triumphs, and suffered those periods which can sometimes seem even worse, when nothing at all happens, neither for good nor ill, when one's life seems to have stopped, when you might as well be dead—but *this* was the worst. To be made a fool of, a laughingstock, before the entire world. To have one's plans exposed as the vaporings of a simpleton, a dunce with no grasp on reality, an ass, an egotistical buffoon capering in the streets—this was the way he described himself to himself, in his mind. His self-loathing was such that he positively strove to punish his cheeks, grinding and gnawing, biting till he couldn't stand it any longer, then biting again. The tears glistening in his eyes, which might have been caused by humiliation, or rage, or regret, or despair, were from pain.

This house belonged to a friend of Ginger's in the music business, and a smallish room behind the kitchen reflected this vocation. The room was soundproofed, and built into the walls was a complete small studio of recording and playback equipment. The furnishings were simple and quiet, with leather swivel chairs and Formica-topped small tables. A console along one wall contained the instrumentation for all the equipment, plus three keyboards. Two heavily draped windows looked out on not much at all; some shrubbery, the tall paling fence belonging to the neighbor next door. It was to this room that Peter retired, once the interminable horrible ghastly program was over, to sit in one of the leather chairs, unmoving, staring at the floor, enveloping himself in pessimism and despondency and self-hatred.

But such feelings about oneself cannot last. They are too painful to be endured for very long; soon we must either forgive ourselves or punish ourselves, with the strongest form of punishment for the strongest level of self-loathing being death. Peter was not a man to willingly end his own life—he was too utterly the center of his universe for that—so that soon he began to shift his angle of view and to see things in a slightly different way.

*He* wasn't the one who had gone wrong. He had remained true to his ideals, true to the plan and vision of Revolution, while those others had fallen by the wayside. Eric Mallock! Who could believe such a failure from Eric Mallock? Had they castrated him?

It was true that Peter hadn't fully researched all ten people before putting their names on the list, it was true he personally knew fewer than half of them, even at the level of nodding acquaintance, but surely a few years ago the reaction would have been very different. There wouldn't have been more than one or two at the *most* who would fail to rally if placed on such a list. What had happened? *Peter* had remained constant, what had happened to all those others? Only three would even answer the call; one a renegade Panther, one an internationalist whose primary involvement wasn't with the Second American Revolution anyway, and one a simple bank robber. Those three could rot in prison, they meant nothing to Peter at all.

It was the others, the seven. What a betrayal! Never mind that they'd made Peter look like a fool, it was the *Movement* they had betrayed, the *Movement* they had held up to public scorn and ridicule, the *Movement* they had turned their backs on. Peter's self-hatred reversed itself, extended outward, enveloping the seven who had made this horrible thing happen.

The day would come when they would pay. Did they, like most Americans, think the Revolution was dead? Quiescent, yes, but the same problems of power and responsibility still existed, the same separation of the governed from the governing, the same potential for the misuse of power and for horrors done in the name of the people but without their cognizance or their will. Those who now held power would be unable forever to restrain themselves from using it; the Revolution was a bomb with a fuse that only the Establishment could light, but *they would light it*. And on that day, Peter's list would still exist. And the people on it would pay, they would dearly pay.

He had gone this far in his thinking when Ginger entered the room, took a chair facing him, and said, "Well, what now, genius?"

Peter barely heard the sarcasm; his mind was already too full. Nor had he yet considered Ginger's question. What now? He had no idea. "We go on," he said. "If we were willing to be stopped by temporary setbacks, we would never have succeeded at all."

"Temporary setbacks!" Ginger's true astonishment superseded his half-artificial scorn. "You call this a temporary setback?"

"We still have Koo Davis."

"Oh, for God's sake, Peter, get out of that dream! You don't think you're going on!"

"What else can we do? Give up? There's no *way* to give up."

"Let Davis go," Ginger said. Waving one hand in a frail parody of his usual ebullient style, he said, "I'll buy you tickets out of the country. *You* people go to Algeria."

"With our tails between our legs? No, Ginger."

"While you still *have* tails and legs. Peter, you are a very very silly person, I understand that now, it's undoubtedly what attracted me to you in the first place." Bit by bit, Ginger was regaining his normal stance toward life; this disaster seemed, if anything, to have improved his spirits. "You and your little friends go play pattycake in Algeria," he said. "La grande affaire est finie."

"No," Peter said.

Ginger made shooing motions. "C'est dangereux. Allez vous en."

"No, Ginger."

Angry and flippant at the same time, Ginger waggled a nervous accusatory finger at Peter: "Je tiens à ce que vous partiez *immédiatement!*"

"I'm staying," Peter told him. "And Koo Davis is staying."

"Vous voulez rire!" Ginger turned aside to an imaginary audience, spreading his hands and saying, "Ecoutez cet homme!"

"And *you're* staying."

Ginger was startled briefly back into English: "What? I certainly am not! Il y va de ma vie! Je pense à mon avenir!"

"And *my* future." Peter was unassailable. He had stopped grinding his teeth, and the resurgent blinking had once again disappeared. He didn't know what was going to happen next, where or how he would move from this abyss, but nevertheless he was calm, secure, confident in himself to a degree he'd never known before. He had touched bottom, and was no longer afraid. "You are tied to me, Ginger," he said, "and if things go badly for me they'll go *just* as badly for you."

Ginger seemed truly depressed now, and not merely playacting at gloom.

"J'ai mal à la tête," he said, slowly getting to his feet. "Je vais me coucher."

"Sit down, Ginger," Peter said. "And speak English."

Ginger's shrug was exquisitely Gallic. "Pourquoi?"

Peter surged to his feet, his right hand whipping around so fast that Ginger never saw it coming. The sound of the slap was a quick flat cracking noise in the soundproofed room, leaving a reddening blot on Ginger's astounded face. "Sit *down*," Peter said. "No more playing. Sit down, speak English, and stop pretending you're not a part of this."

"My God, you *struck* me!"

"Will you sit down, or will I *strike* you again?"

Slowly, unbelievingly, Ginger backed to the sofa, lowered

himself into it, and turned aside as though for thought or self-composure, touching his fingertips to his red cheek. When he next looked over at Peter, his eyes were blank, all his fey mannerisms gone, leaving not a monkey but a monkey-god, stone-faced and unforgiving. "You have just made, Peter," he said, "perhaps your most serious mistake of all." Except for the red mark on his cheek, his face had drained of color.

"You aren't leaving this room," Peter told him, "until you really do understand that you're as deep in this thing as I am. Don't you think I know what you had in mind?" He parodied Ginger's former manner, more insultingly than accurately: " 'Oh, I have a headache, oh I'm going to bed.' Right out the door, you mean, a quick stop for the anonymous phone tip to the police, and then off to Coldwater Canyon or some such place to work up your alibi—'I was screwing this young thing, Officer, I never *did* go to that place in Malibu, it's all some horrible coincidence.' "

"Horrible, at any rate."

That Ginger neither denied the charge nor made fun of it was disturbing, but it confirmed Peter in his guess. "I didn't want you in this, Ginger," he said, "but now you're in, and you have to ride it through with the rest of us."

"Why am I in it? How did the police happen to poke around that house anyway? Some *other* misjudgment of yours?"

"I have no idea," Peter said. Privately, he suspected that Mark might have done something, either deliberately or inadvertently, during the time he was gone from the house after the fight with Larry, but he was hesitant to say so, because the accusation might get back to Mark. Peter was not prepared to challenge Mark directly; it was better to keep that killer rage directed outward. With Ginger, on the other hand, the direct approach was best: "The point is, we had to move, and here we are, and now you're no longer merely our backer, you're part of the action."

"And if I walk out? Or do you intend to stand guard over me twenty-four hours a day? Can you really keep an eye on two prisoners at once?"

"If I'm arrested," Peter said, "the first name I speak will be yours."

Ginger was still considering that threat, his expression calm but his lips thrust out, when the door opened and Larry entered, looking earnest and troubled and eager to be of help. "Can I join the conversation?" He left the door open.

Peter said, "Where's Mark?"

"Joyce says she thinks he's gone for good." Larry sat to Peter's right, saying, "Peter, do you have any idea what to do next?"

"As a matter of fact, I do." It had just come to him, while looking at Larry's obtuse face. "Ginger, I want to make a tape."

"For the police?"

"They're my only audience."

Ginger rose, turning toward the recording equipment, while Larry leaned closer to Peter, speaking in a low and confidential voice, saying, "I was thinking, Peter, maybe we ought to cut our losses."

The sweet predictability of Larry cheered Peter enormously, after the intricacies of Ginger. Almost laughing, he said, "Larry, you want to turn Koo Davis loose. The answer is no."

"I just thought—"

"I know what you thought, and what you always think."

Ginger said, "Sit in this chair here. You want to make the tape yourself?"

"That's right." Peter switched chairs, and Ginger positioned a microphone on the white countertop in front of him, saying, "Don't sit too close when you talk. Just the way you are now."

"All right."

"We should close that door. We'll get outside noise."

"*Leave* it." Peter was irritable, impatient. "We're not interested in *high fidelity*. They'll understand the message."

Ginger shrugged. "Let's make sure we're using blank tape." He turned away, seating himself at the controls. He hit switches, and a faint hissing sound came from concealed loudspeakers.

Larry said, "Peter, are you sure you don't want to discuss it first, get it down on paper?"

"I know exactly what I want to say."

"All right," Ginger said. "It's clean. Give me a sentence for level."

Peter looked at the microphone. "This is Rock," he said, "Commander of the People's Revolutionary Army." 'Rock,' the original meaning in Greek for the name 'Peter,' was the code name he'd used ever since first going underground.

Ginger touched switches and dials, and from the speakers Peter's voice sounded, repeating the sentence. Listening, with that sense of foreignness that people invariably feel when hearing their own recorded voices, Peter decided he approved; the voice sounded determined, cold, capable of backing up its words with action.

"All right," Ginger said. "Start from the beginning."

The beginning was to repeat that self-identification, and go on from there: "We are holding, as a prisoner of war, a collaborator named Koo Davis, and have demanded in exchange for his return the release of ten political prisoners in American jails. The official response has been a farcical television broadcast, in which seven of these ten have been obviously, blatantly forced to claim they do not want to be released.

"The American public will not be deceived, and the People's Revolutionary Army is not deceived. Does the U.S. government think it can fool the world? Can seven out of ten people not want to leave prison? The staging of this mockery was as clever and professional as we might expect from an organization with all the resources of the United States government behind it, but the result can't hold up. Simple reflection will show that it can't be true.

"Therefore, our demand remains the same. The ten people on the list will be removed from their prisons and flown to Algeria, where they will be free to make any statements they choose. If any of them wish to return to prison, of course they may, but let's hear them say it once they are free of the threatening power of the United States government.

"The speed with which the government's comedy was assembled shows that our original deadline was not too tight. This is Thursday night. By noon tomorrow, California time, the government will announce its decision. If the answer is no, Koo Davis dies. If the answer is yes, the government will then have twenty-four hours, until noon on Saturday, to release the ten prisoners and place them on public view in Algeria. If the government fails, Koo Davis dies. There are two deadlines; noon tomorrow for the government response, noon Saturday for the release of the prisoners. Fail to meet either deadline and Koo Davis dies. There will be no more negotiation. A second television farce like the first will result in Koo Davis' immediate death. As a demonstration that our patience is exhausted, and that the comedy is finished, we are enclosing one of Koo Davis' ears."

"Good God, Peter!" Larry cried.

Clapping his hand over the microphone, Peter said to Ginger, "Did that stupid exclamation get on the tape?"

"If it is, I can erase it." Ginger was noncommittal. "You really mean to do this, don't you?"

"Yes."

"Even though you know none of those people on television were forced."

"The laughing has to stop," Peter said.

"So you do intend to kill Davis."

"To strengthen our credibility in the future."

"Credibility." Ginger shrugged slightly, then said, "And the ear?"

"*Peter* won't do that," Larry abruptly said, angry and scornful. It wasn't like Larry to show scorn and he was awkward at it, the result looking more like petulance. Turning to Peter, he said, "You'd have Mark do it, go cut the man's ear off, but Mark isn't here, he's run away. Can you do it yourself?"

"I intend to." Getting to his feet, Peter said, "You two come along, to hold him down."

# 26

Koo opens his eyes from confused dreams of family and flight, to find Joyce looming over him, staring down at his face with great intensity. Orienting himself, seeing the mirrored ceiling with himself and Joyce reflected in it like a bad genre painting, Koo clears his husky throat and says, "The soup lady."

She blinks, as though she'd been lost in thought, then turns to look over her shoulder at the door. "We don't have much time," she says.

"We don't?"

"I'm getting you out of here."

Koo sits up, astounded. "Careful now," he says. "*I'm* the one tells the jokes."

"It isn't a joke. I'm a…a double agent."

*A crazy.* Koo pastes a happy smile on his face. "That's terrific," he says, in the style of the ultimate naïf. "A double agent. Afterwards, you'll be able to collect unemployment insurance twice a week."

"They signaled me during that television show."

"Is that right? Fancy that."

"I can see you don't believe me, but it's true. Didn't you notice the one thing he said that wasn't *about* anything? St. Clair; he said, 'Two-thirteen Van Dyke.' Remember that?"

As a matter of fact, Koo does; it had been an unexpected anomaly in the middle of the program. But the program itself had been such a catalogue of horrors that Koo—and probably everybody else watching it—had promptly forgotten that quick enigma. "What is it, your code name?"

"A phone number." There's something about the very intensity of her manner that forces him to believe her. "The two-thirteen is the area code."

"Los Angeles," Koo says, in some surprise. "This very metropolis, in fact."

"I worked for them for a few years, and that's always the way they got in touch with me. An area code, and a phone number done as a name. Van Dyke sometimes, and sometimes Lydgate. If I hear one of those names, and the area code, I know how to make contact."

"You dial the seven letters. Van Dyke."

"That's right." Looking uncertain for just a second, maybe even oddly saddened, she says, "It's been years since they signaled me. A long long time."

"Probably, they were busy."

"I called them," Joyce says, and double agent or not there's something wild-eyed about her, something unhinged. "And they said I should get you out of here now."

"I agree with them."

"But we must be very quiet."

"I agree with *you*."

Holding a finger to her lips, she moves away across the room, opening the mirrored door, leaning out, then gesturing Koo to follow her, which he does.

This is his first view of the rest of the house, and it's disappointingly ordinary after that bedroom. There's also the sound of surf, faintly, from a distance; is that why he dreamed about drowning in the ocean?

The house is dim and quiet, but doesn't have the echoing quality of a place without people. Koo is very aware of the unseen presences under this roof, unseen and hostile, as he creeps down the carpeted stairs behind Joyce. He's scared, but at the same time this is exhilarating; finally he's *doing* something.

At the foot of the stairs Joyce pats the air at him—*wait*—then leaves briefly to reconnoiter. Koo is beginning very strongly to feel his vulnerability when at last she returns, waving him to come on.

There's a stone-walled living room through a broad doorway. Koo glances at it, and stops dead when he sees there's someone in there! Liz, the tough one, is seated in an Eames chair, legs curled under her, either brooding or asleep. High again? Koo is afraid to move; won't movement attract her attention?

To his left, Joyce is urgently motioning to him: Come on, come on. He hesitates, then somewhere to the right a door opens and there are voices. In a sudden rush he crosses the open space to the shadowed areaway where Joyce is waiting.

The voices approach. Koo listens apprehensively for Mark, but the first identifiable voice belongs to Larry, saying, "How can you justify this, Peter?"

Peter's voice says, "The Movement can't be mocked. We can't permit it."

They go past the areaway as a third voice, one Koo hasn't heard before, says, "It'll be interesting to see just how far you'll go in practice, as opposed to theory." This voice is nasty, angry, sarcastic.

"As far as necessary," Peter says. They're just the other side of this wall now, apparently in the kitchen; Koo hears drawers being opened and closed. Peter says, "There was a knife here, a long carving knife. Where the hell is it?"

A long carving knife? Koo presses his back against the wall, trying to be one more shadow among the shadows. What are they up to *now*?

The nasty voice says, "Here's a cleaver. Just the thing, I should think."

"All right, give it to me." And one more drawer slams, then the three men march out of the room and start up the stairs.

Joyce grabs Koo's arm, tugs at him. Yes, yes. Those three are going up to where they think Koo is, and they're carrying a cleaver; feet trembling in haste, Koo follows Joyce down another flight of stairs between living room and kitchen, and through a door into a sudden rush of cool moist air. Joyce closes the door, hurriedly but silently, and whispers, "Come on! We have to hurry!"

"Check."

No outcry yet from above. They run out from under the cantilevered deck into thick sand, hard to move through. The ocean is out there, under a half moon in a clear black sky. Where is this place? No way to tell; it could be any one of a hundred spots between Newport Beach and Oxnard. Koo looks back, trying to guess where they are from the look of the houses, but Joyce pulls at his arm, crying over the surf. "Come *on*! Hurry!"

"Yes. Right." But she's urging him directly toward the ocean, not along the beach. "Where—" The exertion of running through the sand is rapidly using up his strength. "Where—"

"They have a boat. We're supposed to meet the boat. Hurry!"

The hard sand of high tide line; Koo moves more quickly, Joyce dropping back. A boat? Koo trots forward, gasping, arms pumping, staring out at the black sea with its eerie line of phosphorescence forming and rolling and dying way out there in the cold dark. A boat? Seeing nothing, Koo turns his head to gasp another question, and behind him, rushing at him ahead of Joyce's savage straining face, is dull moonlight striking yellow from the blade of a long knife. A knife held in her raised fist.

"Jesus!" Koo backpedals, turning, tripping over his own feet, trying to run backward away from the slashing knife, throwing his arms up to fend it off, and the blade slices across his forearm, grating on bone, slitting the flesh like cutting through raw veal. There isn't pain, not at first, but there's the horrible *knowledge*; his flesh has been cut. Koo screams, falls backwards, rolls and rolls, blood spraying from his arm in red showers, and the panting mad girl lunges after him on all fours, stabbing downward, scraping the dull side of the blade along his ribcage, jabbing the knife into the sand, pulling it out with both hands, holding it high in both hands, following him on her knees.

Koo is mindless with terror, gibbering, *"Don't don't don't don't* NO JEE-SUS!"

"You're tearing us apart," he hears her mutter, through the crash of surf. "Tearing us apart." And she struggles to her feet, the knife huge and straight and unbending in her hand.

Koo tries to rise, falls back, throws his arms up again and she slashes twice, back and forth. Great triangular strips of flesh hang from his arms, and even in his agony the gag interpretation rises in his shocked mind: *She's filleting me.* "Let me go! Let me go! I won't tell!"

She stops, the red-clouded knife hovering as she sways over him. "Peter would hate me." Her eyes are also clouded, voice swollen as though her mouth and throat are already clogged with his blood. "We can survive if you're dead." And she drops on him, slashing down again, as Koo screams, the loudest harshest most final scream in the world—and all at once Joyce flings herself back from him, as though flying.

No; she doesn't fling herself, she is thrown. A black figure has come out of the ocean, moving with the speed of dark, a blur of vicious motion; it swarms over Joyce, compelling, irrevocable. Something dull and hard is in its upraised fist, thudding down, thudding again, over and over, the sound first dry and then wet.

Koo struggles to get up, but can barely lift his head. His blood-streaming shredded arms have no strength. "Oh," he whispers, in what was meant to be a cry for help. "Oh, God."

People now are running this way from the house. There's no escape, no safety anywhere. The figure hulking over what had been Joyce turns to him, throwing away the dark sea-rock, dropping to his knees beside Koo, murmuring, "Easy. Easy."

Koo can barely recognize Mark in this beatific nurse, bending over him, carefully touching his arms. "Don't," he begs.

"Lucky fat man," Mark says, almost tenderly. "We'll fix you at the house."

"Mark," Koo whispers. "You're all wet."

It's true. From head to foot Mark is wet, as drenched with water as Koo is drenched with his own blood. Mark's eyes gleam like that far-off phosphorescence. "I've saved your life," he says, quick and low and triumphant. "It's mine. We start fresh."

The other people are pounding across the beach, are nearly here. "Mark," Koo whispers. "Help me."

"You're mine again," Mark tells him, slipping his arms under Koo's body, preparing to lift him.

"Help me. You're the only one," Koo whispers, and as Mark lifts him he faints.

## 27

The trouble outside roused Liz at last. She rose from the Eames chair, looking around in a dazed way like someone coming out of hypnosis, and became aware of blurred movement out on the beach, fitful in the dim moonlight, capering silhouettes against the far-off lines of wave-phosphorescence. Sliding open one of the glass doors, she stepped out onto the cantilevered deck to see the obscure cluster of figures split in two; while a part remained behind, involved with something flat on the beach, another part moved this way, weaving and tottering through the sand. Leaning on the rail, peering hard into the darkness, Liz saw that the thing approaching was a person, carrying another person. They approached, they entered the trapezoid of yellow lightspill from the house, and it was Mark, struggling through the soft sand. And in his arms; was that *Davis*?

They disappeared beneath her, under the deck, and she went back inside, turning the corner from the living room to the central hallway in time to see Mark struggle up the stairs from the beach door. That *was* Davis in his arms, unconscious or dead, and both men drenched with water and blood; survivors of some water cult's sacrificial rite. Daubs and spatters of blood painted Mark's face, like a marauding Iroquois. Davis was smeared all over with blood, some dripping and spraying as Mark jolted up the stairs. Liz saw the knife-hilt angling from Davis' side just as Mark reached the first floor; she stared at it, not understanding anything she saw, and on the way by Mark said, "Bandages. Tape. *Anything*."

"Yes." But she'd been so self-involved till now that she'd barely registered her surroundings, and couldn't remember in this strange house where the bathrooms were. She hesitated, looking back toward the living room, then ahead toward the kitchen.

Meantime, Mark continued on up the stairs toward the second floor, hurrying and yet trying not to shake Davis more than absolutely necessary. The second floor; that's where the bathroom would be. Liz followed, while blood drops polka-dotted the gray staircase carpet.

At the head of the stairs Mark turned left, through the open doorway into the room where they'd been keeping Davis, while Liz half-instinctively went right, fumbling for a light-switch on the wall, clicking into existence a large bland bedroom with an open mirrored door off to the right. Through that she found the bathroom, a long elaborate double-sinked room with masses of storage space, most of it empty. But there were gauze bandages, there was adhesive tape, there were first-aid powders and ointments; she grabbed up a double armful and hurried to the other room, where Mark had laid Davis out on the bed, and now she saw his forearms, which didn't look human anymore. "Jesus God," she said, more awed than repelled.

Mark, his face grimly expressionless, slapped the supplies out of her arms onto the bed. "Cloth," he said. "Clean cloth."

"Yes." Back to the bathroom she went, this time gathering up white towels and a handful of small white facecloths. In the bedroom again she found Mark tenderly folding down the flaps of flesh on the lacerated arms, sprinkling antiseptic powder on them, wrapping gauze to keep them in place. Dropping the cloth on the bed Liz said, "What happened?"

He didn't seem to hear her. "Scissors," he said.

Scissors. A third trip to the bathroom, and she brought back other things as well, aspirin and witch hazel, not knowing what

Mark might need. "Strips of tape," he said, as she walked into the room, not looking up from what he was doing. One forearm was now completely wrapped in gauze, like a mummy, like a Red Cross volunteer; he was working on the second.

She cut strips of tape, but as he prepared to tape the gauze on the first arm they both saw the blood already seeping through. A strange sound came from Mark's throat then, a kind of animal noise, half bark and half whine. And he stopped, he seemed directionless all at once, as though someone had pushed a button that disconnected him from his motivations. In the humming silence he hesitated, rocking slightly, looking down at the spreading stains of blood.

Liz said, "More gauze," to prompt him into movement, but he shook his head: "Isn't any more. Used it up."

She looked around at the jumble of things on the round purple bed. "These," she said, holding up the small facecloths.

"Yes." The solution didn't make him pleased, or excited, it merely reactivated him. He took facecloths, folded them around the bleeding arms, wound lengths of adhesive tape to hold them in place. Watching, Liz said, "Not too tight. The circulation."

He ignored that. He ignored everything but what was already in his head. Finishing the arms, he went to work on the wound in Davis' side. He said, "Blankets. We have to keep him warm."

The mirrored walls were in fact doors; she searched, and behind one mirror was a linen closet with sheets and blankets, all in tones of red and purple and orange. She helped Mark move Davis closer to the middle of the bed and then they put blankets over him, so many that by the time Mark was satisfied it looked like a great fat man lying there on the round bed; Old King Cole, perhaps, exhausted from his revels. But a very pale reveler, with very shallow breaths.

Liz and Mark were on opposite sides of the bed, from

spreading the blankets. They both stood a moment, gazing at the unconscious man, and Liz was about to ask again what had happened when Mark, his manner cold and dismissing, said, "That's all."

She looked at him, momentarily surprised, but then realized Mark had been essentially alone through all this. He had needed her temporarily, as he had needed the scissors or the facecloths, but *he* was the only one who actually existed in this room. He and Koo Davis. What is there between them? she wondered, and was surprised that the question had never occurred to her before. There *was* something between them, some extra element none of the others knew about. It was that unsuspected weight which had thrown them all off-balance from the very beginning, creating an environment that drove the others crazy without ever knowing why. Liz said, "Did *you* cut him?"

He was surprised at the question, but in a remote way. Shrugging, he said, "Of course not."

"You came *out* of the ocean. To help him?"

Mark looked at her with his closed secret face. "Go away," he said.

She shook her head. "It's too late anyway," she said, glanced with fading interest once more at Koo Davis, and turned away.

Downstairs, she found Peter and Ginger snarling together in the studio with all the electronic equipment. She had looked for them to find out the story, but the instant she walked in Ginger turned to her, half-whispering, "Did he see me? *You* were up there; did he see me?"

It hadn't taken Ginger long to win Liz's contempt. "No one can see you," she said.

Peter said, "What's going on up there?"

"Mark bandaged him. What happened before?"

"Joyce," Peter said. "She went crazy." Peter himself looked crazier than usual, his eyes staring, his cheeks gaunt. His jaw kept making chewing motions, as though he were gnawing on a rubber band.

Liz said, "Joyce? What did *Joyce* do?"

"She let him go. Davis." Peter gestured wildly, to indicate that he understood nothing of motivation in all this. "Don't ask me why. She let him out of the house and took him down to the beach and tried to kill him."

"With a knife," Ginger said, smirking in Peter's direction. "The very knife we'd been looking for ourselves, to do our *own* slicing."

"Mark stopped her," Peter said. "He—he killed her. Larry's out there now, he's burying her in the sand."

Liz looked from face to face. "So it's all over," she said.

Peter's jaw clenched, his eyes glared. "It is not," he said. "It isn't over till *I* say it's over. *My* way."

"Whatever you want," Liz said, not caring, and left the room, crossing the living room to go out onto the deck. The moon was lower now, the night darker. She could barely make out the hunched figure way out there across the sand.

Liz was back in the Eames chair when Larry came in. She was thinking about death, and didn't hear him when he first spoke to her. Then he spoke again, and called her name, and she frowned at him in irritation, becoming doubly irritated when she saw he'd been crying. She said, "What is it?"

Larry gestured toward the stairs. "What are they arguing about?"

Now she became aware of it; intense voices, not extremely loud but nevertheless vibrating with rage. Mark and Peter, upstairs. "What does it matter?" she said.

Ginger was also in the room, standing over by the window,

and now he turned with his nasty smile, saying, "The Koo Davis ear."

Liz frowned, more irritable than interested. "His ear? What about it?"

Ginger said, "Peter wants it, to send to the FBI, and Mark won't let him have it."

At moments, it seemed to Liz she must still be tripping, that Ginger for instance could have no external reality at all but must be merely a floating atom inside her own brain. At other moments, it seemed her trip had merely served to remind her how unbelievable the real world is; it was Ginger and Peter and Mark who existed, while the white rats in the swimming pool had been imaginary.

Larry was blustering, saying, "Peter's gone mad! What does he hope to—? I'm going up there!"

"Don't," Liz told him.

He undoubtedly didn't really want to; that Larry was afraid of both Mark and Peter had been common knowledge for years. With a show of barely checked determination, he said, "Why shouldn't I?"

"Mark won't want you on his side."

Ginger cackled, while Larry actually blushed. Liz deliberately twisted the knife: "And you wouldn't do any good. Let them work it out for themselves."

Larry dropped onto the sofa, fretfully rubbing his hands together. "I don't know what to do, this is all getting so—" His expression turned tragic, he looked over at Liz and said, "Just tonight, I finally told Joyce I loved her."

"Maybe that's what drove her crazy."

Ginger cackled again. Liz swiveled the Eames chair around to face him, but said nothing. She watched Ginger wordlessly till he stopped and looked away, with an angry shrug, saying, "It's *my* house." Then he said, "And I believe I'll drink in it," and walked briskly away, pretending Liz hadn't driven him from the room.

The angry voices continued upstairs; Peter was doing most of the talking, but Mark's short replies had not weakened. Larry said, nervously, "I wonder who'll win."

"Win?" Liz looked at him with a surprise she didn't feel.

# 28

There are many different kinds of bribe in this world. Money, actual cash, is the bluntest and often the least effective bribe of all, since each of the participants finishes with a sense of contempt for the other. At the other extreme, mutual back-scratching is the noblest and cleanest form of bribery, because the participants—if all goes well—finish by being grateful to one another.

One of the policewomen manning the phones on the Koo Davis case was named Betty Austin, and her secret vice was songwriting; Dory Previn, with a touch of Bessie Smith. With no suggestion of return, Lynsey Rayne had offered to see to it that Marty Rubelman, musical director of Koo's TV specials, was shown some of Policewoman Austin's material. With no suggestion of return, Policewoman Austin had offered to let Lynsey know the instant there were any new development in the kidnapping case. Each was made happy by the offer of the other.

Phone. Telephone. Clanging again and again. Lynsey opened her eyes in the dark bedroom of her small house in Westwood, and for the longest time she couldn't understand what that noise was or why it was going on for so long. There was no sleep-over man in her life right now—hadn't been for nearly a year—so the phone would continue until either she answered it or the caller gave up; but she'd had so little sleep the last two nights that she just couldn't seem to break through this grogginess. Damn! *Damn!*

Tossing her head, trying to clear it, she saw the illuminated numerals on the digital clock-radio, but without her glasses couldn't read the numbers. The desire to know what time it was drove her up that extra little bit toward consciousness so that suddenly, on about the tenth ring, she cried out loud, "The phone!" and lunged to answer it.

The caller, a woman, spoke quietly, as though afraid of being overheard: "You ought to come over now."

"What? What?"

"*You* know who this is."

And then Lynsey did; it was Policewoman Austin. "What's happened?"

"Just come over." Click.

"Oh, my God," Lynsey said. In the darkness she couldn't hang up the phone, find her glasses, find the light-switch, read the clock—"Oh, my God, oh my God." Glasses. Clock reading 4:07. "Oh, my God."

The receptionist in the outer office at ten minutes to five in the morning was male and uniformed and initially unresponsive. "Something's happened," Lynsey insisted, "and I want to know what it is. Who's here? Inspector Cayzer? Is the FBI man here, Mr. Wiskiel?"

"Ma'am, if there's anything new, I'm sure they'll get in touch with—"

"Go in and tell them I'm here. Just *tell* them."

He didn't want to, but finally he shrugged and said, "I'll see if there's anybody here."

There *was* somebody here; Lynsey heard voices when the policeman opened the inner office door. He looked back at her, grudgingly, and closed the door behind himself.

What was happening? What was going on? It wasn't that Koo had been rescued; there'd be no secrecy about *that*. Had they found him dead? Terribly injured? Did they know where the kidnappers were keeping him? What was going *on*?

The policeman returned, followed by Mike Wiskiel, looking irritated and upset. The irritation was because of her presence, but why was he upset? He seemed troubled, disturbed, unhappy. Afraid of what that might mean, needing to know the worst right now, she stepped forward before he had a chance to speak, saying, "What's happened? Something bad, I can see it in your face."

He would try, of course, to deflect the conversation: "Ms. Rayne, how did you know to come here?"

"Mr. Wiskiel, *please*. What's happened?"

He was closed away from her. "Davis isn't dead, if that's what you're worried about," he said, as though that crumb would satisfy her. "Believe me, I'd tell you."

"There's *some*thing," she insisted. "If I were family, would you tell me?"

His laugh was surprisingly harsh: "You mean you'll drag Mrs. Davis down here to ask the questions? You're more family than she is."

Lynsey was surprised that Wiskiel had had the wit to make that assessment, but she wouldn't be distracted. "Then tell me," she said.

He shook his head. "Ms. Rayne, you're not accomplishing anything by coming here this way. When there's something constructive, I'll let you know."

"It has to be very bad," she said. "All right, he isn't dead, I accept that, but it has to be very bad for you to fight me like this."

He hesitated, indecision finally appearing in his eyes. Was he acting from the old macho idea that grimness should be kept as much as possible away from the sight of females? He was certainly capable of such an attitude. Should she reassure him, promise him she could deal with whatever he was keeping from her? No; it was best to let him work it through for himself. Her part would be to make it absolutely clear she wasn't going away.

And at last he sighed and shook his head and said, "Okay. I was sent out here to *not* tell you, but you're right, if you were family I'd have no choice."

But at that point he ran out of words and stopped. She looked at him, waiting, and saw that he was helpless, trying in vain to find the right combination of words. After half a minute of silence, while the fear built in her, she gave him a sad smile and said, "There's no soft way, is there? So just say it, whatever it is."

"They cut off his ear."

She stared at him, at first failing to understand the meaning of those words, and then she heard herself laugh, as though it was a joke: "They didn't!"

"I'm sorry. They want to show the world how tough they are."

"They— His *ear*?" It was still meaningless, incomprehensible. "That's— That's like savages, it's primitive man, it's…"

"Once people lose the social thread," he said, obviously telling her something he deeply believed, "they're capable of anything."

"But his—" Floundering toward something recognizable, she said, "Is there another message?"

"Not his voice. A new voice."

"I want to hear it."

"Ms. Rayne, I don't—"

"And I want to see the ear."

She wasn't going to be stopped, and he must have seen that. With another sigh, he shrugged and said, "Come along, then."

In the workroom were three men: Jock Cayzer, the tape technician, and Maurice St. Clair, the FBI Deputy Director from Washington, whom Lynsey hadn't yet met but had seen on that television program. As Lynsey and Mike Wiskiel walked in, the technician was saying, "—interesting about this tape." But then he stopped, as the three men became aware of Lynsey's presence.

St. Clair, big and meaty and red-faced, lunged up from the folding chair he'd been sitting on, shouting, "For Christ's sake! Mike, Mike—"

"It's all right, Murray," Wiskiel said.

She had already seen the box. That had to be it, sitting alone on a worktable, a small black box bearing the stylized white letters "i magnin." As Wiskiel went through the stupid formalities of introducing Lynsey to St. Clair, she crossed directly to the box, opened the lid, and looked inside.

How awful. How pitiable. It was small, wrinkled, pale, fleshy, stained with rust-colored dry blood, and utterly pathetic. Lynsey pressed her palms onto the table to both sides of the small box, clenched her jaw, stood unblinking, and gazed into the box.

The men had become silent, and it was Jock Cayzer who came over to stand beside her, saying nothing, also looking into the box. Quietly, Lynsey said, "It's so small."

"Well, it's off a living man," he said, "so it would have bled some; that'd shrink it." His manner was calm, sympathetic but unemotional, reducing this horrible thing to something that could be looked at, discussed, absorbed into one's mind and memory.

She needed that. She needed something to make this *ordinary*, so she could go on from it. "I've never seen a thing like this before," she said.

"Oh, I have." And still he was calm, judicious, merely reporting a fact.

"Tell me about it."

She felt him glance at her, study her profile, make a decision about her. Then he said, "Some of the boys back from Nam, they brought Cong ears with them. Anyway, they *said* they were Cong ears, and they were sure ears. And what they mostly looked like was dried peaches."

"This one is fresher."

"Yes," he said, and reached out as though casually to close the lid on the box.

She looked at him, seeing a man who was truly strong without making a point of it. "Thank you," she said.

"My pleasure, Ms. Rayne."

"May I hear the tape?"

"Of course."

The technician already had it cued up, and this new harsh voice snarled from the loudspeakers with its self-serving self-righteousness. Lynsey listened unmoving—she was deadened, at least for now, free from high emotional reactions—and at the end she said, quietly, "They are just beasts, aren't they?"

Cayzer said, "The television broadcast must have been a shock to them."

Obviously uncomfortable, St. Clair said, "Miss Rayne, there just wasn't any way to soften that blow. I mean, telling these bastards what answers we got from their former friends. We simply had to tell them the truth."

"I realize that." Then she sighed, and shook her head, and said, "What happens now?"

"We'll send this tape to Washington," St. Clair told her, "for the next response."

"But there *is* no next response, is there?"

St. Clair frowned unhappily at her—the third man in five minutes to wonder if she could survive the truth—and then he said, "Myself, Miss Rayne, I can't think of any."

"What they ask is impossible."

Beneath his restraint St. Clair was very angry. "And they *know* it," he said. "In the first place, we *can't* just talk half a dozen people out of jail against their will and deport them out of the country. Maybe in Russia you can do that, but not here. There's such a thing as due process, and if we tried any such stunt there wouldn't be a lawyer in the nation out of work for the next two years. And in the second place, even if we could do such a thing we wouldn't, because what this son of a bitch Rock really wants is *other* buddies of his in Algeria to take revenge on those people for standing him up."

"Showing him up," Wiskiel said.

"Both."

"So this is just propaganda," Lynsey said. "They're going to kill Koo and they'll try to put the blame on the government."

Wiskiel said, "So we've got to find them before they do it."

Lynsey shook her head. "If the deadline isn't real, if they're going to kill him anyway, why would they wait?"

"One last propaganda blitz," St. Clair suggested. "Another tape, or maybe even a phone call to a television station, something like that, just at the deadline. Davis will be useful to them right up until twelve noon."

"But how are you going to find them? They left that house in Woodland Hills, and this time there's no message from Koo."

Wiskiel said, "We have one lead. There was something funny about the Woodland Hills house being so available, and we're trying to find the owner."

"*Trying* to find him?"

"He's a rock musician named Ginger Merville," Wiskiel said, "and he's supposed to be in Paris on tour, but he and his tour manager both checked out of their hotel two days ago. The manager flew to Tokyo, where Merville is supposed to perform this weekend, but Merville himself flew to New York. So far, we haven't been able to find out where he went after that."

"Ginger Merville." Lynsey knew the name, knew something of the man's career. She said, "Did you check with his agent?"

"One of my men saw him this afternoon. Or yesterday afternoon, I guess, by now. He didn't know where Merville was."

"Nonsense," Lynsey said.

Wiskiel looked surprised. "Beg pardon?"

"The agent knows where Merville is," Lynsey said. "People hide from their wives, their creditors, their employers and the police, but they don't hide from their agents."

"Are you suggesting the *agent* is part of it?"

"No, I'm not." Lynsey paused, choosing her words carefully. She didn't particularly want to antagonize Wiskiel and the others, but she wanted them to understand. "Back in the sixties," she said, "when law enforcement was being used against the wrong people, many people lost the habit of cooperating with the authorities. A rock musician's agent would undoubtedly have sour memories of the FBI."

Wiskiel obviously couldn't believe it. "To the extent," he said, "that a legitimate theatrical agent would refuse to help us save Koo Davis? We *told* him what we wanted Merville for."

"He didn't believe you," Lynsey said. "He assumed you were lying, which is something else lawmen did a lot in the sixties." Maurice St. Clair was looking thunderous, she saw, while Jock Cayzer was almost but not quite grinning. Smiling thinly, she said, "It's called chickens coming home to roost. You people treated the entire American public as an enemy population. You were the garrison force, foreign conquerors. And now you want cooperation."

"But that's all *over* now," Wiskiel said. (St. Clair nodded emphatically.) "Whatever mistakes people made, excesses that maybe happened, they're all over now."

"Maybe," Lynsey said. "Give me the agent's name, I'll see him first thing in the morning."

Wiskiel was very angry about this, but there wasn't much he could do. He glanced at St. Clair, who was also red-faced and angry, and who nodded curtly. "All right," Wiskiel said. "His name is Hunningdale."

"Chuck Hunningdale. I know him slightly."

"Fine." Apparently needing a distraction, Wiskiel turned away, saying to the technician. "When we came in you were saying something about the tape."

"Yes, sir. It's not like the other two."

"In what way?"

"Well, it's much better quality. Those other two, you could buy them in Woolworth's. Not this one."

"What's so special about it?"

"Well, it's high bias," the technician explained. "The brand is TDK, which is very good, and it's rated SA, that's the highest quality there is. This is an expensive piece of tape."

They were all interested now. St. Clair said, "Who could use that sort of thing?"

"Musicians. Record industry people. People who have professional recording and playback equipment in their own homes."

Lynsey said, "Ginger Merville."

But Wiskiel shook his head. "No, there wasn't anything like that in Merville's house."

The technician said, "Excuse me." When he had their attention he said, "I heard something else this time. In the tape. I'd like to try an experiment; all right?"

"Try anything you want," St. Clair told him.

"Thank you, sir. What I've done, I've damped the bass and boosted the treble. You see, I'm not interested in the voice this time, but the background. I'll also have to play it louder. Listen behind the voice." And he started the tape.

The voice sounded even more hysterical this way, very loud and with its low tones gone; reminiscent in a strange way of old recordings of Hitler making speeches. Lynsey tried to hear past this haranguing repulsive voice, tried to hear whatever it was the technician had found in the background…

…and there it was. Faint, irregular, slowly paced, a kind of rushing hiss, rising and falling, irregular but continuous. Lynsey frowned, listening, trying to figure out what it was. It sounded familiar, somehow: hhhhiiiiIISSSsssssshhhhhhhhhhiiiiiiiiiIIIIII IISSSSSSSSSHHHHHHhhhhhhhiiiisssssSSSSSS—

"The ocean," Jock Cayzer said.

The technician snapped his fingers. "I *knew* I knew it."

"By God," Wiskiel said, "you're right. That's what it is. Waves, on a beach."

The technician switched off the tape, and they all looked at one another. Cayzer said, "A beach house somewhere."

"Filled with professional recording equipment. But somebody didn't know how to use it. They left a door open." Wiskiel frowned, saying, "Does that narrow it enough? Who do we go through? Equipment suppliers. Jock, can we set that up with your people? First thing in the morning, we canvass every wholesale and retail outlet of high-quality recording equipment in the Greater Los Angeles area."

"And repairmen," the technician suggested.

"Right. We want the address of every customer with a beach house. Somebody must have installed that equipment, and somebody services it."

St. Clair said, "Mike, it's needle-in-the-haystack time."

Cayzer said, "I could maybe put forty people on it, in the morning."

While the others talked, Lynsey drifted over to the worktable again, unable to keep away from the small box and its grim contents, and now as she looked down into the box, holding the lid open with one hand, she suddenly laughed aloud, saying, "Why—! It's a joke!"

Turning to smile broadly at the men, she saw them all staring at her. Feeling a kind of hysterical relief, she said, "It isn't Koo."

Wiskiel came forward, expression troubled, saying, "Ms.

Rayne. I'm sorry, but no. There's no way you can recognize an ear."

"Oh, yes, there is." She could hardly keep from peals of laughter. "You look at that ear," she said. "Look at the lobe. You can take my word for it, Mr. Wiskiel, Koo Davis does *not* have pierced ears!"

## 29

Koo's arms hurt. They don't sting or burn, the way you'd expect from a cut, they *hurt*, with a heavy mean aching pain, as though he'd given himself a very bad bruise. Under the covers he can feel the bandages swathing him from wrist to elbow, and inside the bandages is the throbbing pain, as unrelenting as a cramp. And his side, right above his hip, where the knife went in, feels like the blade is still in there, cutting him apart.

Koo has been awake for some time, but he doesn't want to admit it, not with Mark sitting right there on the edge of the bed. Who knows what Mark might do next? The goddamn boy can't seem to make up his mind whether he wants Koo alive or dead, and Koo is in no hurry to get the latest bulletin. So he's lying here under this mound of blankets, peeking at Mark from time to time through slitted eyes, and pretending to be asleep. While Mark just sits there, a bit to the right of Koo's feet, hunched forward, brooding, gazing away at nothing in particular.

Koo remembers everything, and wishes he didn't. Joyce, the only one he'd ever thought normal enough to maybe help him, had turned out to be the craziest of them all. The memory of that knife blade flashing in the moonlight is terrifyingly clear in his brain, and his arms hurt, his whole body *hurts*. Joyce was determined to kill him, and he's been lying here trying to figure out why, and now he believes he's worked out at last what she had in her excuse for a mind. She'd felt the kidnapping was causing too much stress for her pals and she wanted it to end— particularly after that show on television—but the others wouldn't agree to just quit. If she'd released Koo on her own hook they would have been sore at her, so she planned to get Koo out of the house and down to the water's edge, kill him there and let the waves carry the body out to sea. Then, so far as her friends would ever know, Koo had escaped on his own and disappeared.

Jesus H. Christ, but these arms hurt! By the time I get out of this, Koo tells himself, I won't have any resale value left at *all*.

"We can talk now."

Koo is so startled by the quiet sudden sound of Mark's voice that his eyes automatically pop open; and then it's too late to go on faking sleep because Mark has turned half around and is looking at him.

Well, it was too late anyway; Mark obviously has known for some time that Koo was conscious. *Needing* to know what Mark is like at this moment, Koo apprehensively studies that face and sees it calm, almost blank. The rage that usually suffuses and informs those features is gone, at least for now, leaving emptiness in its wake; without his passion, Mark seems as personless as a department store mannequin. And when he speaks his voice is soft, rather light in timbre, barely recognizable when not choked with fury. He says, "My mother's name was Ruth Timmons."

The name means nothing. Koo frowns, gazing at Mark, trying to remember a Ruth Timmons. A one-night stand somewhere? Thirty or more years ago?

Still in the same dispassionate manner, Mark says, "You knew her as Honeydew Leontine."

"Honeydew!" Surprise is almost immediately succeeded by pleasure, at the simple reminder of Honeydew Leontine. She was the first, the very first blonde on the very first USO tour; the first and in many ways the best. For six years she'd traveled with Koo—not always, not every trip, there had been other blondes on other tours along the way—and when she'd quit show business he'd been briefly saddened, because he already

knew that most of the blondes were cold and tough and barely
worth getting a hard-on over, while Honeydew Leontine had
been warm and sweet and *natural*. Not the brightest girl in the
world, but good-hearted. A friend as much as a fuck. But then
she'd quit and...

She quit because she was pregnant; that's right. Koo had an
office on the MGM lot then, and he came in one afternoon
to find a message from Honeydew, whom he'd last seen two
months earlier on their return from a tour to Alaska and the
Aleutians; '47 or '48, that was, between wars. He almost never
saw Honeydew socially, had virtually no contact with her other
than the tours, so he was surprised to get her call, and not at all
happy when he phoned back and the first words out of her
mouth were, "I think I'm in trouble."

Koo's response was immediate: "Let's have dinner. How
many you eating for?"

"I think, two."

"That's what I figured."

He took her to Musso & Frank, *because* it was a prominent
place, full of show business people. If he'd taken her to some
out-of-the-way joint (as had been his first impulse) she'd start
feeling sorry for herself, and maybe she'd take it out on Koo.
Besides, he knew what he wanted her to do, and Musso & Frank
was the proper setting for the discussion. "Your career," he
kept saying, and the word *abortion* was never actually spoken
aloud. She cried a little into her veal parmigiana, not enough to
be noticed by anybody but the waiter, whose job it was to mind
his own business, but except for the tears and a general aura of
sadness and one wistful comment—"Gee, it seems too bad"—
she didn't argue back or disagree very forcefully at all. (Now he
realizes he should have mistrusted such easy compliance; at the
time, he was simply relieved she wasn't going to cause a lot of
trouble.) At the end of the meal he said, "There's a doctor I can

call," but she shook her head: "I'll take care of it, Koo, don't worry about that. It's just the—finances. I'm sorry, I'll need a little help with that."

"Sure," he said, and drove her home, and sent her into her house with a chaste kiss; then the next day he mailed her a check for five hundred dollars and a note containing a crass joke: "Hope everything comes out all right." And that was the last he ever saw or heard of Honeydew Leontine. The next time it occurred to him to get in touch with her, a couple years later when he was putting together his first Korean tour, her agent said Honeydew had quit the business, so he got somebody else. And that was that.

"You're smiling," Mark says. "I didn't expect you to smile, I don't know what it means."

"Honeydew," Koo explains. "I liked her." He very nearly said *I loved her*, which is ridiculous. Also, he doesn't know how far he can trust this new calmness of Mark's, and he suspects the phrase *I loved her* might be just the thing to trigger Dr. Jekyll's next transformation. Feeling nervous, a bit confused, he scrabbles in his memory for a fact about Honeydew, and comes out with the first thing he finds: "The stones," he says. "She had that incredible collection of stones, one from every beach she ever walked on. Carried them all around in little cloth bags. Carried them everywhere."

"That's right," Mark says, and now one corner of his mouth lifts in a not-pleasant smile. Is this Mr. Hyde returning? "I threw them away," he says.

Koo frowns at him, not sure he understands. "The stones?"

"When I was fifteen." Mark shrugs, almost as though embarrassed. "It was very hard to make her cry."

"She cried the last time I saw her."

"Did she? Too bad I wasn't there."

"You were there."

"Oh. Yeah, I see what you mean." The shrug again, of just one shoulder; Mark *is* embarrassed. "She didn't cry when I threw the stones away. Tough old bitch."

"Wait a minute. You were *trying* to make her cry?"

"I've had two goals," Mark says, "since the day I was born. One to make her cry, and the other to make you dead."

"Well, you do work at them."

"I'd see you in the movies, I'd see you on television. *That's my father.* I never said that to anybody, but I'd sit and stare at you and try to kill you with my mind. But you were too far up, and I was too far down."

Dangerous territory; Koo eases them away from it, saying, "But what did you have against your mother?"

"Me." The coldness of his memories is seeping into Mark's face; it's like watching a chill breeze ruffle icy water. "I ruined her life, to hear her tell it. So I figured I might as well make it a *good* job."

"Ruined her life?"

" 'You ruined my life! I was a *star!*' " Mark's falsetto imitation of a woman's voice contains all the fury of his normal self. " 'I didn't *have* to have you, you little brat! Your father gave me *five hundred dollars* to get *rid* of you, and I swear I *wish I'd done it!*' "

"She wasn't like that," Koo says. He's actually shocked to hear Honeydew spoken of this way. "She wasn't like that at all."

"You didn't know her after I ruined her life."

"Jesus." Koo can see it, the sentimental romantic decision to have the child, then to keep it. She would have had some money at the beginning, left over from her career; it would all have seemed possible at first. But it wasn't possible, and by the time she understood the implications of her mistake it was too late to change. She must have been about thirty when the kid was born; a couple of years as a hausfrau, out of the business, quickly forgotten (starlets are *always* quickly forgotten, like the individual leaves on a tree), her blowsy good looks very easily going to seed, going to fat, the lost world irretrievably in the past and receding farther and farther every day; when a good old girl like that turns bitter she can undoubtedly be hell on wheels. Koo shakes his head; then, trying to find *something* good in it, something hopeful, he says, "Didn't she ever marry?"

"When I was two, a fella named Ralph Halliwell. I carry his last name."

"What happened?"

"It didn't last. He was part-owner of a restaurant in Santa Fe, I guess he married my mother because she'd been in the movies, he thought it would be an attraction for the restaurant. But something happened, I don't know exactly, he was stealing from his partner or his partner was stealing from him. Something like that. And he thought my mother must have money because of being a movie star. So one day when I was four he beat the shit out of her and left." Mark smiles, angrily and hopelessly. "I was present for that one. It's just about my earliest memory."

"Where, uh. Where is she now?"

"Dead." The word is flat, spoken as though without meaning. "She died six years ago. Breast cancer. She wouldn't do anything about it until it was too late, but that was her style, right?"

All at once, the tears are coming. Koo blinks and blinks, turning his head from side to side as though to duck out of the way, but there's no stopping them, they're like a warm flood building up inside him, overflowing, feelings he didn't even know he owned, emotions and remorses welling inside him, burning in his throat, groaning in his mouth, bursting out through his eyes. "Gah—God," he says, struggling to say something that will paper over this crack, but there isn't a joke in the world, all the jokes are told and gone. "Gah—Gah—God. God.

Oh. Jee-sus." And he's sobbing, actual racking sobs that shake his whole body and grind like tanks through his throat.

Mark has risen from the bed, is staring at him as though affronted, and now he says, "What've you got to cry about, you son of a bitch? You fucking hypocrite, what are *you* crying for?"

"I never—" But the sobs are too much for him, he can't push words through them, can't stop them, can't get away from all this misery. "I never—*knew*," he cries, and drags his aching heavy arms out from under the blankets, trying to get the stiff cold fingers up over his face.

But Mark lunges forward, one knee on the bed, slapping at his hands, shouting, "Don't you cover up! Never knew *what*? About me? My mother? *Anybody*?"

"I just—" The worst of the attack is over, the sobs becoming half-gasps as Koo strains to catch his breath, recapture control. "—went through life," he finishes, and gestures helplessly with his leaden arms, like a bug on its back.

If there was a risk that Mark would explode into his usual rage it seems to have subsided as abruptly as it came. Still leaning forward with one knee on the bed, his expression now merely impatient, he says, "Don't sentimentalize. If you loved everybody, you didn't love anybody."

"But it could have been—" Koo wants to believe this, wants to find a way to phrase it that won't sound false to himself. "*Somehow*."

"No," Mark says. "If you'd ever learned about me, I'd simply have been an embarrassment. You'd have spread a few dollars on me, like Noxzema on a sunburn."

"But I'm not—*now* I'm not—"

"Now you're sick, and scared, and wounded, and old, and you're probably gonna die. You're a set-up for the sentimental reaction. *Anything* would break you down now; a puppy, a daffodil, an orphan boy."

Astonishingly, through the sobs and the gasping for breath, Koo finds himself smiling, looking up at this mad boy with something very like pleasure. "Where'd you get to—" He has to pause for a spell of coughing and snorting, then finishes: "—be such a smart-ass?"

"It runs in the family," Mark says, and turns abruptly away, leaving the bed. Koo watches him as Mark opens mirrored door after mirrored door, finally returning with a box of tissues, dropping them on the bed beside Koo and saying, "Here. Blow your nose. You look like a science-fiction monster."

Koo struggles upward to a semi-seated position against the padded headboard, using his elbows as he would normally use his hands, then takes several tissues to blow his nose and wipe his face. His fingers are fat white sausages with hardly any feeling, but he persists, while Mark stands beside the bed watching him, a faint smile on his lips. Finally Koo discards yet another tissue and lifts his face, saying, "How am I?"

"Less disgusting."

"That's terrific. Can I ask a favor?"

Mark's face subtly closes down, as though he's afraid Koo is about to take advantage of this altered relationship. "That depends."

"I could really use a drink."

Mark relaxes, with the first honest uncomplicated grin Koo has ever seen on that face. "Sure thing," he says. "And you ought to take your pills, too."

"My schedule's so thrown off, I don't even know which ones to take."

"I'll bring you the case."

This is ridiculous, Koo thinks, watching Mark move around the room; I think I'm happy. Under the circumstances, that must mean I've flipped out completely. And why not?

Mark first brings the pill case and a glass of water, and Koo thanks him, then says, "You know I ought to be in a hospital."

"Not yet."

Koo frowns hard, trying to read something constant in that ever-changing face. "What's going to happen?"

"We play out the hand," Mark says. "I'm not changing that. Peter wants to kill you, you know, but I won't let him."

"Because of the TV show."

"That's right. He sent the Feds an ultimatum they can't accept, then he'll have the excuse to kill you and blame them."

"Lovely."

"He was going to send them one of your ears, but I wouldn't let him."

"My *ear*? Good Christ!"

"We took one off Joyce instead," Mark says, his manner calm, merely informational. "She still had one in good shape. Scotch and water?"

"Oh, definitely."

Trying not to think about people who want to cut off his ears and ultimately murder him, Koo browses among his medicines until Mark comes back with a very strong Scotch and water. Mark sits on the edge of the bed, watching Koo drink, his expression soft, even friendly, and for a moment or two neither of them speaks.

Koo sighs. The liquor is relaxing him, easing his mind and the pain in his arms. He says, "I hope you didn't inherit my stupidity."

Shrugging, Mark says, "I must have got it from *some*where."

## 30

Liz awoke with Peter's hands on her body. "Don't move," he said, his voice low and teasing. Uninterested but not repelled, she remained where she was, on her back on the large bed in the master bedroom, with reflected sunlight amber on her closed eyelids, while Peter manipulated her with his hands, prodding and kneading her breasts while his finger nuzzled her clitoris. He was impatient and too rough, so it took longer than if she'd done it herself, but finally the familiar pressure began to build, the growing tension through her body until the magic instant of transformation, when this caterpillar yet again burst into a butterfly; only to subside, twenty seconds later, into the same caterpillar as before, long-bodied and ground-locked, with stiff limbs, abraded skin, angry mind.

(There had been a time, years and years ago, when orgasm had spread a warming beneficence through her mind and body that might last for hours, even for an entire day, but that was part of a past so dead that Liz hardly remembered it. These days, orgasm was a quick almost-angry relief, a sudden spasm of pleasure, used up in the instant of its birth, leaving no residue at all.)

"Now me," Peter said.

Liz opened her eyes at last. By day this bedroom proved to be done in shades of tawny green; avocado, some lighter tones. The effect was vaguely unpleasant, like the metallic color of a rental car. Sunlight streamed through sheer curtains gauzing the view of sea and sky. Peter, wearing only a shirt, had shifted around to sit with his back against the headboard, bare legs extended, erect cock jutting up at an angle like the stubby cannon on a courthouse lawn. He was smiling at her, with a kind of challenge in the smile. "Come on," he said.

She sat up, turning sideways toward him, and reached out her left hand to hold and stroke his cock. She felt no sexual interest at all, but had no objection to bringing him off with her hand.

But he had different ideas. Still with the same obscurely hostile grin, he said, "No, honey, it's round-the-world time."

"Not today," Liz said. "I don't feel like it."

"You will. We'll start with the mouth."

Looking at him, she understood that the setbacks of the last two days had left him with the need for revenge. He had tried to dominate the world and had failed; he would soothe his wounds by dominating her.

Up to a point. Her hand motionless, she said, "If it hurts, if anything hurts, we stop."

"Sure." He grinned more broadly, shrugging. "You know me."

"Yes, I know you," she said, and twisted around to lie on her stomach with her head in his lap. Could she make him come fast, get this over with? But she'd barely put the head of his cock into her mouth, now stroking the shaft in short quick movements of both hands, when he said, "All right. Next, next."

He was in a burning hurry. She rolled onto her back and he descended on her, poking between her legs. "Easy," she said. "You're scraping me."

"What are you so dry for?"

There was no answer that wouldn't be insulting. She remained silent, and the natural juices solved the problem, and almost immediately he was out of her again, kneeling back on his haunches and saying, "Roll over."

"Not dry, goddamit."

With a schoolboyish laugh, he reached over to the bedside

table and showed her the tube of K-Y jelly. "I thought of everything."

So she rolled over, lifting onto her knees while her cheek and shoulders remained on the sheet, and the cool jelly was pleasant on the rim of her anus. "Take it slow," she said, lips moving against the sheet. "We haven't done this for a while."

"Yes yes, sure."

The first stroke was a shock, making her fingers close into fists grasping bunches of sheet, and she was about to tell him to quit, that's all, forget it for today, but he paused unmoving at the end of the thrust, and now at last he became gentle, murmuring words to her and stroking her long back, his fingers soothing over the old scars. When he moved again it was slowly, carefully, and she was prepared for it; and each stroke after was better.

The anal orgasm was rare enough to be always a surprise, and something of a shock; less pleasurable than the normal way but equally powerful, and at the same time somehow grim, grinding. If the normal was a transformation from caterpillar to butterfly, this was from corpse to vampire. Liz groaned with it, arching her back, biting the sheet, and soon afterward he came to his own triumphant finish. Withdrawing, he patted her on the rump in easy conquest before going off to the bathroom. Liz rolled over and pulled a blanket up across her body, ducking her head under it, closing her eyes. She didn't like it that she'd come.

She heard him return from the bathroom, but remained under the blanket. Again he lightly slapped her buttock, saying, "Get dressed now, come on downstairs. We have things to do. We're ending it today."

Peter felt cheerful and in charge as he trotted down the stairs. He wasn't grinding his cheeks, he wasn't worried about the future, he wasn't troubled by the past. Decisions, whether they turn out to be right or wrong, have a satisfying calmative effect in themselves.

The only residual annoyance, in fact, was that the Feds hadn't as yet made the latest tape public; were they trying to outbluff him? Well, it didn't matter; they'd *have* to release the tape after Davis' body was found.

Ginger was at the kitchen table, morosely eating a bowl of soup. He looked up at Peter's entrance, saying, "Your friend should have brained that idiotic woman with a rock *before* she used up all our food."

"We won't be here much longer," Peter said carelessly. "What's that, the Scotch broth?"

"*I* won't be here much longer, at any rate," Ginger said, glowering at Peter's back as Peter found a bowl and filled it from the pot on the stove. "I leave for Tokyo this afternoon."

"Very good idea." Peter sat to Ginger's left and shook salt and pepper over the soup. "By tonight, we'll all be out of the country." Casually, as though an afterthought, he added, "We'll need money."

"I'm not sure I can do anything about that." Ginger was remaining surly, despite Peter's good temper.

"Oh, but you can, Ginger. You can hardly do anything but. You want us safely out of the country just as much as we do."

"How much do you want?"

"Twenty thousand."

Ginger slapped his spoon on the table, more exasperated than angered. "Peter, you're such a *fool*! How am I supposed to get you twenty thousand dollars *today*?"

"Out of the bank."

"Peter, honestly, living the way you do, you just don't know a *thing* about the adult world. In the first place, if I *had* twenty thousand dollars in the bank, I wouldn't withdraw it all at once for any reason on earth, because all transactions over five thousand dollars are reported to the government."

Peter was astounded. "They *what?*"

"You're fighting the system and you don't even know what the system is. The justification is, they're looking for tax swindlers."

"But that's invasion of privacy!"

"*I* know that." Having been given this opportunity to flaunt his expertise and make fun of Peter along the way, Ginger's mood was improving dramatically. "In the second place," he went on, "I don't even *have* twenty thousand dollars in the bank, I very rarely have more than three or four. All my money goes directly to my accountant, who handles my finances, pays my bills, makes my investments, and gives me dribs and drabs when I ask him pretty please. If I demand twenty thousand dollars all in a heap, he'll most certainly want to know why I want it. And if he *doesn't* want to know why I want it, I'll *fire* him."

As Ginger's mood improved, Peter's soured. There were always problems, nit-picking minor stupid problems that had nothing to do with anything, but were just there to get in the way. It was barely possible to keep an overall plan in mind, much less act on it in a direct and sensible manner. "All right," he said. "Five, then. Or forty-five hundred, so you won't be reported."

"Don't have that much," Ginger said cheerfully. "Not readily available."

Peter watched him, not liking what was happening but seeing nothing to be done about it. "How much do you— How much can you let us have?"

Ginger considered, his little eyes amused, his natural monkey glitter returning at last to his features. "Two," he finally said.

"Two! That's barely enough to get us out of the country."

Ginger shrugged, and returned to his soup.

Two thousand dollars. Peter's teeth began absentmindedly to gnaw at his cheeks. Should he travel alone after all? He'd originally intended to dump the others after this operation, leave for Algeria alone, but now that a further operation would be necessary he needed to keep the group together. The remnant, Larry and Liz, really, that's all there was; Mark was another problem.

One possibility was Canada. They could go there, lie low for a while, then kidnap a prominent Canadian and hold him for the same ransom; an interesting complication for the United States government, to risk the loss of another country's citizen. Of course, the list of prisoners to be released would be much more carefully compiled this time. Peter would have to find ways to make absolutely sure there had been no changes of heart among those to be freed. And the subject for kidnapping would have to be a more serious figure; the effort to go over the government's head to the heart of the people had not been altogether successful.

Liz came into the room while Peter still brooded; her presence activated him again, reminding him that he was still in charge, the group was still his to control. And to remind him also of his cheeks; damn, he'd been biting them again. Consciously stopping, he said to Ginger, "All right. Two thousand it is. But you'll get more to us later?"

"Of course," Ginger said blandly, obviously not caring if Peter believed him or not. "You'll get in touch with me the usual way, let me know where you are, and I'll send you as much as you need."

You're lying, Peter thought, looking into those spiteful monkey-eyes. You're lying, but it doesn't matter. When the time comes, you'll pay. "That's fine," he said aloud.

Liz had found a can of Tab in the refrigerator. She snapped

it open and stood leaning against the counter, watching the two men at the table, saying nothing.

Ginger said, "I'll go to the bank now."

"Wait. I want you to take Mark with you."

Ginger looked insulted. "To be sure I don't run away?"

"Good God, no," Peter said. "You're smarter than that. You weakened last night, but now you know what's sensible."

"I know what's *possible*," Ginger said, a surprising bitterness briefly on his face.

"Whatever. The point is, I need Mark out of the house while Liz and I take care of Davis."

Liz shifted position, staring at Peter, but still didn't speak. Ginger frowned at the two of them. "Take *care* of Davis? I don't suppose you mean to let him go."

"Of course not."

"To what end, Peter?"

"We start building now toward the next effort. Credibility is all we can hope to emerge with from this episode. Which reminds me; I'll want you to help me make one more tape, to leave with the body."

Liz said, "Why send Mark away? I thought he was…the one to *do* this sort of thing."

Suddenly angry, or nervous, Ginger said, "Don't talk about these things in front of me."

Ignoring Liz, Peter turned toward Ginger his coldest smile. "It's too late for you not to know, Ginger," he said. "Haven't you accepted that yet? It's too late."

## 31

There was a kind of dormitory upstairs in the Police Head-quarters Annex, where they permitted Lynsey to get a couple hours' sleep, on a narrow cot under a rough wool blanket. Policewoman Austin, the songwriter, woke her with a conspiratorial wink and grin at 7:30; she made what repairs she could in the ladies' room, and went downstairs to find Mike Wiskiel sitting in moody exhaustion at his desk, drinking a plastic glass of pale orange juice. Her own, when he poured a glass for her, was less pale; it must have come from a different container. "Ms. Rayne," Wiskiel said, as he handed her the glass, "you look like hell."

"Good. I wouldn't want to feel this way and not show it. Has anything happened?"

"We're creeping forward, in our fashion. Jock's men have started interviewing hi-fi equipment places. The New York police Telexed; they've checked all likely hotels in their area and Merville isn't there."

"You think he's here."

"I *hope* he's here. I want to sit down with him and have a good long talk." He drank some of his orange juice. "Let's see; what else? Oh. Washington's decision on the new tape. We're to ignore it."

Lynsey stared in astonishment. "Ignore it? For Heaven's sake, why?"

"Well, that isn't Koo Davis' ear. Also, it isn't a voice we've heard before. Also, Davis' voice isn't on that tape. Also, the tape itself is a different kind. It all adds up to the reasonable possibility that the tape is a hoax."

"But that *was* an ear, a human ear! What kind of hoax would—"

Wiskiel shrugged elaborately, spreading his hands. "The decision came from Washington," he said. "I'm just passing it on. The assumption is, if it *is* a hoax we're better off not confusing the actual kidnappers by responding to it. And if it isn't a hoax, our silence may push them to make contact some other way."

"By *really* cutting off his ear."

"Let's hope not." Looking at his watch, he said, "It's eight o'clock. Can you call now?"

"He won't be there yet, but I'll leave a message."

She phoned, got a sleepy-sounding receptionist, and left her name and number: "Please tell him it's urgent, and I'd appreciate it if he'd call me first thing."

Eight o'clock. Less than four hours to go.

It was five past nine—two hours, fifty-five minutes to go—when Hunningdale finally called back. "How are you, dear?" he said. His voice was a light calm baritone; an excellent tool for negotiation.

"Upset," Lynsey told him. "You know I handle Koo Davis."

"Oh, do you? Of course, I'd forgotten. Wait a minute—does this have to do with the FBI visit I had yesterday?"

"Yes."

"Lynsey," the voice said, calm and comfortable but also with warning in it, "I've known Ginger Merville for years and years. He may be a little flaky, but he wouldn't kidnap anybody."

"He knows some strange people, though," Lynsey said. "Doesn't he?"

"We all know strange people, dear. For all I know, I'm strange people myself."

"The FBI just wants to *talk* with him, that's all."

"Lynsey, are you suggesting I change my story from yesterday's version, call myself a liar? On the *phone*?"

No, this couldn't be done on the phone, Lynsey could see that. She said, "I'll come to your office. Could you see me this morning?"

"There's really no point in it, dear. And my schedule is absolutely jammed. By the time I get there—"

"Where are you now?"

"I'm calling from the car."

"*Where* are you?"

"Where?" A little pause, and then he said, "Pasadena Freeway. Why? Do you want to hitch a ride?"

"Yes. What's your route from there?"

"This really is a waste of time, Lynsey."

"Chuck," she said, "they're going to *kill* him. Maybe it is a waste of time, but I've got to do *some*thing."

He sighed, then said, "Very well. I take the Harbor and the Santa Monica to Overland, then up to Century City."

"How far are you from the Hollywood Freeway now?"

"With this traffic? At least twenty minutes."

"I'll meet you there," she said. "Just after the change from the Pasadena to the Harbor. At the end of that ramp there. You know the place?"

"Far too well."

"What's your car?"

"A gray Bentley, license O CHUCK. But, Lynsey?"

"Yes?"

"If you're not there, I can't wait, you know."

"I'll be there," she promised. Then she hung up and turned to Wiskiel, saying, "Can you get me there in twenty minutes?"

"The Harbor Freeway from here? We'd better take a car with a gumdrop."

"Gumdrop?"

They were already walking out of the office. Making a circular motion over his head with one hand, Wiskiel said, "Flashing light."

"Oh. Gumdrop."

It was Lynsey's first trip in a fast-moving police car, with siren wailing and gumdrop flashing, and she found the experience invigorating; as though the simple fact of such forceful forward motion was itself accomplishing something. A uniformed policeman drove, with Mike Wiskiel trailing in his own car. They ran down the Hollywood Freeway, mostly on the right shoulder, past the sluggish heavy southbound morning traffic, and reached the interchange with the Harbor Freeway with time to spare. They stopped at the appointed place, and Lynsey said, "Thank you."

"My pleasure, ma'am."

Lynsey got out of the police car, and it spurted away. Mike Wiskiel stopped his Buick beside her and leaned over to call out the open passenger window, "I'll trail you."

"Okay, fine. But don't let him know it. I don't think he'll talk if he thinks the police are hanging around."

"I'll stay well back," he promised. Then he waved and drove off.

Lynsey waited five minutes, while several passing drivers made comments or suggestions, all of which she ignored. Then at last the gray Bentley nosed out of the slow-moving lanes of traffic, yellow letters on the royal blue background of its license plate reading O CHUCK. A good-looking red-haired girl in a pale blue jacket was driving, with a large man indistinct in back. Lynsey opened the rear door and slid into a fusty closed compartment rich with the aromas of coffee and cigar. Chuck Hunningdale, a large stout man in a well-tailored pearl gray suit with white shirt, rose-pink tie and pink chrysanthemum in his buttonhole, was on the phone. He smiled and nodded at Lynsey, gesturing with the hand holding the cigar for her to take the fur-covered seat beside him, and went on with his call.

Lynsey settled herself as the Bentley moved forward. This rear seat was divided by a console, containing the telephone, an ashtray and other equipment; putting his cigar in the ashtray, continuing to talk on the phone, Hunningdale pointed at his own mug of coffee on the console and raised his eyebrows in question. Yes, coffee would be a good idea; she nodded, and he pointed at the dispenser built into the back of the front seat. (The glass partition was up between here and the chauffeur's compartment.) Lynsey opened the small door, found more mugs, took one, turned the little chrome handle that produced coffee from the spigot, and followed Hunningdale's gesturing hand to find powdered cream substitute and sugar.

Meantime, Hunningdale was explaining on the phone that "if you want my boy, you've gotta stretch a little. A best-of is nice, but that's just gravy on the vest. What's actually on the *plate* here?"

Lynsey and Hunningdale were both talent agents, but of very different types. She handled a total of six clients, all of them major figures, where the question of *selling* the client almost never came up; she made a very good living, but there was no pressure to flaunt it. Hunningdale, on the other hand, probably had fifty clients in the music business, was hustling them all the time, and his lavish façade was part of the hustle.

Finishing his phone conversation, inconclusively, Hunningdale smiled at Lynsey and said, "My dear, you look as though you haven't slept for a week."

"That's almost true."

"Nothing happens the way it should," he said. "You have a client you have absolute affection for, and he's kidnapped. I have clients I would gladly put in a sack and drown, and *nobody* kidnaps them."

Lynsey gave that a thin smile, saying, "I'm terribly worried about him, Chuck."

"Of course you are. But, Ginger..." He shook his head, frowning, pantomiming long and careful thought. "I just don't see it."

They drove past Mike Wiskiel's maroon Buick Riviera, parked on the shoulder. Lynsey said, "Chuck, it really does look as though Ginger's involved."

"Because of the house. But wasn't that just happpenstantial, criminals stumbling into an empty house?"

"It couldn't be," Lynsey said. "They'd have to be sure they were safe, sure nobody would come to the house while they were there."

"Lynsey, all they had to do was read the trades. Ginger's tour was adequately reported."

"But he always rents his house when he's away. This time he gave it to the same realtor, but he insisted on *double* the regular rent."

Hunningdale frowned, bothered by that. "Are you sure that's true?"

"Absolutely."

"And what do you take it to mean?"

"That Ginger wanted it to *look* as though the house was for rent the same as always, but he actually wanted to be sure it would stay empty."

"Dear dear dear." Hunningdale pursed his lips, staring away at the traffic. "I know Ginger *used* to be involved with some very iffy types," he said. "Way back when, you know. But *every*body was involved with iffy types in those days. I myself had people in my own house ten years ago that today I shudder at the thought."

Lynsey forced herself to be patient, say nothing, let Hunningdale work it out for himself.

Hunningdale said, "When the FBI came around yesterday, I assumed it was merely the coincidence of the house, and they'd looked in their old files or dossiers or whatever, they saw Ginger's old-time connection, and they jumped to a conclusion."

"Of course."

"I mean, that's what the FBI does."

"I know that," Lynsey said. "Guilt by non sequitur. But this time, there's more to it than that."

Hunningdale lowered his head, brooding at his large stomach. "The situation could be awkward," he said.

"You mean, because you told the FBI you didn't know where Ginger was."

"Well, in fact I don't know where he is, not exactly. I do know he's in Los Angeles."

"He is!"

Hunningdale turned his troubled expression toward Lynsey: "You can see my difficulty. I tell you Ginger's in town, you tell the FBI, they get upset because I didn't cooperate."

"You won't come into it at all," Lynsey promised him. "I'll be the one who found him."

"By talking to me."

"By using my contacts."

"Mm." Hunningdale brooded some more.

Lynsey said, "We've never dealt directly with one another, Chuck, but you must know my reputation."

"Of course."

"We can deal."

Hunningdale smiled slightly. "There is a certain appeal in being Deep Throat." But then, shaking his head, he said, "But I truly don't know where he is. Somewhere in town, that's all. I could leave a call with his service, he'd undoubtedly get back to me."

"You know his friends, Chuck. You could find out where he

is." Then, gambling, taking a leap, she said, "He might be in a beach house somewhere. A musician friend."

"A beach house?" Hunningdale gave her a frankly curious look, saying, "There's even more to this than you're telling me, isn't there?"

"Yes?"

"Mm." Putting down his cigar, picking up the phone, he said, "And Ginger was always such a good client. Reliable, profitable, talented, and even interesting to chat with from time to time."

Lynsey said, "We'd like to know where he is, but I don't want to talk to him."

"Of course, of course. Let me just make a few calls. Beach house, beach house." And he pressed the number buttons on the phone.

It took four calls, with Hunningdale explaining each time that he needed Ginger Merville immediately for a new "project" with NBC television, and that an answer had to be given before noon today. The first three offered to help him look, but the fourth, someone called Kenny, knew exactly where Ginger Merville could be found. "Bless you, Kenny," Hunningdale told him, broke the connection, and said to Lynsey, "That was Kenny Heller. Ginger's staying at his beach house, in Malibu."

"Thank you, Chuck. Thank you."

"Poor Ginger," Hunningdale said.

# 32

"You look like wet shit," Koo tells his image in the mirror. "No reflection on *you*, of course." Then he turns and walks some more around the room, slowly and carefully, bandaged arms folded across his chest. He's testing his strength and capacity, struggling to get this battered body functioning again. Approaching another mirror he says, "Listen, guy. You gotta stop following me around." Then he glances worried beyond his mirrored self at the deeper reflection of the half-open mirrored bathroom door; from inside there, the buzz of the electric razor continues.

Why is Mark shaving off his beard? Koo's life depends on Mark now, even more than earlier, but Mark is remaining as erratic and unpredictable as ever. Back when they were actually talking together, when a relatively calm Mark was telling Koo about his mother, it seemed they could find an infinity of connectives, a seamless link of identity between them; but it wasn't so. Mark has lived with pain and hatred too long, there are too many ways to tap into that underground river of rage. Watching the emotions cross Mark's face like clouds on a windy day, Koo kept backing away from subject after subject, until it seemed there was *nothing* safe to say. The conversation didn't so much run down as slowly strangle on its own constrictions. The silences grew longer, and increasingly uncomfortable.

It was during one of those silences that the knocking came at the door. Mark answered it, and spoke briefly in the doorway with the leader, Peter. Koo listened, needing to know what these people were saying to one another, but didn't entirely understand what he heard:

Peter: "Our friend is going to the bank. I want you to go with him."

Mark: "No."

Peter: "No? Mark, you know that little weasel's just looking for a chance to run out on us."

Mark: "Let him run."

Peter: "*After* we get his money. But you'll have to go with him to the bank or he won't come back."

Mark: "You go with him."

Peter: "That wouldn't do any good, he isn't afraid of me."

Mark laughed at that, then said, "Nobody's afraid of you, Peter."

Peter was becoming more obviously irritated. "For God's sake, Mark, why refuse this simple request? Go with Gin—our friend. Oh, what difference does it make? Ginger. Go with Ginger to the bank. I mean, why *not*?"

Mark: "Because I'm staying here."

Peter: "Here? In this room?"

Mark: "That's right."

Peter: "We're nearing our deadline, you know."

Mark: "We'll see."

Peter: "There's no question about *that*, Mark. Don't get any ideas in your head."

But Mark didn't respond to that. Merely shaking his head, he moved back a step and shut the door.

Koo said, "What deadline?"

"It doesn't matter," Mark told him, his manner so flat and final that Koo didn't dare question him again. Then Mark patted the black brush of beard on his face and said, "I think I'll shave."

So that's what he's doing now, in the bathroom, first having snipped and hacked away with a pair of scissors and now using an electric razor. While Koo paces—no, *plods* is more like it—while Koo plods back and forth out here surrounded by mirrors, plagued by more and more unanswerable questions. *What* deadline? Who is this new person, Ginger, of whom Koo has never heard before? *Why is Mark shaving off his beard?* What does Mark plan to do? What does *Peter* plan to do?

The razor buzz stops. Koo halts in the middle of the room, looking over at the bathroom doorway. From this angle, the mirror of the half-open door shows him the reflection of another mirror across the room, in which he can see himself from the back. It isn't a pleasant view. He looks old, weak, tired, bent. He looks like a junk-wagon horse at the end of a long hard day.

Water splashes in the bathroom then stops. Koo moves obliquely to the left, till he can no longer see that depressing view of himself, but the door also moves, following him, and Mark comes out, stroking bare cheeks and looking awkward and a bit sheepish.

Koo essays a shaky grin and a shaky joke: "What are you gonna grow next year?"

"Corn," Mark says. "It's time for a money crop."

"Corn always sells," Koo agrees. "Believe me, I know."

Mark turns to study himself in the nearest mirror, leaning forward, angling his head upward slightly, gazing over his cheekbones at the image of his face. "Come here," he says.

Koo approaches, not sure what the boy has in mind. "What's up?"

"Come *here*. Next to me. Put your face next to mine."

"Listen," Koo says, understanding now and feeling a sudden panic. "Are you sure this is a good idea?"

"Cheek to cheek," Mark insists, leaning ever closer to the mirror. "Come *on*."

Thirty years ago, when Honeydew made her phone call, the thought did cross Koo's mind that the child might just as readily not be his, that Koo might simply be the handiest or the richest or the most vulnerable of the potential fathers, and now he remembers that thought and is made afraid by it. At the time, it was easier to pay the five hundred dollars, but now the question is more vital. When he puts his cheek next to Mark's and studies their joined faces in the mirror, will it be an echo of himself that he sees, or an echo of some long-ago actor, producer, agent, or even Army officer, unidentifiable but ubiquitously there? Or Mel Wolfe, Koo's most frequent gag writer in the old days, who was no mean hand with the blondes himself; if it's Mel's face he sees next to his own in that goddamn mirror, Koo won't know whether to laugh or cry.

Hesitantly, like someone entering a too-hot tub, Koo stands with his shoulder touching Mark's shoulder, his neck stretching as his face nears Mark's face. But then Mark reaches a hand up behind Koo, grabs him by the neck and yanks him closer, strong fingers firm, pressing the side of his face to Mark's cold cheek, and for a long moment of silence they study themselves, Mark with a kind of scientific intensity, Koo in hope and fear… and longing. To see himself renewed, even in the features of this lost crazy boy, would be wonderful.

Doubtfully, Mark says, "The eyebrows?"

"No," Koo says. "Yours are more curved, like your mother's."

"Jawline."

Koo squints. "Do you really think so?"

Mark slowly shakes his head, the smooth-shaven cheek sliding with a strange cold intimacy on Koo's face. "No," Mark says. "Nothing."

Koo might disengage now, safely move away from Mark's cheek and from the hand gripping the back of his neck, but he's reluctant to give up the search. Mel Wolfe is *not* in that face, nor is there anyone else Koo recognizes, except for the faint traces of Honeydew herself. "Goddamn it," he says, peering at their two faces, "I must have the weakest genes in the history of the human race."

"Why?"

"Neither of my other boys looks like me either."

Mark chuckles, but it's a warning sound, like a growl.

"Lucky man," he says. "You said that just right."

"Said what?"

"Your *other* boys." Mark's gripping hand clenches briefly, painfully, on Koo's neck, and Mark says, "If you'd said it any other way, I'd have broken your neck right now."

"You're a tough audience," Koo tells him, very shaky again, and this time he does disengage, easing slowly away. Mark's hand drops, letting him go, and Koo moves awkwardly to the bed, feeling much weaker. Seating himself, he rests his forearms in his lap while watching Mark continue to study his own reflection.

This could be dangerous. Koo is convinced there's still murder inside Mark, just waiting to be triggered. Is that what this is all about? This whole delay here, this strange new sequence in which Mark almost seems to have changed sides, to have joined the prisoner in an alliance against his jailers, could simply be the waiting period until Mark can find again the proper circumstances for murder. The boy has to get into the right frame of mind before he can kill his father; the search of their faces could simply have been the way to psych himself up.

Still in the mirror, Mark says, "Do I look like anybody *else* you used to know?"

"Wait a minute," Koo says, in a fresh panic. *He* can harbor such doubts about paternity, but does he dare permit Mark this further grievance? On the other hand, how can he quickly, immediately, *now*, drive the idea out of the boy's head?

By direct attack; dangerous, but the only choice. "Believe me, Mark," Koo says, "I only pay for my own mistakes."

Mark turns slowly away from the mirror and gazes at Koo for a long time, a small crooked smile on his lips. Then, speaking very softly, he says, "And have you paid enough?"

"I don't know," Koo tells him. "You're the one keeping the books."

Mark considers that, nodding, still with the small smile. Then he says, "The FBI coming to the house—did you have something to do with that?"

"What house?"

"The first one. That's why we moved. Somebody came through, saying he was from the gas company."

"Oh." Now it's Koo's turn to smile; it *did* work after all, and he's pleased with himself, even though it ultimately doesn't seem to have helped. "Yes," he says. "I guess that was me."

"I knew it," Mark says, not threateningly but as though he too is pleased with Koo's accomplishment. "The others didn't think so, but I knew it was you. How'd you do it?"

"That room I was in. I saw it in the movies once, when a director named Gilbert Freeman owned the house."

"Gilbert Freeman. You said that name, on one of the tapes."

"I called him my favorite host in all the world."

"Right." Mark frowns, thinking about that. "How does that tell anybody anything?"

"I hardly knew Gilbert Freeman. He's never been my host."

Laughing, *very* pleased with Koo, Mark says, "Sly old man. I'm glad I met you."

"Well," Koo says. "Uhhh. I'm not sure the feeling's mutual."

"No, I suppose not," Mark agrees, the laughter giving way again to the small almost absentminded smile. "Well, time will tell, won't it?"

"If it does," Koo says, "I'll never tell time again."

"Ugh. You can do better than that."

"Not right now I can't," Koo says.

# 33

Peter walked with Ginger out to the car, a white reconditioned 1958 Ford Thunderbird; an early Thunderbird, from back when Ford had it in mind to build a sports car. Beside it, Peter's Impala looked like a gross unpleasant animal; an alligator next to a swan. The two cars sat side by side in the carport, a doorless concrete-floored insert on the highway side of the house, directly beneath the room in which Koo Davis was being held. Beyond the cars, as Peter and Ginger emerged from the house, traffic flashed by on the Coast Highway in bright sunshine. Across the road, the scrub-covered hills rose steeply toward the north.

Peter said, "You'll be back in an hour?"

"Depending on traffic." Ginger was impatient to be gone.

"Don't make us wait too long," Peter said. "Remember, we also have to get out of the country today."

"I'll be as quick as I can. How many times do I have to say it?"

"That's fine, Ginger."

"Goodbye." Reaching in his pocket for his keys, Ginger went around to the driver's side of the Thunderbird.

Peter watched in silence while Ginger unlocked the door, but then said, "Ginger, one last thing."

"What *now*, Peter?"

"A threat," Peter told him. "You know what's going to happen to Davis. If you don't come back, I assure you the police will find Davis in a way that connects him to *you*."

"You're a very stupid person, Peter," Ginger said. "You have alienated me for no good reason at all. I'll bring you your two thousand dollars, I'll get myself out of this little swamp of yours, and that will be the end of it."

Was Ginger right? *Had* Peter unnecessarily alienated him? But there had been nowhere else to go with Davis, once the first place became known. Chewing on his cheeks, keeping himself with difficulty from adding yet more verbal threats (which he knew full well could only make things worse), Peter watched Ginger insert himself behind the wheel of the Thunderbird, start the engine, and without another look in Peter's direction back briskly out to the sunlight. Peter followed, walking slowly forward, wishing there were some way to reconstitute their former relationship, but knowing it had become hopelessly spoiled. If *only* they hadn't had to move from the house in Woodland Hills. God *damn* the FBI! And God damn Mark or whoever was responsible for tipping them off.

The Thunderbird swung backwards in a tight quarter-turn, then slid forward like a fish, joining the flow of traffic. Peter, shielding his eyes, stepped out into the sunlight far enough to watch the Thunderbird out of sight around the next coastal curve to the east; then he shook his head and walked back into the house, hardly noticing the pain in his cheeks.

What a disaster this operation had been! It had seemed so clear and simple in the planning, such an unmistakable public statement, and it was ending in confusion, death, humiliation.

Peter had made mistakes, he fully acknowledged that, but on careful reflection he didn't believe that *he* had made a fool of himself. *Time* had made a fool of him, time and accident and the frailty of human beings; none of which could be fully guarded against.

It had been so much easier a decade ago, when the Movement was a true and active force, when a leader was someone who sensed where the crowd intended to go anyway and got out front to yell, *Follow me!* But where was the Movement today? Where was the crowd, the consensus; where were the willing masses for a leader to lead? There seemed to be no direction at all, no communal grievance or belief, no goal, hardly even any adversary. What was a leader to do in such muddled times? In a way, Peter could understand the defection of those seven in jail; it's hard to be a revolutionary when revolution isn't popular.

Peter was now regretting that he hadn't spent more time and thought on the *theory* of the New American Revolution; but when things had been going well it hadn't seemed to matter. Each person had his capabilities, his strengths, and the Movement could use everyone in his appropriate place. Larry, for instance, was wonderful at theory, Larry truly understood what the Revolution was all about, but Larry was no leader. Larry couldn't lead a dysentery victim to the men's room.

That was another of the problems. In the rich days, it had been almost inevitable that the leaders would feel a kind of paternal contempt toward the theorists, and old habits do die hard. Peter needed Larry now, to give him the dialectical underpinnings for their goals and their methods, but Peter could not bring himself to go to Larry humbly, as a student to a teacher, he simply could not reverse the leader-follower roles in that ignominious way. More and more, lacking both the tidal pressure of a mass movement and the magnetic pull of a clearly defined theoretical goal, Peter was reduced to improvisation and to patchwork solutions of immediate problems. The murder of Koo Davis, on which he was determined, had no revolutionary significance (as the death of an influential senator, say, or an undercover CIA agent, could be significant in that it would to some extent affect and alter history), but the death of Davis had become for Peter an absolute tactical necessity, the only means he could think of to overcome the stigma of his failure.

There were three radios playing in the house, all tuned to the same news station, but to no effect. The noon deadline was almost here, and the authorities had not so much as acknowledged receipt of the latest message. That had been a frequent governmental tactic over the last several years—"toughing it out," "stonewalling"—and if Peter had been interested in further negotiation he might very well have given in; presented new messages, offered new deadlines, broadened contact with officialdom. As it was, their tactic meshed perfectly with Peter's own, and assured that *next* time they would be less cavalier.

Liz was in the living room, once again seated with legs curled beneath her in the Eames chair. Beyond her, through the glass doors to the deck, Peter could see Larry sunk in thought. Could he rely on Larry now, for *anything*? No; the simplest request would surely provoke weak and cowardly remonstrances, complaints, accusations. It would not be possible to convince Larry that Peter's past errors of judgment—or other problems in the past—were not at the moment the point. The point at the moment was to make the best of a bad job, recoup as much as possible, and get out of here.

Which meant the death of Davis, a tactical action of which Larry would undoubtedly disapprove. Not wanting to place them all in a position where Larry would have disobeyed a direct order, Peter was forced to adjust his thinking to a plan with a cadre of one: Liz. He entered the living room, turned down the radio, sat near her, and said, "When Ginger gets back, we'll leave."

"All right," she said, not looking in his direction.

She obviously didn't care what happened next, but Peter had to explain his plans to *someone*, and she was all he had. "We'll fly to Vancouver," he said. "You still have that safe passport?"

"Of course."

"Before then, before Ginger gets back, we have to take care of Davis."

Now she did look at him, saying, "Shouldn't we wait till tonight? How do we get him away from here?"

"We don't. This is where they'll find him."

She lifted an eyebrow. "What does that do for your friend Ginger?"

"Ginger no longer wants to be a part of us," Peter explained. "He's made that very clear. So it's no longer necessary for us to protect Ginger."

"He'll give your name to the police."

"Good. I'll *want* the authorities to know this was my operation, so they'll be more circumspect with me next time."

"Next time." She said it without inflection.

"We have to act *now*, Liz," Peter said, emphasizing his words in an attempt to capture her attention. "And it's only the two of us. Larry is useless, and Mark has gone completely over the edge."

"There's something between him and Davis," Liz said.

"I know that. I can't figure out what it is." Peter's irritation was surfacing more and more. "When I wanted Davis alive, Mark was determined to kill him. Now when I want Davis dead, Mark stands over him like a faithful collie. We have to take him out, Liz, just you and I."

"Take *Mark* out?"

"We can do it. There are two of us and he won't expect—"

"No no," she said, slapping the air to make him stop talking. "I know we can do it. I'm surprised you *want* to do it. There aren't many of us left."

"Mark has already chosen to be in opposition to us."

Liz shrugged; nothing ever surprised or baffled her for long, a trait Peter was frequently grateful for. "Then we'll have to kill him," she said. "If we just draw him away, he'll make trouble later."

"That's right. What we'll do, you'll knock on the door, talk to him, get him to come out of the room. I'll be partway down the stairs, where he won't be able to see me until he's completely out in the hall. When he comes out I'll shoot him. Then it'll be your job to keep the door open. I don't want Davis locking it from the inside, forcing us to batter the damn thing down before we can get at him."

"What if Mark won't come out?"

"We need an inducement." Peter frowned at her. "What about sex? Could you get him out that way?"

Laughing, she said, "Not a chance." Her face and the sound of her laughter were both harsh. "Not with Mark," she said. "He's even worse than you."

What did she mean by that? Choosing not to pursue it, Peter said, "Something else, then. Tell him something, I don't care what. Get him to just step across the threshold, that's all."

"Let me think." She half-turned to gaze out toward the glass doors and the deck. Peter looked in the same direction, seeing Larry slumped in an orange butterfly chair out there, like a TB victim getting a final infusion of sun. Beyond the deck, the beach and ocean were lightly peopled by swimmers, surfers, hikers, sunbathers. The amazing thing was that this place could at the same time be so public and yet so private. Hundreds of people moved up and down the beach out there, past the long row of dwellings, never guessing what this one beach house contained.

Liz said, "I'll tell him you caught Larry trying to call the police."

"You mean—to turn himself in?"

"To turn us *all* in."

Peter looked out again at the despondent figure on the deck. "God knows it's believable."

"That's the point, isn't it?" With a lithe movement, Liz un-coiled herself out of the chair. "If we're going to do it, let's do it."

"Wait. I have to get the gun."

Peter's luggage was in the room where he'd made the two tapes; the one they'd sent last night to the authorities, and the one he'd made this morning, to be left next to Davis' body. Now, while Liz waited at the foot of the stairs, he went into that room and took from the bottom of his suitcase a small revolver; a .32 caliber Colt Cobra, with a two-inch barrel. Also in the suitcase were a Browning .380 automatic, a Ruger .357 Black-hawk revolver, and a .38 Colt Police Positive Special revolver; all larger, heavier guns than the Cobra. Peter had collected these guns over the last few years, buying them all legally, but he had no real interest in or liking for guns and had never become comfortable with any of them. He did not practice shooting, didn't entirely trust guns, and whenever he felt the need for one he invariably chose the Cobra, being the smallest and lightest and therefore the least intimidating.

Liz had already started up the stairs, and was waiting now three steps from the top. Peter followed, stopped two steps below her, and whispered, "Go ahead."

"Are you close enough?"

"Yes yes! Go on!"

It was necessary for Peter to clench his jaw to stop the teeth from grinding; he couldn't afford that distraction now. Pressing his left side against the stairwell wall, he held the Cobra in both hands, out at arm's length, his left arm braced against the wall, the revolver barrel pointed at a head-high spot directly in front of that bedroom door. Although Peter disliked guns, he knew himself capable of using them effectively at short range; twice before he had shot people, once fatally and once wounding a policeman in the side. There would be no difficulty now with Mark and with Davis.

At the bedroom door, Liz paused and looked down at Peter, who nodded to her that he was ready. Without hesitation, she knocked sharply at the door, and a few seconds later Peter heard the rumbling voice of Mark; though he wasn't near enough to make out the exact words.

"It's Liz."

Mark rumbled again.

"I have to talk to you. Come on, Mark, don't make me yell through the door."

Peter's perceptions were so acute now that he could see the doorknob turn. He watched it disappear as the door opened inward, but Mark did not immediately appear.

Now, however, Peter could hear what Mark was saying: "What's the problem?"

"It's Larry." Liz's manner seemed to Peter offhand and mechanical; shouldn't she sound more troubled? Or was this more appropriate to her style?

"What's the matter with Larry?" Not a bit of Mark showed beyond the doorway, not even a shadow.

"Peter caught him calling the police. He wanted to turn us all in."

The familiar snarl of Mark's laughter made Peter hunch more closely against the protecting wall. When would the damn man come out of there? The waiting was difficult; it was getting harder and harder not to grind his teeth.

Mark said, "That's Larry, all right, always the wrong move at the wrong time for the wrong reasons. Did Peter stop him in time?"

"Yes, we think so. But Peter needs help, he wants you to come down and help him."

"Help? With *Larry*?"

"Peter's holding him," Liz explained, "but we can't trust Larry anymore, we don't know what he'll do next. Peter can't deal with him alone."

"You mean he wants Larry put out of the way, and he's too much of a coward to do it himself."

Oh, am I? You'll soon learn about *that*.

"That isn't it." Liz sounded as impatient as Peter felt. "He can't control Larry all himself, that's all. Come down and *help* him."

"This is all too stupid," Mark said, but grudgingly, meaning he was about to give up. Peter could tell by the way Liz stepped back from the doorway that Mark was coming out now. Here he—

"Peter, there's trouble out—"

Larry's voice! Peter swung around, stunned, and Larry was at the foot of the stairs, gaping upward, bewildered: "What are you—?" Then, understanding: "Mark, look out!"

Swinging back, Peter saw Mark just stepping into the hallway, looking in this direction—beardless! That surprising naked face was also seeing this tableau, understanding it, and even as Peter was bringing the gun up Mark was flinging himself backward. *Damn!* Peter fired, knowing it was no good, too late, then fired a second time even more uselessly, as the door slammed shut.

Liz was shouting something, Larry was shouting something. Peter bounded up the stairs, twisted the knob, but the door was locked from the inside. Enraged, he emptied the Cobra into the closed door, hoping the bullets would go through the wood and glass, would hit *something* in there, and then he turned to fling the empty pistol in rage and frustration down the stairs at Larry, who merely sidestepped it, crying out, "Peter, have you gone *crazy*?"

"That son of a bitch," Peter growled, and he wasn't sure

himself whether he meant Mark or Larry. To Liz he said, "Does Mark have a gun in there, do you know?"

"What a mess *this* is," Liz said, as though it was Peter she blamed.

"*Does he have a gun?*"

"How would I know?"

"We have to assume— Oh, Jesus, can't *anything* go right?"

Larry by now had reached the head of the stairs, his expression astounded and disapproving. "You were going to *shoot* Mark!"

"Yes, by Jesus, I was, and you fouled it up!"

"But *why*?"

"Because we have to kill Davis, and Mark's in the way."

"But we don't have to—"

"Don't argue tactics with me," Peter said, his finger poking out at Larry, his patience finally gone for good. "You're a weak sister, you always *have* been a weak sister, and you won't tell *me* how to run this operation."

Larry's face closed down; he made an obvious effort to attain dignity. "I'll tell you," he said. "I'll tell you what I came in to report. They've cleared everybody away from our area of beach."

"They? Who?"

"I don't know. Lifeguards, police, what difference does it make?"

"Maybe somebody saw a shark."

"They haven't just cleared everybody out of the water, they've moved them away from the beach, too. It looks as though they're setting up sawhorse barriers two or three houses away on both sides."

"There's got to be some—" But then it all overflowed, and Peter yelled, "You *did* call the police! You bastard, bastard, bastard—"

Liz got between them, preventing Peter from hitting Larry, while Larry stumbled backward, as angry as Peter himself, crying, "I didn't call anybody! I should have, I should have, but I never—"

Liz turned on him, saying, "Shut up, Larry. Let's find out about this."

"Look for yourself," Larry told her.

"I intend to."

Peter watched Liz enter the master bedroom, followed by Larry, saying something to her, justifying himself in some way. Was it Ginger, then, who'd turned them in? The strange thing was, it didn't even matter. Peter wished he still had the pistol in his hand, wished the pistol were still full of bullets; he would shoot Larry now, in the back, shoot him down and then put another bullet in his worrying head; not for any specific crime but out of years of frustration; and because *someone had to die*.

Liz slid open one of the glass doors on the far side of the bedroom, leading out to the upper deck. Cautiously she looked out, to left and right, while Larry nattered behind her. Peter moved forward, his eyes and attention on Liz, waiting for her to say the word, and after a minute she turned back into the room, looking at Peter in a closed and somber way, saying, "It's them, all right."

"We haven't run in luck this time, have we?" Peter felt cold, remote from himself, aloof from the consequences of the world around him. There was no fear or panic in him, no thought that he personally was in danger; whatever happened, he remained convinced he would end the day in Vancouver, he and Liz, prepared to await a more propitious moment, a more fortunate operation, a more successful plan. A miserable humiliating failure (which could be risen above) was the worst he visualized in his own personal future.

Again Liz and Larry both spoke to him; again he didn't listen. Stepping around Liz, he carelessly slid the glass door completely open and stepped out onto the upper deck, squinting against the bright sunlight as he moved unhesitatingly across the deck to the rail. The blinding pain in his cheeks seemed to belong to someone else.

Directly below was the cantilevered main deck, empty but for the orange canvas butterfly chair in which Larry had been doing his brooding. The width of sand between here and the water was, as Larry had said, empty of people, as was the immediate vicinity of ocean. Joyce is buried, just about *there*, Peter thought, his eyes glancing off the spot, and then he turned to look to the right.

A crowd of people, gaping this way. The sawhorses, perhaps a hundred fifty feet from here, stretched from house-line to waterline, damming up a flow of curious humanity. There were no obvious policemen visible, but they were undoubtedly close by. "If we had rifles," Peter muttered aloud, staring from under his sun-shielding hand at the people beyond the sawhorses, "we could pot a few of those gawkers." Then, with merely a quick establishing glance at the similar barrier-plus-spectators down the beach in the opposite direction, he went back into the house.

The bedroom was empty, but Larry was vacillating in the hallway; when Peter emerged, Larry said, "Maybe we could still make a run for it. Malibu Canyon Road is just down that way, we could—"

"Don't be foolish," Peter said. "We hold out till dark, then we slip away. Probably down the beach, swim around behind the police line. Where's Liz?"

"She went downstairs for guns, but I don't—"

"She's right. Good girl." Then Peter noticed Larry staring at him in a peculiar horrified way. "What's the matter?"

"There's blood coming out of your mouth."

Peter swallowed, wiping his mouth with the back of his hand. "I cut myself." Then he turned his attention to the bullet-pocked door protecting Davis and Mark. "We have to break that door down."

"What for? Before the police are set up, we still could—"

"They're already in *place*, get that through your head. Besides, whatever else does or does not happen, Davis dies." Peter saw Liz coming up the stairs, pistols in her hands. Speaking over Larry's objections, he said, "Good. We finish Davis now."

# 34

Ginger's bank was in Woodland Hills, down in the flat part of the Valley, not far from his house. However, he was barely a quarter mile up Topanga Canyon Boulevard from the Coast Highway when he saw the flashing red light in his rearview mirror.

Was he speeding? No; but there were cops who liked to hassle expensive or unusual cars just for the hell of it. Irritated, thinking of this as simply more of the bad luck dogging him lately, Ginger pulled into a gravel turnout and rolled to a stop. The Sheriff's Department car stopped behind him, its red warning lights still revolving, and the driver—deliberately intimidating in his crease-ironed khaki uniform and dark sunglasses—came striding forward in the unhurried fashion of traffic cops everywhere.

Ginger already had his window rolled down and his license and registration waiting in his hand; the object was to get this interruption over with as quickly as possible. The policeman arrived, Ginger wordlessly handed him the documents, and the policeman wordlessly took them. He studied both with glacial slowness until Ginger, hunching his neck so he could look out the window at a steep angle upward to see the policeman's blank tanned face, finally said, "What's the trouble, officer?"

"You're Mr. Merville?"

"Yes, sir." Ginger was always very polite when under the direct gaze of Authority.

"And this is your vehicle?"

"Yes, sir." Ginger was faintly aware that another car, a maroon

Buick Riviera, had also pulled off onto this turnout, and was stopping ahead of the Thunderbird; but his primary attention remained on the policeman.

"Just wait here a moment," the policeman said, and crunched away across the gravel toward his own car. Ginger, annoyed and upset but not alarmed, watched him in the rearview mirror, and when next he looked out ahead of his car two men had emerged from the Riviera and were walking in this direction.

Now, belatedly, Ginger got worried. He still didn't really believe the events in the beach house could have a serious effect upon his own life—for years Peter had only been amusing, a joke, Ginger's private joke—but the first twinges of doubt, and even of dread, crossed his mind as he watched the two men approach his car. Both were big, tough-looking, middle-aged. One hung back near Ginger's front fender while the other came forward to speak. Ginger waited for him, and in sudden terror recognized the man just as he spoke:

"Mr. Merville, I am Michael Wiskiel of the Los Angeles office of the Federal Bureau of Investigation. I'm afraid I must ask you to step out of the car for a moment."

Wiskiel; the man on television. "FBI?" Ginger desperately tried for a smile. "For a traffic violation?"

Wiskiel, opening the Thunderbird's door, said, "If you'd just step out of the car for a moment."

Drive away. Shift into first, run the second man down (the second fantasy slaughter-by-automobile in fifteen minutes), accelerate over the hills and into the Valley and disappear. Except that it wasn't possible; how many times had Ginger acknowledged to himself that the life of the fugitive was not for him? Whatever Peter did with his days and nights, however he survived from year to year, Ginger could not possibly live the same way. Whatever happened, Ginger was a creature of civilization, limited to a life within society. Feeling unutterably sorry for himself—the unfairness of it all!—Ginger struggled out of the Thunderbird. Hopelessly but automatically he maintained as much of the pretense as he could: "Is something wrong?"

"You just came from Kenny Heller's beach house."

They've been watching me! "Well—umm…" He couldn't quite bring himself to admit it, though he already knew there was no point denying it.

Wiskiel didn't wait for him to resolve the problem, but went on, asking, "Who did you leave there?"

"No one." That lie was instinctive.

And not believed: "No one?"

And here, at the edge of doom, hope was born. Wasn't he after all shrewder than this heavy-jawed cop? Ginger had first begun lying himself successfully out of scrapes when he was barely in kindergarten, and his tongue had never lost its skill. He was clever and devious and bright, and there would never be any reason to abandon hope. "The place was empty," he said. "At least, no one answered when I rang."

"You were *in* the house."

"But I wasn't." Confidence was flowing again, Ginger was pulling himself back from the brink of despair. "Kenny loaned me the place," he said smoothly, "but I couldn't find the key. He always *used* to keep it atop the lintel, but it wasn't there. I drove over this morning, tried to get in, rang the bell, then went for a walk on the beach. Leaving the car at the house, of course. When I got back I rang again, but still no answer, so I gave up."

Wiskiel frowned; was uncertainty coming into his expression? He said, "So you saw no one."

"Not a soul. Obviously, Kenny loaned the place to someone *else* recently who simply walked off with the key."

"So if there's anybody in the house, you wouldn't be able to help us with information."

"I'm terribly sorry, but no. And I do *wish* you'd tell me what this is all about."

"An FBI matter," Wiskiel said, being officially distant but not actually hostile. Then, surprisingly, he extended his hand toward Ginger, saying, "Sorry to have troubled you."

"Not at all," Ginger said, smiling broadly, in love with himself, reaching out to shake Wiskiel's hand.

And Wiskiel clamped Ginger's hand in an incredible grip, so astonishing that Ginger cried out and actually rose on tiptoe. Squeezing, crushing Ginger's hand in his fist, Wiskiel rasped his thumb and fingers back and forth, grinding the bones of Ginger's hand. Broken hand—can't play the bass—extreme pain—these things flashed through Ginger's mind as he reached in agony with his left hand, clutching at Wiskiel's blunt hard fingers, crying out, "My God! Don't!"

Wiskiel pressed forward, his grip hard and tight, his pressure forcing Ginger back against the side of the Thunderbird. "Put your left hand down at your side," Wiskiel ordered, his voice low and mean, "or I'll break every bone in your hand."

"You *are* break— *Ow!*" But Ginger obeyed, unable not to obey; his left hand flew to his side and trembled there, clenching and unclenching, while he danced on the balls of his feet, imprisoned by this grip. "Oh, don't! Oh, please!"

"How many are in the house?"

No, he couldn't, he couldn't give himself away like that. *"Please!"*

Now Wiskiel gripped his own right thumb with his left fist, and ground the knuckles of his left hand into the back of Ginger's hand, over the small delicate bones. This was *ten* times the pain, so sharp and severe that the strength went out of his knees as swiftly as though someone had pulled a plug. He would have fallen except for the pressure with which Wiskiel held him against the side of the Thunderbird. *"Now,"* Wiskiel said, through clenched teeth, and what happened to Ginger's hand made him scream aloud. But Wiskiel wouldn't stop, and the blood was draining from Ginger's head, and he thought: Let me faint, let me faint.

The grinding knuckles paused, but the gripping right hand remained. Wiskiel said, "How many in the house?"

"Oh, please, my hand." Another police car had pulled up next to the Buick; to take Ginger away, he knew that now. Passing traffic slowed to watch, but no one would stop, no one would rescue him.

A brief excruciating grind: "How many are in the house?"

"*Oh! Oh!*"

"How many are in the *house*?"

"FIVE!"

The crushing grip eased, ever so slightly. "Good," Wiskiel said. "Who's the leader?"

"Peter—Peter Dinely."

The second man had come up beside Wiskiel, with notepad and pencil. Ginger was aware of him writing down Peter's name, as Wiskiel said, "Who else?"

"Somebody named Mark—Larry—I don't know their last names. And a woman named Liz."

"What about Joyce Griffith?"

"Joyce." Although Wiskiel was now merely holding Ginger's hand in an ordinarily tight grasp, the waves of pain still flowed up the length of his arm and spread through his body, shattering and distracting him. Joyce; he had trouble thinking, remembering the creature making all that food... "She's dead."

"How?"

"Mark—Mark killed her. She's buried in the sand in front of the house."

"And Koo Davis? Alive or dead?"

He had admitted everything else, but still he hesitated. Koo

Davis. To acknowledge familiarity with *that* name was to slam the door forever.

But Wiskiel was implacable. Another reminiscent squeeze, dragging a groan from Ginger's throat, and Wiskiel said, harshly, "*Is Koo Davis alive or dead?*"

"Alive! Alive!"

"Good. Where are they keeping him?"

"Upstairs bedroom. Enclosed, no windows."

"An inner room," Wiskiel said. "All right, good. What guns do they have?"

"I don't know. I *swear* I don't know."

"All right." And the punishing hand abruptly released its grip. "You can go with these two gentlemen," Wiskiel said.

Ginger tucked his throbbing hand into his left armpit, hunching down over it. He would *not* tell them Peter was undoubtedly killing Davis this very second. Petulant, frightened, angry, spiteful, he glared at Wiskiel through tear-filled eyes: "You're not supposed to *treat* me this way!"

Wiskiel looked at him without expression. "Tough shit," he said.

## 35

Mike watched in grim satisfaction as Ginger Merville was led away to the other car. He felt no sympathy for such creatures. Five years ago, seven years ago, you could understand and almost forgive all those people who flirted with the kind of anti-social behavior they liked to mislabel 'revolution'; you could understand it because most of them were merely dupes, sheep going along with the popular sport of bad-mouthing Authority. (And also, of course, he had to admit, because it was an unsettled time, a difficult time, and he was as glad as anybody that it was over.) But to continue now in such actions was no longer forgivable, no longer merely a fad or a sport. Ginger Merville had played with fire too long, and he was about to get very badly burned, and Mike was happy to be the one to strike the match.

Dave Kerman, putting away the notepad in which he'd copied down what Merville had had to say, said, "Nice work, Mike."

Mike shrugged, pleased with himself but trying not to show it. "All I did was shake the little bastard's hand." To the Sheriff's Department officer, who had just come over from his own vehicle, Mike said, "Have someone pick up this car, okay?"

"Will do, sir. He was what you wanted, was he?"

"Just what the doctor ordered."

"I still have his license and registration."

"He won't need them for a while. Leave them with the car."

"Yes, sir."

The car containing Merville drove off as Mike and Dave Kerman walked back to the Buick. It was Mike's private car, but

Dave drove, freeing Mike to get on the radio. As Dave swung around in a U-turn, heading back toward the Coast Highway, Mike called Jock Cayzer down at the beach house site, telling him, "They're there, Jock. We got confirmation from Merville."

"Very nice," came the pleased voice, crackling through the static.

"And our information is, Koo Davis is still alive."

"Praise the Lord."

Dave Kerman laughed at the phrase, and made the right turn onto the Coast Highway. Mike said, "Keep them bottled up, Jock. We'll be there in five minutes."


The problem was, the area was so thoroughly public. The Coast Highway itself was four lanes wide, being not only the scenic route along the coast but also the main road to Oxnard and Santa Barbara and beyond, filled with traffic all day long; rerouting all those vehicles up through the hills would be complicated and arduous. Besides that, the entire beachfront from Malibu State Beach just west of the house to Las Tunas State Beach several miles to the east swarmed with people, who would have to be safeguarded. All of which meant that a lot of preliminary work had to be done, and there was no way to do it without attracting the attention of the people inside the house. They could only hope the kidnappers wouldn't panic, wouldn't kill Koo Davis or do anything else stupid once they became aware of the tightening net.

A mobile command center had been set up in two trailers in a diner parking lot on the shoreward side of the road, just east of the target house. When Dave Kerman angled the Buick around the police-line sawhorses and into this parking lot, Mike saw there were now six trailers, the other four all being connected with the media; three TV remote units and one documentary film unit. "The vultures are here," he said.

Dave Kerman grinned. "Why not? When else are they gonna get Koo Davis on the program for free?"

At times like this, the final moments of the hunt, when the TV and newspaper people began to cluster and swarm hot-eyed for blood, Mike felt a certain disgust for the media and all its representatives. As far as he was concerned, though his own work might become messy and dirty in the heat of the struggle, both the motives and the result were clean; the media, on the other hand, was engaged in the unhealthy task of pandering to unhealthy desires. Now, striding from the car to the main trailer, he grimly ignored the two camera crews recording his progress and refused either to listen or respond to the questions of the microphone-waving reporters who trotted to his side. His ear-lier embarrassed pleasure at becoming in a small way a media celebrity was washed away by this repugnance. "Out of the way," he said to a reporter who had become just a little too bold, and stepped into the trailer.

A dozen people were crowded into the long narrow cream-walled space inside the trailer, among them Jock Cayzer and Lynsey Rayne. Lynsey came forward at Mike's entrance, looking frightened but elated, saying, "Is it true? He's certainly alive?"

"According to Merville." But then he quickly softened that, preferring to have her optimistic: "And he was telling the truth, no question about that. He opened up like a flower."

Some toughness in his tone startled her, and she looked at him more closely. "What did you do to him?"

She's still a liberal, Mike reminded himself; we get Koo Davis back by fair play only. "Believe it or not," he said, "the only time I touched him was when I shook his hand."

"Just so Koo's all right," she said. Meaning fair play was no longer an issue?

"He isn't all right yet," Mike told her. "We still have to get him away from those people." And he stepped deeper into the trailer.

The furnishings were a grab-bag of bits and pieces; some folding chairs of various styles, a couple of folding-leg card tables, one sturdy wooden table and a couple of small battered gray-metal desks. At one of these sat Jock Cayzer; approaching him, Mike said, "Is our phone line in?"

"Let's see." Jock lifted the receiver of the phone which was the only thing on the surface of his desk, listened, and shook his head. "Not a thing." Cradling the receiver again, he called toward the other end of the people-filled trailer, "How much longer on the phone?"

"One minute!" The person who answered was a big bearish young man with shoulder-length blond hair and shaggy blond beard. He was dressed in work pants, a yellow T-shirt and a large tool-filled workbelt around his waist, and he was kneeling on the floor at the far end of the trailer, a screwdriver in one hand and a telephone receiver in the other. "Just checking with the operator," he called, waved the screwdriver, and went back to work.

Mike said, "I'm assuming that place has a phone and we know the number."

"It does," Jock assured him, "and we do."

"Good." Then Mike added, "According to Merville, they killed our inside girl."

"I'm sorry to hear that," Jock said. "We didn't do her any favor."

Lynsey had followed Mike, and now she said, with new worry, "If they've already killed once, they don't have anything to lose anymore."

"These people started killing years ago," Mike told her, and went over to the wooden table, which was filled with an untidy Rube Goldberg assembly of electronic parts and wiring. Half of it comprised a two-way police radio, at which an operator sat, receiving occasional messages from elements at the perimeter of the siege area. The rest was the recording equipment, being fussed over by their regular technician from the Burbank office. Mike said to him, "You ready to tape phone conversations?"

"I *think* so." The technician looked harried, very unlike his normal calm self; he apparently didn't like being transported out of his comfortable home environment. "I won't know for sure," he said, "until they get the phone working."

"They say that'll be just a minute."

"They always say that," the technician said.

The radio operator said, "Sir?"

"Yes?"

"An L.A. Sheriff's car on the beach just reported. The word's got around, and the offshore is filling up with small boats."

"Boats! Are they looking to get killed?"

"I guess they're just looking, sir."

Mike pointed to the array of radio equipment. "Can you get the Coast Guard on that thing?"

"I believe so, yes, sir."

"Get onto them, explain the situation, and tell them we'd appreciate their cooperation clearing that area. And if they feel like sinking a couple of those stupid bastards out there, we leave them to their own initiative."

The radio operator grinned. "Yes, sir."

"Try your phone now!" cried the young man from the far end of the trailer.

Mike watched as Jock picked up the phone and listened. "Sounds good," Jock called.

"Terrific." Mike said to the technician, "You set?"

"I need to hear a conversation."

"Right. Jock? Dial the weather or something."

Jock waved an okay, dialed the number, and the technician fiddled with his dials and switches. Suddenly a female voice filled the trailer: "—perature seventy-eight degrees, humidity—"

The technician hit another switch, and nodded in embattled satisfaction. "Set," he said.

"Good."

Mike crossed to the other desk, sat down, and drew its telephone close. As he did so, Lynsey, standing in front of the desk, said, "Is that supposed to make me feel better?"

Mike looked at her, not knowing what on earth she was talking about. "Huh?"

"Telling me they started killing years ago. Why should *that* make me feel better?"

"Oh. Because it isn't new to them," Mike told her. "They're less likely to panic, because they've already known for years the consequences of getting caught."

"I see," she said, surprised. "I see what you mean."

"Now do you feel better?"

"Not really. I won't feel *good* till this is all over and Koo is safe." Then she added, "May I sit by you?"

"Of course. Drag over a chair."

She did, bringing one of the lightweight metal folding chairs and placing it at the side of the desk. Meantime, Mike asked Jock for the beach house phone number, and dialed it as Jock read it off. Lynsey sat down and Mike nodded at her, listening to the phone's ring-sound in his ear.

She said, "What if they don't answer?"

He held up a finger, meaning he didn't want to talk right now. He was counting the rings: five, six, seven…"We'll wait for them," he said. Eight, nine…

In the middle of the fourteenth ring, someone picked up at the other end, but at first didn't speak. Mike waited, hearing the faint sound of breathing, and finally he said, "Hello?"

It was a woman's voice: "Wrong number."

"Peter Dinely, please," Mike said.

There was a sharp intake of breath, then silence. Would she hang up? No; she said, "Who is this?"

"Michael Wiskiel, of the Federal Bur—"

"Hold on. Hold on a minute."

"Sure."

He heard the receiver clatter onto a hard surface. Looking at Lynsey's expectant face, he pressed the phone hard against his ear, trying to hear what was going on in that room at the other end, but heard nothing until the new clatter of somebody picking the receiver up again. A wary voice said, "Yes?"

"Peter Dinely?"

"Where did you get that name?" The voice sounded like the one on the final tape, but less harsh; the same voice without the rage. Which answered the question about the tape's authenticity, now that it no longer mattered.

"Ginger Merville told me," Mike said.

Surprisingly, the man at the other end laughed. "Poor Ginger," he said, but not as though he actually sympathized. "Did he come to you or did you go out and grab him?"

"We grabbed him."

"So he couldn't even make a deal. I imagine he's *very* upset."

"I imagine you all are," Mike said, trying to sound as though he cared. "Merville told us Koo Davis is still alive."

"Oh, did he?"

The voice now seemed to imply that Merville was wrong.

Mike looked away from Lynsey's eyes. "You're in a lot of trouble, Dinely," he said, "but you could stop now before you make things worse."

"Are *you* stupid, or do you think *I'm* stupid?"

"Neither," Mike said. It was obviously necessary to stroke this fellow's ego a bit, and Mike was more than willing. He was willing to do whatever was needed to get Koo Davis back, safe and sound. "You're smart," he told Dinely, "you've proved that the last few days, but there's just too many of us. It didn't matter how smart you were, you couldn't pull this off and get away with it."

"But we *have* gotten away with it, so far." Dinely's air of self-confidence was almost convincing; almost. "And we'll go on getting away with it," he said, with just a bit too much bravado. "I take it you want Davis back."

"Alive."

"Of course. We'll make a deal."

Mike closed his eyes and pressed his lips together, knowing what was coming. The clear route to the airport, the plane waiting, Dinely's promise to release Davis once he was aboard the plane. Mike would agree, of course, because once the gang was out of the house and in motion there would be a thousand different ways to stop them. But without endangering Koo Davis even further? Very aware of Lynsey's presence, but keeping his eyes shut, Mike said, "Let's hear it."

"We have our own car," Dinely began. "The green Impala in the carport."

"Yes."

And Dinely went on to outline exactly what Mike had expected. The Coast Highway was also California State Highway 1, which south of here at Santa Monica went inland, along Lincoln Boulevard, down to Los Angeles International Airport; that was the route they would take, and the plane that was to be waiting for them should be equipped for flying over water. Davis would be released at the airport. Sure.

"It'll take a while to set up," Mike said.

"Not *too* long," Dinely told him. "You don't want us to get nervous here."

"And we need assurance," Mike said, now opening his eyes and looking at Lynsey again, "that Koo Davis is still alive. Let me speak to him."

There was a brief uncomfortable silence, and then Dinely said, "That isn't possible right now." His voice sounded odd; Mike couldn't quite figure out what was wrong. It wasn't as though Dinely were lying about Davis still being alive, but almost as though Dinely were in some strange way embarrassed about something.

Apparently Mike's reaction was showing in his face, because Lynsey suddenly looked alarmed, instinctively reaching out, not quite grasping him by the forearm. Speaking slowly into the phone, choosing his words carefully, Mike said, "Is there some sort of problem?"

"Davis is, uh, locked up," Dinely said. "And it's not—*possible* just this second to unlock him. Give me your phone number there."

"Listen," Mike said. "Is Koo Davis alive or isn't he?" And now Lynsey did hold his arm, her fingers a tight bony pressure.

"*Yes*, he's alive." Dinely sounded exasperated. "Give me your phone number and I'll call you back when he's—available."

"It's four two six," Mike said, "nine nine seven oh. But, listen." Too late. Dinely had hung up.

## 36

Peter hung up. He stood a moment, thinking, his fingertips resting lightly atop the telephone receiver. His teeth ground softly, absent-mindedly, almost tenderly, against his cheeks. Bright sunlight flattened the view of beach and ocean into a two-dimensional snapshot, simple in composition and overexposed. A few small boats bobbed far off, in the water. What would it be like to be a person on one of those boats? Peter concentrated, trying to push his mind, his particularity, out through his eyes and across the intervening space and *inside* the head of a person on one of those boats—*that* boat, right there. Feel the movement, taste the salt spray, grab the cold chrome rail, smile broadly with uncut cheeks and gaze toward shore with easy amused pity for those people mired there.

Liz said, "It won't work."

Peter looked at her with cold distaste. His army. Liz, standing near him, narrow and pinched and dead for years. And Larry over at the foot of the stairs, forehead deeply puckered with worry, mouth open like a victim of brain damage. Peter's army. He said, "*What* won't work?"

"All that car to the airport business. They'll mousetrap us along the way."

"We'll have Davis."

"We don't have him now," she pointed out. "Mark has him, and he won't give him back."

Peter's fingertips left the telephone and moved up to touch his cheek, reassuringly. Perhaps it was only this pain that kept him going. "We'll go talk to Mark," he said. "Maybe he'll listen to reason."

"And if he doesn't?"

"We'll shoot the lock out of the door." In suddenly savagery, Peter said, "In *any* case, the first chance I get, the *first* chance I get, Mark dies."

Lynsey watched Mike's face while he talked with the man called Dinely, and the instant he hung up the phone she said, "What are you going to do?"

His face closed down when he looked at her. "I'm going to stop them," he said.

"Please, Mi— Uh, may I call you Mike?"

He seemed surprised. There was an occasional unexpected boyishness in him that confused Lynsey. He said, "Sure. Mike. Why not?"

"Mike," she said, knowing it was important that communication between them remain open, knowing she was likely to be the only effective restraining influence on him, "Mike, I hate it when I see you turn off that way. You look at me and I can almost hear you saying to yourself, 'Bleeding heart liberal.'"

"Oh, well," he said, moving his hands in awkward embarrassment, and the fact that he even blushed, faintly and briefly, confirmed that she'd been right.

"It's true," she said. "And we have to get past it. For instance, you *know* I don't care more about the criminals than I do about the victim; certainly not in *this* case."

His grin acknowledged the point. "Old habits die hard," he said.

"Yours, or mine?"

"Both." He nodded, heavy and thoughtful. "You're right. I look at you and I see somebody who doesn't want me to do the most effective job."

Honesty deserves honesty. She said, "And I look at you and see somebody who's dangerous because he thinks it's a *game*."

"But it *is* a game," he said. "It's all moves and counter-moves; dangerous, you play it for keeps, but it's a game."

"No," she said. "It's all right for the criminals to think it's a game, they're sick, that's why they're on the wrong side of the law. But if *you* think the same way, then the game becomes more important than the people. You'd sacrifice Koo to win the game."

"I don't know how to answer that," he said. "I know you're thinking about the mistake I made—"

"No, I wasn't," she said, surprised. "I mean, that's part of it, but I wasn't thinking about that. That didn't *give* me my belief, it was just confirmation of what I already believed."

"Which is?"

"All right," she said. "Using your terms, that it's a game. *You* think the point of the game is to capture or kill those people over there. And *I* think the point of the game is to get Koo back, alive and well."

"We want to do both," he said. "Naturally."

"Naturally. But if you had to sacrifice one for the other, you'd kill Koo to capture the people, and I'd let the people go to save Koo. And *that's* the difference between us."

He looked bleak. "I won't lie to you," he said. "You're absolutely right."

Mark looked at the furniture piled up against the door. Both night-tables were there, upside down on the floor, with drawers from the built-in dressers stacked among the night-table legs. A wicker bathroom hamper, weighted with all the bottles and tubes from the medicine chest and bathroom storage shelves, lay on its side atop the drawers; beyond it, the mirror, cracked and splintered by Peter's bullets fired through the door, reflected a crazy-quilt pattern of white wicker. Above that were the reflection of Mark's newly naked somber face and the image of Koo, frightened and exhausted, seated on the bed in the background. "The television set next," Mark said, and moved across the room.

Koo said, "Mark? What's going to happen?"

"They're going to try and break in. We won't let them."

"I mean, after that."

"We'll know when we get there, Koo."

Mark didn't like that question, because he not only didn't know the answer but didn't *want* to know the answer. The astonishment of having actually had a pistol fired at him by Peter had forced him to a sudden awareness of his true position, so that now he *knew* he was living minute by minute, even second by second. He didn't recognize himself anymore, and without identity he couldn't begin to think about direction. He was like a person waking from a three-week binge to find himself in the hospital, fed and dry but charged with a variety of felonies about which he has no recollection; *this* moment is bearable, but any conceivable movement from here is bound to be a change for the worse.

Various wires led from the back of the television set into the darkness of the closet. Mark traced the power-lead, treating that with respect and carefully unplugging it from the wall outlet, but the other wires—aerial, external speakers—he simply ripped loose, then carried the heavy set over to place it on top of the hamper, leaning back against the shattered mirror. Then he turned to look around the room for more barricade material, ignoring Koo's questioning gaze.

He had always thought of himself as separate from other human beings, isolated and alone, but he'd been wrong. *Now* he was estranged; in this current situation, he was the only person on the face of the Earth that both sides wanted to shoot at.

There was nothing else to pile against the door. Either what was already there was heavy enough to do the job, or it wasn't. Since for Mark all potential endings were bad ones, it hardly mattered whether the barricade held or not; to some extent he was doing all this merely because it was the most appropriate action under the circumstances.

So long as he remained in this room, so long as the stalemate continued outside between Peter and the authorities, then Mark still had one lifeline, one thread tying him to the human race; this complex, absurd, contradictory, useless, incomprehensible relationship with Koo Davis. Last night, suicide had seemed the only possible choice, because that moment had been unbearable. Now, the present instant had its nourishing qualities—if he didn't know better, he'd almost think he'd become happy—so he had lost the thirst for destruction, self or otherwise; still, when the black wave did eventually get here, as it would, he would close his eyes uncaring.

Should he take his father with him?

"Mark! Mark!" It was Peter's muffled voice, followed by a knocking at the door. "Mark, can you hear me?"

Koo sat up straighter, sending Mark a frightened look. Turning casually to the door, Mark rested his hands on the waist-level television set, smiling with easy familiarity at his fractured images in the broken mirror. He wasn't particularly worried about Peter shooting through the door at him; those last bullets had penetrated the wood and cracked the glass, but they hadn't entered the room with any force. Mark called, "Yes, I can hear you."

"We made a deal with them, Mark."

Mark waited, but apparently Peter expected him to comment, and the silence lengthened. Mark *had* no comment, he didn't live on the same level of reality as Peter, so he merely waited, mildly, for Peter to speak again.

"*Mark!* Did you hear me?"

"Yes, I heard you."

"They'll give us a plane. They'll give us a clear route to the airport."

Mark smiled at the silliness of it. In his mind's eye he saw the sharpshooters on the rooftops, the curve or corner where the car would of necessity briefly slow to a crawl, the side windows starring and splintering all together, and suddenly everybody in the car dead but Koo. Turning to Koo, Mark grinned and pantomimed a sniper with a rifle shooting down from a rooftop. Koo looked blank, then suddenly nodded in comprehension. "Right," he said. "But with my luck, the guy'd sneeze."

"With my luck, so would I."

"One bullet," Koo said. "Right through the both of us."

"You're an incurable romantic, Koo."

"Oh, I can be cured. I can be cured."

Peter's ragged voice sounded again: "*Mark! There isn't time for this!*"

Mark shook his head at Koo, and turned back to the door. "Go away, Peter," he called. "There's nothing going to happen here."

"We have to let them speak to Davis on the phone. They have to know he's alive before they'll deal."

Mark made no response. To Koo he said, "Come over here. Lean your weight against this stuff."

Getting to his feet, Koo said, "We expect visitors?"

"They'll shoot the lock off in a minute."

"What an exciting life you lead."

Peter again: "Forget what happened before! Everything has changed now! We need him alive, he's our passport!"

"It's nice to be needed," Koo commented, leaning his back against the hamper and the TV set.

"*Mark!*" came Peter's hysterical voice. "*For the last time!*"

"Promises, promises," Koo said.

The sound of the shot wasn't terribly loud, but the vibration of its impact pulsed through the jumbled pieces of the barricade like a preliminary earthquake tremor, and Koo's side twinged painfully. "That's a bigger gun," Mark said.

"You suppose they got nukes?"

The second shot thrummed into the door; bottles tinkled together inside the hamper.


Seated at the small desk in the crowded trailer, Mike looked up when the radio operator called, "Mr. Wiskiel!"

"Yes?"

"Report of shooting from the house."

"No," Lynsey said; too low for anyone to hear but Mike. The color drained from her face, as though she might faint, and he noticed how clawlike her hands became when she clutched at the edge of the desk for support.

Mike concentrated on the radio operator, saying, "Anybody hit?"

"No, sir. They want to know what's their response."

"We don't shoot first," Mike said. "But we return fire."

"Mike, please!" Lynsey's whisper was shrill with urgency.

For her benefit, Mike added, "And nobody fires at sounds. We only respond to direct attack."

"Yes, sir."

The radio operator turned back to his seat, and Mike held a hand up to stop Lynsey's protests before they could start. "Listen," he said. "The guy hasn't called back. You know what that probably means."

"You can't be sure what's going on in that house," she said. "They might be arguing among themselves."

"Fine. If they are, and if Koo Davis is alive, then he's still where Merville said he was—in an interior room without windows. Firing from outside the house won't endanger him."

"You can't be *sure* where he is!"

"I can't be sure of anything till it's over," Mike said. "But I'm not prepared to order my people not to respond when attacked." Picking up the phone, he added, "I'll talk to them again."

"Good."

But they weren't answering. He let it ring eighteen times, then all at once the line went dead. When he dialed again, he got a busy signal.

"More shooting at the house," the radio operator said.

Mike slammed the phone into its cradle; pushing back from the desk, he said, "I'm going down there and see what's what."

"I want to come with you."

He looked at her wryly. "What choice do I have?"

"None," she said.

After Larry shot the telephone, he felt foolish but defiant. He stood there with the revolver in his hand, the shattered phone on the living room floor, and Peter came blundering down the stairs, his voice high-pitched with a new querulousness, crying, "What's the *matter* with you? What's the matter with *everybody*?"

"We can't take anymore," Larry told him. "It has to end."

Peter stared at the phone. "You utter *fool*! Now how can we *deal* with them?"

"Oh, Peter, do you still believe in it all?"

Larry no longer believed. His long morning of thought had led him at last to the understanding that it had all been a mistake, a stupid tragic mistake. He was remembering now something he hadn't thought of in years; a motto on the wall of his parents' bedroom back home, cut from some old magazine by his mother and put in a frame from Woolworth's: *Things done in violence have to be done over again*. Why had he never read that, or remembered it, or understood it? Why had he always behaved as though meaningful change in the world must be instantaneous, violent, and total?

Hell *is* paved with good intentions, and Hell was where Larry now found himself. Good intentions had led at last to mere absurdity; himself pushing on a barricaded door, armed with a revolver, trying to get at a terrified old man. Shame and self-disgust had grown in him while he and Peter pressed uselessly at that door. The endless insistent ringing of the telephone had finally been the last straw, and this emptying of the revolver Larry's last violence. "I'm giving myself up," he said. "You do what you want. I'm giving myself up."

"Oh, no, you're not! No, you're not! If we're going to get out of this, we have to show a united front."

Larry stared. "Get out of this? Peter, we're going to *die* here today!"

"*I'm* not!" Peter's eyes were open wide and glaring, and pink spittle flew with the agitation of his speech. "I'm going to *live*, I'm going to come *back*, I'm going to go *on*." Then he blinked down at the destroyed telephone. "Extensions," he muttered. "We can still make a deal." And he hurried away to the kitchen.

Weary, Larry sagged onto the sofa and sat there leaning forward, head drooping, the empty revolver held slackly between his knees. He didn't care what happened now.

Peter came back from the kitchen, calmer and colder. "Well, you've done it," he said. "The phone's out of order."

"It doesn't matter, Peter."

"It does matter! Larry, I'm not going to finish here. I'm getting out, and you're going to help. You're *going* to."

Apathetic, Larry looked up. "What do you want?"

"Convince Mark to come out. You can do it. We can't force our way in there. Convince him we just need Davis as a hostage, so we can get away. Convince him nobody's going to get hurt."

"Mark knows you mean to kill him."

"Not anymore," Peter said. He came across the living room, closer to Larry. "It's true, I swear it. You know what the circumstances were, but now they've changed. I won't hurt Mark. He can just let Davis out if he wants, he can stay in there by himself. Or he can come along, and he'll be perfectly safe. But we *need* Davis."

"You don't have the phone anymore."

"We'll show Davis out on the deck. We'll have a white flag of truce, and we'll let them see Davis on the upstairs deck." Peter abruptly dropped onto the sofa next to Larry, his gaunt-cheeked face anguished and intent. "*Please*, Larry," he said. "Please! I can't end here!"

Larry had to look away, embarrassed by this nakedness; that Peter should beg, and particularly that he should beg *him*. "Peter, it won't do any good. Mark won't listen to me, he never has."

"You can try. Just *try*."

Larry closed his eyes. Would it never be possible to stop? "I'll try," he said.

The highway side of the house was windowless, avocado in color, and contained only the door leading in from the carport. Mike and Lynsey drove past this featureless wall, and Lynsey said, "It looks like a fortress."

"Fortunately, appearances are deceiving."

All normal traffic had been diverted from this part of the road. Nearly three hundred police officers were here, representing half a dozen commands, including the State Police, the FBI, the County Sheriff's Department, and even a few men from Jock Cayzer's Burbank force. Several police cars were parked across the highway from the house, with uniformed men carrying rifles and shotguns as they waited on the far side of the cars.

More men, more uniforms, more guns, more official cars, were down on the beach itself, at the nearer barricade. The

civilian spectators had been moved farther back, behind a second
line of sawhorses, but here there was still a crowd; grim-faced,
well-armed and obviously becoming impatient. Mike and Lynsey
left the Buick, walked to the barrier, and stood next to one of
the Sheriff's Department sharpshooters, who was watching the
house through the scope of his rifle. Mike said, "Anything happening?"

"There's a woman in that upstairs room. I get an occasional
glimpse of her. That's about it." Then he offered the rifle, saying,
"Want to see?"

"Thanks." Mike peered one-eyed through the scope, found
the house, the upper deck, the glass doors. There were curtains;
was that movement behind them? He couldn't be sure. Lowering
the rifle, he said to Lynsey, "Want to look?"

She shook her head, gazing at the rife in distaste. "I can see
well enough. Thank you."

"Sure," he said, and raised the rifle to look again.

Liz stopped looking out the window at the police. Letting the
curtain fall back into place, she walked from the bedroom to
the hall, where Larry was leaning against that other door, talking
in his stodgy well-meaning manner at Mark, who was not answering; probably not even listening. Liz said, "You're wasting
your breath."

Larry turned away from the door. He looked haggard. "I know.
Peter insisted." Shaking his head, he said, "I wish it would end.
I wish it was over."

Liz spent her last smile. "You want it to end? It can end right
now."

He frowned at her. "What do you mean?"

"Come along and watch," she said, and went back into the
bedroom.

○

"There she is!" Mike said. He was still watching through the rifle scope.

"I see her," Lynsey said. "She's coming out."

The woman was pushing open the sliding door, stepping out to the sunlight, a slender blonde girl, raising her arm and pointing in this direction. Startled, Mike said, "She has a gun! She's—" he saw the gun jerk up in her hand "—going to—" he heard the shot, he heard the sudden grunting sound, he looked around to see the sharpshooter, the man who'd loaned him his rifle, falling backward with astonishment on his face, his hands reaching for his chest. "My God!"

From the bedroom doorway, Larry yelled, "Liz! For God's sake, don't!"

Out on the deck, in plain view, Liz turned about and shot once at the police line in the opposite direction along the beach to her left. Then she turned back to shoot again to the right.

Half a dozen men fired. Staring through the scope, Mike saw glass shatter beside the girl, but saw that no one had hit her; all firing too hastily, too unexpectedly. The gun in her hand, pointing this way, jumped again.

No. Mike's finger found the trigger, his cheek nestled against the wood stock, the butt formed comfortably against his shoulder, he squeezed, and the rifle *kicked* against him. He blinked, brought the barrel down, saw the girl staggering back against the glass doors, and knew she had been hit solidly in the body. There was more and more firing all around him now, a growing fusillade, but he knew it was his bullet that had struck home.

At the sound of the first shot, Peter leaped to his feet from the living room sofa, staring around in terror and disbelief. *This* wasn't the right way! He started instinctively toward the glass doors leading to the cantilevered deck, wanting to see what had

gone wrong, but then the firing started in earnest, and two of
the glass panels ahead of him shattered as they were hit. "No
no *no!*" Peter cried, backing away, making patting motions at
the outer world with both hands. Not like this! Not like this!

Mike wanted more. Hurrying to stay ahead of everybody else,
but at the same time striving to be meticulous, accurate, correct,
he *squeezed* again. Yes! High on the right side of her chest,
puffing a ragged red-black hole, straightening her against the
glass door when she might have fallen forward. And again, the
cartridge leaping from him to her, embedding in her body,
thumping in, holding her in place, not letting her fall.

Thump. Thump. Thump. Like spikes into rotten wood, like
stakes into soft clay, he pounded the wads of metal into her
flesh, watching each bloody crater blossom. Forty or fifty guns
were rattling now, light-reflecting glass shards were spraying,
the bedroom curtains were whipping and snapping as though in
a high wind, other men's bullets were biting into that body, but it
was still first and foremost *his.* Thump. He spaced them, timed
them, placed them to keep her upright, prevent her from falling.
Blood and meat obscured the details of her now, someone else's
magnum cartridge swept the top of her head away as though
with a scythe, but Mike kept punching, punching, punching into
the torso, seven, eight, nine, ten—and the rifle didn't kick. That
was when he knew it hadn't fired, it was empty, and at last the
ragged thing on the porch toppled forward, jerking as it was hit
several more times on the way down.

The bedroom was full of buzzing. Angry metal bees swarmed
everywhere, stinging and biting, knocking Larry down as he
tried to run through the bedroom door into the hall. Eleven
bullets struck him, leaving him broken, impaired, profusely
bleeding, unconscious, but alive.

o

Peter, mad with fear, clawed at the carpet, trying to dig down through the living room floor. Blood and saliva ran from his open mouth, tears ran from his eyes, and all he could hear was everything in the world breaking, cracking, splitting, shattering as the bullets flashed through the rooms. He lay chest-down on the floor, gasping, staring wide-eyed at nothing, scrabbling with raw fingertips, shredding his nails, until something burned the back of his neck; a spent bullet, hot from its journey through the air. Screaming, Peter leaped up into the trajectory of half a dozen more.

Mike lowered the rifle. The shooting went on and on, like strings of firecrackers on Chinese New Year, the officers around on the roadside firing now as well, pumping hundreds of bullets into the featureless front wall. Mike, breathing heavily, as dazed as though he'd come out of a movie house to bright sunshine, turned and saw Lynsey staring at him in shock, comprehension and rejection.

## 37

"I want to warn you about something," Koo says. "I did too much USO; when I hear gunfire, I go into my act." He and Mark are sitting side by side now on the floor at the foot of the bed. In here, the massed shooting outside the house has the lightweight mild quality of dried beans ratting in a coffee can.

"That isn't the cops," Mark says. "It sounds like the critics found you."

"Their aim never was any good." To Koo's right, another mirror cracks. "Jesus," he says, trying to keep the tremor out of his voice. "So far, that's a hundred forty-seven years' bad luck."

They're safe in this room from all that heavy firing, but it doesn't *feel* safe. The occasional bullet penetrates the house deeply enough to hit one of the surrounding mirrors from the back, and then that mirror cracks or splinters, so that by now over half the mirrors are broken, the reflections of the room becoming increasingly fragmented and crazy. With the room's color scheme of black and white and purple and red, with the furniture piled up against the door and all the mirrors sharding and shattering so that wherever Koo turns he sees reflected the images of disjointed parts of himself and Mark, sometimes weirdly linked, the effect should be nightmarish; but it's merely ugly and dangerous, and rather trite. Koo says, "I'd be ashamed to tell a dream like this to a psychiatrist." Putting on the standard comic's Viennese-psychiatrist accent, he says, "Vot's dis mit de broken mirrors? Ged adda here, you'll be coming in mit de freight trains next. Vot are you, some kind a *normal* or something?"

"In my flying dreams I always go economy fare," Mark says, "and my luggage winds up in Chicago. What does that mean, Doctor?"

"It's ein deep-zeeted neurotic reaction. Vot does dis inkblot look like to you?"

"A four-dollar cleaning bill."

Koo laughs, in surprised pleasure. "Nice," he says, in his own voice. "Very nice. I don't think I heard that one before."

Mark seems highly amused by that: "You only like jokes you recognize?"

"Old friends are best."

This patter started back during that ludicrous terrifying few minutes when Koo and Mark were braced side by side against the barricading furniture while Peter and the others struggled to push open the door. Much of comedy is a way of trying to deal with tension and fear, both of which Koo now possesses in abundance, so it was in a spirit of whistling-in-the-graveyard that he looked across the barricade at Mark and said, "Maybe we should just *take* the magazine subscriptions."

And Mark immediately answered, "*Collier's*? *Life*? I don't trust these people; keep pushing!"

The jokes and gag-lines have been running ever since, a lengthening routine which almost distracts Koo from the truth of his surroundings and circumstances, and which in any event delights him. *Mark* delights him. Neither of Koo's sons—his other sons, he has to be careful about that—neither of them has followed in Koo's funnyman footsteps. Frank has a kind of salesman's hearty good humor while Barry sports a self-amused wit, but neither has Koo's love for or skill with *gags*. Astonishingly, down inside that raging murderous beast which has apparently always been Mark's surface persona, there lies a *comic*. It doesn't matter if the jokes are good—we're going for quantity here, not quality—the point is that they're jokes and they're delivered with a natural sense of style and timing, and to Koo's joy and bewilderment he and Mark *work well together*. This, he thinks, aware of the exaggeration but not caring, must be what Abbott felt when he met Costello, Hardy when he met Laurel. "Well," Koo says. "This is *another* fine mess you've gotten me into."

"Hush," Mark says; seriously, not part of any routine. "Listen."

Koo lifts his head to listen, and realizes it's stopping. The war is coming to an end out there. The rattle and clatter of gunfire is reducing rapidly to a mere scattered popping, it's thinning out, thinning…one last distant *crack*. "Somebody's always late," Koo says.

Mark doesn't answer. There's silence, stretching on. Looking around, Koo sees jumbles and shards and geometric segments of the room, all ricocheting back and forth among the fractured mirrors; a crazy quilt in glass. When he raises one bandaged arm, bewildering quick movements flash from the mirrors all around, like a flight of tiny birds. And the silence stretches on. "Peace, it's wonderful," Koo says.

And still Mark says nothing. Koo looks at him, suddenly apprehensive, and Mark's head has lowered, he's brooding with hooded eyes at the floor between his feet. In profile he seems cold and humorless, reminding Koo uncomfortably of the Mark he'd known at first. Suddenly very nervous, not wanting to lose their connection, Koo says, "What's up?"

Mark makes no response.

"Listen," Koo says, keeping it light even though his old terror of Mark is rapidly returning, "just 'cause I won't kiss on the first date, you don't have to get sore."

Now Mark shakes his head, with a small brushing-away hand gesture, but he won't meet Koo's eyes, and he still doesn't speak.

"Mark," Koo says. He feels it all slipping away, and he *must* hold onto it. "Mark, for Christ's sake, what's happening?"

"It's coming to an end." And Mark turns to show Koo a

painful bitter smile. "It's all over," he says. "The law's on its way."

"And the west will never be the same again."

"Neither will I." Lifting his head, his expression almost playful, Mark says, "I was trying to decide whether to take you with me."

Koo doesn't get it, and it alarms him when he doesn't understand Mark. Peering intently at the boy, he says, "Take me with you?"

"Oh, I'm gone, Koo." Mark chuckles, not pleasantly, and shakes his head. "I've been gone since last night. I just came back to help you with Joyce, that's all."

"Take it easy, Mark," Koo says, and rests his hand on the boy's forearm.

But Mark shivers and pulls his arm away, as a horse sometimes flinches from being touched. "Better not, Koo," he says. "I don't know who I am right now. I don't want to kill you by mistake."

As so often before, Koo's fear of Mark leads him to face the boy directly, insist on the clarifying statement. Heart in his mouth, he says, "The question is, do you want to kill me on purpose?"

"That's the question, all right." Mark glances toward the door. "And I don't have much time to find the answer."

"Mark, listen, it doesn't have to be this way. We can work things—"

"Don't make promises!" The harshness in Mark's voice shocks Koo into silent rigidity. "What are you gonna do, sign me up with a contract? Make me second banana on your TV shows?"

"I thought I'd let you handle my negotiations with the network."

Mark grunts in amusement, but then once again shakes his head.

"Listen," Koo says, putting all the sincerity he can muster into his voice. "We *can* work something out. You're not—"

"I will kill you, Koo." Mark's eyes as he gazes at Koo are as cold and empty as a northern lake. "If you sweet-talk me to save your life, I'll strangle you this second."

Koo blinks and blinks, staring into those clueless blank eyes. Mark wants something from him, he knows that much, but if he tries to give what he wants the boy will accuse him of hypocrisy. And the finish *isn't* resolved in Mark's mind, the old need to kill is still inside him, like snake venom. Whatever Koo does now is wrong, and whatever mistake he makes is fatal.

It's too much. The seconds go on, and Koo remains impaled here, and at last there's nothing left to do or say, no more twists and turns. Koo closes his eyes, his head dropping back to expose his throat; finally, after all this time, he's giving up. "Do what you want," he says. "Take me with you if you have to."

"Do you want to be with me?"

Something strange in the wording, and in the boy's voice, plucks at Koo's attention, bringing him back from defeat. But he's too tired, he's been through too much, he can't defend himself anymore. He doesn't move. He waits for it to happen, the hands on his windpipe or whatever it's going to be.

"Koo? Do you *want* to be with me?"

Since it doesn't matter, the simple truth will do: "Yes," Koo says. His eyes remain shut, his body is limp and relaxed, his voice weak and without inflection.

Mark says, "Your place or mine?"

Koo could never resist a straight line; not even here, on the brink of the grave. In doubt and wonderment, with great reluctance to answer the bell for yet another round, he nevertheless lifts his heavy eyelids, looks at Mark's expressionless face, and says, "Mine."

Mark is about to answer, express some mistrust, but then his eyes flicker, and Koo hears it, too: Voices outside the door, coming up the stairs. "Sounds like the cavalry," Mark says, then glances toward the barricade. "Still, they'll take a while to get through all that."

"Mark."

The head swivels back, the eyes study Koo's face. "Yes?"

"I'm about to say something stupid."

"Go ahead."

"I—" Koo hesitates, tries to find a more self-protective way to phrase it, fails, and goes on: "I want you to love me."

Mark stares. There are people in the hall, just outside the door, shouting to one another, but Mark and Koo both ignore them. Mark says, "You want me to love you. So I won't kill you?"

"No. Regardless of anything. I just want it, that's all."

"I thought you were smart, Koo."

"You were wrong."

"I sure was."

In sudden rage, Mark says, "You complete schmuck, why do you think I *wanted* to kill you? It's because I *wanted* to love you, you asshole!"

"What?" Koo can't follow this last turn.

"You've been my father all my life," Mark says; then in sudden disgust he twists away from Koo, scrambling to his feet. "Oh, the hell with it. The hell with *you*. What made me think you were worth struggling over?"

Mark begins with quick angry movements to dismantle the barricade, pushing the television set away, tossing dresser drawers to left and right. Outside, the voices are calling Koo's name. "In here," Koo shouts, as much to recapture Mark's interest as to answer the voices, but Mark pays no attention. Koo struggles to rise, having trouble because it hurts to put pressure on his arms, and in a hurry because there's something left to say to Mark. He doesn't know what it is, but he feels the urgency and he believes the words will come of their own accord if he can ever get up on his damn *feet*.

But it takes too long. He is barely standing, weaving, when the final pieces of the barricade are shoved out of the way by people on the outside pressing against the door. And now they all burst in, and a pistol butt flashes through the air, and Mark reels backward, blood pouring from his temple.

"Mark!" Koo tries to catch him, but the boy is falling, and his weight drags Koo down onto the floor with him; Koo bouncing at a tangent off the edge of the bed, finishing in a seated position on the floor among all those uniformed legs, with Mark's bloody head in his lap.

Koo looks down in astonishment. Mark's eyes are half-open, barely conscious; the blood pulsing from the forehead gash is rich and dark. And the room is filling with people; cops in uniform, plainclothesmen, men with pistols and rifles in their hands.

"Mister Davis! Mister Davis!"

Koo raises his head, seeing a face he saw on television. This face is saying, "Mister Davis, thank God you're alive! I'm Michael Wiskiel of the Federal Bureau of Investigation."

"Yeah, yeah, I caught your pilot. Is there a doctor in the house?"

"Mister Davis, we'll get you medical care at—"

"Not for me. For this boy here."

Wiskiel's expression, when he looks at Mark, becomes stern, disapproving: "Somebody get that creature out of here."

"Wait wait!" As hands start reaching, Koo leans over Mark's head, spreading his own aching arms protectively above the boy's body. "He's not— Listen, he's not what you think."

Before Wiskiel can respond to that, he's shoved unceremoniously to one side, and there's Lynsey Rayne. She's crying, she's laughing, she's yelling out loud, and now she drops to her knees in front of Koo and flings her arms around him hard enough to about knock him out. "Koo! Koo! Baby!"

Koo's painful arms go around her, he pats the back of her head, he says, "Hello, Lynsey. Hello, darling."

"You're alive!" Leaning back to look at him while still holding him tight, her face shiny and tear-streaked and beaming with a huge smile, her glasses crooked on her nose, she says, "I didn't really believe it anymore, Koo. I'd given up. I was sure you were dead."

"Me, too."

But people are pulling at Mark again, and the boy has become conscious enough to struggle with them, feebly. Clutching Mark's arms, Koo says to the cop-faces all around, "What are you doing? What's the idea?"

Wiskiel, standing over them, says, "Mister Davis, your ordeal is over now. Let that fellow go."

"No. He's—" And Koo is aware of Mark looking up at him, eyes glinting in the bloodied face. "He's my *son*."

"Koo, Koo." It's Lynsey, patting Koo's cheek, looking at him in maternal worry, saying, "Koo, don't. You've been through so much—"

Squatting down next to Lynsey, the FBI man says, "Mister Davis, it's normal for kidnap victims to become emotionally involved with their captors, dependent on them."

"I'm telling you, it's true. He's not—" But can he claim Mark wasn't part of the kidnap plot? Things are about to get very complicated, Koo can see that, but first things first. "He's my son, and he stays with me."

Mark mutters, barely loud enough for Koo to hear, "You're gonna hate yourself in the morning."

"You shut up," Koo tells him.

Lynsey says, "Koo? Are you sure you know what you're doing?"

"I don't have the first idea what I'm doing, Lynsey," Koo say. absently patting Mark's cheek, "but one thing is definite, and no fooling. This is my son. He's my own absolute son, and I want you to be nice to him. He's the only person I've ever met who needs love more than I do."

ah, but will you respect me in the morning?"

The audience roars; they've heard the line a hundred times, over the radio, on the big screen, on the tube. And now in person. And it's always a scream.

But he thinks of Mark as he says it, and a look of concern briefly crosses his features. The custody, the trial—and what will come after? What kind of life will they have, separately or together?

But as the laughter crests and starts subsiding, as the big light turns toward him and the camera dollies forward on its track, the next line rises to his lips, the next gag; and the cloud that crossed his features passes. The audience leans forward.

Koo Davis is home.

·

**Don't Let the Mystery End Here.**
**Try These Other Great Books From**
**HARD CASE CRIME!**

Hard Case Crime brings you gripping, award-winning crime fiction
by best-selling authors and the hottest new writers in the field.
Find out what you've been missing:

# 361

## by DONALD E. WESTLAKE
### AUTHOR OF 'THE COMEDY IS FINISHED'

The men in the tan-and-cream Chrysler came with guns blazing.
When Ray Kelly woke up in the hospital, it was a month later,
he was missing an eye, and his father was dead. *Then things
started to get bad.*

### PRAISE FOR '361':

*"My personal favorite of [Westlake's] hard-boiled period
and, to my mind, the first book in which
he found a voice that was uniquely his."*
— Lawrence Block in
MYSTERY AND SUSPENSE WRITERS

*"Classic hard-boiled style…prose so clean it's like
Hemingway threw away his thesaurus."*
— Booklist

*"Neat and tight, like a well-delivered right cross."*
— Steve Vernon

**Available now at your favorite bookstore.**
**For more information, visit**
**www.HardCaseCrime.com**

**More Great Suspense from
Donald E. Westlake's Legendary Alter Ego**

# Lemons
## NEVER LIE
### by RICHARD STARK

When he's not pulling heists with his friend Parker, Alan Grofield runs a small theater in Indiana. But putting on shows is expensive and jobs have been thin, which is why Grofield agrees to listen to Andrew Myers' plan to knock over a brewery in upstate New York.

Unfortunately, Myers' plan is insane—so Grofield walks out on him. *But Myers isn't a man you walk out on…*

RAVES FOR 'LEMONS NEVER LIE':

*"This first-rate hard-boiled mystery…reads like
Raymond Chandler with a dark literary
whisper…of Cormac McCarthy."*
— Time

*"The prose is clean, the dialogue laced with dry humor,
the action comes hard and fast."*
— George Pelecanos

*"Lemons Never Lie is a delight—
a crime story that leaves you smiling."*
— Washington Post

*"The best Richard Stark ever."*
— Paul Kavanagh

**Available now at your favorite bookstore.
For more information, visit
www.HardCaseCrime.com**